I0717010

PRAISE FOR BRANDON MCNULTY

"Enthralling, mysterious, and absolutely terrifying. Readers beware: these twists and turns could break spines."
    —Felix Blackwell, bestselling author of *Stolen Tongues*

"With his suspenseful, imaginative storytelling, Brandon McNulty is a writer to watch!"
    —Jeff Menapace, author of *Bad Games*

"[*Entry Wounds* is] an action-packed, surprise-filled, outrageously thrilling novel!"
    —Jeff Strand, author of *Wolf Hunt*

"*Entry Wounds* is a harrowing supernatural thriller filled with shootouts, bloodshed, betrayal—and best of all, a cursed revolver."
    —Jeremy Bates, author of *Suicide Forest* and *The Sleep Experiment*

"Clever and gripping, *Entry Wounds* is a tour de force that moves as fast as the bullets from the cursed gun within its pages. You're going to want to read this ASAP."
    —Robert Swartwood, *USA Today* bestselling author of *The Serial Killer's Wife*

"*Entry Wounds* makes the reader question whether, in the face of unstoppable lust for death, a predator is as tormented as his victim."

—L.C. Barlow, award-winning author of *The Jack Harper Trilogy*

"*Bad Parts* asks the intriguing question, 'What would you give up to make your body whole again? Can you put a price on your dreams?' A page-turning tale of Faustian bargains, bad choices, and hard lessons."
—Alma Katsu, author of *The Deep* and *The Hunger*

"*Bad Parts* is a non-stop thrill ride! It starts out breakneck fast and keeps accelerating—the twists keep coming tighter and darker as the novel races toward its grisly, unexpected, and thoroughly satisfying finish. "
—John Everson, Bram Stoker Award-winning author of *Covenant* and *The Devil's Equinox*

"McNulty has crafted one of the most original horror novels in recent years. [*Bad Parts*] reads like *Needful Things* if it had been written by Richard Laymon."
—Tom Deady, Bram Stoker Award-winning author of *Haven*

"*Bad Parts* gives body horror the heart replacement it needs, and this heavy metal love song about a deal with a unique kind of devil hits all the right notes as it flies by."
—Michael Arnzen, Bram Stoker Award-winning author of *Grave Markings*

"Open *Bad Parts* at your peril: you won't be putting it down until the final page is turned."
—Frederic S. Durbin, author of *A Green and Ancient Light* and *Dragonfly*

THE HALF MURDERS

BRANDON MCNULTY

MIDNIGHT
POINT
PRESS

THE HALF MURDERS

Copyright © 2024 by Brandon McNulty

This book is a work of fiction. Names, characters, businesses, places, events, locales, and incidents are either the products of the author's imagination or used in a fictitious manner. Any resemblance to actual persons, living or dead, or actual events is purely coincidental.

All rights reserved. No part of this book may be reproduced, stored in a retrieval system, or transmitted in any form or by any means, electronic, mechanical, photocopying, recording, or otherwise, without the prior written permission of the author, except for the use of brief quotations in a book review.

Published in the United States by Midnight Point Press.

Cover Design by Damonza.

Paperback ISBN-13: 978-1-952703-09-6

Hardcover ISBN-13: 978-1-952703-08-9

eBook ISBN-13: 978-1-952703-10-2

Audiobook ISBN-13: 978-1-952703-11-9

For Joni & Fran

1

K elly O'Neill received a green envelope in the mail every September, whether she wanted it or not.

It usually arrived on the nineteenth. Today was Monday the nineteenth, and she avoided her mailbox as though it were emitting fatal levels of radiation. She couldn't even look at the thing. She locked herself in her upstairs office, shut the curtains, and braced for the worst.

When the postal truck rumbled down the street, she jammed a finger into each ear. She went through her breathing exercises, popped a Vistaril, and smoked a cigarette. The anxiety passed. Life went on.

That afternoon, she picked up her twins from school, coached their soccer practice, and rushed home to prepare a mac-and-cheese casserole. Though dinner was late, it was a hit with the kids and her husband DJ. Monday the nineteenth proved to be another harmless, uneventful day.

Then, halfway through dinner, DJ opened his cheese-smeared mouth and asked the only question she didn't want to hear: "Hey, where's the mail?"

Kelly clutched her fork like she might have to use it in self-defense. "No mail today."

"You sure?" He scratched his shaggy brown beard, then checked his phone. "I got a notification saying my computer parts arrived."

"Maybe they were misdelivered."

"Ugh, great." He leaned back and grimaced. "Can't wait to go door-to-door bothering the neighbors."

"I'm sure whoever got it will drop it off later."

"But I want to clone my SSD tonight. My laptop's begging for a storage upgrade." He glanced toward the living room. "Wonder if our mail came late."

"I doubt it." She smiled at Aiden and Zach, hoping her six-year-old twins might change the subject. Both boys were licking cheese from their plates in an effort to delay their bedtime. "We should get these two to bed."

"Nooo," Aiden groaned. "I just finished eating."

"Late dinner doesn't mean late bedtime," she said. "C'mon, you two."

"Mommy, please," Zach said, licking more cheese, "we can't go to bed."

"Oh, yes you can." She reeled in their empty plates. "Say goodnight to your dad."

The boys hugged their father, dragging out their good-byes until she chased them upstairs to the bathroom. She watched them brush their teeth then tucked them into bed.

When she came downstairs to wash the casserole dish, DJ was heading for the front door. She froze on the spot. "Wh-what're you doing?"

"Right now?" He rubbed his generous gut. "Digesting noodles."

"Real funny. I mean, where are you *going*?"

"To find that package."

"Y'know, I could use help with the dishes."

"Already got the casserole tray soaking." He pumped his fist then reached for the doorknob.

"Wait!" She swatted his hand away. For a moment, things were awkward. Then she tucked her long red hair behind one ear and flashed a sly, sexy smile. "If you finish the dishes, I can...get ready."

His bespectacled eyes widened with understanding. "Ah, so we're heading down to the Batcave?"

They kept an air mattress in the basement, and on those rare nights when the kids were asleep and Kelly had the energy, she and DJ snuck downstairs to remind each other what sex was. Tonight she was in no mood and had no energy, but if it kept him from retrieving today's mail, she'd find a second wind.

"Consider those dishes done," he said. "But first let me double-check the mailbox."

Before she could stop him, he was out the door.

Kelly trudged into the kitchen and smacked her forehead against the fridge. It left a woozy, tingling sensation above her eyes. She wondered how hard she would have to hit her head to forget about the green envelope. Maybe she could crack her skull like an egg and let the bad memories ooze out.

Her phone buzzed in her pocket. The name Emma flashed across the screen. Kelly blinked in disbelief. *Wow. First time Emma's called in nearly a year. Did she have a change of heart?*

Kelly answered. "Hey, Em. What's up?"

Static burst through the phone. Then a distant, muffled voice.

"Em?"

The call ended.

Seemed Emma had dialed her by mistake.

Of course. Never should've gotten my hopes up.

The front door squealed open. DJ marched into the living room hoisting a cardboard box like it was the World Cup trophy. "*Neither rain, nor snow, nor sleet, nor hail!* Can't wait to fire this baby up."

"So much for you firing *me* up," Kelly muttered.

"Relax, I'll inflate the air mattress in a sec." He slapped a stack of mail onto the kitchen table. A bright green envelope corner poked out like a scorpion tail.

Her chest went tight. She reminded herself she didn't have to open the envelope. She could toss it in the garbage. Pretend it never arrived. After all, it said the same thing every year.

But this year might be different. This year, the envelope's contents might offer forgiveness—a reason to stop feeling horrible about what happened.

Soon as DJ went downstairs, she plucked the envelope from the pile and ripped it open. Inside was the usual twice-folded sheet of paper.

Why do I do this to myself? God, I'm such an idiot.

After unfolding the paper, she saw a black-and-white printout of Anissa Norwell's obituary. In the accompanying photo Anissa was posing in her college soccer uniform, smiling with fierce, energetic eyes. Kelly didn't need to read her teammate's obituary; she had the whole thing memorized.

Behind it was a second sheet of paper. Four short sentences were printed at the top: "Twelve years ago today my daughter passed away unexpectedly. Do you miss her? You should visit her grave. I do every day."

The letter was signed by Nancy Norwell.

Kelly swallowed hard. Chills snaked down her arms despite the warm September night.

Twelve years now. Can't believe it. All I had to do was finish college like a normal girl. Ride out the rest of soccer season on the bench. I didn't have to be such a monster. Didn't have to—

Her phone buzzed again.

She answered. "Emma? You there?"

"Mom?" Static crackled through the line. "Can you hear me?"

The sound of her teenage daughter's voice left Kelly speechless. Heat spread across her cheeks as she blinked back tears. She cleared her throat. "Y-yeah, Em. You're a little choppy, but yeah."

"Uh, so... Remember you said if I ever got stuck at a party, I could call you and you'd pick me up?"

"Of course." Kelly snatched her keys off the kitchen counter. "Give me the address, I'll be right there."

"And you said if you picked me up, you wouldn't tell my dad?"

"That's the deal, yep."

"And there'd be no questions asked?"

"Emma, *yes*. Where are you?"

Another burst of static. "I'm not sure."

"Ask someone at the party."

"It's not a party," Emma said. "I mean, it was, but we left and went to another house. I'm upstairs in the attic. I'm stuck."

Stuck? That was odd. Kelly had broken into houses on dares when she was Emma's age, but she never got stuck. "Can you check your location on your phone?"

"Uh, lemme—"

Her voice dropped out again.

Come on, come on.

"—ail Road."

"What?" Kelly said.

"Red Trail Road, number 88. It's twenty minutes outside Scranton."

Kelly punched the address into her GPS app. "Stay there. I'll see you in twenty."

She ended the call and grabbed her purse.

"And where do you think you're headed?" DJ asked, climbing the basement stairs.

"Emma's at a party. I gotta pick her up."

"What?" He launched into the kitchen, his shoes squeaking on the tiles. "But she's been shutting you out for a year now."

"Right, and that's about to change."

"Be careful, babe." He set his hands on her shoulders. "I don't want to see you get used."

"I'm not getting used." She shrugged free. "If Emma needs help, I'm gonna help her. Besides, it's not like she's asking for money. She just wants to get home safe."

"Why didn't she call her father?"

"Because Rick would probably arrest her."

"Eh, that's true." DJ crossed his arms and sighed. "Well, if you're going... Want me to tag along? I can ask the lady next door to babysit till we get back."

"Thanks, hon, but I need one-on-one time with Emma." Kelly slipped into her shoes and took a deep breath. "I think this is gonna work out. I really do."

"Let's hope so." He flicked his head toward the basement. "Maybe later we can celebrate."

"Maybe." She pecked his cheek and hurried into the garage.

2

Kelly braked for a stop sign and tapped a cigarette out the minivan's window. The nicotine failed to calm her nerves. Her foot jittered onto the gas pedal, and she exited the well-lit Scranton suburbs, heading northwest toward Redbrook Township. The shadowy, woodsy area was well outside her comfort zone. Not a Starbucks for miles—or even a Dunkin' for that matter.

Driving through the winding roads of rural Pennsylvania at night could get tricky, but what really bothered her was the thought of approaching Emma. *How should I act? What should I say? Will Emma even want to talk? On the phone she insisted no questions be asked, but I should still engage in some sort of conversation.*

At the next stop sign, Kelly began to light another smoke before she realized she'd arrived. Red Trail Road. Pretty dumb name considering the road itself was black and the surrounding trees were exclusively green, orange, and copper. Even the stop sign was discolored to a darkish pink.

Her stomach full of hornets, she drove on. The GPS

said her destination was right ahead, but all she saw were thick trees swishing in the nighttime wind.

She flicked on her high beams.

Hanging oak leaves hid a rusty mailbox. She squinted at the numbers before a sloping driveway appeared out of nowhere on her right.

She stomped the brake. Her tires squealed to a stop.

She reversed and turned into the crumbling dirt driveway. Birch trees formed a tunnel-like canopy overhead. The van rumbled uphill, and when things leveled off, her headlights landed on overgrown grass and bushes as shaggy as her husband's beard.

Beyond the bushes stood a towering two-story home. An elegant wooden veranda wrapped both sides. The house was a duplex, two identical housing units separated by a central wall. *What an odd place to build a duplex. Usually people moved out to woodsy areas to distance themselves from their neighbors, not share a building with them.*

As she rolled closer, Kelly noticed the entire right side showed signs of fire damage: melted window shutters, blackened vinyl siding, exposed underlying brick. Strangely, the left side showed no burn markings whatsoever. The difference baffled her. She hoped this wasn't the correct house.

With a sputtering heart, she dialed Emma.

"Mom? Where are you?"

"I'm outside a duplex."

"What's a duplex?"

"Two houses in one."

"Oh—that's it. I'm in the good side."

Kelly exhaled. "Okay, you can come out."

"I can't—I'm stuck in the attic, remember?"

"Stuck how? Like you need a ladder?"

"Somebody locked the attic door. It won't budge."

Kelly killed the engine. "I'll come get you. How do I get inside the house?"

"Back window. Waaay in the back. You'll see it. And watch out, there's glass on the floor."

As Kelly approached the building, she kept glancing between the two halves. The left unit was in pristine condition, the right unit ruined. *So strange.* Though it was possible that a firewall had protected the left side, there should've been at least some exterior damage. Then again, maybe the damage had been restored. But why fix one side and not the other?

She stepped onto the veranda. The wooden planks creaked beneath her feet as she rounded the house, where she spotted two toppled garbage cans in the back. Several feet above them was the open window that Emma had presumably climbed through.

The garbage cans didn't look sturdy enough to stand on, so Kelly tried the back door, a French door with rectangular glass panes. Locked. She noticed rocks in the dirt and grabbed a pointed one. Three good strikes shattered the glass panel near the doorknob. She carefully reached inside and unlocked it.

Upon entering, she stepped on broken glass—not just the panel she'd busted to unlock the door but countless shards of all shapes, sizes, and colors. Beer bottles, most likely. Yet the place didn't smell of booze. Instead, when she inhaled she caught a foul odor that reminded her of oily, unwashed hair.

She shined her phone's flashlight down the hall. Nearby was an empty kitchen: countertops, cupboards, and a sink, but no table or chairs. The living room was also barren aside from a ceiling fan. Not a single piece of furniture. Just glass everywhere.

A staircase rose near the front door. Dust tickled her nostrils as she climbed the glass-covered steps. On the second floor her foot kicked an empty bottle into a spin. It rattled off a nearby baseboard. When she shined her light toward it, she noticed words carved into the wall: "Half Murder House."

How lovely.

She called Emma's name but got no reply.

She checked the upstairs rooms. More broken glass. In one room she spotted an empty pill bottle. Her eyes lingered on the translucent orange container until a thumping sounded overhead, from the far end of the hall.

Kelly hurried into what appeared to be the master bedroom. The place stank like a sewer. A soiled, sunken mattress lay surrounded by spent needles, busted bottles, and used condoms. *No questions asked. No questions asked.*

Another thump sounded above.

"Emma?"

Shining her light toward the ceiling, Kelly spotted a rectangular wooden door with a brass knob. She discovered a metal bucket in a corner and used it as a footstool to reach the knob. She grabbed it and tugged. It didn't budge. Not until she twisted it.

The door dropped open. A metallic screech sounded as an extension ladder slid free. The ladder banged against the floor beside the mattress.

Kelly pressed a hand over her pounding heart. She shined her light toward the opening in the ceiling. After catching her breath, she said, "Em, you can come down!"

"I need help." Her daughter's voice echoed.

"What's wrong?"

"Please just come up here. I'm really stuck."

It hurt to imagine why her daughter couldn't come

down. Was she injured? Trapped under something heavy? Handcuffed to something as a joke?

Whatever the reason, Kelly set foot on the ladder. It wobbled and screeched as she ascended into the darkness above.

3

The attic was hot, dusty, and unthinkably dark.

Kelly stepped off the ladder onto the floorboards. Her toe bumped something hollow. Whatever it was rattled away woodenly before thudding to a stop. Trembling, she shined her light and illuminated an arm—a pale gray mannequin arm. She spun the light around the wide, high-ceilinged attic. The floor was covered with similar parts: plastic legs, heads, torsos. Some bodies had limbs attached, most were in pieces.

Great. First the broken glass, then the sleazy mattress, and now these freaky mannequins. Emma, you sure picked a lovely house to get stuck in.

Using her foot, Kelly swept aside plastic limbs to create standing room. The place was a mess. Ahead stood a maze-like arrangement of wooden bureaus, cabinets, and grandfather clocks. Dusty cardboard boxes lay stacked upon tables and shelving racks.

"Emma, where are you?"

"Over here." Her voice echoed from the attic's center.

"I'll be right there."

Kelly entered the maze, taking careful steps to avoid rolling an ankle on the scattered mannequin parts. She continued toward the back wall. There stood a row of full-length mirrors. Despite the dusty air, the mirrors remained relatively polished. She caught her reflection in them, souring at how worried she looked.

No questions asked.

Nearby tables were burdened with cardboard boxes and wooden crates. Plastic fingers poked from one container. Another overflowed with plastic heads, their eyeless faces staring blankly at her.

Fresh sweat trickled down her back, tracing her spine like a wet fingertip. She upped her pace, kicking through waves of hard plastic. Everything rattled and crunched, louder and louder. Then something grabbed her knee.

She flinched.

Gasped.

"Mom, it's me!"

Kelly dropped a nervous hand over her rioting heart. She glanced down.

Emma sat on the floor, leaning against a wooden cabinet. Her red hair stuck to her sweaty, freckled face. Her expression was exhausted, her blue scoop-neck top soaked with perspiration. She looked relatively normal—until Kelly noticed a shower curtain wrapped around her daughter's waist like a makeshift skirt.

Kelly aimed her light toward it. "What's with the—"

"You promised no questions," Emma said, her tone high with embarrassment. As the light reached her bare feet, she outstretched both hands. "Help me up."

Kelly grabbed her daughter's wrists and hoisted her. Once upright, Emma threw her arms around Kelly and squeezed tight. Emma had always been a hugger, but tonight she held on as though she might otherwise collapse. Kelly wanted to ask a zillion questions, but instead she returned the hug. It was nice to hold her daughter again.

"We can leave now," Emma said, breaking their embrace. Her shower curtain swished. She took two steps before stumbling against a shelving rack. Her eyes met Kelly's. "Mind helping me walk? My legs are acting weird."

Kelly let Emma wrap an arm around her. Together they staggered toward the attic entrance. There, Emma paused. She seemed nervous about climbing down. To get her onto the ladder, Kelly had to lift her daughter by the armpits and lower her through the opening. It required arduous effort, and Kelly dreaded the lower back pain she'd be waking up to tomorrow.

Now secured against the ladder, Emma hesitated. Her hands clutched the side railing. She glanced below. Took shallow breaths. She lifted one foot and lowered her toes onto the next step.

Then she slipped. She tumbled backward and landed hard on the soiled mattress.

An icy spike slammed through Kelly's heart. She rushed down the ladder in a panic. "Are you okay?"

Emma lay sprawled, her legs bent awkwardly beneath the shower curtain. Her face was constricted with pain. Kelly lifted the plastic curtain to straighten Emma's legs and noticed she wasn't wearing anything underneath.

"What the hell, Mom?" Emma pushed the shower curtain over her ankles. She struggled to sit up and caught her breath. They both did. Then she eyed the glass-covered floor. "Do you have an extra pair of shoes in your van?"

Kelly set her jaw. So many red flags, so many unanswered questions. Maybe once they left this freaky house, Emma would calm down and explain herself.

"They might not be your size, but yes," Kelly said. "Wait here till I get back."

"Thanks." Emma forced a smile. "And remember, no questions."

Kelly was finding it harder and harder to keep that promise.

4

Kelly had never associated silence with her daughter. Emma had always been a yapper. Her mouth would fly in a thousand different directions as she raved about TV dramas, criticized her teachers, and mocked her stepmom's fashion sense. One subject would pour into another until Kelly encouraged her to start a podcast or steal someone's job at SiriusXM. Then Emma would laugh until she caught her breath before jabbering on about other topics.

Tonight, however, there was no yapping, no laughing, no jabbering. The only sound came from the minivan's grumbling motor as it rolled through downtown Scranton.

At each stoplight Kelly glanced sidelong at her daughter. The nighttime breeze tossed Emma's red hair as she stared outside at parked cars and empty sidewalks. Every few seconds she adjusted the shower curtain around her waist. She would then rest her hands atop her thighs, acting like such a wardrobe choice was normal. Kelly played along.

"I broke into a house once," Kelly said, trying to sound casual. "Must've been around your age. The floors weren't covered in broken glass or plastic limbs, but I did get chased by a Doberman." She shook her head, chuckling. "You wouldn't believe why I broke in."

Emma didn't reply. Didn't care.

So much for making conversation.

Kelly drove up a one-way street, attempting to shave a minute off her drive time. Instead, traffic stalled near a shady hole-in-the-wall bar. Horns blared while a drunk girl stood in the street ranting about someone named Kimberly. She kept pronouncing it "Kim-Blurry," which went from funny to annoying real fast.

Kelly leaned toward Emma. "See what you have to look forward to in college?"

Emma gave a noncommittal shrug.

Once Kim-Blurry and her friend ducked into a car, traffic resumed. Things ran smoothly until Kelly reached a series of red lights. The stop-and-go rhythm made her want to scream. Every time she hit the brake, she studied Emma's shower curtain and wondered where her daughter's pants and underwear had gone. She hoped it was part of some stupid game. If it wasn't—if someone had touched her—Kelly would kill them, plain and simple. She would—

No. Don't think about it. Just let it go.

But then she noticed the bottom of Emma's shirt. It was cut in a strange uneven way, as if someone had taken scissors to it. And not in a fashionable way.

A horn blared from behind. Kelly snapped alert. Green light. She stomped the gas pedal and fled the Electric City.

As they headed north, Emma repeatedly poked and squeezed her thighs. At one point she leaned forward and stared at her feet. She rotated her ankles in circles. Her legs seemed to be loosening up.

After exiting the highway, Kelly hung a left into Peachwood Acres. Streetlamps gleamed in welcome. The lavish development sprawled with wide streets, rolling lawns, and jumbo-sized homes. The van groaned as it climbed a hill toward her ex-husband's house.

In the passenger seat Emma straightened herself up. "Can you drop me off a couple houses down the road? That way, we won't wake Dad."

"How's your father these days?"

Emma shrugged. "Total zombie."

"What do you mean?"

"Every night after patrol duty, he drops into his recliner and stares at the TV. Just flips channels. Doesn't even watch anything. When he's on duty, though, he's like a different person. He calls me up, cracks jokes, listens to my every word... I kinda wish he was always working."

Kelly was surprised her daughter was suddenly so talkative. She invited Emma to vent further. "Your stepmom still driving you nuts?"

"Not really. I barely see her these days. She works thousand-hour weeks, always running financials for a new client or whatever. At least she stays outta my way."

"Nice."

"Yup."

Kelly parked along the sidewalk and unlocked the doors.

Emma didn't move. She glanced at the shower curtain.

"Wait here," Kelly said. "I might have some extra gym shorts in the trunk."

She ran around back, found the shorts, and gave them to Emma.

"Thanks." Emma tugged them on beneath the shower curtain. She shed her plastic skirt and opened the passenger door. Cool air rushed in. She eyed the sidewalk with the severity of someone about to leap off a cliff. Then she swung both feet outside. Upright, she held onto the door.

"Huh." There was a pleasant note in her voice. "My legs feel better."

"You sure?"

"Yeah..." She marched in place, then chuckled with relief. "Hey, thanks for picking me up. I was afraid to call Dad."

Kelly leaned over the armrest. "You have my number if you ever get stuck again. Or if you just wanna talk."

Emma forced a smile. She swayed awkwardly before saying, "I have a soccer game tomorrow if you wanna go."

Kelly flinched. A mix of icy nerves and cozy warmth spread through her chest. "I-I'd love to. Where at?"

"It's a home game. Starts at 4:45."

"I work till five, but I'll be there right after."

Emma grinned. "I made varsity. I'm the starting goalie."

"That's amazing! Goalie is—"

"What you played in college." Emma snorted. "Believe me, I know."

"You'll do great." Kelly blinked back tears. "Before long, you'll be putting Hope Solo and Briana Scurry to shame."

Emma grabbed the door and went to shut it. "Thanks for...not making tonight more awkward than it needed to be."

"I've been there. If you ever wanna talk, I'm all ears." More than anything in the world, Kelly wanted Emma to crawl back into the van and confide in her. Clue her in. Ask for help if she needed it. "Otherwise, we'll pretend this never happened."

Emma glanced at her legs, then at Kelly. "Yeah, let's pretend."

5

Soon as Kelly pulled into her garage, she killed the engine and rested her forehead against the steering wheel. Though it was a poor substitute for a pillow, she dozed. Tonight had worn her out both physically and emotionally. She couldn't imagine climbing upstairs to her bedroom. With each passing breath, she felt herself drifting.

Then a squeal sounded. She glanced out the passenger window and saw the kitchen door opening. Light poured into the garage. A silhouette appeared in the doorway, barely inches taller than the doorknob. Though her sons were identical twins, she could tell it was Zach. His timid demeanor gave him away.

He tiptoed toward the passenger window and knocked. "Mommy?"

"Be right out, cutie." She peeled her forehead off the steering wheel and trudged outside.

Zach ran over and hugged her around the waist. Greatest feeling in the world—even when her lower back was sore.

"You should be in bed," she whispered.

"I couldn't sleep." He hugged tighter. "And I couldn't find Daddy."

"He's not upstairs?"

"No." Zach released her and looked up with wounded eyes. "I thought you both left us."

"We would never." Kelly kissed his forehead. She wondered where her husband might be. Then she remembered the air mattress downstairs. DJ probably fell asleep while waiting for her to come home. "Bet your dad's in the basement working on his computer."

"I tried to check, but the door was locked."

As it should be. Back in January, DJ installed an electronic number-pad lock to keep the twins from going near the washing machine. The kids had been banned from the basement after some jerk on their school bus convinced them to drink laundry detergent. They had both gulped enough fluid to warrant a trip to the ER. Absolute nightmare.

Zach tugged on her shirt. "Mommy, your clothes are dusty."

"Yeah, I was...cleaning."

"Oh. Can you rub my head till I fall asleep?"

"Sure."

They went upstairs. Aiden was fast asleep in his own bed. Zach climbed under his Incredible Hulk comforter and rested his head on the pillow. Kelly sat alongside him and ran her fingers through his curly red hair, barely a shade darker than her own. She liked that about her twins. Facially, they resembled their father, but they had her hair, just like Emma.

She rubbed Zach's head with gentle circles until he dozed.

At some point she dozed too.

MORNING ARRIVED like a kick to the head.

Kelly groaned as the twins' Bluey alarm clock jingled, playing the cartoon theme song. Both kids snoozed despite the noise. She reached over to smack the alarm and sat up, her back against the headboard. Her brain felt swollen to the size of a watermelon.

Sunlight flared between the slit in the curtains. The thought of enduring eight hours of customer phone calls made her want to dive headfirst out the window. Her gaze wandered over the twins' dresser, which was cluttered with Spider-man action figures and soccer participation trophies. She wished she were a kid again. Or even a teenager. She missed having more energy and less responsibility.

Beside her, Zach snored. She shook him awake. Then she called out to Aiden, who flinched but pretended to be asleep.

"C'mon, boys," she said. "Brush your teeth and head downstairs for cereal."

"Can we have Pop-Tarts?" Aiden asked.

"Pop-Tarts are for dessert."

"Nuh-uh. Ethan at school eats them for breakfast."

"Ethan at school doesn't have me for his mother. Brush your teeth, please. You too, Zach."

"I want Pop-Tarts," Zach said. "Please, Mommy?"

Aiden started chanting. "Pop-*Tarts*! Pop-*Tarts*! Pop-*Tarts*!"

Zach joined in.

She raised her voice. "If you two aren't in the bathroom in five seconds, you'll eat broccoli for breakfast. One... two...three..."

Both boys darted into the hallway.

Kelly wandered down the hall and found her bedroom empty. No husband in sight. She went down to the basement and discovered DJ asleep on the air mattress. He lay sprawled on his back wearing only a pair of boxer briefs and his Batman mask. In their nine years together, he'd always insisted on wearing that thing during sex, even on their wedding night. Why he required a Batman mask to maintain a hard-on was a mystery. She asked him about it once, and he freaked. In the end she let him bury that particular secret; after all, she had hidden many of her own.

This morning, his snoring sounded like Velcro ripping. Each time he exhaled, his beard floated away from his lower lip. She liked his beard. It made him look manly. If she weren't dead tired, she might've peeled off her jeans and hopped onto him. It had been, what, two months since their last go? Three? Tempting as that was, she needed to get the kids to school.

She kicked the air mattress.

"Huh?" He stirred awake. Sat up. "Oh, you're back. How'd it go with Emma?"

"Good. Kinda."

He frowned. "Wanna talk about it?"

She hesitated. "Maybe another time."

"All right." He flashed a hopeful grin. "So... We sleeping down here?"

"It's morning, dummy."

"Really?" He grabbed his phone off a nearby shelf. "Whoa, already after seven?"

"Yepper." She rubbed her temples and headed for the stairs.

"Hey, Kelly?"

"Yeah?"

"How about tonight?" He patted the mattress. "I mean, it's been ages."

"It certainly has, but Emma invited me to her soccer game tonight."

He winced. Soccer disgusted him for some reason. Last year when Kelly had signed up the twins for a youth league, he went berserk. Said the sport was too dangerous and cited how thousands of kids landed in the ER each year due to soccer injuries. She pointed out that most of those injuries were sustained by kids older than twelve, but he kept piling on statistics. In the end, she ignored his concerns, and he refused to attend the kids' games on principle.

"Well, it's great that you and Emma are reconnecting," he said, genuine warmth in his tone. He removed the mask and slid his glasses onto his nose. "After the game, you should take her to that Thai place she likes."

Kelly perked. "Good idea. I'll have to ask her."

"Yeah, give it a shot." He pulled his shirt on. "Worst-case scenario... If you get home early, we can order takeout, send the kids to bed, and then, y'know..." He held his mask up with two fingers. "Batman versus Poison Ivy."

Kelly rolled her eyes and started upstairs.

"What?" he said. "Would you rather dress as Catwoman?"

She paused halfway up the steps. "I'd rather you dress as DJ."

6

Gametime was in less than nine hours, but first Kelly needed to survive her workday. After dropping off the twins at school, she headed home, brewed fresh coffee, and hiked upstairs with a steaming mug in each hand. Reluctantly, she sat at her desk and powered on her computer. Beside the keyboard lay her headset. She clipped it to her ear and wished someone would shoot her.

Instead, a robotic jingle sounded.

She tapped a button on the headset. "Hi. This is Kelly from HomeTekk. How can I help you?"

"Your name's Kelly?" asked an elderly man. "With a Y or *IE*?"

"With a Y. How can I help you?"

"Well, Kelly with a Y, this morning my microwave had itself a tizz."

"A tizz?"

"Yep. Never had problems with it before."

"But now it's...having a tizz?"

"Sure is."

"What's wrong with it?"

"I don't know. You tell me."

I'm about to have a tizz myself, she thought.

The geezer complained about his microwave for ten straight minutes before asking about his freezer's power settings. Then, out of nowhere, he began quoting passages from his dishwasher's instruction manual, speaking in a strong, reverent tone, as if he were reciting the Old Testament.

After transferring him elsewhere, Kelly received a message from her boss ordering her to assist the credit department with an influx of emails. She hated working with numbers. Worse yet, she hated doing other people's jobs. *God, I should've finished my degree.*

She caught her reflection on the computer screen and imagined putting her fist through the glass. She often wished she could somehow beat herself bloody. Just step outside her body, turn around, and unload punch after punch. That would make her feel much better.

Then again, so would wine. And after last night, she deserved an early drink.

Soon as the local liquor store opened at 10 a.m., she signed off for a bathroom break and hopped into the van. Sweet relief was two left turns and a traffic light away. She pulled into the strip mall lot and parked beside a faded blue handicap spot.

A bell jingled as she opened the shop's front door. She knew exactly what she wanted: Sunset Blush boxed wine. Back wall, bottom shelf. She hurried down the center aisle, pausing as the potent scent of spilled wine nipped her nose. Near the back wall, a pair of WET FLOOR signs guarded a shattered bottle.

"Hey, K-Lady!"

Kelly whirled around and saw her lifelong friend Brittney Mathis. Tall, with thick dark curls, Brittney wore a burgundy work apron over a gray t-shirt with the words "You Can Wine To Me" printed across the front. She was all smiles as the two of them embraced like teenagers—big squeeze, little giggles, swaying back and forth.

When they stood at arm's length, Kelly marveled at Brittney's new hairstyle. Sideswept and chin-length, it covered one cheek while revealing the rest of her radiant, adventurous face. Her smooth dark skin glowed as she grinned.

"So, what do you think?"

"I love it!" Kelly said, gesturing for her to turn around. Brittney did a little twirl—something she'd obviously been practicing—and her curly hair floated before settling back into place. Kelly squealed. "You have to tell me where you got it done—right after you tell me what spilled over there. It smells delish."

"It's a Spanish red. And you're right, it's *muy bueno*."

Kelly gave a mischievous grin. "Did you have a sip?"

"Off the floor? Girl, get outta here. This isn't college."

Kelly flinched at the mention of college. The green envelope flashed in her mind. Rather than dwell on it, she wet her upper lip and asked, "How much for that Spanish red?"

"Triple what you normally pay."

Groaning, Kelly grabbed her usual and carried it to the sales counter.

Brittney followed and rang it up. "Cash or credit?"

"Cash. Can't have DJ getting a purchase alert from the wine store."

"Certainly not before noon," Brittney said. "You must have one rough day ahead."

"Yeah, but it should be a great night. Emma invited me to her soccer game."

"Oh, nice! See, I told you she'd come around. What'd she say?"

"Long story." Kelly grabbed her keys. "Sorry, but I gotta get back to work."

"Ooo, you know what?" Brittney enthusiastically knocked on the counter. "We should get drinks this week-end. My brother's coming in, so I won't have to babysit Mom and Dad. You free Friday?"

"I wish."

"Saturday?"

"I wish."

"Sunday?"

"I wish."

"Oh, come on." Brittney flipped her sideswept curls. "I want to test my new do, see how many heads I can turn. You telling me you can't carve out one night?"

"It's tough with the kids."

"Ask DJ to cover for you. Say, 'Sweetie-poo, can you shut your laptop and watch the kiddos this weekend?'"

"First of all, I'd never call him sweetie-poo."

"You're missing my point."

"And second—" Her phone buzzed. She feared it might be her boss, but it was a notification from Emma. Smiling, she held the phone up to show Brittney the message: "Thx for everything last night. Coolest mom everrrr!"

Brittney laughed. "Look at you being Mom of the Year."

"Don't hand me any awards just yet."

"It'll work out." Brittney stepped around the counter for

a quick hug. "And you can tell me all about it this weekend. Pick a day, find a sitter, and we'll have ourselves some fun."

Kelly grabbed her wine, raced home, and logged back on her work computer. She immediately received a call from some guy whose stove was having a tizz. She let him rant while she filled her wine glass. The familiar strawberry scent soothed her. After taking a sip, she responded to Emma's message.

"Ready for your big game?"

"Yup!!! And I need a HUGE favor. I left my purse in that attic. It's bright blue. Can you plz get it for me?"

Kelly shivered in her office chair. No way was she returning to that creepy house. She sipped more wine—which now tasted a little too sweet—and mulled over a reply.

"How about I buy you a new purse?"

"But my old one had something important inside."

"What? Credit cards? You can always cancel them."

"It's not those. It's a good luck charm."

"Do you need it before your game?"

"No. But I do need it. Plz get it for me?"

Kelly pinched the stem of her wine glass. Her mind wandered to DJ's warning from last night—the part about her getting used by Emma. *Would Emma be messaging me now if she didn't need that purse? Will the messages dry up once she gets it back?* Disappointment seemed likely.

Then again, Kelly had been invited to tonight's game. That was a good sign. Last night Emma could've exited the van without a word; instead, she invited Kelly back into her life. They'd be seeing each other today and hopefully again in the future.

Though Kelly dreaded returning to that house, she couldn't afford to disappoint her daughter. Not now.

She typed back, "Tonight after your game I'll go get your purse."

"Thx Mom!!! Be careful!"

Kelly gulped more wine. Her headset rang, and she accepted the call. Whatever the customer said, she wasn't listening. All she could think about was making Emma happy.

7

At five o'clock Kelly hit the road. She reached Emma's school and parked in the first spot she could find. Then she ran toward the soccer stadium, her stomach in a full-on tizz. She liked that word, *tizz*. It amused her. Got her through her workday. Even now, it calmed her nerves as she passed through the ticket booth.

In the distance came the sounds of the game: the thud of a kicked ball, the shouting of coaches, the cheering of parents and students.

This'll work out. Emma wants me in the stands. Wants me back in her life.

Two sets of bleachers faced the field, which glowed yellow-green in the late-afternoon sun. The wind carried a grassy scent that made Kelly nostalgic for her own high school soccer days. Back then, she dominated at every position and earned the nickname Kickin' Kelly while leading her team to the state semifinals as a junior. Had she not gotten pregnant with Emma the following summer, she might've won the state championship as a senior.

Now, it was Emma's turn to dominate. And as Kelly

jogged along the sideline, she saw her daughter run up to make an easy save.

"Yes!" Kelly clapped. "Go, Em!"

From the bleachers boomed a familiar roar of approval. Kelly's ex-husband Rick sat in the fifth row, behind everyone else, wearing his blue police uniform and sunglasses. His bald head shined with sweat. After Emma made another save, the whole stadium knew it when his voice thundered.

Kelly climbed the bleachers and tried sneaking up on him for a cheap scare.

"Don't do it, Kell," he said as she came within arm's reach. "I'm in game-mode right now."

She laughed. "I can see that. How's Emma doing?"

"You tell me. You're the soccer expert."

"Did the other team score?"

"No."

"Then she's doing great." Kelly sat beside him and picked at his uniform sleeve. "Surprised you didn't take the evening off to watch the game."

"That was the plan, but my asshole captain had other ideas. Best I could do was take my lunch break when— Yo, wait!" Rick pointed to a girl on the other team who slid to knock the ball away from Emma's teammate. "Are they allowed to do that?"

"Do what? Tackle?"

"That's not a tackle. She nearly tripped her. Shouldn't that be a red card?"

"It's legal, Rick."

"Better not happen to Emma. Anybody tries that shit, I'll show them what a real tackle is."

She snorted. "That I'd like to see."

"Know what *I'd* like to see? You explaining why you drove Emma home last night."

"Oh, geez." She swallowed hard. Usually she got along great with Rick. They had been high school lovers who were pressured into marrying after Emma was conceived. Because of the shotgun wedding, they never took their marriage seriously and actually bonded over the absurdity of the whole thing. They'd had nothing to fight over in the divorce, and afterward they embraced their roles as co-parents. Unfortunately, Rick often disagreed with her parenting methods.

"C'mon, Kell. Let's hear it."

After a deep breath, she said, "When Emma started middle school, I told her to call me if she ever got stranded at a party. I promised I'd pick her up, no questions asked."

"That's good, but you should've kept me in the loop."

"I didn't want to break her trust."

"Well, now you're testing mine," he said. "Tell me, was she drinking last night?"

"No."

He raised a finger. "Don't lie to me, Kell. I hate when you lie."

"I'm not lying. I didn't smell anything."

The crowd emitted a collective gasp.

Rick turned his attention toward the goal. He leaped out of his seat. "Come on, Em! Get in position. Get... Yeah! BOO-YAH!" His thick hairy hands clapped thunder. "That's my girl!"

The parents below smiled awkwardly.

After a high punt, the game resumed with lots of passing and dribbling around midfield. When Emma's team drove toward the opposite end, Rick sat down.

"So, no booze?" he asked.

"No booze."

"No drugs either?"

"Nothing."

"Then what was she doing last night?"

Kelly shifted uncomfortably. Only Emma herself knew the answer. How she ended up in that attic wearing a shower curtain was a mystery. "Honestly, I don't know."

"From now on," he said, craning his neck to follow the action, "if she calls you, you call me."

"I promised her otherwise."

"Relax, I won't say anything to her—I just want to know what's going on."

Kelly crossed her arms to contain her frustration. "If I rat her out, she won't call either of us next time. Is that what you want? Remember, she's a teenager. She's gonna explore her boundaries whether we like it or not."

He made a noncommittal face. "Just keep me in the loop, okay?"

"Sure."

"I'm serious. We can't—"

Static burst through the radio mounted on his shoulder. "Unit three, come in, unit three. Over."

Rick clicked his radio. "Copy. Over."

"Got a 10-82 in Taylor. Here's the address."

He jotted it down on an old-school notepad and told dispatch he was on his way.

"Need a favor, Kell." He stood and massaged his knee. "You mind driving Emma home after the game?"

Kelly perked up at the opportunity. "Not at all. Be careful, Rick."

Once he was gone, she focused on the players from both teams, judging footwork, positioning, and stamina. Eventually she found herself zeroing in on Emma. The longer

Kelly watched, the more she noticed something about Emma's footwork was off. Her movements looked stiff and unnatural—same as last night.

The other team came storming Emma's way. A forward slipped behind a defender and passed the ball. The striker caught it on the side of her foot, made a move that sent ponytails flying, and dribbled toward the goal. The crowd released a collective gasp as the girl swung her leg back and launched the ball.

It rose off the grass, speeding toward the net.

Emma dove after it. Caught it on her chest.

The bleachers erupted in cheers. Parents clapped wildly. Students chanted Emma's name.

The celebration died down as the ref blew the whistle.

There was an injury timeout. Emma wasn't getting up.

8

The ref blew the whistle again as Kelly stormed down the bleachers and onto the field. She and the coaching staff sprinted toward the penalty box, where Emma lay clutching the ball against her chest. Her upper body twisted with discomfort, but her legs weren't moving.

Kelly dropped to her knees beside her daughter. The girl's eyes were alarmingly wide, pupils narrow as pinpoints. She hugged the ball so hard that it popped from her grasp like a champagne cork and bounced off a nearby teammate.

"Everyone give her space," Kelly said, shooing people away. "Em, what's wrong?"

"Cramp."

"Like last night?"

"Yeah."

Now what? Call 911? Call Rick? Probably best to let Emma ride this out. Then again, waiting hadn't helped last night. What *had* helped was propping her upright in the van.

"She's had an issue like this before," Kelly said to the

coaches. "She needs to sit. Can someone move her over to the bleachers?"

Two tall brunettes hoisted Emma off the ground. Her legs dangled while they carried her to the sideline and lowered her onto the bottom bleacher. People everywhere were watching. Emma stared at the ground, face red as a sunburn. Kelly settled beside her and secured an arm around Emma's trembling shoulders.

"She'll be fine," Kelly said to her teammates. "Finish your game. Win it for her."

The team failed to. They lost 3-0. Every time the ball hit the net, Emma flinched like she'd been kicked in the throat. After the game ended, she remained seated. She hugged her legs to her chest like a turtle retreating into its shell.

Players, coaches, parents, and students vacated the field. One student loitered on the third row of bleachers—a stoner-looking kid with messy hair and a Nirvana t-shirt. He eyed Emma until Kelly shot him a dirty look that sent him packing. Everyone else left except one of Emma's teammates, a platinum blonde who ran over.

"Em, you played great," the girl said. "That one save you made was amazing."

"Thanks, Cassie."

"How's your cramp? Is it worse than it was in chem class?"

"It's fine," Emma said defensively.

Cassie tilted her head, unconvinced. "Well... Hope you feel better by Friday's game."

The girl jogged off, leaving Kelly and Emma alone on the bench.

"How are you really feeling?" Kelly asked. "Want me to call your dad?"

"No—don't," Emma said. "Promise me you won't tell him about this."

Kelly recalled her chat with Rick. "That's asking a lot, Em. Losing control of your legs like that... He should know."

"It's no big deal. I'll be fine."

"Do you even know what's wrong with your legs?"

Emma shrugged.

"You don't know?" Kelly grabbed her keys. "Then we're going to the hospital."

"Wait. I do know. I just don't want to talk about it. Can we please ignore this?"

Kelly squeezed her daughter's elbow. "When you called last night, I dropped everything to make sure you were okay. That's important to me. So no, I will not ignore this, and you will not ignore me. I need to know you're healthy."

"I am."

"Then what's wrong with your legs?"

"I slipped and fell in that attic, okay? I landed hard on one of those plastic heads."

"You might've pinched a nerve. You should see a doctor."

"I'm fine. Really. My legs are better than they were last night. Honestly, I'm more worried about my purse. You're still gonna go get it, right?"

Kelly hesitated. She didn't like this at all. Not only was Emma shutting her out, but the girl still expected a huge favor. Maybe DJ was right. Maybe Emma *was* using her.

No. Emma invited me here today because she wants to reconnect. There's still a chance to make this work. I need to set the right tone.

"Here's what's gonna happen," Kelly said, her voice firm. "Tonight I'll get your purse like I promised. But once I have it, you're not getting it back until you either visit the doctor or tell me what happened last night."

Emma gave a sheepish smile. "Y'know what? I'll just go get the purse myself."

"No you won't. And if you even try—"

Kelly's phone buzzed. Rick. He must've heard the news.

She answered. "Hey, Rick."

"What the fuck were you thinking?" His hostile tone startled her. "I told you to drive Emma straight home—not to the mall."

"The mall?" Kelly paused, dumbfounded. She glanced at Emma, who leaned closer to listen in. "Rick, what're you talking about? Emma isn't at the mall."

"Oh, but she *was* fifteen minutes ago. And now she's at the police station because she got caught shoplifting."

"Shoplifting?" Kelly laughed humorlessly. "Whoever's giving you that info is either stupid or messing with you. Emma's here with me."

"Bullshit. I'm staring right at her."

Kelly opened her mouth to correct him. Then she remembered what Emma said last night about Rick cracking jokes while on duty. "Ooookay, Rick—real funny. You fooled me. Now what do you want?"

"*What do I want?*" he snapped. "You're unreal."

He hung up.

Kelly sat, baffled. Of all the phone calls she'd received in her lifetime, none fit the WTF category better than this one. Rick must've carried out a drug bust and inhaled some hallucinogens. Either that or he was trying to catch her off guard so she might fess up about what happened last night.

"What was that about?" Emma asked.

"Your dad lost his mind." Kelly shook her head,

annoyed. "He thinks you got arrested for shoplifting—while you were here at the game."

Emma turned pale. She opened her mouth, then shut it.

"Em? What's wrong?"

"Nothing." Emma struggled to her feet and took a few experimental steps. They were an approximation of successful. "I'm ready to go home."

9

Before leaving her house that night, Kelly lied to DJ about where she was headed. Rather than mentioning the creepy attic and Emma's purse, she claimed she'd been invited to Emma's to binge-watch something on Netflix. She said she'd be home late, that he shouldn't wait up. She kissed him and the twins goodbye, and that was that.

Later, while speeding toward Redbrook Township, Kelly chided herself for lying. There was no reason to lie. And yet she had, because she didn't want her husband pointing out that Emma was probably using her. That was Kelly's biggest fear—that her relationship with her daughter would vanish once she retrieved the purse.

She popped a Vistaril and smoked a cigarette before she reached 88 Red Trail Road. For the second night in a row, she overshot the driveway. It was like the house didn't want to be found.

She parked near the front porch. Tonight the surrounding area seemed darker. Quieter. She held still, listening. The wind rustled the trees, and a stiff fear pushed against her chest. She gazed up at the towering duplex, remembering the words *Half Murder House* carved into the second-floor wall. Visions of ax-wielding psychos danced in her head.

Years ago, Rick had encouraged her to carry a pocketknife. He had given her one for Christmas, though she buried it in her glove compartment with no intention of using it. Now, however, she grabbed it and unfolded the blade. She squeezed the rubber handle and exited the van.

The air smelled of fresh woodsmoke, maybe from down the road. The neighboring homes were several hundred feet away. Too far away.

Knife in hand, she rounded the creaky wooden veranda and opened the back door. Her phone's flashlight pierced the darkness. She stepped inside. Glass crunched underfoot till she paused. Then a thick, overpowering silence flooded her ears. It reminded her of being underwater. She darted straight for the stairs, then paused again.

A scratching noise, clock-like and hypnotic, came from the living room. When she shined her light, it lit only an empty room.

The scratching grew louder as she ascended the stairs. Fear weighted her feet. It felt like climbing Mount Everest, minus the snow. Her head went fuzzy. Her lungs struggled to expand. She felt alone yet surrounded. She wanted to turn back, but even that seemed dangerous.

Reaching the second floor, she aimed her light down the hallway. Every door was open. Her heart pounded at an unthinkable rate as she approached the master bedroom.

Inside, the attic door was shut. She couldn't remember if she had shut it last night. For the sake of her sanity, she told herself she had.

She tugged it open. The ladder slid loose and banged the floor. The echo shook the room.

She stepped onto the ladder. It wobbled as she climbed into the hot, stuffy attic. Dust tickled her nostrils. Her mouth went dry. Sweat soaked her clothes.

Clutching her knife in one hand, she shined her light around with the other. Broken mannequins lay scattered everywhere. Piles of them. Different shapes and sizes. All as gray as fading smoke.

Where's your purse, Emma? Where'd you leave the thing?

Kelly sidestepped between tables on her way toward the rear wall. Her shoulder brushed something hanging from a rack—dirty old wigs. Whoever had lived here must've owned a clothing store. Either that or they had a severe mannequin fetish.

Upon reaching the spot where she'd found Emma last night, Kelly kicked away plastic limbs, hoping the purse might appear. All she found were the words *HALF MURDER* carved into the floor, the jagged letters the scrawl of a madman.

Her pulse thundered in her ears.

Where's that stupid purse? On the floor? On a table?

Kelly swung her light toward the far end of the massive room. Strangely, both housing units shared the single attic. No wall separated the two sides. Instead, a mannequin-covered valley stretched from the front to the back of the room. Across the center ran a thin, polished strip of wood where no dust had settled. Tables, bureaus, and mannequins seemed to avoid this dividing line. Kelly wanted to avoid it herself until she noticed something glinting on the other side.

A blue sequined purse lay atop a nest of plastic body parts.

Her shoulders sank with relief. She approached the

purse then hesitated. Something about the attic's dividing line bothered her. The floor was too clean. Too polished. Too unnatural.

Or maybe I'm just seeing things. I'm stressed, I'm tired, and it's unbearably hot up here. I need to head home and sleep.

She pocketed her knife and leaned forward to grab the purse.

Then came a harsh noise—a *whoosh*, like a swinging tennis racket, distant but louder as it approached. The noise intensified, howling and howling.

Terrified her skull would explode, she slapped her hands over her ears and screamed.

Then the noise dropped away.

Complete silence.

She cautiously removed her hands from her ears.

Suddenly, a sharp burning sensation pierced her navel. She growled between her teeth. Jagged pressure cut into her abdomen, ripping through tissue and muscle. Heat radiated toward both hips.

Gasping, she reached toward the pain. Her fingers smacked against a waist-high barrier—an invisible surface.

I'm dying. I'm dying and I can't even see what's killing me.

Fire swallowed her chest. Nausea flooded her gut. She coughed and tasted blood.

I'm imagining this!

I'm imagining this!

I'm—

Scorching pain tore through her lower back, striking her spine. She moaned through the grinding pressure. When she looked down, blood poured from her waist like a dark red skirt.

Then came the sick pop-crunch of breaking bone.

She wailed as her spine snapped.

Tears flushed her eyes as she toppled helplessly forward. Her face dropped toward a pile of plastic limbs. She opened her mouth to scream again—as if crying out could somehow stop this—before her chin struck something hard.

Everything went blurry.

Twisting her neck, she looked over her shoulder and saw the impossible—her jeans standing upright, no upper body attached to them. A bleeding stump protruded from the waistline. Red liquid spilled over her belt as she watched her torso-less legs topple backward.

She whimpered. Pressed a hand to her side. Traced her fingers down her ribcage to her waist to her—

Nothing. There was nothing below her navel.

My legs—I need them back.

That nonsense was her last thought before she began to shiver.

She glanced toward her daughter's purse.

She reached for it. Closed her fingers around it.

Then the world went dark.

10

Birds. Chirping somewhere. Chirping nonstop.

The high-pitched noise burrowed into Kelly's head like a rusty claw. It pried at her skull, ripping her from the haze of sleep. This morning her pillow was rock hard, her mouth tasted of dust, and her skin was sticky with sweat. When she tried sitting up, the bed shifted beneath her and made strange clicking sounds, like when Aiden dumped his Legos on the floor.

Then her eyes opened. She found herself in near-total darkness. Slivers of light filtered through the ceiling above.

This wasn't her bedroom. This was the Murder House attic.

She tensed. Her memories smeared into focus. She recalled being sliced in half. Was that even possible?

With shaky hands, she patted her sweat-soaked shirt. Her fingers traced a path from her collarbones to her navel. She feared there might be nothing below, but both thighs were attached, the flesh warm and slick with perspiration.

Her head sank back in relief.

Then she realized her pants were missing. Same with her underwear, socks, and shoes.

Panic flooded her. She reflexively squeezed her legs together, afraid something had been done to her last night. Was this what had happened to Emma?

Trembling, Kelly sat up and frantically dug around for her phone. When she found it, the battery was dead. That meant she was stuck in a dim, cluttered attic with nothing to see by other than faint sunlight coming through the roof. She would have to feel her way along the walls and furniture till she found the exit.

But what if whoever removed my pants is still here?

Kelly realized she was breathing rapidly. As she wobbled to her feet, she noticed someone lying in front of her.

Two muddy shoe soles faced her, the toes pointed skyward. This had to be her assailant. Whoever this pervert was, he was wearing her shoes and jeans.

Kelly grabbed the nearest object. A mannequin leg. She brandished it like a weapon, its bolt facing forward. She trembled, agonizingly aware of her nakedness. Her bare feet itched against the dusty wooden floor. She crept toward the sleeping figure, lifting her makeshift club overhead, ready to attack.

Then she realized the person on the floor wasn't some pervert.

It was a woman. And not just any woman.

It was her.

The person lying before her *was her.*

Kelly scrambled backward, dropped the mannequin leg, picked it back up, then inched forward. The thud of the dropped leg hadn't woken the person. The person that was her.

No. Impossible.

She took another step forward. The woman was naked from the waist up, and she wore no makeup or earrings. Aside from that, she was a perfect replica, like something from a wax museum.

But this replica was no simple wax sculpture. The flesh looked real. The face was identical to her own. Same with the rest of the body, right down to the freckle patterns on the cheeks, shoulders, and breasts, which rose and fell with sleep.

Kelly pressed a finger to the woman's belly. It was sweaty. Fleshy.

Human.

The woman twitched. Her eyes opened.

Kelly stared at her. It was surreal. Hypnotic. Like looking beyond a mirror.

The woman gasped. She shot to her feet and retreated behind a wooden cabinet.

Kelly dashed away in a retreat of her own. She ducked behind a stack of cardboard boxes like a frightened tabby cat. Her pulse slammed within her neck, her thoughts spiraling in all directions. One moment she considered hiding, then running, then screaming, then attacking that other woman. *Why is she here? Why does she look like me?*

Kelly inhaled dusty air. It irritated her throat but settled her nerves. Her thoughts started falling into place. She needed to stay calm, then escape this attic and drive away.

But there was a problem. Her keys were in the front pocket of her jeans. She would have to get them back from that woman.

With great hesitation, Kelly stepped out into the open. She spotted a shoe—her shoe—sticking out from behind a wooden cabinet. After a dry, nervous swallow, she called, "Wh-who are you?"

"Me?" the woman said. "Who the fuck are *you*?"

That voice. It was her own. Though she had quit using profanity after Aiden and Zach were born, there was no mistaking that voice.

"Give me my shirt back," the woman said.

"But this is my shirt," Kelly said.

"Listen, bitch," the woman snapped, "I don't know what kind of kink club this is, but give me back my clothes and point me to the exit. Where the hell are we, anyway?"

Kelly cleared her throat. "Red Trail Road."

The woman paused. "Oh, shit. You're right." She peeked out from behind the cabinet. Her eyes squinted before they went wide. "Holy fuck, you look just like me. But...how?"

"Not sure." Kelly trembled. "Last night, some crazy invisible force—"

"Cut me in half."

They both went quiet.

Birds chirped.

Kelly didn't know what to say. This person, this thing— it couldn't be human. It had to be a trick. A hallucination. Someone was messing with her. Someone wanted her scared. Someone had gone to sick lengths to make it happen. Could this be Norwell's doing?

Kelly tightened her grip on the plastic leg. "Are you with Nancy Norwell?"

"Me? With Norwell? Hell no."

"But you know who she is?"

"Yeah, she sends me mail every year."

Kelly hesitated. "Who are you?"

"I'm Kelly," the woman said. "Kelly O'Neill."

"No you're not," Kelly snapped. "I'm Kelly O'Neill. You're..."

Something else.

The woman crossed her arms. "Look, I don't know what the fuck happened last night, but I know for certain that I'm Kelly O'Neill. If you're also her, then...I don't know what to say."

The sunlight dimmed, threatening to leave Kelly in total darkness. She lifted the mannequin leg overhead.

"Seriously?" the woman said. "You're gonna hit me with that?"

"I might."

"Then what? Go home and cry to *DJ*?" She spat his name like poison.

"I never cried to DJ about anything."

"You did on your wedding night. When he wouldn't take off his stupid Batman mask."

That comment startled Kelly. She had never told anyone about her wedding night. *How could this imposter know the truth?*

Kelly had no idea who she was dealing with. But she knew one thing—an imposter who shared her appearance and memories could walk out of this attic and impersonate her without anyone knowing the difference. There was no telling what this woman wanted or what she was capable of. And for that reason, she couldn't be allowed to leave.

Kelly clutched the mannequin leg and charged at the woman.

Plastic rattled underfoot. Thin bars of sunlight flickered.

The woman opened her mouth in surprise.

Kelly swung for her face, cutting the air with a whoosh. She missed.

But on her second swing, she smacked the side of the woman's head, right above the ear. The impact pulsed through Kelly's arm, energizing her. She swung again, but this time the woman ducked. Kelly whiffed, which left her exposed.

The woman took advantage and shoved her backward. Kelly stumbled from light into shadow, feet skittering over mannequin parts. She bumped into a table then hit the floor, landing hard on her elbow.

Darkness hung around her.

Movement sounded—plastic rumblings, dead ahead.

The noise grew louder.

A sweaty odor filled the air.

Kelly launched to her feet. Swung hard.

Then again.

And again.

Finally a satisfying impact shook the weapon in her grasp. The imposter cried out. Kelly repeatedly smacked her until the woman went down and stayed down.

Seizing the opportunity, Kelly squatted beside the imposter and tugged off her shoes, socks, pants, and underwear. She dressed with Olympic speed. Then she grabbed Emma's purse, located her phone and knife, and raced for the exit.

Her heart drumming, she descended the ladder and slammed the attic door shut. She twisted the brass knob, locking it in place. That woman—that *thing*—would be trapped for now.

Kelly wondered if there was anything else she should do.

Footfalls sounded overhead.

She fled the house in an adrenaline-fueled panic.

11

Kelly sparked a cigarette and drove away in a daze. Her eyes barely registered the sunlit road. She couldn't focus. Couldn't make sense of what had happened at the Murder House.

Nightmarish questions cluttered her mind. Was the house cursed? Did witches meet within its walls? Was Nancy Norwell one of them? Norwell had to be involved somehow, especially since this year's green envelope had arrived the same day that Emma had been trapped in the attic. Could Norwell have lured Emma there as part of some sinister revenge scheme?

No. No way. This can't be happening.

When Kelly reached I-81, she lit another cigarette and talked herself into the idea that she'd been drugged last night. That fire-damaged house was probably full of an airborne chemical that caused her to imagine herself being chopped in half. This morning, there was probably so much of the drug in her system that she'd hallucinated a doppelgänger. That sounded reasonable. And now that she was inhaling fresh air through the van's open windows, she was seeing and thinking clearly again. Her experiences at the Murder House had been illusions. Nothing more.

There was, however, a strange uneven cut along the bottom of her shirt—just like Emma's. Kelly fingered the frayed edge and wondered.

Maybe Emma would know more.

Kelly grabbed her portable charger and plugged in her phone. It buzzed to life with a thousand texts and missed calls from DJ. Those could wait. She dialed her daughter. It went straight to voicemail, so she called Rick instead. He picked up on the second ring.

"What, Kell?" He sounded irritated. "Make it fast. I'm on my way out the door."

"Is Emma there? She's not answering her phone."

"That's 'cause she's grounded from her phone. Shoplifting, remember?"

"I need to talk to her."

"She just hopped on the bus. I'll have her call you later."

Kelly couldn't wait till later. She needed answers now.

RAIN SPLATTERED the windshield as Kelly parked the minivan across the street from Northvale High School. The weathered brick building sat like a miserable old geezer between two state-of-the-art athletic fields. Yellow buses chugged by, unloading students and diesel fumes. Kids trudged through the morning drizzle. There was no sign of Emma.

While waiting, Kelly noticed strange chills in both feet,

like ice cubes were stuck between her toes. She wiggled them to warm them up, but cold spread toward her ankles. She reached down to massage them when another bus pulled in.

Emma stepped onto the sidewalk wearing earbuds.

Kelly sprinted across the street, yelling her daughter's name. Emma didn't notice. She approached the school entrance until Kelly seized her elbow, startling her.

"Jesus, Mom." Emma removed an earbud. "What're you doing here?"

"There are two of me."

Emma's eyes went wide.

Before Kelly could continue, a horn blared behind her. Her minivan's front door hung open, partially blocking traffic. She dragged Emma toward the vehicle. They climbed inside, where the van's smoky odor clashed with Emma's perfume. Kelly pulled into the student parking lot, passing numerous upperclassmen.

Emma shrank away from the window. "Can we talk after school?"

"This can't wait," Kelly said. "Where's your... Where's Emma Number 2?"

Silence.

"Honey, where is she?"

More silence.

"*Emma.*"

"She's at home, okay?" Emma blurted. "She's hiding till my stepmom leaves."

Kelly's mouth went dry. She'd been hoping her daughter would act confused. Laugh it off. Call her crazy. Instead, the girl confirmed her worst fears.

"Did I hear you correctly?" Kelly squeezed the steering wheel. The blood between her knuckles boiled.

She wanted to scream. "Are you saying there are *two of you?*"

"I gotta get to homeroom. Can we please talk later?"

"*Later?*" Kelly snatched her daughter's forearm. "Are you kidding me?"

"Please. I'll tell you everything later."

"You should've told me everything yesterday."

"I couldn't."

"Why not?"

"Because... How was I supposed to explain it?"

"Any way at all!" Kelly smacked the steering wheel. "If you had said something, there wouldn't be another *me* in that attic. Do you realize the mess I'm in?"

"Stop yelling at me!"

"I'm not yelling!" Kelly shouted.

"Look, I didn't think you'd get split," Emma said, gesturing frantically. "Remember how you went into the attic to help me? Nothing happened then, so I thought you couldn't get cut in half. If I'd known otherwise, I never would've asked you to get my stupid purse." She sighed. "Sorry for asking. Sorry for calling you, period."

Emma looked at her with watery eyes. She was only a scared kid. It was easy to forget that in the middle of this bizarre situation.

At least Emma wasn't facing this alone. In spite of everything, Kelly was glad to be involved. "Em, it's okay. You were scared. You did the right thing by calling me." She took her daughter's hand. "All things considered, how're you feeling?"

"Still adjusting." She scratched her thigh. "My legs are the worst part."

"Have they acted up since your soccer game?"

"Yeah. When I'm at school, they get cold."

Kelly flinched. "Wait, my feet are freezing up."

"That's where it starts. You're too far away from her."

"From who?"

"Your twin."

Kelly took a deep breath and tried to process this.

"The farther apart you are," Emma said, "the faster the cold creeps up your legs. And as time goes by, it only gets worse."

"Worse how?"

"Like, colder. Yesterday in homeroom my legs were chilly; by lunch they were basically filled with snow. But don't worry—on my way home, they warmed up. And when I gave my twin a hug, everything felt normal again."

"You *hugged* her?"

"Yeah. When I do, everything gets toasty warm. And if I close my eyes, it's like we're one person again."

Kelly gawked in disbelief. "Honey, you should be on your guard around her. You don't know what she is."

"Sure I do. She's me. She acts a little immature and laughs at the stupidest things, but she's definitely me. I know it's a crazy situation and all, but she's not a bad person. She's like...a best friend who looks and thinks like me. And she makes my life easier. Like, last night we got our homework done twice as fast, then we watched TikTok videos till bedtime."

"Has she tried to hurt you?"

"What? No." Emma sounded offended. "Why, did your twin attack you or something?"

Kelly ducked the question. "Listen, we have to do something about our doubles. I don't know what they are, but they shouldn't exist. We need to fix this somehow, get back to normal." She glanced outside at passing students. "Does anyone else know about that house? Did your friends go inside?"

"Nope."

"You went in alone?"

"Yes, Mom." Edge in her voice. Emma was hiding something.

"Why'd you go alone?"

"Someone dared me to."

"Who?"

"I don't know. There were like a million people there. Everyone was afraid to go near that creepy house, and when I said I wasn't scared, people dared me."

"Who? Was an old lady there?"

"No. Everyone was my age."

"Who dared you?"

"Like, everybody at once."

"But who first suggested it?"

"I don't know!" she snapped. "Jesus, Mom. There were tons of people there and it was the most terrifying night of my life. I barely remember anything."

Emma started breathing heavily. Probably wasn't smart to push her any harder—even if she was lying.

"We'll get through this." Kelly squeezed her daughter's hand. "There's gotta be a way to get us back to normal. I'll search every inch of that Murder House if I have to." Of course, that would mean revisiting the attic, which she would prefer to keep locked. Though Emma had vouched for her own double, Kelly wasn't convinced that the creatures could be trusted.

The school bell rang.

Emma jumped. "I gotta go."

"Wait, here's your purse." Kelly grabbed it from the backseat and handed it over.

"Thanks." Emma checked the main compartment. She fished out a piece of multicolored rope. Both ends were frayed. It looked like it was cut from a little girl's jump rope.

"Is that your good luck charm?" Kelly asked.

Emma tucked it away and opened the door. "Bye, Mom."

"Hold on," Kelly said. "Where's your twin hiding?"

"My backyard—in the garden. Why?"

12

Kelly parked one street over from Emma's house and snuck through the neighboring yards until she spotted the garden. Ornate and try-hard, it was the stepmom's passion project. The colorful kidney-shaped island stretched through the lawn, sporting bright yellow chrysanthemums, pale purple asters, crimson roses, and many varieties Kelly didn't recognize. Last year she had received the full lecture on them, but rather than paying attention, she'd slurped wine and suggested starting a vineyard.

Now, as she approached the garden, she noticed it was still attracting bumblebees. That was somewhat surprising for late September, but what surprised her more was that Emma Number 2 had chosen the garden for her hideout. Ever since Emma had been stung by a swarm of hornets on Memorial Day, she had avoided anything that flew around and buzzed.

A dirt walkway wove between the bushes. Kelly kept her head low—the stepmom was home, after all—and crept toward the heart of the fragrant garden. There she found Emma Number 2 sleeping under a rhododendron bush.

Unbelievable. She looks exactly like Emma.

The double snored. She wore a gray track hoodie that Emma hadn't put on in years. It looked tight around the armpits, and the sleeves didn't reach her wrists. The hood was drawn around her face, and a chair cushion served as her pillow. Compared to the vibrant pink flowers she slept under, the girl looked drab. Bags underlined her young eyes, and her forehead ran with sweat that gleamed beneath the morning sun.

Flower petals tickled Kelly's hand as she reached out and shook the girl awake.

Her eyes snapped open. She flinched. "Mom? What're you doing here?"

That voice was authentically Emma's.

Kelly brushed hair from the girl's sweaty cheek, studying the shape of her face. There could be no doubt. This was her daughter. Or, rather, a perfect copy.

"How'd you know I was here?"

"You told me," Kelly said. "I mean, the *other* you told me."

The girl gasped.

"Relax." Kelly gestured toward her abdomen. "I'm going through the same thing."

"Wait, there's another you? Where is she?"

Kelly's cheeks burned. After seeing how Emma trusted —maybe even cherished—her double, Kelly couldn't help but feel guilty about locking up her own. "Listen, do you remember who dared you to enter that house the other night?"

"Uhhh..." The girl chewed her lip. "Not sure. Lotta people were there."

Same thing Emma had said earlier. Maybe she hadn't been lying.

"What time is it?" The girl peeked over the bushes. "Did Step-O leave yet?"

Step-O. That was Emma's derogatory nickname for Olivia back when the woman first married into the family. Until recently, Emma refused to call her stepmom by anything else.

"Not yet," Kelly said. "Her Land Rover's in the driveway."

"Wait, look!" The girl pointed past the bushes. Olivia stood at the kitchen window, hunched over the sink, her gold hair flashing in the sunlight. "Step-O's washing her coffee mug. She's leaving!"

Olivia must've heard because she glanced up.

Kelly pushed Emma's double to the dirt and hushed her with a finger to her lips. They waited, holding their breath, listening.

Robins chirped. Bees buzzed. Olivia's Land Rover growled to life and then drove away.

"Finally!" the girl exclaimed, rising and dusting herself off. She left the garden, walked toward the house, then paused. With an excited little hop, she turned and said, "Hey, Mom, wanna come inside and watch *Outer Banks*?"

Kelly was touched by the offer. She couldn't remember the last time Emma invited her to watch TV. "I'd love to, but not now."

"Oh, come on." The girl grabbed Kelly's wrist and tugged. "It'll be fun!"

"I can't, sweetheart."

"Please?" Desperation tinted her voice. She tugged harder. "Pleeeease?"

"Another time. First I need to figure out how to get things—" Kelly almost said *back to normal*, but she didn't want to scare the girl. Revealing that the plan was to erase her from existence would freak her out. "Look, once every-thing's under control, you can have all the fun you want. Until then, make sure you stay hidden. And no more shoplifting."

"I know, I know," she moaned. "Dad already grounded me. Two whole weeks without my phone—and that includes weekends. Can you believe that?" She lifted a potted plant off the back porch and collected the emergency house key from underneath. With a hopeful grin, she said, "Sure you don't want to watch Netflix with me?"

"Sorry, I can't."

The girl pleaded with wounded eyes. "Not even for five minutes?"

Kelly melted on the inside. Then, without thinking, she pulled her daughter close and kissed her forehead. "Another time. I promise we'll—"

The girl twisted free and sulked toward the house. Without a word, she stepped inside and slammed the door behind her.

Kelly stood there, wondering how she always managed to disappoint her daughter. Even now with two Emmas walking around, she couldn't make either of them happy.

13

Icy teeth bit into Kelly's ankle. They chewed and chewed like starving mice. She managed to walk back to the van, but the discomfort hindered her stride. According to Emma, things would only get worse. At some point Kelly would have to return to the Murder House and reunite with her double.

But right now she wasn't ready for that. Things were happening fast, and she needed time to decompress. More importantly, she needed to learn everything she could about that house. Hopefully an internet search would help.

She headed home and settled behind her work desk. The moment she fired up her computer, her headset jingled. A customer complained about his stove not lighting. Too bad. She put him on hold and typed "88 Red Trail Road" into Google.

The top result was a local news article about the Murder House catching fire last month. The article described the house as abandoned and said that squatters had been living there. An improperly discarded cigarette had likely caused the fire. There was plenty of info about the blaze, but what stole Kelly's attention were the photos. They depicted only a single housing unit—the right-side unit—with an empty lawn beside it.

The Murder House's entire left side was absent from every photo.

Her tongue turned chalky. She checked real estate websites and found pictures taken before the fire. Those also showed a single housing unit beside an empty lawn.

How is this possible?

Her fingers trembled over the keyboard as she sought more info. Apparently the homeowner, Jessica Ruminsky, had died last year after living in Vermont for the past decade. Ruminsky had inherited the house from her father, who died nearly fifteen years ago. His obituary mentioned that he passed away at home unexpectedly but gave no further detail.

Kelly clicked every webpage associated with the family but found nothing related to mannequins, murder, or Norwell. A dead end.

Work calls jingled in. Kelly pretended to listen while she did more research. Nothing led anywhere. Sadly, there were no how-to guides for restoring two identical people into the original body. As the morning went on, she realized that if she wanted answers, she would have to explore the attic. She dreaded the thought.

Around noon, coldness crept from her ankles to her knees. Hoping to offset the chills, she donned knee-high socks, then wrapped her legs with an electric blanket. It had no effect. During her lunch break, she drew a steaming hot bath and sat in the tub. The water burned her fingers, but her legs remained icebergs beneath the surface.

Emma wasn't kidding. These chills don't go away.

Kelly returned to her desk and poured herself a glass of wine.

Her iPhone buzzed. It was DJ. He asked why she hadn't come home last night. She made excuses about falling asleep at Emma's house. He didn't seem happy with her reply.

Later, when she picked up the twins from school, frost surrounded her thighs. By the time her shift ended, the discomfort had traveled to her navel and stopped there. Her upper body remained warm; everything below was frigid.

Numbness suffocated both legs while she drove her kids to soccer practice. The pain intensified with each passing mile. She was wearing shorts, and at each stoplight, she glanced at her thighs, expecting them to be blue. She clutched the steering wheel and prayed she wouldn't crash.

At the practice field, she opened her door and carefully lowered both feet to the dirt. She walked gingerly to the sideline and sat in a bright patch of grass, her legs outstretched. The sun warmed her face and arms, but her lower body felt bloodless.

Both legs appeared normal and felt warm to the touch. She massaged her thighs, rubbing vigorously until her fingers ached.

Soccer moms and dads pulled into the parking lot and dropped off their kids. Some wandered aimlessly like Zach. Others joined Aiden, who was kicking a ball at the boarded-up concession stand nearby.

Kelly tried to stand, but numbness overpowered her legs. Defeated, she settled back on the grass, closed her eyes, and wondered how she would survive the next hour.

"Sup, Coach?"

Kelly flinched at the smooth masculine voice. Her assistant coach Lance Davis stood over her, one hand on his hip. The other clutched a bottle of lemon-lime Gatorade. He wore a red Arsenal jersey, black shorts, and a casual smirk that made him seem impressed with himself. She too was impressed—especially when he pushed back his dark, chin-length hair. It was wet today, and as the wind picked up, she caught the scent of ocean-surf shampoo.

He nodded at her outstretched legs. "New yoga position?"

She sat up, laughing. "No, actually, I'm...uh..."

"Tanning?"

"God, no. I don't tan. I burn like an Irish vampire."

He snorted. "Better get outta the sun then. C'mon, Coach. On your feet."

"Give me a sec." She rubbed her knees. "My legs are killing me. Haven't felt this bad since I tore my ACL in college."

He grimaced. "I know that feeling."

"You tore yours too?"

"Yeah. Snapped it like an old brake cable. It kept me from winning the World Cup."

She smirked. "You mean, it kept you from *attending* the World Cup."

"Listen—had I been healthy, the U.S. would've won it all in 2018."

"Riiight."

"I'm serious—you should've seen me in my prime."

"You should've seen me in mine."

"Didn't realize yours ended."

Kelly laughed, hoping her cheeks weren't blushing. "You're such a suck-up."

Lance sat beside her on the grass. Their shoulders brushed; the touch sent her stomach into a tizz, which was a welcome distraction. He sipped Gatorade and nodded at the team. "The kids look like giants from down here. Sure beats watching them from the bleachers."

"For Sunday's game, we should make the soccer moms sit on the grass."

"All of them?" he said. "Including you?"

She narrowed her eyes at him. "I am *not* a soccer mom. I'm a soccer *coach*."

"Who drives a minivan and lives in the 'burbs."

"How would you know where I live? Are you creeping on me, you creeper?"

"Creeper?" He winced. "Ouch. That stings."

"It should." She elbowed him. "*You creeper*."

He laughed. It was a great laugh. She could listen to it all day. Sure, the guy could be arrogant, but it was hard not to like him. He'd signed on as an assistant coach so he could spend time with his nephew; when the boy's dad had been deployed overseas, Lance stepped into the role of father figure, a response she couldn't help but admire.

"C'mon, let's go." Lance bounced to his feet and offered his hand. "It'll sink the team's morale if their coach lounges through practice."

Kelly took his hand. One strong tug brought her upright. She ignored the numbness in her legs and paced the sideline while leading the kids through warm-ups. After they finished stretching, she blew her whistle and ordered everyone through dribbling drills. While the kids zigzagged between strings of orange cones, she jogged alongside them, keeping her legs active. Movement distracted her, so she trotted around, refereeing their scrimmage.

When practice ended, she was a sweaty mess, but she felt better. She even caught Lance eyeballing her.

What a creeper, she thought, burying a smile.

On the drive home, her legs thawed with each passing

mile. When she pulled into the garage, her lower body remained chilly, but it was an improvement, as though she'd migrated from the freezer to the fridge. She decided that once everyone was asleep, she would return to the Murder House.

That evening, she went through the motions. She reheated chicken leftovers, paid her bills online, helped the twins with their homework, and kissed them goodnight.

Then she sat on the living room couch next to DJ while he tapped away at his laptop. She thought about confiding in him, but he was a rational guy who worked with codes and numbers for a living. She couldn't picture him believing a word about the Murder House. And if he did believe her, knowing him, he'd play hero and march into that attic for answers. She loved how brashly supportive he could be, but now wasn't the time. The last thing she needed was for him to be split in half too.

And so, instead of broaching the subject of the Murder House, she asked him how his day went. Then he asked her how hers went. Typical surface-level conversation. She wondered how long it had been since they'd had a truly personal talk.

"You free this weekend?" he asked.

The question caught her off guard. "Uh...Saturday I've got work. Sunday morning is the kids' game. And I've gotta buy groceries at some point. Why?"

He scratched his chest. "I was thinking we should do something. Maybe golf on Sunday. Or you know what? In Dunmore there's a cider tasting event Saturday night."

"Hard cider?"

"Of course."

She smiled. "Sounds fun."

"Want me to order tickets?"

"Not yet." Though she liked the prospect of going on a date, she didn't want to make any commitments until the Murder House situation was resolved. "Hold off. Just in case something comes up."

Her legs visibly twitched.

He squinted with concern. "You okay?"

She wanted to tell him. She really did. Instead she downplayed it. "I'm fine. Just some soreness. Muscles are acting up from one of my old soccer injuries."

He nodded solemnly. "It's a dangerous sport."

"Only at the higher levels."

He must've sensed an impending argument, because he shut his laptop and announced he was going to bed.

She joined him upstairs. Soon as he started snoring, she struggled to her feet and headed out the door.

14

S weet warm relief.

It started in Kelly's hips and trickled through her thighs. She eased back against the driver's seat, savoring the change in temperature. It was as though icy socks were being peeled away from her legs. She could freely bend her knees and rotate her ankles. The numbness faded. Sensation returned. She stomped the gas pedal with confidence as she exited the highway toward Redbrook Township.

Crickets chirped in the surrounding woods, cheering her on as she upped her speed. Her headlights pushed through the shadows until she reached the Murder House. By that point, she was freely wiggling her toes again.

But now wasn't the time to celebrate. She didn't come here for pain relief; she came here for answers. She needed to search the attic, but first she had to do something about her double.

Kelly grabbed her knife. Hopefully she wouldn't have to use it. Hopefully her double would cooperate, like Emma's had.

With a thrumming pulse, Kelly marched upstairs to the

master bedroom. She opened the attic door, and heat pulsed from above. It was like the ceiling separated Earth from hell.

Kelly yelled, "Hello?"

No reply.

Then came the familiar sound of mannequin parts rattling.

She shined her light through the opening. "Hello?"

More rattling.

"You there?"

More movement. Faster than she was comfortable with. She readied her knife and pointed her light toward the noise.

Red hair swept into view. Her double squatted along the edge of the attic, elbows on knees, hands dangling in front, a dirty towel wrapped around her torso. Her eyes closed as the flashlight reached her face—the face of Kelly O'Neill. The double's forehead was bruised from their scuffle this morning.

"Hi," Kelly said, tucking her knife in her jacket pocket. "I'm back."

"Back?" The woman's voice came out raspy. "What the fuck? How could you lock me up like that?"

Not the politest reaction. Then again, Kelly couldn't blame the woman for being upset after spending all day in that attic.

"Sorry, I panicked earlier," Kelly said. "I think we should talk."

"I wanna leave." The double blinked, adjusting to the light. She turned her hands over and scrutinized them as if checking for a sliver. "I was losing my mind up here. It's like a million degrees, yet my head and hands were freezing."

"Really? What about your legs?"

The double squinted, confused. "No, my legs were fine.

But my head felt like it was filled with crushed ice. Same with my chest and arms."

Huh. So while my lower body was freezing, the same happened with her upper body. Creepy. Though, given that we were chopped in half at the waist, I guess it makes sense.

"I had the same problem with my legs," Kelly said.

"Oh, fuck. What's happening to us?"

"The same thing that's happening to Emma. She told me her legs get numb when she's separated from...the other Emma."

The double tilted her head, considering. "So when we're apart, we suffer?"

"Right. That's why I came back."

"Glad you did." The double glanced down at the broken glass. "Can you get me some shoes so I can leave?"

Kelly tightened her grip on the knife. Though her plan had been to remove this woman from the attic, now the thought of doing so made her uneasy.

"What's wrong?" the woman asked.

"It's just... I don't know what you are or what you want."

"I'm Kelly O'Neill," the woman said. "And I want food, clothes, and a shower."

"Then what?"

"Then...I don't know. I guess I'd like to apply for a new job."

Kelly snorted. The comment wasn't terribly funny, but it was achingly true. It was something she'd often thought about but never voiced. Hearing it out loud was cathartic. Part of her wished she could have a glass of wine with this woman.

No. Forget that. I need to stay on my guard. Just because

she looks and thinks like me doesn't mean I can trust her. And even if she is harmless, I can't afford to be seen with her—there's no telling how the world would react if we were spotted together. I have to be careful. Once she's out, I need to hide her somewhere so I can come back here and search the place.

"Please," the woman said. "Can we leave?"

"Before we do," Kelly said, "let's establish some ground rules."

"Ground rules? What am I, five?"

Kelly narrowed her eyes. She didn't appreciate snippy remarks. "We have to take this seriously. First rule is that we can't be seen together. If anyone realizes there are two of us, we'll be in major trouble."

"Couldn't we just say we're sisters?"

"Not if someone recognizes us," Kelly said. "Second rule is that we can't be in two public places at once. That means if I go pick up the kids from school, you can't go grocery shopping at the same time."

"Wait, you expect me to go grocery shopping?"

"It's just an example. Now the third thing—"

"Listen, I'm starving." The woman's head drooped. Hair spilled over her knees. "Can we write this rulebook later?"

"Sorry, but—"

"You don't sound sorry," the woman snapped. "Do you realize I've been trapped in this hot dusty attic all day with no food or water, and it was so dark I couldn't see two inches in front of my face? And what did I do to deserve that? All I did was wake up, then you started whacking me like a fucking piñata."

"Calm down," Kelly said, clutching her knife. "This morning I didn't know what you were."

"Well, I didn't know what *you* were, but I didn't beat your face in."

"I'm sorry, okay?"

"Sorry? Pfft. Just get me some clothes so we can leave."

"Forget it. We're not going anywhere till you settle down."

The woman groaned. She sat, her bare legs dangling beside the ladder. After taking a breath, she said, "Are you mad at me because of my comment this morning?"

"Which comment?" Kelly said. "The one about me running and crying to DJ?"

"Look, I didn't mean to insult you—it just slipped out. I'm tired of him and his Batman mask bullshit. He's a good dad but a total weirdo, y'know? And it's getting harder and harder to talk to him. He won't even open up anymore. It's like the longer we know him, the less we understand him."

Kelly knew that feeling. It ate through her day after day like acid. She missed the early years with him, when they would go jogging together each morning and talk all night; on weekends they'd stay out late then wake up early to watch the Premier League. Strangely, he never had an issue with soccer until she signed up the twins. She wished she understood what his problem was, but like her double said, everything with him was a big secret anymore.

Kelly relaxed her grip on the knife. She looked up at the woman. "You really are me, huh?"

"I told you—I'm Kelly O'Neill."

That idea still made Kelly uncomfortable, but she supposed she would have to deal with it until things returned to normal. "Okay. Third rule is that once we leave here, you need to do what I say. I know that doesn't sound fun, but we need to be careful. We can't let this situation get out of control. So no shoplifting or anything like that. Got it?"

The double nodded. "Got it."

Kelly took a deep breath. Glass crunched as she stepped back from the ladder. "Wait here. I'll bring you some shoes."

15

Kelly drove away from the Murder House with a pounding heart. Her eyes bounced between the road and the passenger seat, where her double gobbled a protein bar and chugged Gatorade. Before leaving the attic, the woman had dressed in Kelly's old gym clothes. She now sported a wrinkled t-shirt, yoga pants, and discolored Nikes. Across the shirt was printed YES, BUT FIRST COFFEE.

The woman pointed to the quote. "Can we get Starbucks? I want a caramel macchiato. Haven't had one in forever."

Kelly couldn't tell if she was being serious. "I don't think they're open."

"Okay. Tomorrow then."

So far, the woman had proven tame. No sudden movements, no hostility. Despite the good behavior, an anxious cloud expanded within Kelly's chest. She didn't trust this creature, and once they got home, she would have to keep the woman contained. But how?

Kelly needed a plan. That, and a cigarette.

She poked one between her lips and lit it.

"Eww, gross," the woman said. "Quit that shit already."

Kelly blew smoke outside. "Wait. You're supposedly *me*, but you hate smoking?"

"It's nasty and bad for you. And every time you finish a cig, you hope it'll be your last." The woman smiled. "You know I'm right, Kelly."

"Interesting. You just called me Kelly."

"It's our name."

"Not *our* name. I'm not calling you Kelly."

The woman chewed her protein bar. "But it's on my birth certificate, my license—"

"Pick another name." Kelly tapped ashes out the window. "Use one of our old nicknames."

"Ooo! Remember what Coach Fernandez called us in high school?"

"Kickin' Kelly?"

"Yeah, but then he shortened it."

"K2?"

"Yes!" The woman hopped excitedly. "K2 sounds *amazing*."

"Okay. I'll call you K2. Makes sense, since I already consider you my number two."

"No way! I was thinking the same thing. Except to me, you're *my* number two."

Kelly shifted uncomfortably.

Both women stayed silent as they reached the section of the highway where Anissa Norwell had died twelve years ago. Attached to the guardrail was a roadside memorial: a homemade cross and artificial flowers that marked the spot where Anissa had crashed her car. According to newspapers, the impact whipped her against the steering wheel and broke her neck. Though she had been drinking that night, it was never confirmed whether her death was an alcohol-fueled accident or a suicide. Either way, Anissa's mother blamed Kelly for it.

Now, as the headlights glowed across the guardrail, she clutched the steering wheel and shifted into the passing lane. She thumped the gas pedal and passed tractor trailers until the roadside memorial faded behind her.

She and K2 exhaled simultaneously. The timing was eerie yet oddly comforting.

"Should've taken another route home," K2 said.

"I usually do."

"I know."

Kelly flung her cig outside. "You think Nancy Norwell is involved?"

"With what?"

"Our situation." Kelly tightened her grip on the wheel. "Think about it. She sends those green envelopes every year, and this time her letter arrived on the exact day that Emma got trapped in the attic. It can't be a coincidence."

"Shit, good point." K2 sipped more Gatorade. "Then again, Norwell's had twelve years to punish us. Why wait till now?"

Kelly didn't have an answer.

She took the next exit and stopped at a red light. Home was mere minutes away. Her stomach floated. What was she supposed to do upon arriving at the house? K2 couldn't be allowed near the kids, yet Kelly couldn't think of anywhere to hide her.

The stoplight turned green. While weaving through traffic, an idea sprang to mind. She could lock K2 in her backyard shed. It was the perfect spot; DJ and the kids never went near it. The only tricky part would be luring K2 into the shed and convincing her to behave once inside. If she made noise, the neighbors would come looking.

"When we get home," Kelly said, "you'll need to hide somewhere."

"Basement?"

"No, DJ could wander down there."

"How about our office?"

"No, it's right next to the kids' room."

"So? I'll lock the door."

"What if they see you before you get inside?"

"Then I'll tell them to go back to bed. Remember, I'm their mom."

"But you're covered in bruises."

"And whose fault is that?"

Kelly cleared her throat. She turned onto Byron Street and rolled downhill toward her house. Luckily none of her neighbors were outside. Nothing in sight but empty vehicles parked beside empty lawns. A lone streetlight lit the bottom of the dead-end street.

Her lungs heaved as she pulled into the garage. After she killed the motor, there was nervous silence. She reached into her pocket for her knife. Without looking, she unfolded the blade and held it against her thigh where K2 couldn't see it.

Kelly's next words needed to be chosen carefully. If things turned ugly, K2 could take over her house, her life, everything.

"You know what?" Kelly said in an offhand tone. "Why don't you hide in the shed?"

"The shed?"

"Sure, why not?"

"Well, for starters, it's cluttered with the lawnmower and all that other junk."

"It'll only be for a few hours," Kelly said. "Just till DJ and the kids leave."

"Can I please sleep here in the van?"

Kelly pretended to consider. "No, too risky. Besides, I gotta drive the kids to school. Please spend the night in the shed. It'll make things easier. Then we'll regroup in the morning."

K2 shrugged. "Okay. Whatever. Just don't lock me inside."

Kelly frowned. "But the lock is always on it."

"What's your point?"

"Well, what if DJ notices?"

"Ohhh, I see." K2 smirked. "You don't trust me."

"That's not—"

"You can admit it. Go on."

"Listen," Kelly said, steadying her voice. "I need to do what's best for my kids. If you really are me, you should understand that."

K2 met her eyes with a long, unnerving gaze.

"Fine."

16

That morning a green envelope arrived in the mailbox. Same shade of green as the one from three days ago. Kelly tensed at the sight. She checked over both shoulders, afraid someone was watching from the street. The envelope was postmarked, no return address. The handwriting across the front was distinctly Norwell's.

Kelly retreated into her kitchen, where her second pot of coffee was brewing. For a moment she considered calling 911 before frantically tearing open the envelope.

Inside was the usual twice-folded sheet of paper. A single line printed at the top said, "Bring yourselves to my daughter's grave or you'll understand my pain."

She reread it several times. The word *yourselves* alarmed her. Sure, it could've been a typo, but the spelling might also be deliberate. Did Norwell know there were two Kellys? And that "you'll understand my pain" line—was that a threat against Emma? Aiden? Zach?

Fresh coffee pattered against the glass pot. The aroma spread through the kitchen, but Kelly no longer needed caffeine. She was now wired.

She dialed the admin office at her sons' school and requested that the boys be kept inside until she picked them up this afternoon. Then she ran around the house locking doors and shutting curtains. Once everything was fortified, she peeked out the front window. The dead-end street was motionless, silent. Danger could be hiding anywhere.

She dialed Rick.

"What, Kell?"

"Remember Nancy Norwell? The mother of the girl who died twelve years ago?"

"That wacky lady who sends you mail every year?"

"Right. She sent me two letters this week. The one I got today says, 'Bring yourselves to my daughter's grave or you'll understand my pain.' It sounds like a threat."

He cleared his throat. "Where are your kids right now? School?"

"Yeah. I told the admin office to keep them indoors for recess."

"Good. Now whatever you do, don't visit that grave. Stay away and stay calm."

She took a deep breath. "Okay."

"Watch your boys. I'll worry about Emma. Do you know where Norwell lives?"

"The envelopes didn't include a return address."

"I'll look into it. Once I find this lady, I'll straighten her out. Till then, is there anything else I should know? Has anything unusual happened?"

Her gaze drifted out the kitchen window and settled on the backyard shed.

"No, nothing."

THOUGH RICK INSISTED he would worry about Emma, Kelly decided to warn her daughter immediately. She called the high school and said it was an emergency, that she needed to speak with Emma. Five minutes later her daughter's voice came through the line.

"Mom?"

"Em, are you okay?"

"My legs are cold, but yeah. Why do you sound so hyper? Something wrong?"

Kelly paced about the kitchen. "There's this lady named Nancy Norwell who has a grudge against me. She sent me a nasty letter on the day you went into that attic. Today I got another letter. I think she knows about what happened to us."

"*What? How?*"

"Stay calm, Em. Your father and I will get this under control."

"Wait—you didn't tell him about the attic, did you?"

"No, I haven't told anyone. For now, we'll keep this quiet. But I need you to be careful. Don't go anywhere except school and home. No parties, no goofing off, nothing. And tell your twin not to goof off either."

"Okay." Emma sounded scared.

Kelly's mouth went dry. She drank some coffee to moisten her tongue. "Everything will be fine. Your father's tracking down Norwell, and tonight I'll search that attic for answers."

"You're going alone?"

"Yep."

"Mom, you can't go alone."

"Relax, I'll be fine."

"Let me go with you. I'll back you up."

"Honey, I don't want you in danger."

"And I don't want *you* in danger." Emma's voice cracked. "You're the only other person who understands what I'm going through. If something happens to you—"

"Nothing will happen to me."

"If you believe that, then take me with you. We can look out for each other. Plus, we'll be able to search the attic faster."

"I'd rather you stay home."

"If you don't pick me up tonight, I'll go there anyway."

"Emma, no."

"Pick me up at nine-thirty."

"Emma—"

The phone line went dead.

17

The shed remained locked all afternoon. Kelly refused to let K2 out, even when a downpour began around dinnertime. The shed roof often leaked when it rained, and if that were happening now, K2 would have to dodge random spills until the storm clouds dried up. The thought made Kelly shiver. She felt rotten about imprisoning her double.

But what choice do I have? I can't unlock the door—not after that threatening letter. Norwell is probably connected to the Murder House, and for all I know K2 could be part of her plan.

Rain splashed the kitchen windows while Kelly ate mac-and-cheese leftovers with her family. After every bite, she glanced outside and wondered about K2. Perhaps it was time they had a chat.

Once DJ wandered upstairs for a shower, Kelly ran outside under an umbrella and knocked on the shed door. "K2, I have a question."

"So do I," K2 answered in an agitated voice. "Why the hell haven't you cut me loose? I'm getting soaked in here."

The wooden door shook within its frame. "C'mon, let me out!"

"Quiet down."

"I will once I'm outside." K2 kept pounding the door.

"Quiet!" Kelly looked over her shoulder at the upstairs bathroom. The light was on, but thankfully DJ hadn't bothered to look outside. "Listen, today I got another letter from Norwell."

The pounding stopped. "You did? What'd it say?"

"She threatened Emma and the twins."

"Holy fuck. Did you call the police?"

"Rick's looking into it." Kelly took a breath. Time to see if K2 knew more than she was letting on. "There's another thing... Norwell knows there are two of us."

"*What?* How'd she find out?"

"I don't know. Do you think she's behind this whole thing?"

"Well, she must be if she knows about us."

"Tell me something," Kelly said, squeezing the umbrella handle. "While you were in that attic, did she contact you?"

"Contact me?" K2 sounded insulted. "Where are you going with this?"

"Just asking a question."

"Really? Because it sounds like an accusation. And, no, Norwell didn't contact me."

"Thanks. That's all I wanted to know."

"Why do you always assume the worst with me?" K2 said. "Seriously, what have I done wrong? Name one thing."

Kelly didn't reply.

"See?" K2 said. "You can't. Now will you please unlock this door?"

"Not now. I gotta go check on Emma. I'll let you out tomorrow."

"Tomorrow?" K2 pounded the door. "You can't leave me here all night. It's damp, it smells, and I have to pee."

Kelly grimaced. K2 didn't deserve this, but it was hard to trust her right now. "I'm sorry."

"Bullshit. If you were sorry, you'd unlock this door."

Kelly couldn't afford to. Not until after she and Emma finished searching the attic. For now, it was best to remain cautious. "Soon as I get back, we'll talk."

"I don't want to talk," K2 said. "I want out. Please!"

"Tomorrow, okay?"

"Why not now?"

"Because I'm not comfortable letting you out."

"*You're* not comfortable? What about me? You think I'll be comfortable using a fertilizer bag for a pillow tonight?"

Kelly sighed. "I'm really sorry."

"The hell you are."

Kelly fell silent. They both did. The only sound came from the rain pounding against the shed roof. It grew louder and louder, as if the shed were ready to explode.

18

After picking up Emma around ten o'clock, Kelly went into protective-mother mode. By the time she parked at the Murder House, she was hyperalert, searching every shadow for fear that Norwell might be nearby. She regretted bringing her daughter along but knew that if she hadn't, Emma would stubbornly show up regardless.

Kelly killed the headlights. Darkness flushed in from all sides. With no streetlamps nearby, the only illumination came from a crescent moon as thin as a clipped fingernail. She grabbed two flashlights from her purse, handed one to Emma, and headed into the damp, brisk night. Kelly shined her light in every conceivable direction before approaching the house.

"This is so cool," Emma said as they stepped onto the veranda. "We're like detectives. Someday I wanna be a real one, like my dad."

"Your dad's a patrol cop."

"Yeah, but you know what I mean."

Kelly allowed herself a smile. "It'll be funny if you outrank him someday."

They continued along the veranda and let themselves in through the back door. The place was silent aside from roaches scuttling through the glass-covered hallway.

"I know you hate bees," Kelly said. "What about roaches?"

"They're gross, but at least they don't sting."

"I was surprised E2 slept in your garden. Lots of buzzing going on."

"Yeah, E2's weird. She looks like me and has all my memories from before Monday, but she's not afraid of bees."

"And she shoplifts."

Emma laughed uncomfortably. "Hey, so are your legs okay?"

Kelly paused outside the living room, only now noticing the chill creeping up her shins. "For now, yeah. How about you?"

"Eh. Feels like I'm wearing a cold pair of socks."

"And those socks keep getting pulled up higher and higher?"

"Right? So annoying."

"Let's head upstairs. Got your pepper spray ready?"

"Uhh, I forgot it."

"*Em.*"

"Sorry."

"Stick close and stay behind me."

Kelly readied her knife and climbed upstairs. She and Emma encountered nothing but roaches on the second floor. Glass crunched as they approached the master bedroom. The attic door remained open, the ladder extending into the hot, dusty darkness above. Emma started toward it, but Kelly grabbed the back of her hoodie.

"Wait down here."

"Why?"

"Someone should guard the ladder. Especially since you were trapped last time."

"We won't get trapped."

"You don't know that."

"Actually, I do." Emma scratched behind her ear. "See, I found out that E2 locked me up there."

"What? Why?"

"She woke up before me and panicked."

"She panicked? That's no excuse." Kelly was furious. Though she'd done the same to K2, the thought of it happening to her daughter—her *original* daughter—sickened her. "Why didn't you mention this?"

"I just did." Emma grabbed the ladder. "Come on, let's search."

Kelly locked the bedroom door to be safe, then climbed up into the poorly ventilated attic. Within seconds she was sweating and struggling to breathe. She removed her hoodie and tied the sleeves around her waist. Beside her, Emma peeled off her own hoodie, revealing a low-cut sleeveless blue top.

"Seriously?" Kelly said. "You go around dressed like *that*?"

"What?" Emma said innocently. "We knew it'd be hot up here."

"I don't mean now. I mean when you're out with your friends."

Emma crossed her arms beneath the neckline. "I like this top. It's comfy."

"Does your dad know you have it?"

"Probably not. I do my own laundry."

Kelly sensed this conversation was morphing into an argument. Having endured the silent treatment for so long, she decided it would be unwise to further criticize Emma's wardrobe. No teenager wanted to hear it, and one wrong word could alienate her daughter for months. Not worth the risk. Besides, they had other priorities.

Mannequin limbs clicked against the floor while Kelly and Emma tore apart cardboard boxes. Each contained plastic body parts, heaps of dust, and little else. Emma pushed aside a full-length mirror and discovered a hidden wall rack covered with blonde wigs. Unfortunately, the tags inside the wigs provided no names or leads of any kind.

Kelly checked every crate, drawer, and container on the left side of the attic before approaching the dividing line to continue her search.

"Em, I'm gonna check over there."

Emma shuddered. "You don't think it can cut us in half again, do you?"

"Let's hope not."

"Careful, Mom."

Trembling, Kelly paused before the polished dividing line. Her legs twitched, more from nerves than from being separated from K2, she suspected. Bracing herself, she extended her foot over the divide. Though she feared it might get chopped off, that perhaps a K3 would appear, nothing happened. Nor did anything happen when she stepped forward and crossed over without incident.

She gasped with relief. Pressed a hand over her drumming heart. Her entire body was zinging. She reached into her purse for her pills, shaking one into her palm before adding another for good measure.

"Hey!" Emma snapped. "You're not supposed to take pills."

"My doctor says otherwise," Kelly said.

"But you're not supposed to. Not anymore. Not since..."

"Since what?" Kelly said. "Since that night in our apartment when you were a little girl? Em, those were *sleeping* pills. And I took way, way too many. These—they're just antihistamines. They calm me down." Her hand shook so hard that she almost dropped them. "God knows I need to calm down."

Emma crossed her arms. "You promised."

"Promised what?"

"Don't you remember? After I found you lying on the kitchen floor that night, I called Dad and he made you puke up those pills. When you left the hospital, you swore you'd never take pills again." She cocked her head in a teenage way. "You promised."

"I promised I'd never take *sleeping* pills again," Kelly said. "These are different."

"Are you supposed to take two at once?"

"Honey, relax."

"Stop taking them."

"How about this? I'll stop taking them if you stop wearing tops with low necklines."

"Don't change the subject."

"Why not?" Kelly said. "If you keep dressing like that, I'll be a grandmother next year."

Emma winced, a wounded look in her eyes. She turned away and feigned interest in a dust-covered table.

Now I've done it, Kelly thought. *Accusing my own daughter of making mistakes she hasn't made. Wonderful job, Kelly, you idiot. No wonder she avoids you.*

"Em, I'm sorry. I didn't mean—"

Emma stormed off between two rows of tables.

With a sigh, Kelly dropped the pills back into the bottle and resumed her search.

The attic's right side offered more cardboard boxes. Most contained plastic limbs, but she did find one packed with books—old leatherbound hardcovers with wrinkled brown pages. Some were medical textbooks. Others focused on stage magic.

She flipped through them. Eventually she found a faded diagram that showed how to perform the classic magician's trick of cutting an audience volunteer in half. The diagram depicted a person lying inside a coffin-like box that used a trap door to hide the volunteer's legs. Sadly, the book said nothing about spawning doppelgängers. She shoved the box aside in frustration.

"What's wrong?" Emma said, appearing at her side.

"Nothing," Kelly said. "Found some old books."

"Really? So did I."

"Where?"

Emma disappeared behind a nearby table. Mannequin parts rattled until she returned with a cardboard box.

It mostly contained dictionaries and *Farmer's Almanacs*, but crushed underneath them was an old diary, not much larger than a pack of cigarettes. The pages were brownish, the handwriting hideous. The first entry, dated 1934, read, "I still believe it's out there." *Creepy*. The following entries were barely legible, but the words *misery* and *starvation* appeared several times, likely in reference to the Great Depression.

"Wonder who wrote this." She flipped pages and squinted. It would be easier to read in daylight, so she tucked it away in her purse for later. "Find anything else?"

Emma glanced over her shoulder. "Somebody carved the words *Half Murder House* into the floor."

"Yeah, someone carved that into the upstairs hallway too."

"What do you think a half murder is?"

"Probably what happened to us."

Emma trembled. "So we're dead?"

"No. We just gotta figure things out."

"Guess we should keep looking then."

"Right." Kelly risked a smile. "By the way, I didn't take those pills just now."

Emma shrugged and walked away. It seemed like she was always walking away. Even as a baby, she had taken her first steps toward Rick and her grandparents, giving Kelly the cold shoulder in the process. That had been the first heartbreak Kelly endured as a mother—the first of many.

Now's my chance to move on from all the heartbreak—to redefine myself as a mom. I need to get us out of this mess.

Kelly searched the remainder of the attic. Between two tables she found a tall metal safe protected by a combo lock, evident fingerprints around the dusty chrome dial. The words *We Burn* were scratched into the metal beside the lock. Her gut told her something important was inside. She checked nearby, hoping to find the code written somewhere. No luck.

The safe didn't look like it could be pried open, but there might be a way to cut through it. She considered dragging it back to the van, but when she tried pushing it, the thing wouldn't budge. Turned out it was nailed to the floor, and the nail heads were rusted. She wondered what else she could do.

Her thoughts were interrupted by a shriek. Emma cried out in pain.

Kelly grabbed her flashlight and rushed across the attic. She found Emma lying on the floor clutching her knees.

"What's wrong?"

"My legs," Emma said through gritted teeth. "Ugh, get me outta here."

Kelly's own legs were frosty, but it wasn't debilitating.

She helped Emma to her feet and served as a human crutch until they reached the van. Her daughter spent the entire drive home twisting in her seat and grimacing against the window.

Even when Kelly pulled up to Emma's house, her daughter remained in obvious pain.

It seemed E2 had snuck out tonight.

19

Kelly struggled to fall asleep that night. Before dawn, she wandered outside to smoke cigarettes. Byron Street was silent aside from the whistles of insects and the occasional rumble of distant traffic. She paced the front porch, anxious to learn whether her daughter's legs had improved. Emma being grounded from her phone meant Kelly would have to call Rick for an update.

At sunrise she dialed him and asked to speak with Emma. He insisted their daughter needed to sleep after being up all night vomiting.

"Vomiting?" Kelly asked, alarmed. "What's wrong with her?"

"Probably a stomach bug," he said. "She's staying home from school today."

"Can I talk to her?"

"She just fell asleep. I'm not waking her."

"Please, Rick. I'm worried. Especially after that letter from Norwell."

"That reminds me," he said. "I found some info on the old lady. According to tax filings, she hasn't lived anywhere in three years. That means she's either homeless or shacking up with somebody."

Kelly tensed as she remembered that article about squatters living at 88 Red Trail Road. "So Norwell could be anywhere?"

"Right, but I doubt she's a legit threat. The fact that she mails you letters suggests she's afraid of confrontation. If she really wanted to hurt you, she'd have taken action."

She may already have, Kelly thought. *Could E2 have been targeted last night? Attacked? Kidnapped?*

"Rick, can you please put Emma on the phone?"

"Not now. She'll call you later."

"Please—two minutes."

"Bye, Kell." He hung up.

She lit another cigarette.

After dropping off the twins at school, she slogged through her workday. Every phone call seemed deliberately obnoxious. Grown men and women whined about noisy dishwashers and squeaky fridge doors. Tizz after tizz. Kelly wanted to snap.

That afternoon, she picked up the twins from school. They chirped about all the fun they had in art class. Zach had made her a clay pot that looked like Frankenstein's monster. Aiden had made her a clay starfish. Kelly couldn't bring herself to enjoy either gift, but she sparked to life when Aiden said they had to write a journal entry for homework. That reminded her of the diary she found last night. She needed to check it out.

Back at her desk, she opened the diary. The first entry— "I still believe it's out there"—gave her the shakes, even in daylight. She flipped pages; day after day went by in 1934. She squinted at the scribbly handwriting and noticed the word *house* kept popping up. Seemed the author had been searching for the Murder House.

Oddly, however, the writer kept mentioning Las Vegas and Boulder Dam. Apparently he had worked construction on the dam. His days were spent on the job while his nights involved tracking down the house. But why would the Murder House have been near Vegas?

Midway through the diary, the author mentioned the "miracle in Arizona"—whatever that was. It had apparently transpired months before the first entry in this book. That led her to believe there might be another diary. Maybe it was buried in the attic somewhere.

She continued flipping pages. Night after night, the author failed to find the Murder House. Then she came across bizarre entries written with dots and horizontal lines. It resembled Morse code, but there were also half circles, uneven triangles, and sideways lightning bolts. Running across the middle of each page was a blank stretch without writing. It reminded her of the polished line that divided the attic.

What happened to this guy?

Those bizarre etchings covered the next few dozen pages. Toward the end, English entries reappeared, in which the author gloated about a series of successful magic shows. He was evidently enjoying his nightly performances until his "other half" botched a magic trick and ruined his reputation.

The final entries mentioned that he wished to rid himself of his other half by "doing what was done in Arizona." Unfortunately for Kelly, the diary's last page had been ripped out. She could only torture herself as she wondered what details had been scribbled on it.

She reread the diary until her shift ended and DJ arrived home.

It was time to visit Emma.

NOBODY ANSWERED the bell at Emma's house, so Kelly unlocked the back door using the emergency key. Inside, the place smelled of Lysol. She rushed upstairs and found Emma snoring in bed, her skin tinted yellow by the sunlight from the window. A bottle of Nyquil stood on her nightstand.

Kelly shook her daughter awake.

Emma groaned. Both eyes remained shut as she writhed against her mattress.

"Em, you okay? Where's your twin? Did she come home? Did she say where she went last night?" Kelly realized she was asking too many questions of someone emerging from a Nyquil coma. After a deep breath, she asked, "How you feeling?"

"Bad." Emma's unwashed hair lay smeared against the pillow. "It's like knives are stuck in me."

"In your legs?"

"Everywhere." Emma grunted. "Everything hurts."

"Where's E2?"

"Not sure. She never came back."

Kelly swallowed hard. "Back from what? A party?"

"Yeah. She went with Cassie last night."

"Where was the party at?"

"Caraway."

"Caraway *University*?" Kelly's pulse tapped within her neck. Caraway parties were notoriously wild. Anything could've happened. The double-body situation worried her most. If Emma's legs were in pain last night, E2's upper body would've suffered as well.

What if E2 collapsed among strangers? How would people react? Would someone drive her to a hospital? Would someone take advantage?

Kelly asked for the address then looked it up on her phone. The street view showed a two-story house with a spacious porch and front yard. Thick evergreens surrounded the property. It looked familiar—Kelly had likely partied there during her college days. She enlarged the image and spotted Greek letters on the front of the building.

A frat house. Great. E2 had gone to a frat house.

And not just any frat house—the one where Anissa Norwell had last been seen alive.

20

Kelly motored toward Caraway University with icy legs and fiery determination. Nothing could stop her, certainly not the speed limit. Her van darted up I-81 while she envisioned herself kicking down the frat house door and demanding answers. If those scumbags didn't tell her where her daughter was, she would make them.

Her fantasy was interrupted by a numbing pinch around her ankles. Seemed she was straying too far from K2.

Kelly checked her GPS. Her destination was twelve miles out. As she continued up the highway, sensation faded from her knees, thighs, and hips. Numbness seeped through her bones, between her joints, into her muscles. Her lower body began to suffocate.

Before long, she couldn't sense her foot against the gas pedal.

Horns honked as traffic swerved around her. An SUV whizzed past her window, nearly taking out her side mirror.

Rattled, Kelly pulled over to the shoulder.

Caraway's campus was too far. Though she hated to

admit it, she couldn't continue while K2 anchored her in the opposite direction.

Defeated, Kelly veered onto the next exit ramp and drove home.

When she stormed into the living room, DJ and the kids were running around shooting each other with Nerf guns. Laughter and foam darts filled the air. Aiden invited her to play, but she ducked into the kitchen. She reheated a container of barbeque chicken and hurried it out to the shed. She removed the lock, then checked over both shoulders to ensure that no neighbors were watching.

After a deep breath, Kelly ripped the door aside like a Band-Aid. The shed interior stank of urine and gardening supplies. Water dripped from the leaky ceiling. K2 sat with her back against the far wall, her eyes baggy, her hair a crumpled mess. On her arm above the elbow was a cut that had scabbed over.

"Are you okay?" Kelly asked. "What happened to your arm?"

K2 glared at her.

"Seriously, what happened?"

K2 nodded at a nearby shelving rack. "Tripped and cut myself while I was dodging roof leaks. Thanks for taking such great care of me." Her eyes found the container in Kelly's grasp. "Oh, wow. Reheated leftovers. Must be my lucky day. What's on the prison menu for tomorrow?"

"Forget about tomorrow. We're leaving."

K2's bitter demeanor shifted toward confusion. "Leaving?"

Kelly nodded. "Emma's in trouble."

"What kind?"

"Here, eat this while I explain." Kelly handed over the Tupperware container and a fork. K2 ate ravenously but stopped chewing when Kelly recounted the darker details. Before long, K2 had set aside her food and was staring back with wide, worried eyes.

"You sure E2 is still at the frat house?" K2 asked.

"That's what I need to find out," Kelly said. "I can't drive there without my legs turning to icicles, so I'm taking you along. Please don't make this difficult."

K2 scowled and held up a hand. "Whoa. Hold on. I didn't make anything difficult. Remember, you're the one who beat *my* face with a plastic leg and then locked *me* in here. If you want my help, that all has to stop. I want to sleep inside our house from now on. No more shed. We clear?"

Kelly squeezed the padlock till her knuckles ached. She didn't want K2 inside the house. Not with the kids around. Not in a million years.

But with Emma's well-being at stake, Kelly couldn't afford to waste time. If Emma had trusted her double, then maybe Kelly should trust K2 this once. Besides, there had been a sincere, wounded look in K2's eyes when she learned of E2's disappearance. That had to count for something.

Kelly stepped outside. Glanced at her house. Glanced at K2.

"From now on," Kelly said, crossing her arms, "whenever DJ and the kids are home, you will stay in my office with the door locked. That's nonnegotiable. We can discuss other rules later. Deal?"

K2 stepped outside. She gestured at the padlock in Kelly's hand. "Gimme."

After Kelly handed it over, K2 flung it into the woods behind the shed. It struck a tree and sent birds scattering. "Now we have a deal."

21

Moving K2 into the house meant Kelly needed to send DJ and the kids away. She interrupted their Nerf gun battle and announced they'd have to get McDonald's for dinner because she had to visit Emma. DJ offered to cook pasta, but Kelly promised the twins that if they left for McDonald's now, they could have Pop-Tarts for breakfast tomorrow. The boys sprinted into the kitchen for their shoes.

"What's going on with Emma?" DJ said, gathering up foam darts. "This is like a nightly thing now."

Kelly picked at her earring. "Em's going through a phase."

"Okay, but what about Aiden and Zach? Every night they ask when you're coming home. Zach's been losing sleep."

"That's why I'm leaving now," she said. "Hopefully I'll be home sooner."

He shook his head, dismayed. Then a smile broadened within his beard. *Must've had one of his epiphanies,* she thought.

"How about we all go visit Emma?" he said. "Maybe seeing Aiden and Zach will cheer her up."

"I don't think so, hon. She needs space."

He looked perplexed. "She needs space...yet you're visiting her?"

"You know what I mean. She needs me."

"For what exactly?"

"Advice. Comfort. Support."

"Rick and Olivia can't provide that?"

"God, DJ, do I have to spell it out for you? Emma's having girl problems—issues with boys and stuff. She doesn't trust her stepmom, so she needs me."

"I see." He turned his back to her. He always got like this when they disagreed. Rather than addressing the problem, he would silently withdraw until she confronted him. A mild dispute would ensue, apologies would be exchanged, and the status quo would return. Rinse and repeat till death do us part.

Soon as he and the kids left, Kelly fetched K2 and rushed her upstairs to the bathroom. K2 brushed her teeth and took a quick shower to wash away the stink. Afterward she headed into the bedroom, plopped onto the mattress, and said, "So, what're we wearing?"

"Does it matter?"

"Sure it does. We're going to a frat house. We need to blend in."

Kelly entered her walk-in closet. The options were limitless. Her closet was overloaded with impulse buys she had never worn. Party dresses, off-the-shoulder tops, leopard-print blouses, and countless other outfits of every color, style, and fabric. Most wouldn't fly at the grocery store or her kids' soccer games, but tonight anything was fair game.

Great. Now what do I wear to a frat house at age thirty-four?

Kelly tried on different tops while her double tried others. It accelerated the process; she wished K2 had existed back in high school during those long weekends inside mall fitting rooms.

"Here's our winner," K2 said, posing in a purple off-the-shoulder top. The neckline dipped beneath Kelly's comfort zone, but K2 insisted it fit the occasion. "Remember, this isn't a PTA meeting. Those frat guys'll laugh you out the door if you dress like your usual errand-running self."

Kelly slipped into a beige cardigan. "How about this?"

"Seriously? *That's* your entry ticket?"

Hands on her hips, Kelly turned her shoulder toward the mirror. The cardigan downplayed her features. "I'm trying to find E2, not trying to hook up with some sleazebag."

"At least do better than a cardigan, you frump. A cardigan at a frat house is like lingerie at a funeral."

Kelly threw her hands up in frustration. "Fine. Hurry up and pick something that's frat-worthy but tasteful."

"Tasteful frat attire...riiight." K2 dragged hangers back and forth until she selected a black V-neck top with lattice sleeves that Kelly bought last month. It looked like a fair compromise between sexy and conservative.

She tried it on. Aside from being tight around the shoulders, it fit comfortably. The black brought out her cheeks and hair, and the lattice sleeves exposed skin in a sophisticated way.

K2 fixed the shoulders. "Personally, I'd pair it with a miniskirt, but knowing you, you'll insist on wearing jeans."

Kelly nodded at the mirror. "Yep. Jeans. Now let's get moving."

22

Kelly couldn't remember the last time she drove while wearing heels. Probably around the time of her last job interview, which had been three years ago. Tonight that lovely streak ended with sharp discomfort along her foot. The stop-and-go traffic near Caraway University was torture, and she berated herself for not bringing slip-ons.

In the passenger seat, K2 touched up her eyeshadow. It was eggplant purple, matching her off-the-shoulder top. Though Kelly had ordered her to wear jeans, K2 rocked a white miniskirt with fuck-me heels. The woman possessed a shameless enthusiasm that Kelly hadn't displayed in years. It left her feeling disgusted as well as envious.

After fixing her eyeshadow, K2 tossed some cinnamon Tic-Tacs into her mouth and switched on the radio. It was tuned to a station the kids enjoyed, but she spun the dial until Rihanna's "We Found Love" burst through the speakers. "Ooo, haven't heard this one in forever. It's like we're back in college."

"Yeah. Literally." Kelly turned left, into the heart of the Caraway campus. The place was so well lit it resembled a cloudy day despite the nighttime hour. Students skittered along the sidewalks, some racing toward the dining area while others approached the campus' dark edge. Kelly followed the latter group, squinting through the stiff breeze coming through her window.

According to her GPS, the frat house was minutes away. "God, I hope E2's okay."

"Relax," K2 said, flattening out her skirt, "I'm sure she's all right."

"Based on what? She's been missing all day."

"So? Maybe she was goofing off with some sorority girls."

"But Emma's bedridden. Why would E2 feel any better?"

"Listen," K2 said, lowering the radio volume, "the whole time I was locked in the attic, I had no trouble moving around. The cold, the numbness—it was never as bad as you described it."

"You said you were freezing."

"Right, but I was never in agony. Whenever you and I are separated, I get a headache. At first it hurts like hell, then it wears off. I'm not sure if it's because the pain receptors in my brain go numb, but once that initial headache passes, I feel better."

"And you think the same thing happens to E2?"

"I don't see why not."

Kelly exhaled. "I hope you're right."

"She'll be fine," K2 said, tucking her damp hair behind her ears. "After we take her home, we should go out for drinks."

Kelly scoffed. "Yeah, right."

"Oh, come on. You desperately need a cosmo, and I'm

dying to get plastered after the past couple nights. Let's do it."

"Another time."

"You sure? You look awfully thirsty."

Kelly smiled despite the mounting tension in her chest.

Her GPS guided her to the north end of campus, where houses stood along the edge of the surrounding woods. When she reached her destination, she found the sidewalks crammed with parked cars. She nabbed a parking spot farther down the street.

They exited the van and trekked toward the house. Kelly felt exposed. She was out in public with her twin, and while their outfits and makeup distinguished them from each other, they still shared the same height, body type, and hair color.

"These heels are killing me," K2 said, grunting after every step.

"Should've worn sandals."

"Sandals with a miniskirt? Yuck."

"Sandals go with anything."

"That's a lie, and you know it."

"Quiet, we're almost there."

"What, afraid someone might overhear our sandal debate?"

"I'm trying to act casual."

"Debating shoe preferences *is* casual." K2 dabbed a finger under Kelly's eye. "I might've overdone your mascara. You're flaking."

"Shut up till we get inside."

Electronic dance music throbbed from the two-story building. On the front porch stood two dudes with gelled hair. They sipped beer and yapped about girls until the taller guy noticed K2.

"Evening, ladies." He set aside his beer. "Ready for your handcuffs?"

"Handcuffs?" Kelly cringed. "You're kidding, right?"

"No, didn't you hear? It's champagne and shackles night. You cuff yourself to a partner, we give you a bottle of Andre, and the cuffs stay on till the bottle's empty."

"If you two are single," the shorter dude said, grinning, "we can accommodate you."

"We're looking for our friend Emma," Kelly said.

"Emma? Don't know any Emmas."

"We'll find her." Kelly approached the door.

"Whoa, whoa." The short guy jumped in front of her. "Nobody goes in without champagne and shackles."

The tall dude grabbed two bottles of Andre from a plastic cooler. "You want in, you need a partner."

"Don't worry," Shorty said, "we make great partners."

Kelly hesitated, then clasped K2's hand. "Already got one."

"Right," K2 said, playing along. "We're together."

Shorty narrowed his eyes. "Lesbians?"

"Big time," K2 said.

He squinted back and forth. "But you look like sisters."

"We get that a lot," Kelly said.

"Holy shit, you *are* sisters." He pointed to Kelly's cheek, then to K2's. "Twin sisters. Even got the same birthmark."

"Lesbian twin lovers..." The tall dude touched a frosty bottle to his forehead. "Fuck, that's hot."

"No, it's nasty," Shorty said. "That's incest, bro."

"Dude, it's not like they can get each other knocked up."

"Still nasty. Like imagine if your mom and sister—"

Kelly snatched a pair of handcuffs from a cardboard box. She pushed one cuff onto her own wrist and the other onto K2's. "Give me that champagne."

The tall guy handed her a bottle.

Shorty blocked the entrance. "Wait."

"Now what?" Kelly said.

"If you're lovers, prove it."

"Excuse me?"

"Prove it. Or else you're not getting in."

"I'm not doing anything for your amusement, creepo."

"I didn't say I'd be amused."

"Well, then don't—"

Kelly felt two hands grab her cheeks. A moment later her neck twisted toward K2, and before she could resist, K2's lips were all over hers—wet, pushing, sliding, tasting of cinnamon Tic-Tacs. The whole thing was mortifying. Holding hands with K2 was bad enough. The last thing Kelly wanted was to accept her double's tongue in her mouth. But for Emma's sake, she played along. She wrapped an arm around K2's neck and moaned.

Then came the sound of shattering glass. Kelly pulled back and realized the tall guy had dropped the other bottle. His eyes were wide as full moons. Shorty was speechless too.

Kelly fought the urge to wipe her lips as she marched past them.

23

An EDM song pounded Kelly's eardrums as she stepped inside. The main room was smothered in darkness, brightened only by the whipping beams of strobe lights. Each flicker illuminated new waves of unfamiliar faces. Shackled couples gyrated everywhere. Drunken limbs flew as the music built toward a crescendo.

Hoping to find E2, Kelly barreled into the sweaty crowd. Maneuvering around was a struggle, especially with K2 anchored to her wrist. Kelly pushed forward until she found a pocket of open space near the room's center. Here, the frat-boy B.O. was at its stenchiest, and there was enough body heat to melt a diamond.

She begrudgingly sipped from her bottle of Andre. The cheap champagne cooled her tongue and washed away the cinnamon flavor of K2's Tic-Tacs. After another gulp, she handed the bottle to K2.

"Let's get these cuffs off," Kelly said.

"What?" K2 pointed to her ear. "Speak louder."

"Let's get these cuffs off!"

"You telling me to fuck off?"

"No." Kelly raised her cuffed hand. "Get. These. Off."

"Oh!" K2 guzzled champagne. "Want another sip? If you drink enough, maybe you'll forget that kiss."

"Shut up about that."

"Hey, it got us through the door."

"I said shut up."

"Tell me, was I better than DJ?"

"Enough!" Kelly snatched the bottle and emptied it onto the carpet. "Let's find a key master so we can split up and look for Emma."

In a cramped, smoky kitchen they spotted a guy in a jailbird costume. He had a large keyring in hand. When Kelly showed him the empty bottle, he unlocked her cuffs.

K2 went to search the main room. Kelly checked the others. She asked people about Emma and Cassie until a spray-tanned dude said he'd seen Cassie in the backyard.

Kelly stormed past the kitchen guests and headed outside. A fire pit blazed near a dirt trail leading into the woods beyond. Couples huddled around the fire, their rubbery young faces grinning as somebody in an orange jumpsuit cracked jokes.

"Has anyone seen Cassie?" Kelly asked.

"Cassie who?" the guy in orange said.

"High school girl. Platinum blonde hair."

"Oh yeah. She looks like that chick from *Game of Thrones*."

"Is Cassie here or not?"

Right then, a college girl near the back porch screamed. She raced out, full speed, in a bra, panties, and sneakers. On her head was a gorilla mask. She jumped down the wooden steps and stumbled as her shoes hit the dirt. Once she righted herself, she sprinted into the woods. Everyone nearby cheered.

Then some dude in a matching gorilla mask rushed outside in nothing but plaid boxer shorts. He beat his skinny chest, earning roars of approval from onlookers, then ran barefoot into the woods, chasing the girl. He must've stepped on a sharp rock because he hopped in pain before resetting his stride.

Kelly faced the guy in orange. "You still do banana races?"

"Still?" The guy squinted at her. "Why would we ever stop? We've been doing them since I was a freshman."

Actually, a lot longer than that, Kelly thought. She had run many races during her time at Caraway. Whenever a guy challenged her, he was obligated to run barefoot while she kept the footwear advantage. They would race down the woodland trail, grab a banana from the checkpoint box, and sprint back. Winner got to request any favor from the loser. Most winners wanted sexual thrills, but Kelly typically demanded money or the answers to a history test. And then, of course, there was that time she ordered a guy to snap an incriminating photo of Anissa Norwell.

"Haven't seen you before," the guy in orange said. "Are you like a grad student or something?"

"Yep, grad student."

"Cool. I like smart girls." He grinned. "Wanna race?"

"Forget it. I need to find Cassie so I can find my daughter."

"Daughter?" His eyes scanned her body. "You have a daughter?"

"She's sixteen," Kelly said. "She was here last night but never came home."

His smile evaporated.

"Her name's Emma." Kelly grabbed her phone and

showed everyone Emma's picture. "She has red hair like me, she's kinda tall, and—"

A muscular guy snapped his finger. "I saw her."

"Where?"

"Last night she did a race."

Kelly felt the blood drain from her cheeks. "Sh-she did?"

Cheers erupted as the current race ended, the girl sprinting out of the woods, banana in hand. She ripped off her gorilla mask in celebration while her opponent hobbled into the backyard. He lifted his left foot, the bottom of which was smeared with blood. The girl embraced him and whispered something in his ear.

"Oh, fuck—not that!" he shouted.

She bopped his head with the banana and dragged him inside.

Kelly faced the fire pit crew. "What happened after Emma's race? Did anyone see where she went?"

"There were tons of races last night," the guy in orange said. "They all blur together."

"Unblur them! C'mon, think."

The group went quiet.

One guy in a straitjacket costume spoke up. "I remember."

"What?" Kelly said. "What happened to Emma?"

He sipped his beer. "She lost."

24

K elly froze. Her entire body tensed up—head, neck, chest, and everything below. She wanted to ask questions but feared the answers. Part of her wanted to pretend Emma had never come here, let alone lost a silly race to some douchebag. But now wasn't the time to pretend things were okay. Now she needed the truth.

"Where'd Emma go afterward? After losing?"

"Back inside," the straitjacket guy said. "She went with that guy she lost to. Later on, though, she came back out here. Must've lost an earring or something during the race, because she ran into the woods."

"And then?"

He shrugged. "That's all I remember."

Kelly hurried toward the dirt trail. She stumbled in her heels, then corrected her gait and power-walked into the woods.

Please, Emma. Tell me you camped out all night because you were scared or embarrassed or your upper body turned numb. Any reason is fine. I'll take you home now.

Shining her flashlight between the trees, Kelly repeatedly called Emma's name.

No reply.

The trail continued up a steep hill. At the top was the checkpoint box with bunches of freckled bananas inside. Kelly pushed on through waves of oak trees, their branches scratching her face and snagging her hair. While she untangled herself, her flashlight beam sparkled against a familiar blue sequined design.

Emma's purse—same one Kelly had rescued from the attic. It lay on some twigs. Her heart rumbled as she unzipped it. The contents—wallet, cosmetic bag, tampon, breath mints, and the lucky piece of rope—appeared undisturbed.

"Em, you out here?" Kelly yelled. "If you are, then scream, kick something, make noise!"

The woods stayed silent.

Kelly tucked Emma's purse inside her own and pressed on. Busted twigs nipped at her ankles while she swept her flashlight ahead. A waist-high broken branch caught her attention. The dirt below was scuffed with footprints leading deeper into the woods, toward a field of overgrown grass. At its center was a flat spot.

Someone was lying there. Someone in a wrinkled blue skirt.

"Emma!" Kelly fell to her knees beside her prone daughter. E2's face was covered with tangled hair and small leaves. The girl wore a sleeveless black top with a bright blue skirt that matched her purse. Black sandals adorned her feet, which were flecked with bits of forest debris.

"I'm here," Kelly said, flipping her onto her back. "We can leave now."

E2 didn't respond. She lay motionless except for the

nighttime wind stirring her hair and rippling her muddy clothes.

Kelly softly slapped her cheek, then pinched both ears. Nothing woke her. Perhaps the girl was too numb, too frozen.

Need to get her home. Once she's back, she'll regain strength. She has to.

Kelly checked E2's neck for a pulse. As her fingers grazed the throat, she noticed a strange lump beneath the chin. She aimed her flashlight and gasped.

Dark bruises bloomed across the neck.

Someone had crushed her windpipe.

She was dead.

25

Kelly's first instinct was to pinch the windpipe from the sides. Her thumb and forefinger jittered as she reached for her daughter's throat. Once she had a grip, she gently squeezed and tried to uncrush it like a dented soda can. She thought she was making progress, but the cold, oily flesh slid from her fingers.

Nonono. Please work.

After a deep inhale, Kelly rubbed her hands in the dirt and tried again. This time she found a solid grip. She applied pressure. More pressure. More.

The windpipe popped loose and sank down into the neck.

Into her daughter's cold, purple neck.

This was bad. The girl had no pulse, no breath, nothing. Her whole body was frigid, and the cheek that had been touching the ground was reddish and hard, as if blood had settled inside.

Kelly again reached toward the girl's throat.

Her crushed throat.

Someone crushed my daughter's throat.

Memories flooded Kelly's mind. First, she was giving birth to Emma in the hospital, then chasing her across a bright green lawn, then teaching her how to kick a soccer ball. As more images poured through, Kelly choked. Tears flowed. She sobbed over the body, unable to pull herself away.

"Oh, Emma. This can't be real. This can't."

Kelly collapsed onto her side, moaning in the grass. It seemed impossible that Emma—either half of her—could be dead.

You will understand my pain.

Kelly glanced up, hyperalert. She scanned her surroundings. The forest clicked and scratched. Popped and crunched. Hissed and whistled.

It wasn't safe out here. Norwell could be peeking through the trees, watching Kelly and her dead daughter.

No. Emma's not dead. She's at home. At home and in pain. I can still help her. I need to take E2 back to her.

Struggling to her feet, Kelly grabbed E2's ankles and started dragging the body. Gutted and mortified, she could only muster so much energy. The strain on her back and shoulders wore her down, and her heels made every backward step an ordeal.

You will understand my pain.

Norwell was lurking nearby. Waiting in darkness. Waiting to pounce.

Kelly couldn't do this alone. She needed to find K2. Together, they could watch each other's backs. Together, they could carry E2's body.

Kelly stormed back into the frat house. An EDM song thrummed through the humid building, driving handcuffed couples into dancing fits. Champagne splashed the air, soaking Kelly's shoulders. She ignored the noise, the wetness, the discomfort. Her search for K2 led her to the second-floor hallway, which was crammed with people waiting in line for the bathroom. Girls twitched in place, desperate to pee. One knocked frantically on the bathroom door.

"Pleeease," the girl said, pressing a hand to her crotch. "I reeeally need to pee."

"Who's in there?" Kelly asked.

"Some redheaded bitch."

Kelly pounded the door. "K2, open up!"

A toilet flushed. The door opened a crack. K2 appeared with ruddy cheeks and woozy eyes. Behind her was a brightly lit marble bathroom. The toilet seat was up, the shower curtain hanging at a crazy angle.

"What're you doing?" Kelly snapped.

K2 wiped her lips. "Sorry, someone offered me gin."

"You idiot!" Kelly snatched her elbow and dragged her downstairs. K2 moaned, slapping at Kelly as they passed boozing couples and left through the back door. Kelly didn't release her grip until they were halfway up the dirt trail, out of earshot from the backyard. Then she shoved K2 up against a tree.

"What were you thinking?" Kelly growled.

K2 rubbed her elbow. "I was investigating."

"Investigating what? The bottom of a Solo cup?"

"Some guy said he knew Emma. When he offered me a drink, I took it." With a sheepish grin, K2 said, "What about you? Any luck finding her?"

Kelly nodded.

K2 hopped with excitement. "Really? Where is she?"

"In the woods." Kelly swallowed hard. "She's—" No. She couldn't say it. Not even about E2. "I need help moving her."

K2 frowned. "What do you mean?"

Kelly burst into tears. She stumbled sideways. K2 caught her before she hit the ground. They twisted in clumsy circles while Kelly sobbed against her double's bare shoulder.

"What the hell happened?" K2 said. "Did some douchebag hurt her?"

"She's..." Kelly sniffled. Couldn't bring herself to say it. "Follow me. And watch out for Norwell."

"Norwell?" K2 said. "What the fuck happened?"

Kelly didn't answer. She continued ahead.

Soon her flashlight revealed E2's body.

K2 paused, then rushed toward it.

On her knees, she tried to adjust the crushed windpipe.

It was like reliving the nightmare all over again.

26

Long past midnight Kelly's tears ran dry. She grabbed the girl's armpits while K2 clutched the ankles. Together they carried the body back toward campus. The weight strained Kelly's arms and shoulders, but she refused to take a breather. She stumbled several times, fell twice, and swore she'd never wear heels again.

To avoid being seen, she and K2 chose a roundabout path through the woods. Staying hidden proved easy until they approached the sidewalk near the frat house. There the tree line ended. Cars passed beneath bright orange streetlamps.

"Let's set her down," Kelly said, winded. They lowered the body onto a dirt patch. Relief surged through her arms and shoulders, which were so exhausted that she couldn't lift either hand high enough to wipe sweat from her brow. "Wait here. I'll get the van."

Kelly returned and double-parked near the sidewalk. She left the van running while she and K2 rushed to lift the body into the trunk.

They drove off.

Reaching the interstate, Kelly coughed harshly, as if expelling water after nearly drowning. Fresh tears stung her eyes. She squeezed the steering wheel and moaned.

"Hey—slow down!" K2 said.

Kelly checked the speedometer. The needle hovered past ninety. She tapped the brake. Though traffic was scarce and no cops were around, she couldn't risk getting pulled over. Not with her double in the passenger seat and a body in the trunk. She needed to stay calm until she reached Rick's place.

K2 glanced back at the trunk. "Where we gonna put her?"

"We're taking her to Emma."

"Yeah, but we can't hide her in Emma's bedroom. She'll stink up the place."

Kelly hadn't thought that far ahead, but it was true. The body would soon smell, and that odor needed to be contained. She supposed they could seal E2 inside a large bag, but the stench might leak through. If Rick or Olivia caught a whiff, Emma's secret would be exposed. The body would have to be hidden outside the house—but not too far away.

"Let's hide her in the garden," Kelly said.

K2 hesitated. "You mean...bury her?"

Kelly grimaced. That idea was too heartbreaking. Too real. Too final. "No, we'll hide her under some thick shrubs."

"What about the smell?"

"We'll seal her inside a bag."

"Like a garbage bag?"

Again Kelly winced. She never imagined placing her daughter inside a trash bag, but their options were limited. "We can't exactly get her a casket."

K2 shook her head. "This is so wrong."

For once, Kelly agreed with her.

There was a Walmart off the next exit. Kelly stopped and bought a pack of the largest garbage bags they had, along with some duct tape. Then she drove to Rick's. No lights were on inside, so she and K2 lugged the body straight to the moonlit backyard. They located a hiding spot beneath the rhododendrons.

Kelly ripped open the package of garbage bags. Citrus scent escaped the box. She peeled off a large bag, shivering at the scaly plastic texture. Her cheeks blazed. Her eyes watered. She remained still, afraid that if she moved she might start sobbing.

When the tension around her eyes faded, she shook open the bag. With K2's help, she delicately lowered Emma —no, E2—inside.

They triple-bagged her and slid her beneath the rhododendrons.

K2 knelt in the dirt beside the bag. "Should we say something?"

"No," Kelly said, steeling herself. "This isn't a funeral."

"Are you kidding me?" K2 snapped. "This is our daughter. She's gone."

"Our daughter is alive."

"Only one of her is," K2 said, her voice thin. She tugged the bag closer and hugged it against her. "How can you act like E2 isn't real?"

"Of course she's real. I've been crying over her all night."

"Then why can't we say a few words?"

Because Kelly didn't want to. Any sort of eulogy would only make this more painful. Seeing E2 lying in the woods with a crushed throat had broken Kelly's heart and mind.

The less she thought about it, the better. "We need to focus on Emma—on the one upstairs. We only have one more chance to protect her from Norwell."

K2 scowled. "Well, I'm saying something." She laid the lumpy bag flat along the dirt. Placing a hand on the bag, she whispered, "Love you, Em. Every part of you."

K2's voice cracked. That sent Kelly into tears. She knelt beside her double and abruptly hugged her. K2 was startled by the hug, but she returned it, sobbing. A strange warmth spread through Kelly's midsection, and she was reminded of what Emma had said outside school the other day about how nice it was to hug E2.

After breaking the embrace, Kelly crawled through the garden and wiped away their footprints from the dirt. She then sprinkled dead leaves across the area so everything blended.

By the time she finished, the sun glowed orange on the horizon.

Light shined across Emma's upstairs window.

27

DJ was waiting in the driveway when Kelly arrived home. He stood in front of the garage, hands on hips. Sunlight reflected off his glasses. She couldn't see his eyes, but she could tell he was furious. Last night he had texted, asking when she would get home, but she'd been too distraught over E2's death to respond.

Right now, Kelly was so emotionally ravaged that she considered venting the entire story to him. Anything to avoid an argument. She couldn't endure any marital conflict this morning.

"Is it safe to come out?" K2 asked from the minivan cargo area.

"No," Kelly said without moving her lips. "Stay put."

She parked, exited the van, and approached her husband.

His sharp blue eyes glared at her. "The kids were wondering where you were."

She paused before him. The wind tossed her hair across her face. With a shaky hand, she pushed it away. A lump formed in her throat as she met his eyes. "The other night,

Emma went to a frat party. Something...happened to her. Last night I tried picking up the pieces."

DJ's gaze softened. His arms flattened at his sides. "Oh."

She frowned. "Sorry for not texting you, but last night was hell."

"I had no idea," he said apologetically. "Is she okay? Are *you* okay?"

Kelly shook her head. A sob burst from her throat. She stumbled into his arms.

He held her tight. "Didn't know things were so serious."

"Me neither," she said, sniffling.

"Want me to stay home today? I could take care of some chores, make your life easier."

She smiled through her tears. "Thanks, but I'd like some time alone."

"Understandable. Is there anything I can do?"

"You mind driving the twins to school?"

"Kelly, it's Saturday."

"Oh." She blinked. "Right."

"How about this? How about I drop off the twins at my parents' house? That way, you'll have some quiet time." He held her at arm's length. "You calling off from work?"

"I'm out of sick days. It's okay, though—I could use a distraction."

"All right." He gave a reassuring smile. "Let me know if you need anything."

She was grateful for her husband's kindness. When your world was crumbling, it was the little gestures that kept you glued together. DJ always came through when things were at their worst, and this morning she cherished him— him and the kids, who she smothered with kisses at the breakfast table.

Later, after they left for his parents' house, she brought K2 upstairs. Her double took a shower then snoozed on the office couch while Kelly dealt with customers. In between calls, she contacted Rick about Emma. He said she'd been asleep when he went on duty. He also said he'd given Emma her phone back for the weekend. That was great news.

Kelly messaged her daughter and waited for a reply. The waiting was torture. Minutes dragged like lifetimes. Her anxiety festered. She became convinced her iPhone was broken—or maybe the entire cell network was. She restarted her phone several times, yet received no joyous messages saying "Thanks, Mom, I'm fine now!"

Her thoughts were interrupted by her jingling headset. Next thing she knew, she was getting bitched at by Sarah Brundy of Salem, Oregon. The lady was having a tizz over a six-dollar shipping charge that appeared on her AMEX card. Six dollars. Christ. Kelly could only wish her biggest problem was a stupid shipping fee.

Then it happened—her iPhone buzzed.

Finally!

But the message wasn't from Emma. It was from DJ.

"Can you put my grandma's birthday card in the mail?" he asked. "It's on the kitchen counter."

Kelly buried her face in her hands and groaned.

"Hey!" Ms. Brundy yelled through the headset. "Where's my refund?"

Kelly set her jaw and swiveled her chair around. On the office couch lay a sleeping K2. What Kelly wouldn't give to be asleep right now, free from all this stress.

"Excuse me, Ms. Brundy. Let me put you on hold so I can investigate your sensitive shipping issue."

Kelly muted the line and stomped downstairs to grab

the birthday card. She rushed out to the mailbox, only to learn that today's mail had already arrived. A short stack of bills and junk mail waited inside. She grabbed the pile and noticed the edge of a green envelope.

Blood drained from her cheeks. She checked over both shoulders, then retreated into her house, locked the door, and tore open the envelope. She held her breath as she unfolded the note.

Printed at the top were three sentences: "After I lost my daughter, I lost my home. Do you know what that feels like? Join me out on the streets."

Where? Which streets? Kelly would swim to South Korea if that's what it took, but the letter offered no specifics.

Her phone buzzed in her pocket.

This time, a message from Emma: "Still feeling crappy. Legs bad. Arms bad. Everything bad. Going back to sleep."

Not the response Kelly had wanted. She messaged back, asking if there was any improvement, even a minor jump in energy. Emma said no.

That left Kelly with a tangled stomach. If moving E2's body hadn't helped, then there was only one other option. It was time to confront Norwell and get answers.

Kelly considered heading to Anissa's grave, but that seemed like a trap. She needed to act with caution. She texted Rick and asked if they could meet for lunch. He said he was at his usual place—her father's bar.

She hurried upstairs to her office and shook K2 awake.

"Unngh." K2 stirred. "What time is it?"

"Time for you to take customer calls."

"What? Me? No way."

"I have to head out. Got another letter from Norwell."

K2 sat up, alarmed. "Really? What'd it say?"

"I'll explain later. I'm taking it to Rick. He's eating lunch at Dad's bar right now. Hopefully I can catch him before he leaves. Can you please cover for me and not get fired?"

K2 grimaced. "Can I go meet with Rick instead?"

"No."

"Well, I'm not taking calls. Fuck that."

"Please, K2. I don't have time to argue."

"Tell you what. I'll do it if you let me have a night out."

"A night out? Now? With everything that's going on? You can't be serious."

"I couldn't be *more* serious. After these past few nights, all I want to do is get wasted."

"How can you even consider that while Norwell's threatening us?"

"It's *because* Norwell's threatening us that I want to get lit. Think about it—if she came after E2, I'm probably next."

That left Kelly shivering.

"C'mon," K2 said. "Let's text Brittney. If my days are numbered, I want one last girls' night out. Can't I have some fun for once?"

Kelly hesitated. "If I let you go out, will you take calls?"

"Sure. A day's work for a night's play sounds fair."

Kelly dreaded K2's interpretation of play, but they could establish rules and boundaries later. For now, she handed over the headset. "Here. Finish up with Brundy."

K2 made a skeptical face. "Brundy?"

"Don't worry," Kelly said, heading out the door. "She's a sweetheart."

28

The O'Brother Bar shined along the Scranton street corner it had occupied for the past forty years. Neongreen lights glowed in the front windows, hyping up happy hour deals and the hottest boneless wings in Lackawanna County. Beyond food and drink, the place boasted ten ridiculously large TVs, two pool tables, and enough wiggle room to celebrate any goal, touchdown, home run, or buzzer-beater that might transpire.

Kelly tugged open the front door, which responded with a familiar squeak. The place smelled of fried potatoes and melted cheese. Business buzzed this Saturday afternoon, with college football fans wolfing down hoagies, burgers, and tater tots.

Behind the counter, two massive TVs displayed the Penn State game. Between them hung a framed soccer jersey, green with a white number one—Kelly's jersey from Caraway University. Seeing it always brought back rough memories of when she had to juggle school, soccer, and parenting—not to mention the guilt over Anissa Norwell's death. Kelly had asked her father to take down the jersey many times, but he always reminded her that Mom had framed it before passing away.

At the corner barstool Rick was having a laugh with Dad while they watched the game.

Kelly pulled up a stool, the metal feet scraping the floor tiles, announcing her arrival.

Dad cackled when he spotted her. "Kelly, my dear, what brings you in?"

"A whiskey. No ice."

"Oh-ho-ho!" Dad grabbed a bottle of Jameson, poured two fingers into a glass, and slid it toward her.

Kelly set her purse on the counter. The green envelope poked from the side pocket. After downing a searing gulp of whiskey, she said, "I need a minute with Rick."

Dad frowned, drawing out the wrinkles on his face. "And here I thought you dropped by to see your old man." He poured her another whiskey, then wandered into the kitchen, mumbling to himself.

"What's up?" Rick said before biting into his chicken sandwich.

Kelly sipped slowly this time. Whiskey wasn't her thing, but beer wouldn't hit hard enough and wine wasn't available. Once her throat stopped burning, she pulled the envelope from her purse and set it beside Rick's plate. "Norwell sent another one."

Still chewing, he wiped his fingers on a napkin before handling the envelope.

"Third time this week," she said. "One on Monday, another on Thursday, and now this."

He unfolded the letter beside his plate and read it aloud. "'After I lost my daughter, I lost my home. Do you know what that feels like? Join me out on the streets.' Sounds like she's looking for a fight. And that part about losing her home could be a threat against your house. Though, I can't tell if she's serious."

Kelly clutched her glass. "She is."

He leaned closer. "What makes you say that?"

She couldn't admit what had happened to E2. That was more than he could handle. Instead, Kelly went with the first lie that came to mind. "Zach said a strange lady approached him after school yesterday."

Rick's eyes popped. "Really? Why didn't you tell me?"

She shrugged.

"Jesus, Kell." He sipped his Coke. "You need to keep me posted on this shit. I mean, what if it spilled over to Emma?"

Kelly avoided his eyes. "Can you please find Norwell? I know she doesn't have an address, but she's gotta be local because of the postmarks on the envelopes."

"Already have people looking into it." He took out a pen and notepad. "While we have a minute, tell me what happened to Norwell's daughter."

"Why? You know the basics."

"Give me details. When people want revenge, they often try to re-create the harm that was done to them. Poetic justice and all that."

Kelly ran both hands through her hair then clutched the bar railing as if she were at the top of a roller coaster. She took a deep breath and glanced at her framed jersey.

"Heading into my senior year at Caraway, I was the starting goalie. Then I lost my job to Anissa Norwell. I had to warm the bench while she opened the season with two straight shutouts. The girl was unbeatable. It wasn't until our third game that she gave up a goal. We still won by two, but she was pissed about it. She blamed my friend Brittney and the other defenders for spoiling her shutout streak.

That divided the team, and over drinks that night, I asked Brittney to get me back in goal. I told her to do whatever it took. Told her to ruin Anissa. From then on, the defenders started bullying her."

Rick tapped his pen against the counter. "How? Give me specifics."

"It wasn't anything serious," Kelly said. "They lied about practice being rescheduled, stopped inviting her to parties, made up lies about her boyfriend, stuff like that."

He scribbled something down. "Keep going."

"There was one game when Brittney deliberately misplayed the ball and left Anissa one-on-one with the other team's striker. Anissa made the save, but after the game, she and Brittney got into a screaming match. Our whole team ran over. Everybody took sides and started shoving while I watched from the sideline. It was a mess. Girls were pulling hair, throwing elbows, you name it. I thought about intervening, but instead I let my team eat itself alive.

"The brawl got nastier until Anissa and Brittney collapsed in the middle of it. People piled onto them until Coach ripped everyone away and threatened to cancel scholarships. When the dust cleared, Anissa was on the ground clutching her ankle in pain. She was supposed to miss our next game, but she played through the injury and got another shutout. Afterwards, she told me to quit the team and become a stay-at-home mom. That pissed me off."

Rick grunted in agreement.

"The next night our team partied at a frat house," Kelly said. "When I got there, some guy challenged me to this silly race where the winner could make the loser do anything they wanted. After I won, I ordered him to take pictures of Anissa while she was drinking shots and snorting coke. Then I had him post the pictures all over social media and send the link to our athletic director. I hoped it might get her suspended for a game or two.

"Instead, she got kicked off the team and lost her scholarship.

"I started the next game. We won and returned to the frat house to celebrate. Anissa showed up. She didn't talk to anybody. Just stood around drinking and staring at me. She disappeared around midnight.

"The next day, Coach ordered an emergency meeting at the practice field. When we arrived, we learned Anissa had died that morning. Drove drunk into a guardrail. All because of me."

Rick scratched his scalp. "Fuck."

Kelly finished her whiskey. "Anyway, you know the rest. Anissa's death was all I could think about for months. I couldn't focus on school or soccer or even my four-year-old daughter. God, I was such a mess. And then there was that night I swallowed all those sleeping pills."

"Yeah, you're lucky Emma found you on the floor."

Kelly smiled sadly. Emma had been her guardian angel that night. "I never should've let myself unravel like that. Emma never should've seen me in that state. Not then, not ever."

Rick frowned. Slid his plate away. "I gotta get back on duty."

"Wait. Will Norwell come after me?"

"Hard to say. Lock your doors, watch your kids, and don't go near Anissa's grave." He pinched the bridge of his nose. "What worries me is the revenge angle. I wonder if that old cunt is considering hurting Emma—eye for an eye, daughter for a daughter, that sort of thing."

Kelly tensed. "Yeah, I'm worried about that too."

"Tonight when I get home, I'll have a talk with Emma." He climbed off his stool. "One more thing. Your friend Brittney—she still local?"

"Yeah, why?"

"Tell her to watch her back."

29

Kelly headed straight for the liquor store.

Inside, a muzak version of "Margaritaville" was playing. Saturday-afternoon shoppers filled the place, some waiting impatiently at the checkout counter. She scanned the aisles for Brittney, but her friend was nowhere to be found. Kelly feared the worst until the backroom door swung open; Brittney came out to hand a bottle of Grey Goose to a customer.

Kelly sprinted over, panting. "Britt. You're here."

"Hey, K-Lady. Back for that Spanish red?" Thankfully, Brittney looked unharmed. She was still sporting her new sideswept hairstyle. Her face glowed, and she wore a t-shirt under her apron with the phrase "Love the Wine You're With" printed across the front. Her cheerful demeanor dimmed once she noticed Kelly's eyes. "Is something wrong?"

Kelly dragged her into the backroom, a tight, dimly lit hallway lined with stocked shelves and unopened cardboard boxes. A fan hummed inside the employee restroom.

"What're you doing?" Brittney said. "You can't be back

here—I could get fired."

"Remember Anissa Norwell? You know how her mother sends me a letter every year? This week she sent me three. The most recent two were threats."

Her friend's eyes widened to perfect circles. "Really? What'd they say?"

Kelly gave her the cliff notes then asked if she'd received any green envelopes.

"No, never have," Brittney said. "I don't think Norwell knows I was involved back then."

Kelly exhaled. "Then you're probably safe. Be careful though."

"Of course." Brittney glanced out at the sales floor. "Listen, I gotta head back to the register. Wanna get drinks and talk about this? Tonight I have to close up, but tomorrow I'm free."

"Sorry, I can't. Not while—" Kelly stopped when she realized this was a golden opportunity to fulfill her promise to K2. If K2 wanted to get wasted, Kelly could make Brittney play chaperone. "Actually, Britt, I'll take you up on that. But under one condition."

"Name it."

"When we go out tomorrow," Kelly said, "babysit me the entire time. Let me drink, but don't let me near any guys. Remember, I'm married."

"Okay."

"And don't let me go home till I'm completely sober."

"Got it. You can crash at my place if you need to."

"Thanks. And one last thing. I know this sounds weird, but can you take selfies of us throughout the night and send them to my phone? I want the whole night on record."

Brittney raised an eyebrow. "Because of Norwell?"

"Yeah," Kelly lied. "Because of Norwell."

WHEN KELLY RETURNED to her home office, she feared she might find K2 ignoring her duties, cussing out a customer, or pouring wine over the keyboard. Instead, K2 sat upright at the desk, filing her nails while explaining how to replace a faulty door hinge. Her unwavering patience floored Kelly. Bargaining with K2 had paid off. At least for now.

"So what'd our ex-hubby say?" K2 asked after ending the call.

Kelly plopped onto the couch. "He's gonna track down Norwell."

"Nice." K2 blew dust from the edge of her thumbnail. "Did you tell him about E2?"

"No way. Are you kidding? We can't let other people know about this."

"I think we can trust Rick," K2 said. "I mean, it involves Emma."

"That's exactly why we can't tell him. He's overprotective of her. He'd lose his mind if he knew what was going on." Kelly leaned forward, elbows on knees, hands folded. "Besides, I promised Emma I wouldn't tell anyone."

"You're acting like we've never broken a promise before."

"I just don't want to disappoint her." Kelly scratched at her hairline. "Maybe when he finds Norwell, I'll tell him, but until then—"

The doorbell rang. Kelly jumped, then darted across the hall into the kids' room. She separated the curtains and spotted a white van parked along the curb. Her heart rate tripled.

She rushed back to K2. "There's a white van outside."

"Oh yeah. I ordered a Tracfone. Same-day delivery."

"*What? Why?*"

K2 shrugged. "You said I could go out drinking."

"I never said you could get your own phone."

"Well, it's not 1996 anymore. I'll need a phone for Ubers and stuff. Besides, it'll help us communicate while we're separated. Think about it—if I had a phone last night, you could've called me from the woods. We could've moved E2 sooner."

Kelly crossed her arms. "Why didn't you consult me about this?"

"It's just a phone. I didn't think it was a big deal."

"Going behind my back is a *huge* deal."

"I didn't go behind your back. It's not like I tried to keep the phone a secret."

Kelly shook her head, fuming. "How'd you pay for this thing?"

"Don't worry, I charged it to our Discover card. DJ won't get notifications." K2 removed her headset and rose from her chair. "Whelp, time to unbox it."

"Oh no you don't." Kelly blocked the door. She buried the urge to smack her double and said, "I was gonna let you go out with Brittney tomorrow, but now you're staying home."

"Hey, we have a deal."

"We *had* a deal. Then you bought that burner phone, and now I can't trust you."

"But all I'm gonna do is drink and dance."

"You won't stop there. You'll keep drinking till you go home with some random guy."

"Ohhh, so you're jealous?" K2 grinned. "You miss that lifestyle, huh?"

"That lifestyle is behind us. Remember, we're married."

"You are." K2 wiggled her empty ring finger. "Not me."

"You *are* me. And you're staying home tomorrow."

"But Brittney might know something about Norwell."

"I already asked her. She didn't."

"Still, can't I see her? It's okay to hang out with friends, you know? There's more to life than worshiping your kids 24/7."

"I do not worship my kids."

"You slave over them."

"Well excuse me for being responsible." Kelly took out her phone. "That reminds me. I need to message Emma, see how she's doing. Even if her condition improves, you and I still need to—"

Kelly stopped herself. She almost said they needed to restore themselves to one body, but a dark thought spilled through her mind. If Emma's legs fully recovered—which was a big "if" right now—that would mean E2's death had broken the curse. And if E2's death restored Emma to normal, then K2's death should do the same for Kelly.

Of course, this was all speculation. And if it did work, Kelly would have to murder her double, which sickened her on many levels. But if no other solution arose, she might have to consider going through with it in order to get her life back.

"We need to *what?*" K2 asked.

"Need to...visit Red Trail Road," Kelly said, backing into the hallway. "We'll go after work and talk to the neighbors. Maybe I'll let you use that new phone so we can cover more ground."

K2 clapped her hands. "Yes! I knew you wouldn't shut me down."

You have no idea what I'm capable of, Kelly thought.

30

Kelly accelerated past the Murder House. She continued down Red Trail Road, snaking between walls of towering foliage. The tallest trees blazed gold and orange in the autumn sun while everything below lay shrouded in cold shadow. Birds squawked. Insects hissed. The wind tore leaves from branches and spread a spicy woodsmoke odor.

Before long, neighboring homes appeared. She drove door-to-door like a mail carrier while K2 dashed outside to ring doorbells. About half of the neighbors answered—of course it was *half*—but none provided anything useful. Some slammed their doors while others offered the "Gee, wish I could help" routine. Kelly grew restless behind the wheel and fell into a fruitless driving pattern:

Step on the gas.

Hit the brake.

Wait.

Step on the gas.

Hit the brake.

Wait.

Step on the ga—

Something caught her eye in the next yard. Maple trees. Two of them. Bright red ones. The rest of the property had an almost grayish tinge, as if those maples had drained color from the lawn, bushes, and one-story ranch home behind it.

The name on the mailbox was Manganaro. In the driveway sat an old Mazda and a silver Honda Civic. The Honda's rear window sported a familiar lion decal—Emma's high school logo.

Kelly nudged K2. "Whoever lives here goes to Emma's school."

K2 went out and rang the doorbell. An angry dog barked in reply. She waited on the porch for five minutes before returning to the van.

They visited the remaining neighbors then returned to the Manganaro house around nightfall. No lights were on inside. Apparently nobody was home. Kelly decided to park alongside the yard until someone arrived.

While waiting, she burned through cigarettes and took out the diary to reread it.

"What's that?" K2 asked.

"A diary." Kelly tapped her cig out the window. "Emma and I found it in the attic."

"Really? Who wrote it?"

"Some guy who worked on the Boulder Dam."

"You mean the Hoover Dam?"

"Yeah. He lived near Vegas. Also spent time in Arizona, where there was something called the Miracle House."

K2 hopped in her seat. "You think he meant the Murder House?"

"I don't know."

"Can I see that?" K2 grabbed the diary before Kelly

could stop her. She flipped pages until she reached the entries with those bizarre symbols. "What are these?"

"No idea." Kelly blew smoke outside. "I think the author lost his mind."

K2 kept flipping. She paused toward the end. "Huh. It's in English again." She reached the final entry. "Wait, where's the last page? Did you rip it out?"

"No, we found it that way."

K2 gave a dubious glance. "Then where is it?"

Kelly shrugged. She tossed her cigarette and went to grab another when lights flickered within the Manganaro house. A skinny silhouette passed the front window.

"Look, someone's home."

The front door opened. A girl stepped outside. She adjusted her top as she hurried through the lawn toward the driveway. She tapped her key fob, and the silver Honda glowed to life. Its headlights illuminated her platinum blonde hair.

"Wait," K2 said, "that's—"

"Cassie."

Kelly left the van and sprinted after her. She yelled out to Cassie, who jumped before ducking into her car. She started the engine when Kelly reached the driver's window.

"Relax, Cassie, it's me. Emma's mom."

Cassie stared back with wide, alarmed eyes.

Kelly gestured for her to lower the window. "Can we talk?"

The window dropped an inch. "Wh-what're you doing here?"

"Joyriding," Kelly said. "Why are you here?"

"Meeting my lab partner from chem class."

"Manganaro?"

"Yeah. Mike. We have a paper due on Monday."

"Were you here with Emma the other night?"

The girl's face confirmed it. "Listen, I gotta go. I have to study."

"It's Saturday night, Cassie."

"But I have three tests on Monday."

"Before you go, tell me who dared Emma to break into that creepy house—the one down the road."

"Uh...everyone did."

"You included?"

Cassie shrugged. "I mean, sure, yeah."

"Were you the first to suggest it?"

"Does it matter?"

"*Cassie.*"

"Look, it was everyone. Everyone was teasing her. If it really matters, no, I wasn't first. I was terrified of that place. I couldn't believe Emma actually went inside."

"What happened at the frat house?"

"Frat house?"

"Yes, the one you invited Emma to the other night."

"I didn't invite her. She invited me. It was a last-minute thing."

"What happened there?"

"Not much." Cassie's cheeks turned red. "We partied a little."

"Who asked Emma to do a race?"

Cassie laughed uncomfortably. "Wait, she did one of those?"

"Don't play dumb."

"I'm not." Cassie held up her palms. "I was playing beer pong all night. Em hates beer, so she went off elsewhere. We got separated."

Kelly stared into Cassie's eyes. The girl was nervous. It

was hard to tell if she was hiding something or simply feeling uncomfortable.

"Look, I gotta go," Cassie said, putting her car in reverse. "Could you please not tell Emma we talked? I don't want her thinking I ratted her out to her mom."

"Okay. Drive safe."

Cassie backed out of the driveway and motored off.

Kelly returned to the van and updated K2 on the details. K2 suggested tailing Cassie, but Kelly wanted to chat with Mike Manganaro. She marched up the lawn and rang the doorbell, which made the dog erupt.

The front door opened a few inches. The mutt barked as a lethargic voice said, "Whoa, chill out, Snoop."

"Hi," Kelly said. "You must be Mike."

"Huh?" Manganaro squinted through the doorway. He reeked of weed. Sloppy dark hair hung over his eyes like a tattered curtain. She recognized the kid. He'd been at Emma's game the other day. "Uh, do I know you?"

"No," Kelly said, "but you know my daughter, Emma Wallace."

"Emma...yeah." He picked absently at a hoop earring. "Yeah, she goes to my school."

"Was she here Monday night?"

"Yeah. Bunch of people were. Did she forget something? Somebody lost a bracelet. Yo, wait, are you her mom?"

"I just said she was my daughter."

He gave a delayed laugh.

"Listen, Mike, on Monday night—"

"Mango."

"What?"

"People call me Mango. Not Mike."

"Okay, listen, Mango. Emma said on Monday night she

visited an old abandoned house. Would you know anything about that?"

He tugged his earring. "I remember Emma wasn't afraid of the place. Rest of us were like, 'Yo, let's turn back.' Then Em said she'd break into the house if everybody gave her twenty bucks. Then someone dared her to steal something from inside."

"Who dared her?"

"I don't remember."

"What'd she steal?"

"A wig."

"A wig?"

"Yeah. She left it here. Hang on." He shut the door and returned moments later with a dusty blonde wig. He handed it over.

Kelly rubbed the fake hair between her thumb and forefinger. She wondered if E2 had brought it back here after locking Emma inside the attic. "Tell me. When Emma left that house, what was she wearing?"

Mango blushed beneath his sloppy hair. "Wearing?"

"Yeah. You know. Clothing." She tugged her sleeve to demonstrate.

He glanced at the floor. "She, uh, had jeans on."

"No top?"

"Uh, no."

That confirmed Kelly's theory that E2 left with the wig. Now she needed to know more. "How long was Emma inside that house?"

"I don't know. Half hour. Maybe more."

"How did people react when she came back without her shirt?"

"I didn't stare at her," he blurted. "I mean, if that's what you're asking, then no—I didn't stare at her. It was dark, I barely saw anything, I swear." His stoner persona was wearing down fast. It looked like he'd switched from weed to speed. "Besides, she covered herself up with that wig until she borrowed a hoodie."

"Who gave her the hoodie?"

"I did."

"How nice of you." Kelly lifted the wig. "Who dared her to steal this?"

"I told you, I don't remember." The dog barked louder. "Maybe ask Emma."

"I'm asking you."

"Well, I don't know."

"I think you do."

"I don't. Lay off already."

He shut the door.

"Hey!" Kelly pounded her fist against it. "You know Emma's father is a cop, right? I'll call him right now unless you tell me what happened. Open up!"

When he didn't, she took out her phone to call Rick. Ironically enough, she had three missed calls from him. She dialed him back.

"Kell," he answered, sounding exhausted. "Where've you been?"

"My phone was on silent. What happened? Did you find Norwell?"

"No, it's Emma." He cleared his throat. "You need to come see her."

Kelly was afraid to ask why. "I'll be right over."

"She's not at the house."

"Then where is she?"

"The hospital." His voice cracked. "They just moved her to the ICU."

31

A staff member buzzed Kelly into the ICU. She rushed into the wide, hectic area, passing the central nurse's station as she checked the individual rooms along the perimeter. Nurses bustled about, switching IV bags and checking monitors. There was no privacy; each room had an open doorway surrounded by glass walls. Everything beeped, the place reeked of disinfectant, and it was chilly enough that Kelly wanted a scarf.

She spotted Rick in his police uniform standing beside one of the beds. He breathed heavily, his shoulders rising and sinking. His face was whiter than the sheet covering their daughter's legs.

Propped up on pillows, Emma slept, her expression agonized. Her body lay pale and motionless. IV tubes snaked along her arms. If not for the zipping green lines on an EKG monitor, Kelly might've thought her dead. Full-dead.

Kelly rushed to the bedside. "What happened?"

Rick took a labored breath. "Found her on the hallway

carpet. She'd—she'd pissed all over herself. Scared me to death."

Kelly placed an anxious hand on his shoulder to steady herself. With her free hand, she touched Emma's forearm before she reached under the blanket to check her thigh. Both body parts were warm, roughly the same temperature. "What'd the doctors say?"

"Lots of speculation. The MRI and lab results ruled out some stuff, but nobody nailed down a diagnosis. They think she might have something called...uh, wait, I wrote it down." He flipped through his notepad. "Guillain-Barré syndrome. It affects the legs and works its way up the body. So far, only her legs are having issues, but if things get worse, it'll reach her lungs and she'll have to be put on a ventilator."

Kelly knew it wasn't Guillain-Barré, but she wished it was. At least then there'd be a treatment plan.

Rick tugged on her elbow. "The other night, when you picked up Emma from that party... Where was it at?"

She wet her lip. "A few miles west of here. At an abandoned house."

"Shit, Kell, you should've mentioned that. We had a guy at the station who busted into an abandoned house that turned out to be a heroin den." He pinched the bridge of his nose. "I need to search that place. Now."

That wasn't gonna happen. "No, Rick. Where you need to be is here with Emma."

He sighed. "You're right. It kills me that I can't be two places at once."

Careful what you wish for.

"Why not find a nurse?" she suggested. "Ask what Emma could've picked up from an older home."

The nurse explained that the doctors had checked for

wounds—punctures, cuts, anything fresh—and that any indication of exposure would have been addressed. That left Rick withering helplessly beside the bed. He was always Officer Hardass until Emma scraped her knee or got a papercut. Kelly could only imagine his reaction if he learned the truth.

Once the nurse left, he grabbed the bedrail with both hands. Kelly did the same. It reminded her of their honeymoon. Money had been tight, so they spent a weekend in Wildwood, New Jersey. Each night after dinner, they stood on the boardwalk clutching the guardrail, staring into the endless black ocean. Those nights, she wondered how she could spend the rest of her life as a mother. It all seemed impossible.

Now, as Kelly hunched over her unconscious daughter, she felt as if she were staring into another endless black ocean, one deeper than any on Earth. Her daughter was drowning, and Kelly didn't know how to save her.

But there had to be a way. Maybe Manganaro knew something. If not, there might be a clue inside the Murder House—maybe another diary. Either way, Kelly wasn't going to solve any problems by standing around.

"Rick," she said, stepping away from the bed, "can you call me if she wakes up?"

He looked up in a daze. "Why? Where you going?"

She hurried out the door.

32

Approaching the Manganaro residence, Kelly noticed the lights were off and the Mazda was gone from the driveway. The dog went nuts when she rang the bell, but nobody answered. Five, ten minutes passed. She considered breaking in to see if Mango was hiding from her, but she wasn't that desperate. Not yet.

She headed for the Murder House. Her high beams illuminated the entire façade, including the scorched side, which she hadn't yet explored. Burns covered the exterior from foundation to roof. There was no telling how unsafe it was inside—the structure might crumble at any moment—and she hesitated at the thought of entering.

She faced K2 in the passenger seat. "You know what we haven't searched yet? The other half."

"You mean the burned side?"

"Yeah," Kelly said. "I wonder if there's a clue or—"

"Let's go check," K2 said, throwing open her door.

"You're just gonna run in? What if the floor collapses?"

"Emma's in the hospital," K2 said. "We can't sit around."

That response gave Kelly chills—the good kind. Though she and K2 had butted heads, it was hard not to admire the woman's attitude right now.

Together they approached the burned side and opened the front door. An ashy, chemical odor escaped.

Kelly buried her nose in her sleeve. "I'll search the living room."

"Then I'll check the kitchen." K2 cupped her hands around her nose. "Bet I find something before you do."

"Seriously? You're making a game of this?"

"Sure, why not?"

That competitive spirit reminded Kelly of her college self. Back then, everything was a competition. She would treat weekend drives like Daytona, ping pong matches like Wimbledon, and friendly foosball games like the World Cup. Her need to dominate had been insatiable.

After powering on her flashlight, Kelly stepped into the ruined building. The air inside stung her eyes. She blinked rapidly and swept her light around. The layout mirrored that of the next-door housing unit. The only difference was that there was no broken glass on the floors. Instead, debris lay scattered everywhere—piles of ash, soot, and scorched garbage.

Floorboards creaked as she entered the living room, where a ceiling fan lay smashed. Black-and-brown char marks covered the walls. The blaze had consumed most of what the squatters left behind: tattered pieces of fabric, blackened pizza boxes, old shoes, busted syringes. Using her foot, she lifted various chunks of debris but found nothing interesting underneath.

She sidestepped toward the kitchen, where K2 was tearing open charred cabinets and drawers. The woman hesitated after opening one directly beneath the sink.

"Find something?" Kelly asked.

K2 slammed the cabinet shut in frustration. "Junk, junk, and more junk. You?"

"Nothing."

"Let's check upstairs."

K2 led the way, carefully climbing the ruined staircase. Upon reaching the top, she waved Kelly ahead.

Together they searched the second floor. Smoke had discolored the walls, and the floor was smeared with ash. Tattered garbage lay everywhere. In the master bedroom Kelly found a soiled mattress identical to the one in the other housing unit, except this mattress was badly burned. Shattered syringes and the singed remains of condom wrappers lay nearby.

And, of course, above it all loomed the attic entrance.

K2 trudged into the bedroom. "I didn't find anything in the other rooms."

"Neither did I." Kelly glanced toward the ceiling. "Time to search our favorite attic."

Using a nearby bucket as a stepping stool, she grabbed the attic doorknob and twisted it loose. The door swung down. The ladder banged against the floor. An echo sounded, then faded. Neither Kelly nor K2 approached the ladder.

"C'mon," Kelly said, "let's go."

K2 crossed her arms. "You first."

Kelly laughed. "Relax, I'm not gonna lock you up there."

"So you say."

"Look, what happened the other day was a one-time thing."

"Actually it was a two-time thing. You also locked me in the shed, remember?"

Kelly lowered her head and sighed. "I promise I won't do it again, okay? Now can we continue our search? Remember, Emma needs our help."

"She sure does." K2's arms remained crossed. "If you plan on searching that attic, you better get climbing, because I'm not going first."

"Okay, fine." With a nervous step, Kelly approached the ladder. She pressed her foot against one of the bottom rungs. It moaned with a metallic creak. She climbed, the ladder rumbling beneath her. At the top she glanced back at K2. "You joining me?"

"Soon as you're up there."

Kelly hesitated, then stepped into the dusty attic.

K2 approached the foot of the ladder. She paused. Glanced up at Kelly for what felt like an eternity. Then she climbed.

Kelly exhaled when her double reached the top.

"I'm proud of you," K2 said, smiling. "You actually trusted me for once."

"Don't give me a reason to stop."

Together they searched the attic. Every square inch. They moved tables, ripped apart boxes, and flipped through every book they could find. The search proved useless. There were no more diaries lying around. Nor was there anything else of interest, other than that locked safe with the words "WE BURN" etched into it. The combo lock sported sixty digits, so she tried entering various dates from the diary. None of them worked. She grew more aggravated with every fruitless twist of the dial.

Her phone buzzed. Delayed text messages trickled in. They were from DJ. He asked why she wasn't at the hospital.

She kicked the safe out of frustration, then sighed and

turned to K2. "We should head back. DJ's visiting Emma, so I'll drop you off at home."

K2's eyebrows rose. "Really?"

"Yeah. Just make sure you stay in the office."

"Sure thing." K2 smiled then squeezed Kelly's shoulder. "Hey, cheer up. If Emma doesn't get better on her own, we'll find a way to help her. You know we will."

"Let go of me."

K2 frowned before releasing her grip.

After they left the attic, Kelly grabbed the ladder, slid it back into place, and slammed the door shut as hard as she could. It closed with a bang that reverberated through the room. She locked it tight.

"Fuck this place," she muttered and stormed down the hall.

33

Back at the hospital, Kelly found DJ in the waiting room outside the ICU. He was thumbing away at his phone, intensely focused on something. He didn't even notice her until she claimed the seat beside him, at which point he turned and gave her a bearhug.

"Hon, I'm sorry about Emma," he said, squeezing tight. When he pulled back, he adjusted his glasses. "Rick and Olivia are in there now. I thought I'd give them some space. Rick's taking everything real hard. How about you? Wait—where were you? You smell like a campfire."

Kelly hesitated. She decided to feed him snippets of the truth. "Don't mention this to Rick, but I went to an abandoned house. Same one Emma called me from the other night. Thought I might find answers there."

"Really? You're lucky you didn't get hurt. Gotta be careful in those old houses."

"Believe me, I know."

"Is there any way I can help?"

Kelly was about to decline his offer, but she stopped

herself. "Actually, yeah. Weird request, but can you look into someone? Like, really dig around?"

"Sure can." He rubbed his hands together. "What do you need? Deep Web?"

"Anything. Look up a guy named Mike Manganaro. Emma goes to school with him. Check his social media and see what he's been doing this past week."

"Should I look for something specific?"

She twisted uncomfortably. "Just find out whatever you can about him. And look up Cassie Gilbert too."

"You got it." DJ typed their names into his phone and frowned at the search results. "Know what? This'll be way easier on my laptop. You mind if I head home?"

"No, go ahead." She glanced at the ICU entrance. "I'll be okay."

"You sure?"

"Yeah. By the way, where are the twins?"

"At my parents' place. That reminds me—the kids really miss you. Aiden kept asking if you'll be able to coach their game tomorrow."

She rubbed her temples. "I can't make any promises."

"Don't worry about it." He gave her a kiss and left.

At the door to Emma's room, Kelly saw Rick and Olivia holding each other alongside the bed. Rick stood there dazed while Olivia whispered that everything would be okay. Emma didn't look remotely okay.

Kelly approached the opposite bedside. Rick asked where she'd been for the past three hours, and she ducked the question by asking about Emma's condition.

The room went quiet aside from beeping noises.

Time dragged by, slow and merciless. Seconds crawled like hours. Hours crawled like seasons. Kelly felt trapped in an endless moment.

Nothing changed. Emma remained asleep. Rick and Olivia remained silent. Kelly remained anxious. As the hours stretched on, her legs turned from cold to icy. Though taking K2 home had initially seemed like a smart decision, she now regretted it.

A nurse stopped by to monitor Emma. Rick asked questions; nobody liked the answers. Kelly thought to mention the Murder House but hesitated. She didn't know where to begin.

After midnight a new nurse arrived.

There was more monitoring.

More silence.

More waiting.

Waiting.

Waiting.

Around 3 a.m., Kelly stumbled in place. Her legs were numb. If she stuck around much longer, she'd be in a hospital bed of her own.

She glanced at Rick, who was sitting in a chair facing their daughter. Olivia had stepped out for coffee, and he was staring ahead, elbows on knees, hands folded grimly beneath his chin. Kelly could no longer bear keeping Emma's condition a secret. The truth was gnawing through her like a pack of rats. She needed to tell him.

"Rick?"

"Yeah?" He sounded lost. "What?"

"There's something you should know."

He faced her. His eyes were glossy. She'd never seen him like this. Never seen him so broken. So ready to shatter into a million pieces.

"The other night..." She paused. Glanced at Emma. Then at Rick.

"The other night *what?*"

"The other night I..." She swallowed hard. Feared that if she told him, he might drive out to Red Trail Road and get split in two.

"What, Kell?" He launched from his chair. "Say it."

"I..." She sighed. "I promised Aiden and Zach that I'd coach their game." She had never made such a promise, but she needed an excuse to leave the hospital, warm her legs, and regroup. "I have to head home, but I'll be back."

Rick stared at her. Dropped into his seat.

Then he nodded slowly, as if granting her permission to leave.

34

That Sunday afternoon, Kelly was in no condition to coach a soccer game, even one that only required her to tell a bunch of six-year-olds to chase the ball and kick it.

When she arrived at the field, she barely had enough energy to stand upright. The discomfort left her irritable. Every time parents came by to insist that their son get more playing time, she narrowed her eyes in a death stare. It pissed her off that some people couldn't appreciate that their kids were healthy enough to strap on shin guards and run around. She would've given anything to see Emma walk again.

"Sup, Coach?" Lance bumped her shoulder with his own. He was bouncing with energy on this warm September afternoon, practically jogging in place. He tucked his hair behind his ears while he snuck a peek at her clipboard—and probably her breasts. "I scouted the other team while they were warming up. There's one kid, this giant monster boy, who can drive the ball like he's a mini Ronaldo. We might want to double-team him. What do you think?"

"I think it's just a game," she said dully.

"Yeah, but do you want to lose by fifty? We gotta do something about this bruiser. I mean, look at him." Lance clutched the top of her head and turned her so her eyes faced the other end of the field. Near the opposing goal, kids were practicing a passing drill. One kid stood a head taller than the others, built like a torpedo. The midsized kids took turns passing balls to him, and he drilled each one into the net. He was insanely coordinated for a six-year-old.

She glanced at her own squad. Aiden and a few teammates chased each other in circles while Zach and the others stood around talking about *Pokémon*.

"Okay, Lance. Explain to the kids what a double-team is. Have them keep the ball away from Monster Boy." She looked upward. "And get your hand off my head."

Lance laughed, then blew his whistle to round up the kids. When the whistle dropped from his mouth, sunlight gleamed off the wet part where his lips had been. She absently wondered what flavor of Gatorade he'd been drinking.

Right then, a sharp loneliness pinched her. Not just loneliness, but jealousy too. She had no idea why these feelings surfaced—especially while Emma's health continued to nosedive—but she imagined it had something to do with the fact that K2 would be getting drunk tonight and would likely get hit on by tons of guys. Was it possible to envy yourself? It certainly was possible to hate yourself, so why not?

After Lance finished his pep talk, he sent the kids onto the field.

The ref blew the whistle. The game began.

To Kelly's surprise, Zach darted toward midfield, chasing the ball. She'd never seen him so aggressive.

"Lance, what'd you say to them?"

"What do you mean?"

"They're fired up," she said. "Did you promise them a pizza party?"

"Nah, just told them what a double-team is."

The double-team went into effect after Zach knocked the ball out of bounds. Following the inbound toss, Monster Boy got the ball. His chubby legs dribbled toward Kelly's goal. Two kids surrounded the giant. They were able to knock the ball away, but an opposing player got a foot on it and drove toward the net.

Kelly clapped her hands. Her competitive spirit blazed. "Come on, defense!"

Zach chased the ball. He kicked at it but missed.

The opposing player passed it back to Monster Boy.

"Double-team!" Lance shouted.

Aiden raced over from his position. He tackled the ball toward the sideline. Though the giant was coordinated, he was slower than her jackrabbit son, who dribbled up field.

Kelly raced alongside him. "On the attack—let's go!"

Aiden and his teammates crossed midfield. They hit traffic down the other end. The ball changed possession a thousand times, then squirted free toward the opponents' net.

Aiden stormed after it. He drilled the ball toward the net.

The goalie overplayed it and the ball rolled in.

"GOOOAAAALLL!" Lance bellowed.

Kelly leaped into the air while the kids danced in celebration.

The ref set the ball at midfield. The opposing team kicked off. Monster Boy charged along the near sideline. One of his teammates booted it to him.

"Defense!"

Monster Boy snarled as he got possession. He bullied past one defender and swerved by another, setting up a shot.

Then, out of nowhere, Zach came barreling in. He lunged in front of Monster Boy just as the giant kicked the ball.

It thudded off Zach's leg, popped into the air, and landed near the penalty area.

Monster Boy hunted it down and swung his leg forward.

This time Aiden threw himself in front of the giant.

The ball connected with Aiden's chest. A loud smack, like the sound of a fly swatter striking a kitchen wall, was heard across the field. It sent Kelly and the other parents into a collective gasp. Aiden dropped onto his side while the ball sailed toward the opposite sideline.

Before Aiden could pick himself up, the giant drew back his leg again.

This time his massive foot slammed into Aiden's stomach.

Kelly flinched as though her own gut had absorbed the impact. She thought her tired mind was playing tricks on her—that she imagined the blow—but startled cries from the crowd confirmed the reality. That little asshole had kicked her son.

The whistle blew as Aiden rolled on the ground hugging his stomach. His freckled face was red as a strawberry.

Breathless, Kelly sprinted onto the field. She grabbed his shoulders to steady him. Then she lifted his jersey. An ugly pink splotch stretched across his navel. She pressed her fingers to it and rubbed gently. He grunted but allowed her to keep rubbing.

Finally, he pushed her hand away and sat up. "I'm okay, Mom."

"You sure?" Kelly pulled him in for a hug. As she looked past his shoulder, she saw Monster Boy laughing with his teammates—*laughing*—and gesturing toward his stomach with a mocking expression on his face.

Kelly had never been so furious in her life.

A bizarre thought crossed her mind: *What would K2 do?*

Kelly released her son. Launched to her feet. Stormed after the boys on the other team.

The smaller, skinnier ones fled like mice, but the giant faced her.

She dropped her foot on his toe, the toe that had drilled Aiden's stomach. She pressed down, pinning the boy's foot against the grass. The smug look faded from his face.

"I-I didn't mean to," he said.

"You little shit." She leaned closer, her shadow overtaking him. "Don't you dare kick my son—don't you *ever*."

The kid shrank backward. He lost his balance and thumped onto the grass.

The whistle blew.

Parents stampeded from the bleachers.

The referee roared, demanding order.

Threats boomed among the swarming crowd. Someone grabbed Kelly by the ponytail and tugged hard. She twisted away. Another parent shoved her from behind, and she spun around, looking for a fight. Then someone snatched her wrist. She drove her free elbow into her captor's ribs until she heard Lance say, "Cool it, Kelly. It's me!"

Soccer moms and dads shouted and shoved, pointing

fingers and throwing water bottles at each other. The ref repeatedly blew the whistle but was swallowed by the mayhem.

Kelly lunged toward the chaos, wanting more action, but Lance dragged her away.

"Get your hands off me!" she snapped.

"Yo, cool it!" Lance steered her toward the sideline. She was so outraged she kicked his shin. He flinched but grabbed her shoulders and pushed her behind the bleachers. There, in the shade, she stopped struggling. He pressed her up against a steel beam, looked her in the eyes, and hissed, "Settle. Down."

"That little shit kicked Aiden."

"I know," he said. "Everyone saw it."

She locked eyes with him. "Then why are you blaming me?"

"I'm not." His warm breath tickled her nose. "Not one bit."

Kelly reached behind his head and tugged his lips toward hers. Before she could second-guess herself, the slick, electric pressure of his kiss jolted her. A warm tingling sensation flooded her scalp. She pictured the saliva on his whistle, and her tongue instinctively sought his mouth. She tasted Gatorade but couldn't determine the flavor.

His arms curled around her lower back. He drew her body against his. The contact gave her chills—good chills— as her breasts pushed against his chest. She clutched him tighter. Her thigh slid between his legs, and she rubbed it against his crotch, teasing him.

They spun clumsily together, knocking against the support beam. Kelly moved her mouth against his.

Fruit punch, she thought. *Definitely fruit punch.*

She clawed at his back while his hand snuck under her

shirt. He palmed the padding of her bra. She moaned and surrendered to the urge to grind her body against his. She felt clumsy—felt years out of practice—but she stirred against him, pulsing to the rhythm of the Rhianna song K2 had played in the van the other night.

Whatever this was—whatever was happening right now—Kelly embraced it.

She loved every second of it.

Then a voice called out to her.

"Mommy?"

She froze.

Uncoiled herself from Lance.

Hurriedly fixed her hair.

Zach stared at them with confusion in his eyes, as if he'd spotted a bird flying upside-down. He rubbed the knee where the ball had struck him earlier.

Oh no. What have I done?

"H-honey," Kelly said, stammering. "I-is your knee okay?"

"Yeah." Zach blinked. "The ref said we have to forfeit."

35

Kelly took her kids to Burger King and tried bribing Zach with chicken fries and an Oreo milkshake. He hadn't said anything since she peeled herself off Lance, and somehow she needed to convince Zach that what he saw behind the bleachers *wasn't* what he saw behind the bleachers. Kids imagined the wildest things, and with the right nudge maybe she could make him believe she'd been fighting Lance in the heat of an argument.

Fighting, she thought disgustedly. *Right. Another minute behind those bleachers, and I'd have been fighting to get his shorts off. What was I thinking? I should be visiting Emma now, not running damage control.*

Her order arrived at the counter. Aiden complained; he wanted McDonald's. He insisted he deserved to pick the restaurant because he'd been kicked earlier. While he certainly deserved something—maybe the kiddie equivalent of a Purple Heart—her priority was getting on Zach's good side.

They sat at a window booth looking out at afternoon traffic. She drank a black coffee, wincing at its bitterness.

The twins sat across from her and tore open the bags containing their meals. Warm, greasy air escaped each bag. Zach stared at his food. Aiden wolfed his chicken fries two at a time.

"Aiden, chew," she said. "Don't upset your stomach."

Aiden swallowed, burped, and sipped Zach's milkshake. Usually the boys guarded their food with territorial hostility, but Zach didn't seem bothered today.

After Aiden finished his chicken fries, he said, "Can we get McDonald's now?"

"No," she said.

"But I got kicked."

"I know." She watched Zach intently. He continued to stare at his food.

Aiden sipped the milkshake. "It's not fair that we had to forfeit because you yelled at that kid, Mom."

"What I did was wrong," she said. "I should've kept myself under control."

"But we were winning. That shouldn't count as a loss."

"Yes, it should. I didn't play fair."

"But that kid kicked me. He was the real cheater."

She winced at the word *cheater*. How could she have done that to DJ? Especially after how supportive he'd been the past couple days.

Aiden slid out from the booth. "I gotta pee."

That left Kelly and Zach alone at the table.

Shrinking under her gaze, he grabbed a chicken fry and broke it in half. He eyed his brother's ketchup, then set both pieces on the table.

She sipped her coffee. "You played great today, Zach."
He blinked.

"Never saw you hustle like that before."

Zach peered through the plastic lid of his milkshake. He pinched his straw like he was going to stir, then let go.

"What's wrong, cutie? Something up with your food?"

He shook his head.

"Not hungry?"

He shrugged.

"Zach, you speak English. You can talk to me."

The boy stared at the table.

She sipped more coffee. "Okay, then. You can take your food home and have it for dinner. Anything else you want while we're here?"

He continued staring.

"Zach?"

Still staring.

"Hey!" She slapped the table, making him and two nearby patrons jump. "I asked you a question."

He nervously tucked his food into the bag and grabbed his milkshake. When he looked up at her, he didn't need to speak. His eyes revealed all.

They said, *You kissed him, Mommy. You kissed somebody who isn't Daddy.*

36

Kelly stepped into her upstairs office, shut the door, and punched K2 square in the mouth.

Her fist connected dead on but without the loud, satisfying smack she'd often heard in Hollywood movies. The blow didn't launch K2 across the room either. It barely made her stagger. Kelly had never punched anyone before, and the results were disappointing.

"The fuck was that for?" K2 said, fingering her lip.

"Everything." Kelly shoved her toward the desk.

K2 set her feet and shoved back.

Kelly readied both fists. K2 did the same.

They exchanged glares.

Then K2 let her hands fall to her sides. "Seriously, what's your problem?"

Kelly rubbed her throbbing knuckles in dismay. "Thought hitting you might make me feel better."

"About what?" K2 grabbed a beer from the mini fridge beneath the desk. She touched the frosty bottle to her chin then twisted off the lid. "C'mon, let's hear it."

Kelly clenched her fist despite the ache. "You need to stop."

"Stop what?"

"Everything you do."

"Including breathing?"

"You know what I mean—the show-offy stuff you do to pretend you're better than me."

"Better than you?" K2 sounded baffled. "We're equals. Whatever I can do, you can do."

"That's not true. I have a reputation to maintain."

"Ohhh, I get it. You're jealous that I'm trying to have fun and be happy." K2 gulped beer before letting out a satisfied exhalation. "Want a drink?"

Kelly did. From the moment she'd entered Emma's ICU room yesterday, she had wanted a drink. Countless drinks. However, she shook her head. "No thanks. I've got enough problems."

K2 settled in the computer chair and set her beer aside. She leaned back and interlocked her fingers behind her head. "Know what your real problem is? This room, right here. You spend most of your waking hours rotting behind this sad little desk. You sit here day after day hating yourself —and for what? For health insurance that DJ promised he'd provide? For extra cash to blow on flashy clothes you never wear?" K2 took a sip. "And you know why you never wear those clothes, right? It's because DJ hates going to dance clubs and fancy restaurants. He hates everything you enjoy. The two of you have nothing in common—*nothing*."

"That's not true."

"Sure it is." K2 took another sip. "Now, maybe your marriage would be salvageable if you genuinely loved the guy, but you don't. You won't admit it, but you don't love or even understand him. That means your only solace is your kids, and once you kiss them goodnight, you're stuck with a stranger—a so-called lover who rambles on about computer parts and wears a Batman mask to bed. That's your marriage. That's your life. And that's your problem."

Kelly leaned against the wall and released a humorless laugh. "You spend all morning practicing that speech?"

"All morning? Try the past few years. You've heard it before in your head."

"Listen, I don't need this right now. Emma's in dire straits, I feel like garbage, and this morning I attacked someone else's kid."

K2 swiveled her chair toward her. "You *attacked* a kid?"

"Yeah." Kelly perched on the couch and anxiously scratched her thighs. "This boy on the other team kicked Aiden in the stomach. I got so angry I went after the little monster."

"For real? Good for you, girl."

"No, it *wasn't* good for me. I completely lost my cool. Lance had to restrain me."

"Ooo, I'd like to get restrained by him."

Kelly answered with a defeated smile. "Then you'll be happy to know that after he dragged me behind the bleachers, I made out with him."

K2 hopped in her seat. "Really?"

"Really."

"Wow." K2 rolled her chair closer. "How was it?"

"It was... It ended when Zach came over to tell me we had to forfeit the game."

"So Zach—"

"Saw the whole thing. Yeah."

"Ugh..."

Wind burst through the open window. Kelly shut her eyes against the cool autumn breeze. She dropped sideways against the couch cushion. "Zach hasn't said a word to me since. Not a word."

K2 sat beside her and set a pillow on her lap. Then she propped Kelly's head on the pillow like Mom used to. She even smelled like Mom with fresh beer on her breath. "That sucks." K2 brushed a thumb across Kelly's forehead. "We're not child-psych experts, so there's no telling what Zach's thinking."

"I don't know what to do," Kelly said.

"You could tell him the truth."

"Are you nuts? He's six."

"Little kids are good at adapting. Give him the truth. Tell him you don't love DJ."

Kelly flinched. "That would break Zach's heart."

"He's gonna figure it out eventually. Face it, DJ isn't soulmate material."

"DJ's a great guy." Kelly lifted her head off the pillow and shifted away from K2. "Our marriage is just a little tired."

"Tired? It's been *sleepwalking* since you said 'I do.' Honestly, how much longer can you stand it? Another twelve years until the kids turn eighteen? Is that how you want to spend your life till you're forty-six?"

Kelly ignored the question. "I'll talk to Zach, say he saw a brotherly kiss."

"Wait." K2 took Kelly's hand in both of hers. "Do you want to be the mom who lies to her kids? Do you want them to distrust you? Resent you?"

"I want them to be raised in a happy, loving family."

K2 cocked an eyebrow. "And how's that working out?"

Kelly ripped her hands from K2's. She paced around the office, unsure what to do. If she admitted to Zach that she'd made a mistake, he would have a thousand questions.

She could anticipate some of them, but kids were like mini prosecutors, pressing you on everything you tried to hide. Zach might eventually tell DJ, which would send shockwaves through the household. Somehow, she needed to prevent that. Needed to keep her son silent. But how?

While she stared at the doorknob, an idea crossed her mind. A wild one that might allow her to quiet Zach while also saving face. It would require K2's help and some top-notch acting, but if it worked, it would be the ultimate Band-Aid.

She turned to her double. "I need you to swap clothes with me."

K2 glanced down at her t-shirt and yoga pants. "Why?"

"Once we do, I'm gonna call the kids upstairs and let them see us together."

"Seriously? You sure they're ready for that?"

"Yep. And once they see us, I'll tell them you're my twin sister and that *you* coached their game today while *I* was at the hospital with Emma."

K2 scowled. "You're gonna lie to them?"

"It's the only way to convince Zach."

"That's disgusting."

"Please just do this for me," Kelly said. "I've got enough problems with Emma in the hospital and all. Besides, you owe me for letting you keep that burner phone."

"Owe you?" K2 launched to her feet. "If anything, *you* owe *me* after that unprovoked punch to the face. You want my help? Then cut me a break for once."

"Fine. I'll let you get drunk with Brittney tonight."

"You already promised that. If you want me to lie to the kids, you owe me another favor."

Kelly crossed her arms, breathed deep, and slowly said, "Name it."

"Let me go out with Lance."

"*With Lance?*" Kelly nearly jumped out of her skin. "Are you insane?"

"Face it, the floodgates are open," K2 said. "He's crazy about us, and we're crazy about him. It'd be silly to waste this opportunity."

"You can't be serious. You can't."

"I totally am."

"No. Forget it. Pick another favor."

"Sorry, that's my final offer."

"I'm not letting you go out with him."

"Why?" K2 smirked. "You jealous?"

Kelly opened her mouth to argue otherwise, then stopped herself. Playing along might be her best chance to put Lance off limits. "Fine. Yes, I'm jealous."

K2's smirk evaporated. "Wait, really?"

"Of course," Kelly snapped. "He and I had a moment today. I'm trying to process what happened, and I don't want you interfering."

"Oh." K2 scratched behind her neck. "Didn't realize you felt that way."

"Please pick another favor, okay?"

K2 paused. A smile bloomed across her lips. "How about this instead? Why don't *you* go on a date with him?"

Kelly flinched, then forced herself to play along. "That's all? One date?"

"Yep. Text him. Pick a day and time."

"But Emma's in the hospital and Norwell could be lurking around any corner." Kelly scratched at her hairline. "Besides, didn't you hear me when I said I needed time to process this?"

"I didn't say the date had to be tonight."

"Still, I need time to cool down."

"Then ask him out at practice tomorrow."

"That's way too soon."

K2 stepped closer and cupped her hands around Kelly's cheeks. "Hey. Look at me. I know you're scared, but it's okay to be happy. Just think how much fun you'll have being Cinderella for an evening. You can wear a dress, eat dinner, have some laughs with a hot guy. You deserve this."

Kelly looked away. "I swear you're trying to manipulate me."

"And you're trying to manipulate your kids. If I'm wrong, you're wrong times fifty."

Kelly twisted away in frustration. Unfortunately, her plan to sway Zach could only work with K2's cooperation. That put Kelly in a tough spot. She didn't want to arrange a date with Lance, but if she didn't act soon, DJ would come home from work and hear about what happened behind the bleachers. She couldn't bear to imagine the consequences.

"Do we have a deal?" K2 asked.

Kelly lowered her head and sighed. "Give me your clothes."

37

"Aiden! Zach! Get up here!"

Kelly trembled in her office doorway while her sons thumped upstairs. Aiden led the way, sucking an orange popsicle that was melting over his fingers. Zach trudged behind, his eyes avoidant. He leaned his butt against the wall beneath a hanging photo of Kelly and DJ on their wedding day.

After a deep breath, Kelly relaxed her shoulders. She wanted to be the mom Zach adored, so she put on her most innocent face. "Hey, boys. How was your game? I heard some crazy things happened."

Aiden removed the popsicle from his mouth. "What do you mean 'heard'? You were there."

Behind him Zach watched her with wounded eyes.

She squatted at eye level with the twins. They smelled of grass and sweat from their game. "I have to tell you something. It might sound scary, but I want you to understand what's going on with me."

"Oh no!" Aiden blurted. "Are you losing your memories?"

"Losing my memories?" Kelly laughed. "What gave you that idea?"

"This one girl in our class—her grandpa has memory loss. Sometimes he even forgets her name. Did you forget what happened this morning?"

"No..."

"But you're acting like you weren't at our game."

Kelly smiled. "That's because I wasn't."

Zach craned his neck, looking past his brother's shoulder. Zach had always been the more gullible of the two boys, while Aiden was the skeptic who already doubted the existence of Santa Claus. If she could convince Aiden, she could convince Zach.

"But you *were* there." Aiden pointed with his popsicle. "Mom, you coached our game."

"Nope." She shook her head so fast her hair danced before her eyes. "Today I was visiting Emma at the hospital."

When the words left Kelly's mouth, something crumbled inside her. K2 was right—this was bad. Not only was Kelly lying to her sons, but she was using her daughter's condition to advance that lie. *I should be shot for this. Why do I keep making things worse? I should stop right now, but I'm already neck deep in this lie. Might as well follow through.*

"I left the hospital around noon," she said. "I tried to catch the end of your game, but when I arrived, nobody was there."

"Mom, you were at our game!" Aiden said, flustered. "You drove us there."

"No, I didn't. This is the first time I've seen you today."

"But...no. How can you say that?"

"Here, let me show you." As she rose to her feet, excitement fizzled in her chest. It was like dribbling downfield and luring a goalie out of position. She led her boys into her office and gestured toward the couch. There, K2 was lying in the same long-sleeve t-shirt and shorts Kelly had worn to the game. "Boys, I want you to meet your aunt Kay."

The moment Aiden spotted her, he dropped his popsicle. It bounced on the carpet. His mouth fell open, and he ran down the hall screaming.

"Aiden, wait. Come back!"

He stormed down the stairs.

To her surprise, Zach didn't run. Instead, he hugged the doorway, eyeing K2 with caution. He poked his finger into the corner of his mouth and chewed on it.

Kelly knelt beside him. "It's okay, cutie. She's my twin sister. Your aunt Kay."

K2 waved at him. "Hiya, Zach. We had quite a day together, didn't we?"

Zach hugged the door frame harder. The wood creaked.

Kelly rubbed his back in soothing circles. "I had to be at the hospital, so I asked her to coach your game. I heard you and your brother got roughed up. Are you okay?"

He swallowed hard. "How come we never met her before?"

"Aunt Kay works for the government," Kelly said. "She does secret agent stuff."

"Top-secret stuff," K2 said, adopting a formal tone. "You can't tell anyone about me, Zach. Not even your dad."

He trembled.

Kelly paused, letting him absorb what he'd heard. "Think you can keep this a secret? You can't go around telling people like you did with Grandpa's surprise party."

Zach mumbled something. When she asked him to

speak up, he removed his finger from his mouth and pointed to K2. "Her lips are puffy."

"What?"

"Whoever coached my game didn't have puffy lips."

"Oh—they're puffy 'cause I slapped her," Kelly blurted. She felt like she had taken a step off a tall building and was grasping for a rope. "When I heard she stepped on that kid's foot, I slapped her. And when she mentioned kissing Coach Lance, I slapped her again. She never should've done those things."

"Yeah." K2 lowered her head. "Not sure what came over me."

Zach met Kelly's eyes. His little face scrunched with concentration. "Mommy? So...you didn't take us to Burger King?"

Kelly swung toward K2. "Wait, you took them to Burger King?"

"Forgot to mention that," K2 said sheepishly. "I bought him an Oreo shake."

Kelly scoffed in mock outrage. "Kay, those shakes are pure sugar." She poked Zach in the belly. "You, mister, are not supposed to have those."

"But I barely took a sip!" Zach protested. The moment he went on the defensive, she knew she had convinced him. "Mommy, I didn't even ask for the shake. Really! Please don't take my Nintendo and Nerf guns away. Please." In a desperate lunge, he threw his arms around her and hugged tight, clinging to her as if the floor underneath him might vanish at any moment.

Kelly rocked him back and forth, smiling with relief.

K2 was also smiling, but for different reasons.

38

Though Kelly desperately wanted to return to Emma's bedside, first she needed to calm Aiden down. She spent all afternoon running damage control while he threw tantrums in the living room. Tears spilled down his cheeks as he asked why she never told him about his "Aunt Kay." Kelly reused the same excuse that had worked on Zach—that K2 was a secret agent. Both kids bought the story, and by the time their father called to say he was driving home, they had promised not to tell anyone about K2's existence.

When DJ arrived, Kelly announced she was leaving for the hospital. She couldn't bring herself to look her husband in the eyes, and before he could ask how her day went, she raced upstairs to her office. There she found K2 at the computer, looking at a restaurant menu.

"That where you're meeting Brittney tonight?" Kelly asked.

"Nope. Browsing options for your date."

Kelly rolled her eyes. "Well, at least we convinced the twins."

"What do you think? Italian? Thai? Seafood?"

"Seafood. But I'm not going until Emma's healthy and Norwell's in handcuffs."

"That's fair. But make sure you text Lance and let him know everything's okay between you two."

"That can wait. I'm heading to the hospital now."

"Oh, come on. It'll only take a second."

"Not if—"

A knock sounded at the door. DJ.

Kelly frantically gestured for K2 to hide behind the couch. "Hey, hon? Mind giving me a sec? I'm on the phone with Rick." She pretended to wrap up a conversation before she opened the door. "What's up?"

"How's Emma?" he asked.

"No improvement." And that was the truth. Kelly had been receiving grim updates from Rick. "Hopefully I can cheer her up tonight."

DJ squinted past her shoulder. "You and Rick getting dinner?"

"No, why?" Kelly glanced at her computer screen. The Waterfall Cafe's menu was on display. "Oh—ohhhh! You weren't supposed to see that. I was gonna surprise you."

"Me?"

"Yeah, now pretend you didn't see it."

"Kelly, can I ask you something?" He picked at his beard. "One of the parents from the soccer team texted me."

Her mouth went dry. Had someone seen her and Lance behind the bleachers?

"Wh-what'd the text say?"

"That you ran onto the field and yelled at someone's kid."

"Oh," she said with great relief. When she realized relief wasn't the appropriate emotion, she added, "Unfortunately, yeah. That happened. It's been a stressful week, and everything boiled over when that kid kicked Aiden."

DJ's eyes widened behind his glasses. "He *kicked* Aiden?"

"You didn't hear? That little jerk drilled him right in the stomach. I was furious."

"And Aiden's okay?"

"He's a little sore, but yeah."

"Wow." DJ shook his head, stunned. "Didn't catch that part of the story. When I heard you went after some kid, I thought we'd have to call Saul Goodman." He smiled like he always did after making a corny joke.

She obliged him with a chuckle. "Listen, we'll talk about this later. I need to get dressed and head to the hospital."

After he went downstairs, she donned jeans and a gray long-sleeved top. Though she had dressed rapidly, she needed to wait for K2 to leave the bathroom. Her double came out wearing a black cocktail dress and more makeup than Kelly used in a month. K2 didn't even resemble Kelly, which was a plus. Her reputation might yet survive the night.

"Well," K2 said, adjusting her neckline for maximum cleavage, "how do I look?"

"Let's get going," Kelly said. "I'll distract everyone while you sneak outside."

Kelly gathered her family in the kitchen and announced that they'd be having Little Caesar's for dinner. The boys cheered in celebration. She gave them goodbye kisses before heading into the garage. K2 hid in the backseat, laying low until Kelly drove the van into Scranton.

The Sunday evening traffic was light. Kelly motored around Courthouse Square, passing the Electric Building and its iconic Electric City sign. Though she wanted to lecture K2 on behaving tonight, she kept quiet. She parked near the Backyard Ale House and unlocked her doors.

K2 strutted onto the sidewalk, then paused abruptly. She checked her burner phone and looked back with worried eyes.

Kelly lowered the window. "What's wrong?"

"I got a text."

"From who?"

K2 swallowed hard. "From DJ."

"*From DJ?*" Aghast, Kelly stared out the window. That shouldn't have been possible. He wasn't supposed to know the burner phone existed. "How'd he get your number?"

"I don't know." K2 trembled on the sidewalk. "You're the only one who has it."

Kelly gestured frantically toward the phone. "What'd he say?"

K2 swiped her screen. "He says, 'Forgot to mention... Mike Manganaro doesn't use social media. All I found was that he volunteers at animal shelters and that his mom died two years ago. I'll keep searching.'" She looked up. "Wait, how does DJ know about Mango?"

"I told him, but that's beside the point. Did he mention the burner phone?"

"No." K2 tapped her screen. "Should I reply to him?"

"Don't. I'll sort this out later." Kelly squeezed the steering wheel. Her mind raced, trying to imagine how DJ had gotten K2's number. If the burner phone had been purchased with her Discover card, he shouldn't have known about it—unless he logged into her email account. Regardless of how he'd found out, the real problem was his suspicion. "Let's hope he doesn't start following us around. If he does, that'll create a mess."

K2 nervously lifted her shoulder strap. "Wanna text Brittney and cancel? Would that make things easier?"

Canceling sounded smart, but Kelly feared that K2 would hold it against her later. Kelly was indebted to her double for covering up the bleacher incident, and that came after Kelly had imprisoned her, punched her, and repeatedly treated her like shit. If Kelly didn't cut her a break soon, the woman might drop the "Aunt Kay" performance.

"Please be careful tonight," Kelly said, forcing a smile. "Remember, Norwell's out there. Watch your back, and don't do anything to make our situation worse."

K2 smiled. "Thanks. Let me know how Emma's doing."

Kelly stomped the gas pedal and motored toward the hospital. By the time she parked outside the Critical Care Building, her feet were frosty, but that didn't stop her from sprinting inside. She felt horrible for not arriving hours ago.

In Emma's room Rick hunched beside the bed like a melted statue. He still wore his wrinkled police uniform from yesterday. His B.O. clashed with the hospital's antiseptic smell, and his oily scalp reflected the overhead fluorescent lighting. He was so focused on Emma that he didn't hear Kelly enter the room. Only when she tapped his shoulder did he react.

"How's Em?" she asked. "Was she awake earlier?"

"For a while, yeah. Didn't do much. Wasn't too chatty either."

Kelly felt her heart drowning in her chest. "What'd the doctors say?"

"They're not sure what she has. Guillain-Barré syndrome is still on the table, but they mentioned something called conversion disorder. Basically, they think her brain is tricking her body into feeling symptoms that aren't there."

"They think she's faking?"

"No, it's a mental thing. They're not sure, though. Guillain-Barré seems more likely because she complained about the numbness spreading up her abdomen. Hopefully we'll get answers when they fly her out to Danville tonight."

"*Danville?*" Kelly flinched. Her mind jumped to E2's corpse in the garden. "*Tonight?*"

"Yeah, once a bed becomes available, they're moving her."

"No—they can't."

He gave a puzzled look. "Why not?"

"Because...I want to be near her."

"We can stay in Danville if we have to."

"You can," she said, "but I've got the twins to worry about."

"Then commute back and forth. Either way, Emma's going. End of discussion."

Kelly eyed her sleeping daughter. Emma looked worse today; her pale flesh and sunken demeanor suggested great suffering—suffering that a trip to Danville wouldn't fix. Somehow, she had to get better so she could stay local.

Kelly dug through her purse for a bag of Swedish Fish. The gummy candies were her daughter's favorite. The moment she opened the bag, Emma stirred at their iconic berry-flavored scent.

"Unngghh..." Emma opened her eyes. "Mom?"

"Hey, honey." Kelly rubbed her daughter's shoulder. "Want some candy?"

Emma opened her mouth. Kelly placed a gummy fish on her tongue. Emma slow-chewed it for what seemed like hours before swallowing.

Rick smiled tiredly. "First thing she's eaten all day."

Their daughter ate the entire bag. Afterward, she stared at Rick, which prompted him to ask if she needed anything.

"Name something," Kelly said, hoping for an excuse to send him away. The sooner he left, the sooner she and Emma could sabotage her Danville trip. "Don't be shy. Your dad'll get you anything you want."

Emma caught on and said, "iPad."

"Your iPad?" he said. "That's at home."

Kelly squeezed his elbow. "I'll stay here. Go get it for her."

"If anything changes, call me." Rick hesitated before rushing out.

Kelly leaned over the railing and kissed her daughter's forehead. "How are your legs? Can you feel them?"

"No. And everything above the waist hurts." Emma grimaced. "Did you find E2?"

"I...did."

"Really?" Emma sounded relieved. "Where?"

"Outside that frat house." Kelly didn't want to mention the next part, but with the situation worsening, her daughter deserved the truth. "Someone hurt her."

"Hurt her?" Emma's eyes turned glossy. "How bad?"

Kelly fought back tears. "E2's gone."

"Gone? You mean..."

"I'm so sorry, honey."

"No..." Emma's lips quivered. Her face wrinkled. "But... she's my friend. She's me. She can't be gone. You're lying, Mom. You always lie."

"Not this time."

"You're lying!" Emma burst into tears. The sobbing drew the attention of passing nurses. Kelly shooed them away until her daughter quieted.

"If she's gone," Emma said, sniffling, "what's gonna happen to me? Will I...?"

"Nonono, you'll get better, I promise." Kelly checked over her shoulder to make sure nobody was nearby. "Listen, on Friday night I hid E2 in your backyard. Did that help?"

"Um, I'm not sure."

"Think. Was there any difference when you woke up?"

"I..." Emma looked ready to cry again. "I don't know."

Kelly stared at the tangled IV tubes crawling from Emma's arm. They were hard to look at, especially knowing the drugs could do nothing to save her. Kelly wondered if moving E2's body closer to the hospital would help. Shortening the distance had alleviated Emma's pain when E2 was alive, but now it seemed the effect wasn't as pronounced. Even so, there wasn't a better option. And with Rick intent on sending Emma to Danville, there wasn't much time left.

Kelly explained the situation to Emma and said, "When your father gets back, tell him you don't want to leave. If you make enough of a fuss, he'll side with you—he always does."

"Okay," Emma said. "Mom, promise me that if I don't get better you'll never tell anybody about E2 and the Murder House. Especially not Dad."

"Em, you'll get better."

"You don't know that."

Kelly swallowed hard. She didn't want to imagine a world without her daughter. Seeing E2 dead in the forest had been the single worst experience of her life. The only thing that kept her from falling to pieces was the fact that it was only a half-death—Emma was still alive, and things needed to stay that way.

"Promise me, Mom. That you won't tell Dad."

Kelly glanced at the EKG monitor. "Okay. I promise."

"Promise what?" Rick asked, marching through the doorway with Emma's iPad. He must've broken at least a dozen traffic laws to return so quickly. His scalp was slick with sweat, and his shirt was soaked. Huffing, he approached the bed and set the iPad on Emma's lap. His hyper eyes narrowed at Kelly. "What'd you promise her?"

"That I'll be right back," Kelly said, stepping past him.

39

For the second night in a row, Kelly tiptoed into Rick's backyard with the intention of moving a body. Tonight, lights glowed inside the house, which meant Olivia was home, probably under a deadline to get a client's financials in order. Luckily the woman wasn't paying attention as Kelly stumbled toward the garden on frosty legs.

She approached the rhododendrons until a brutal stench hit her and stopped her in her tracks. It was unlike anything that had ever entered her nostrils. She exhaled and knelt with a shudder.

There must've been a hole in the garbage bag—from either poking branches or gnawing animals. Kelly grabbed it and felt the plastic stretch. The odor intensified, and her eyes watered. She located the ankles and dragged the body to the minivan.

Pinching her nose firmly, she drove back to the hospital. She parked in an empty corner of the lot where nobody could smell what was rotting in her cargo area. Soon as she killed the motor, she jumped out to vomit. With another deep shudder, she wiped her mouth. She chewed a mouthful of cinnamon Tic-Tacs before returning to the ICU.

Rick stood at Emma's bedside, clutching the railing with white-knuckled fists. He glanced over as Kelly entered. His nose wrinkled.

Emma lay against the pillow wearing a look of severe discomfort. Moving E2's corpse into the hospital parking lot hadn't had the impact Kelly was hoping for. Not even close.

Dread consumed her. She thought back to the night in the attic when Emma cried out in agony. That was the moment E2 was murdered, and Emma had been on a steady decline ever since. What if E2's death meant Emma couldn't recover?

No. There's gotta be a way.

Maybe the corpse needed to be moved even closer. Maybe it needed to be touching her. But how was Kelly supposed to move a decomposing body up here? Even if she somehow snuck it up to the third floor, she still had to be buzzed into the ICU. That wouldn't fly. Her only hope was moving Emma outside the hospital.

"Em?" Kelly said. "Want to go home?"

"Don't tease her like that," Rick said.

"I'm trying to make conversation."

"Make a different one."

Kelly wondered if she could manipulate Rick into thinking the doctors were botching Emma's diagnosis. He was already worked up about her condition, and with the right push, maybe Kelly could coax him into taking Emma home. Then again, knowing Rick, he would need a guarantee that Emma's condition would improve, and Kelly couldn't offer that.

Another option sprang to mind. One that made her uncomfortable.

"Be right back," she said, stepping away from the bed. "Gotta run out to the van real quick."

The moment she popped the tailgate, the stench rammed her like an elbow to the nose. She staggered back toward fresher air and collected herself. Then she reached into her purse for her pocketknife and sliced a hole near the center of the bag.

Foul air burned her streaming eyes. She reached inside the bag and located one of E2's hands. She pressed the hand flat and touched her blade to the pinky finger's top knuckle. She hesitated, wishing there was another way, wishing she didn't have to desecrate E2's body. But time was running out.

Kelly shut her eyes and forced the blade down, cutting through the finger like a carrot.

The tip popped loose. She expected blood to gush, but minimal fluid trickled out. She wrapped the severed fingertip in tissues, tucked it into her purse, and slapped the trunk shut.

She rushed back to Emma's room. Rick remained at her side. Kelly needed him gone.

"Your wife left me a voicemail," she lied. "Said you haven't been answering her calls."

"I'll call her later."

"Do it now while I'm here. You don't want to leave Emma alone, do you?"

He grumbled before he left.

Kelly unzipped her purse. Stench filled the room when she unwrapped the severed fingertip. She pressed the rotten flesh to her daughter's forearm, rubbing from wrist to elbow.

Emma's eyes snapped open. She glanced at her forearm. "Mom... Mom!"

Emma's ghastly pale arm was changing color.

To a healthy pinkish white.

Kelly rubbed the fingertip vigorously, as if it were a pencil eraser. The healthy glow spread as she worked the finger along Emma's palms and knuckles. Before long her daughter was curling both hands into fists. When the finger reached Emma's neck, she began to cough—a strong, productive cough. Color returned to her chin and cheeks soon after.

Emma eyed the fingertip—first with horror, then with curiosity. Finally she held out her palm. "Gimme."

Kelly handed it over.

Emma rubbed behind her neck while Kelly guarded the doorway. No nurses were coming, and Rick had yet to return.

"Can you cut off her whole hand?" Emma said, leaning forward to rub her legs. "It would speed things up."

"Not now. I don't want to leave you alone in case..." *In case something goes wrong.* That's what Kelly meant to say, but she was afraid to verbalize it. She didn't want to jinx this miracle.

Emma reached under her hospital gown and rubbed her stomach. She grunted in frustration.

"You okay?" Kelly asked, rushing toward the bed.

"Hurts inside," Emma whispered. "Everything's great along the surface of my skin, but my stomach feels horrible."

"Maybe if I rub your back, it'll seep inward. Roll over."

Emma twisted onto her side. Kelly went to work, brushing the severed fingertip along her shoulder blades and down her spine before tracing the backs of both legs. Once color was restored, she flipped Emma onto her back again.

"Better?"

Emma clutched her stomach. "Not really."

Kelly checked under the gown. "Maybe I missed a spot."

"Wait," Emma said. "Gimme that finger."

Kelly handed it over.

Emma hesitated for a split second before she tossed it into her mouth like a pill.

40

Nobody believed the speed of Emma's recovery. The medical team swarmed her ICU room, asking questions, checking vitals, and running tests. Nurses gossiped outside the door. When Rick returned, Emma reached out to squeeze his hand. That led to a sound Kelly had never heard before—her ex-husband sobbing. His face ran shiny with tears as he asked Emma if she needed anything. She begged to be taken home.

Before long, Kelly and Rick were arguing with the medical staff, who insisted on monitoring Emma. Though her symptoms had resolved, she needed to be cleared by both a neurologist and a physical therapist before she could leave. She was also required to get a psych consultation. Rick pulled some strings—he had friends in the hospital— and sped the process along. When the neurologist arrived, Kelly and Rick stepped out of the ICU to claim seats in the waiting room.

Kelly's legs were frosty, and she was relieved to sit down. Beside her, Rick opened his mouth to say something before he buried his face in his hands. She rubbed his back and whispered, "She'll be fine, Rick."

"What'd you do to her?" he snapped, abruptly looking her in the eye.

"Excuse me?"

"Kell, you lied about Olivia calling you. That was a ploy to get me away from Emma. What did you do while I was gone?"

"Nothing." She shrugged. "Maybe when you left, it took some pressure off Emma. You're stressing her out by being there 24/7."

He grabbed her elbow hard. "What did you do?"

She accepted his glare.

The ICU door opened. A doctor who looked like Al Pacino—complete with expressive dark eyes and a dusty goatee—sauntered over. "Excuse me. Officer Wallace? And are you Emma's mother?"

"I am," Kelly said, tugging her elbow free. "Is Emma done with the neurologist?"

"Not yet." The doc adjusted his lab coat and sat across from them. "She's had quite a recovery tonight. Haven't seen anything like it before."

"Will she be okay?" Rick asked.

"Aside from minor discomfort in her abdomen, everything else is a dramatic improvement. We'll monitor her for twenty-four hours. If she's stable at this time tomorrow, she can head home."

"Why not sooner?" Kelly asked. "Can you make an exception?"

The doc gave her a dubious look.

"I ask because Emma hates hospitals," Kelly lied. "They make her anxious. Can't we take her home?"

"We'd rather not rush this," he said. "And we'd like to understand her condition before sending her off."

"So you don't know what was wrong with her?" Rick said.

"Not yet. We believe it could've been conversion disorder. That's when—"

"I know what it is," Rick said. "But if that's over with, why can't she leave?"

The doctor folded his hands. "Conversion disorder isn't something that can be diagnosed in one visit."

"Then send her home," Kelly said. "We can bring her back later."

"Again, we want to monitor her—"

"I've heard enough," Rick said, launching to his feet. "Emma comes home. Right now."

The doc cleared his throat. "If you rush her out of the hospital against medical advice, we'll have to notify Child Protective Services. Surely you're aware of that, Officer."

Rick grunted and sank back down. "All right. Fine. When's the earliest she can leave?"

AFTER RICK PULLED SOME STRINGS, the hospital discharged Emma around 10 a.m. She finished her psych consultation and walked outside under her own power. She gave Kelly a leaping hug. Despite having barely slept in the waiting room, Kelly had never felt more energized. She squeezed her daughter tight.

Rick drove Emma home while Kelly tailed them in the van, which stank like a mausoleum. They parked in front of his garage. Kelly slammed the van door behind her while Rick helped Emma out of his truck. She carefully stretched both feet onto the blacktop and stood baffled, like she'd set foot on Mars. She looked hesitant. Afraid.

Three steps were all she managed before her legs gave out.

Rick caught her and pulled her upright. Her legs dangled beneath her like noodles.

"What's wrong, chief?"

"Nothing," she said. "I'm fine."

"You don't seem fine." He scrutinized her legs. "Looks like a relapse to me."

"Dad, really," she said, her legs twitching, "it's just pins and needles."

Evidently unconvinced, he lifted her, aiming for the passenger seat. "C'mon, we'll head back to the hospital."

"Rick," Kelly said, "it won't make a difference."

"Sure it will. That's where she got better."

"She can get better here too."

His nose scrunched with confusion. "What're you trying to say?"

"Mom, no!" Emma said, struggling within his grasp. "Don't!"

Kelly met her daughter's gaze. She hated to break her promise, but they couldn't return to the hospital. They needed Rick on their side, and he needed the truth.

"There's a way to help her," Kelly said, glancing at the minivan. "It's in my van."

"What is?" Rick asked. "What's in there?"

"Her other body."

41

The rotting-sweet stench had no effect on Rick. He didn't grimace. Didn't gag. Didn't budge. Either he had developed a tolerance to dead bodies or he was so enraptured that the odor didn't register. He stood silent while Kelly sliced a full-length flap across the wrinkled bag. When she lifted it open, the van's interior lights fell on E2's corpse.

Rick nudged Kelly aside. Other than a twitch of his nose, he showed no emotion. He eyed the body, following its shape from toe to head. The moment he spotted E2's crushed throat, he paused. His expression was unreadable. No blinking, no breathing, nothing.

He mumbled something then turned to Emma, who was sitting on the nearby grass and pinching her nose. He glanced at the corpse, then at her. Finally, with a helpless expression, he turned to Kelly. "What the hell is this?"

She grabbed a fresh garbage bag from the cargo area. "First, let me move the body into the garden. Then we'll go inside and I'll explain."

Rick didn't blink.

THEY SAT across from each other at the kitchen table. Rick sipped coffee while Kelly recounted the past week's events with complete honesty. Now and again, he interrupted with questions. She answered them patiently, relaying every hideous detail.

Despite hearing the unfiltered truth, Rick refused to believe it. This surprised Kelly, who had assumed he would instantly accept E2's existence and punish her for covering it up. She never imagined having to convince him that Emma had a double—especially after showing him proof. Maybe he didn't believe Kelly because of her chronic lying. Or because the reality was so bizarre. Or because he simply couldn't cope.

Whatever the reason, he repeatedly denied that E2's corpse had any connection to Emma. It wasn't until after his fourth cup of coffee that he finally surrendered. He went quiet and stared at a black smudge on the kitchen table, one Emma had made years ago while goofing around with a grill lighter. He rubbed at the smudge, his thumb squeaking against the polished surface. "You haven't told anyone else, have you?"

"About E2? No."

"What about K2? You tell anyone about her? Does DJ know?"

"No."

"Has K2 told anybody?"

"Not that I know of. She wants to keep it a secret for her own safety."

Rick looked up. "Bring her over here."

"Now?"

"Yeah. Got questions for her." He rubbed his eyes.

"Before you leave, write down the address to the Murder House."

"Forget about that. You should focus on finding Norwell."

"I will. Right after I check out that house."

"I'd rather you not."

"Relax, I'll avoid the attic."

"Even if you do, it's still dangerous."

"Didn't ask for a safety lecture. Now give me the damn—"

"Hey, guys." Emma stood in the kitchen doorway dressed in a varsity soccer hoodie and shorts. Bags hung beneath her eyes, but aside from that she looked beautiful. She had eaten another fingertip an hour ago, and her legs seemed to be working. "Dad, please don't go near that house."

Rick rose from his seat. He approached Emma as though she were a glass statue. "How you feeling, chief?"

She frowned. "Did you hear me? Don't go near that house."

He scratched his scalp. "But if I search the place, it could make a difference. It doesn't help if I'm standing around."

"Then stop standing around." Kelly opened her purse and took out the diary. "Here. Figure out who this belongs to."

"What is it?" He flipped pages. "Can barely read anything in here."

"We found it in the attic," Emma said. "Mom thinks it's important."

"Right," Kelly said. "Some parts are written in a language I don't recognize. The English parts mention names and locations. I Googled people's names but couldn't find anything useful. Maybe you'll have more luck."

"There's a page missing." He held open the back cover. "Someone ripped it out."

"We found it that way," she said. "Also, there's an old-fashioned safe in that attic—one with a combo lock. While you're reading, mark down any important dates or numbers."

"Why not just grab the safe? I can have somebody cut it open."

"It's nailed to the attic floor."

He grunted. "See, this is why I need to visit that house."

"*Dad*," Emma protested.

"It's not up for discussion." He slapped the diary shut. "Kell, what's the address?"

Kelly rubbed her throbbing temples. She knew he wouldn't drop the subject till he saw the place, but she didn't want him going alone. "I'll drive you there later."

"Later? Why not now?"

"You want to talk to K2, don't you?"

He considered. "All right, fine, bring her over."

She grabbed her keys. "Be right back."

"Hold up a sec." He marched across the kitchen into the garage. Minutes later, he returned with a polished black snubnose revolver. He offered it to her. "Keep this handy in case Norwell comes after you."

Kelly shied away from the gun. "Rick, no. I mean, it's registered to you. Besides, I keep a pocketknife in my purse."

"Take the damn thing. I can't have you getting hurt." He grabbed her hand and set the revolver in her palm. It was heavy. Definitely loaded.

She sighed and tucked the gun into her purse.

42

Before leaving Rick's, Kelly stole a bottle of Lysol from the bathroom and sprayed the cargo area. Somehow, Lysol made the corpse odor worse. While driving home, she smoked with the windows up to mask the smell. It helped— or at least she told herself it did. She hoped the twins wouldn't notice when she drove them to soccer practice that evening.

As she continued toward her house, a cozy warmth seeped into her legs. That was a good sign. It meant K2 had returned safely after her night out.

But when Kelly checked her office—K2's designated sleeping area—the room was empty. Kelly wondered if K2 had stayed in the backyard shed to avoid waking DJ this morning, but the shed was also vacant. Finally, Kelly wandered into the basement. She found K2 lying naked on the air mattress with her cocktail dress draped over her like a blanket.

Kelly smiled until she spotted a naked man lying behind K2. The sight stopped her cold. The middle-aged stranger sported a gray crew cut and a farmer's tan. Faded tattoos covered his shoulders and wrinkled chest. He must've been at least twenty years her senior.

Kelly frantically shook K2 awake.

"Unnnnghh." K2 stirred against the mattress. "Morning, soul sister."

"Who the hell is *he*?" Kelly whispered.

K2's eyes popped open. "Oh, shit."

"I want him gone," Kelly hissed. "Now."

"Okay, okay, go hide somewhere."

Kelly ducked behind a shelving rack in the shadowy corner of the basement. She heard K2 slap the man's chest repeatedly until he stirred awake. He groggily tried to sweet talk her, but K2 insisted he leave. The guy chuckled as he hopped into his pants. K2 pulled her dress over her head and rushed him upstairs.

When she returned, her face wore a relieved grin. "All gone. Like it never happened."

"Except it did happen," Kelly snapped. "I can still smell his filthy cologne."

"Relax. Easy fix." K2 grabbed a bottle of Febreze and sprayed until the basement smelled like a rainy summer day. "All better."

"No, it's not." Kelly kicked the air mattress. "His sweat is on the sheets."

"I'll wash them."

"You shouldn't have to." Kelly wanted to pummel K2. Knock the beauty out of her face so this couldn't happen again. "What the fuck were you thinking?"

"I don't think I *was* thinking." K2 rubbed her forehead. "Last night's a blur. I don't even remember his name. Jason? Jack?"

"You're outta control. I should lock you in the shed again."

"Hey, I'm sorry, okay? Brittney and I got blasted, and I guess I brought a guy home."

"You guess?"

K2 scratched her arm. "Okay, I definitely did."

Kelly peeled the bed sheets off, careful not to touch the sweat stains. She tossed the soiled lump in the washer and measured out a cup of laundry detergent.

K2 tiptoed over. "So, how's Emma?"

"She's back home."

"Holy shit. She recovered?"

"Not entirely." Kelly poured in the detergent. "But she's doing better."

"That's great!" K2 clapped excitedly. "Wow, so what happened?"

Kelly hesitated. It was best to keep K2 ignorant of the details. Emma's recovery signaled a possible solution to this mess, and if Emma's strange new diet worked out, Kelly might have to follow suit. The prospect of cannibalizing K2 disgusted Kelly beyond words—even now her stomach flipped—but currently there were no other options.

"We're not sure what happened," Kelly said, adjusting the washer settings. "The doctors tried all sorts of medicines —antibiotics, steroids, placebos, you name it. Then out of nowhere, Emma's condition improved. She's doing okay now, but she might have to go back to the hospital. I told Rick to keep me posted. Oh, and I also told him about us."

K2's tired eyes sprang wide. "Y-you did?"

"Yep." Kelly started the washer. A jingle sounded. "Told him everything."

"Everything?" K2 clutched fistfuls of her hair. "Did you tell him about E2?"

"I showed him the body."

K2's hands fell at her sides. Her mouth hung open in

shock. "Oh no... Rick worships the ground beneath Emma's feet. Seeing her dead must've... Is he okay?"

"He'll be fine," Kelly said. "He's tough, and he's got his mind on Norwell anyway."

"Still... Is he okay?"

"You can ask him when we see him."

"We?"

"Yeah. He wants to meet you."

43

Sunlight. Green grass. The distinct *thump* of a punted soccer ball. These things greeted Kelly as she exited the van and approached Rick's backyard. Another punt sounded, which was a great sign because only one member of the Wallace household could kick like that.

Propped between the house and Olivia's garden was a regulation-size soccer net. Emma protected the goal in a tank top and shorts while Rick booted several balls her way. He kicked with the accuracy of a wounded donkey, but she chased down each shot, her red ponytail flowing as her legs propelled her back and forth between the goalposts. When Emma punted a ball toward the neighboring yard, Kelly stopped it with the side of her foot.

"Mom!" Emma yelled. "Take a shot!"

Setting her purse aside, Kelly dribbled toward the goal and kicked the underside of the ball. It whizzed toward the upper corner of the net.

Emma jumped.

Caught it.

Landed hard on her shoulder.

"Shit!" Rick said, hustling after her in a sweaty gray t-shirt.

Kelly held her breath.

But Emma bounced to her feet and flung the ball skyward in celebration. She hugged her father. Kelly threw her arms around them both.

"Told you, Dad," Emma said, laughing. "I'm fine."

"Better stay that way." He broke the group hug and faced Kelly. "Where's K2?"

"In the van," Kelly said. "Listen, don't mention how Emma ate those fingers. I don't want K2 getting any ideas."

"Least you're not naive," he said. "C'mon, let's meet this other you."

Kelly led them to the driveway and opened the passenger door.

K2 stepped out with an energetic grin. "Hey, Emma! Hi, Rick!"

"Holy fuck." Rick wiped his face with his shirt collar. "How do I even tell you two apart?"

"I'm the one with a wedding ring," Kelly said.

They all went inside. The kitchen smelled of blueberry pancakes. A plate of them waited on Emma's checkered placemat. She folded one like a taco and devoured it, explaining between bites that she'd requested pancakes for lunch but got sidetracked by the urge to run outside and play soccer. She didn't seem fazed by K2. The same could not be said of Rick, who sat opposite the woman and narrowed his eyes at her.

Kelly claimed the chair beside him. "So, Rick, what'd you want to ask her?"

He sipped coffee. "First of all, what the hell are you?"

"I'm Kelly O'Neill," K2 said, drumming her thumbs on the table. "Same as always."

"From what I understand, you've only existed for a week."

"Try thirty-four years. If you don't believe me, I can rattle off details from back when we dated. Wanna discuss the raw chicken incident?"

"Ew, gross," Kelly said. "Let's not."

Rick leaned in. "Pop quiz for you. First time we went to a shooting range, what gun did I take away from you?"

"Pump-action shotgun," K2 said. "You hated how I kept pumping it and losing ammo. In the end, you taught me to fire revolvers and pistols."

He sipped more coffee. "Back in high school... How'd you pass your Algebra II exam?"

"I didn't pass it. Miss Harper gave me an exemption."

"Why?"

"Because I threw up on my exam sheet. And I told her I was in the first trimester."

Rick set his mug down. He unloaded more questions. She answered them. The verbal tennis match was mesmerizing. Rick asked about things Kelly hadn't thought about in years, and K2's answers filled her with nostalgia for when she and Rick were high school sweethearts—back when life was simple.

Emma gobbled another pancake. Kelly nibbled one, too. It was cold and rubbery—and definitely needed maple syrup—but otherwise tasty.

After K2 answered a question about the heating bills in their old apartment, Rick turned to Kelly and interrogated her too, presumably because he suspected *she* might be the double.

Several correct responses later, he went quiet. His eyes

drifted to Emma, then toward the backyard where E2 lay hidden among the bushes. He frowned.

Kelly patted his forearm. "I know it's a lot to take in."

"It's not." He slid his chair back and stood. "C'mon, let's go see that goddamn house."

44

Even during daytime the Murder House carried a malevolent air. Its windows seemed to absorb sunlight rather than reflect it, and the building itself cast char-black shadows across the high grass out front. The surrounding trees rioted with every whoosh of the wind, their orange, gold, and copper leaves flapping as if desperate to fly away. A foul, woodsy odor emanated from the property, intensifying as Kelly parked her minivan on the front lawn.

In the backseat Rick leaned forward for a better look. "I don't like this place."

"Wait till you see the inside," she said.

"I don't like this place," he repeated.

"Dad, we heard you the first time," Emma said from the back.

"Well, I don't like it. Something about it."

In the passenger seat, K2 unbuckled herself. "We going in, or what?"

"I can't go in there," he said in a distant tone.

"Can't?" Kelly glanced over her shoulder. "Rick, you wouldn't stop nagging me about this."

"I can't go in there."

"My friends said the same thing," Emma said. "Everyone was scared."

Rick flinched. "Didn't say I was scared."

"So you're going in with us?" Kelly asked.

He eyed the house. His nostrils flared. Sweat beaded along his scalp. Finally, he said, "Yeah, we'll go inside. Lead the way, Kell."

Everyone stepped onto the overgrown lawn. Kelly led the group onto the porch, around the veranda, and through the back door. K2 and Emma followed her in, but Rick paused outside the doorway, visibly trembling. He stared at the broken glass scattered along the floor. His face muscles flexed with strain. His shoulders rose and fell rapidly. Breath hissed from between his lips.

Kelly tilted her head. "Rick? You okay?"

He lifted his foot and attempted to step inside. His toe paused short of the threshold. His eyes, two bulging white orbs, threatened to pop from their sockets.

"Dad?" Emma said, approaching him. "What's wrong?"

Growling like a man trying to lift a boulder, he pushed his foot closer to the threshold. His face turned red. Sweat rolled down his cheeks. His entire body wobbled.

Then it happened. The tip of his shoe crossed the threshold.

He flinched like he'd been bitten and withdrew his foot from the house.

Took one step back.

Then another.

Then started running.

His footfalls pounded the veranda floorboards.

Kelly chased after him, yelling for him to stop. She thought he might retreat into the van, but instead he sprinted down the driveway toward Red Trail Road. She almost reached him when the growl of a diesel motor sounded. A semi truck rumbled by.

He flung himself at its rear tires.

She screamed, "Rick—no!"

His body struck blacktop. He had fallen short of the whirring tires. Both his hands reached after the truck as though it were a missed opportunity. When it faded from sight, he crawled across the yellow dividing line and rolled onto his back.

Emma hurried over. "Dad, what's wrong with you? Get up before you get run over!"

He didn't react. He lay staring at the clear September sky.

Kelly waved a frantic hand before his eyes. Still no reaction.

Another motor sounded in the distance. She seized his arm and tugged him toward the driveway. K2 and Emma grabbed his ankles and helped drag him off the road. Had they hesitated, a Nissan Pathfinder would've rounded the bend and flattened him.

In the driveway Kelly slapped him across the face. "What the hell, Rick?"

He flinched. Sat up. Touched his cheek. "What was that for?"

"You idiot, you could've gotten yourself killed."

He blinked several times. Glanced around in a daze. "Huh. Must've lost it for a second. Staring into that house was like...huh."

Emma dropped to her knees beside him, her eyes glossy. "Dad, what happened?"

"Not sure, chief. Guess I'm not welcome here."

"But why not?" K2 said, pacing nervously. "The rest of us can walk right in."

"Maybe the house has a different effect on men," Kelly speculated.

"No," Emma said. "My friend Cassie was petrified. Same with the other girls."

"Then maybe only redheads can go in?"

Emma shrugged.

Rick rubbed his cheek. "Once I stepped into that hallway, all I could think about was running out into traffic. It was like needing to find a restroom in the worst way. Nothing else mattered." He glanced in the direction of the house. "Bet if I tried again—"

Kelly grabbed him by the shirt. "Don't even think about it."

"But I can't just sit around."

"Then find Norwell. Or figure out who wrote that diary. Whatever you do, don't go near that house again. Promise me. Better yet, promise Emma."

"Please, Dad." She tugged his arm. "Don't go in again."

He sighed before climbing to his feet. "All right. I promise."

But as he said it, his eyes lingered on the Murder House.

45

That evening, Kelly wrangled her twins into the van and drove them to soccer practice. Along the way, they complained about smelling cigarettes, Lysol, and another odor that Aiden described as "worse than puke." She changed the subject and asked about school. Both boys raved about acing their math tests, but she was too preoccupied with the latest Murder House incident to celebrate.

While she was arranging orange cones along the practice field, her phone buzzed in her pocket. Rick. She ducked into her van for privacy and answered. "Rick, you okay?"

"Better than okay," he said in a gloating tone. "I found her."

"Found who?"

"Norwell."

"Really?" Kelly slapped the steering wheel excitedly. "Where?"

"That cemetery I told you to stay away from. I went to Anissa's grave and heard movement coming from the nearby woods. The old lady was rolling up a sleeping bag. She spotted me and took off running, but I caught up to her. And now, Nancy Marie Norwell is in custody."

"Rick, that's amazing!" Kelly jumped and knocked her head against the van roof. She laughed deliriously.

"Settle down. We're not done yet. Still gotta get Emma back to full strength. I asked Norwell about that, and she freaked. Lady's a fucking head case."

"Where is she now?"

"At the station."

"Wait—you got the police involved?"

"Had to," he said. "When I spotted her in the woods, I didn't want to take any chances, so I called another officer for backup. Unfortunately, from here on we'll have to do things by the book, but at least we nabbed the bitch. This'll work out, Kell. We're gonna save Emma."

The confidence in his voice made her smile. "This is incredible. This is—oh, wait."

"What's wrong?"

"I just realized... What if there are two of her?"

"Nope. Only one," he said. "Her body didn't freeze up when we drove her to the station. It was an eleven-mile drive, so it's safe to say there's only one Nancy Norwell."

Kelly leaned back against her seat. Her neck tingled with relief. "Wow. That's great."

"One more thing—and I'm not sure if this is good news." He lowered his voice. "I flipped through that diary you gave me and jotted down people's names. Turns out, back in the 1930s they all lived in a remote Arizona settlement. Place called Separtown. I guess it was a play on the word *separation*. Anyway, there's not much info on the town, but I made some calls and found out the place got torched back in 1934. When that happened, most of the residents were stuck in the attic of a boarding house."

"Oh, no." She swallowed hard. "Could that have been the original Murder House?"

"It's possible."

"How did one end up here in Pennsylvania?"

"Don't know. Right now, I'm trying to figure out who wrote the diary. The author never mentioned his own name, so I'll look into the other names and see if they have a friend in common. If the author's still alive, maybe he can give us answers."

"Or maybe Norwell can."

"Right. Speaking of Norwell, she's about to be questioned. I'll keep you posted."

After he hung up, Kelly excitedly dialed K2.

"Guess what, guess what, guess what," Kelly said. "Rick caught her!"

"Caught who? Norwell?"

"Yes!"

"Woohooooo!" K2 laughed on the other end. "Oh shit, I should probably be quieter since DJ's downstairs. But that's amazing. What happened?"

Kelly recounted Rick's story and began to cry. It was overwhelming to know that she wouldn't have to check over her shoulder anymore. Better yet, they might find a way to help Emma. After wiping tears away, Kelly realized her team was wandering aimlessly around the practice field. "Gotta go. We'll talk later."

"Wait," K2 said. "With Norwell outta the picture, you know what this means, right?"

"What?"

"Daaate niiight!"

"Oh, geez," Kelly said. "Can't that wait?"

"Nope. The deal was that you'd go out with Lance once Emma was healthy and Norwell was in custody."

"We don't know that Emma's totally healthy."

"Oh, come on," K2 said. "Emma was running around her backyard earlier."

"Still…"

"No excuses. If you want me to remain Aunt Kay, you better ask Lance to dinner."

"I hope he says no."

"Don't be such a frump. You should be thrilled. Emma's on her feet, Norwell's in handcuffs, and Lance is gonna be all over you. What's not to love?"

"The consequences."

"Worry about those later. I'll see you tonight. Have fu-u-u-un at practice."

Practice was anything but fun due to the noticeable distance Kelly and Lance maintained from one another. The playful warmth that normally characterized their relationship was gone. Like bad actors in a sitcom, they traded clumsy comments and forced smiles.

When practice ended, she jogged over while he was gathering plastic cones. Her stomach floated. She mentally rehearsed what she would say, all while praying that he'd reject her. *Please, Lance, shut me down. Tell me I'm too old, too married, too complicated. Any excuse will do.*

"Lance, got a sec?" Her voice came out shaky.

He turned toward her, cradling a stack of orange cones against his side. "Sup, Coach?"

She shifted from one chilly leg to another. "So, yesterday morning we…had a moment. I'm not sure how you feel about it, but I was wondering if you'd like to maybe get dinner. I mean, usually two people get dinner before they…do what we did." Kelly turned away and cringed. *What the hell am I saying?*

Lance laughed. "Yeah, dinner usually comes before the other stuff."

She forced a laugh. Met his eyes. This next part scared her more than climbing into the Murder House attic. "I'm free tonight. What about you?"

"Sure. Where we eating?"

"Um, any preference?"

"How about Taco Bell?" When her nose wrinkled, he snickered. "Kidding, kidding. How about seafood? That's your favorite, right?"

Months ago during their first practice, Kelly mentioned she loved shrimp but never got to eat it because DJ hated fishy-smelling restaurants.

"Seafood sounds great," she said.

"Name the place."

"How about the Waterfall Cafe?"

"Perfect."

Kelly smiled. "Eight o'clock?"

"Eight o'clock."

He swaggered back to his Ford Explorer. Was he expecting to get laid tonight? After one date with a married woman? She wasn't sure how she felt about that. Then again, she had come off as ravenous yesterday. He probably pegged her for a nympho. But she didn't want him to think of her like that. She wanted...

She wasn't sure what she wanted.

BACK AT HOME, Kelly lay on her bed texting with Rick. He said their daughter was "eating healthy," which suggested she had gobbled another of E2's fingertips. Norwell, meanwhile, was still being interrogated at the police station. Kelly asked if it was safe to leave the house tonight—she was fishing for any excuse to cancel her date—but unfortunately he gave her the green light.

"Let's go," K2 said, dragging Kelly into her walk-in closet. "Pick out a dress."

"A dress?"

"You know, those one-piece garments that you always buy but never wear. These things." She gestured to a rack of hanging dresses.

"Shouldn't I wear something more casual?"

"Casual? You're going on a date."

"If I wear a dress, it'll raise red flags when I head downstairs."

"Don't worry, I'll distract DJ and the kids while you sneak out."

Kelly rubbed her temples. This felt wrong. Unforgivably wrong. She'd been sneaking around all week, but that had been for the sake of helping her daughter. Tonight, if she went through with this, she'd be betraying her family. Though she liked Lance and certainly found him attractive, she didn't envision herself as a cheating wife.

"Date's off," Kelly said, storming out of the closet. "Too many things can go sideways."

"Like what?" K2 asked.

"Like someone recognizing me and telling DJ."

"Who's gonna recognize you? You only leave the house for errands and PTA meetings."

"Still, all it takes is one person."

"You can't cancel because of that."

"What about Emma? What if she gets sick again?"

"Rick just said she's eating well."

"But I'll be thinking about her all night. How can I enjoy myself if I'm worried about her?"

"Girl, you're not worried about Emma—you're worried about having a good time with Lance." K2 lifted a fiery red cocktail dress from the rack. She rubbed the fabric between her fingers and frowned. "If you want to cancel, fine. But then I'm done with the Aunt Kay routine."

Kelly glanced at the photo hanging above her nightstand. In it, the twins stood waist-deep in a pile of bright orange leaves. The boys were three when the picture was taken, innocent to the world's chaos. Even now they remained oblivious to life's harshest truths, and that was how it was supposed to be. Sadly, Emma had not been so lucky when she was little; Kelly had carelessly exposed her daughter to marital arguments, passive-aggressive parenting, and even her own suicide attempt. Kelly had been a terrible mom on her first go-round, but the moment her twins were born, she vowed to do things right.

"Please, K2. Don't do this to me."

"You're doing it to yourself." K2 shook the cocktail dress at her. "I made the rules clear. If you want me to keep lying to the kids, you have to be honest with yourself about Lance. All I'm asking for is one date."

Kelly eyed the photo of her twins. Though she'd committed a massive screwup behind the bleachers, she still had a chance to maintain her image as Ideal Mom. No child should have to believe his mother was cheating with the assistant soccer coach. That wasn't how she wanted her kids to understand marriage—wasn't how she wanted them to understand her.

Gritting her teeth, she marched into the closet, grabbed a sleeveless emerald midi dress by the hanger, and held it up against her. "What do you think?"

K2 smiled. "I think we have a pair of heels that'll go perfect with that."

46

With a quivering heart, Kelly pulled into the Waterfall Cafe parking lot. The restaurant stood upon a grassy slope along a quiet forest road. There were no waterfalls, rivers, streams, or ponds for miles, but that was part of the place's charm. Back when it first opened, local food critics mocked its name, but the cafe nonetheless built its reputation as a top-notch seafood spot. Kelly had always dreamed of dining here, but with her stomach now in a full-on tizz, she couldn't imagine eating so much as a breadcrumb.

She faced K2 in the passenger seat. "I can't do this. Please take my place. You can wear my dress."

"This is your date, not mine," K2 said. "Now leave the van or else that Lysol smell will stick to you all night. Plus, I need to grab a seat at the bar."

"The bar? You're going *inside*? But you said you'd wait out here. I thought you were only tagging along so my legs wouldn't freeze up."

"I'll be watching." K2 narrowed her eyes. "Gotta make sure you enjoy yourself."

Kelly forced a laugh. Her plan had been to put Lance to sleep by rambling on about her job—if necessary, she'd sour the mood by talking about her husband. She wanted to ensure this date failed, but K2 apparently had other ideas.

"What are you, my chaperone?" Kelly asked.

"More like the total opposite." K2 pulled a blonde wig from her purse. The one they'd taken from Mango. She donned the wig and adjusted the bangs to obscure her forehead. "I wanna see you have fun. If you play things too safe or deliberately screw up, our deal's off."

"You can't change the rules!"

"Not changing anything." She added sunglasses to complete the disguise. "The deal was that you'd go on a date with Lance. Nobody goes on a date to be miserable. I'll watch you from the bar, and if I see you frumping things up, I'll call you on your cell. First call is a friendly reminder. Second is a warning. If I call three times, I'll tell Aiden and Zach the truth."

"Don't you dare."

"Don't make me. Now have a good time."

KELLY WAITED on a stiff metal bench outside the Waterfall Cafe entrance. The night was breezy. Even with the entrance door shut, she could smell the warm, salty odor of shrimp. Her mouth watered, but her stomach spiraled. She clutched her phone, hoping Lance would text her with any cancellation excuse—engine trouble, bad weather, tuberculosis, anything. He was already twelve minutes late, so why not bail?

Then a pair of familiar headlights pierced the darkness along the forest road. Without a doubt, it was Lance's Ford

Explorer. His arrival filled her with a mix of relief and dread. Relief because she admittedly didn't want to be stood up; dread because with K2 watching from the restaurant bar, Kelly felt like a mouse trapped under a see-through bowl.

Lance parked, then sauntered up the sidewalk wearing an untucked white button-down, the sleeves rolled to his elbows. His tanned forearms popped with veins. Kelly wanted those arms around her but also nowhere near her.

Tucking his hair behind his ears, he spotted her. His face lit up, but his expression looked forced, as if he were having second thoughts. "Guess I'm late, huh?"

Kelly didn't know what to say. Then she wondered, *What would K2 say? Would K2 chide him for being late? Hold it against him?*

No. K2 would play it cool.

"You're not late," Kelly said with a wry smile. "I'm just faster."

"Oh yeah? After dinner we should race back to the parking lot."

"I'm game." She rose from the bench. "I'll even keep my heels on so it's competitive."

He laughed and held the door for her. They stepped inside. The restaurant carried a warm, buttery scent. Tables and booths were scattered under dim lighting. Over at the bar K2 nursed a beer, ignoring the flirtations of a pock-faced old man.

A well-dressed host asked Kelly whether she'd prefer to sit indoors or on the patio. She chose the latter. Sitting outside would distance her from K2.

The host grabbed menus and strolled outside rambling about lobster bisque and seasonal desserts. Kelly and Lance took their seats at a tiny metal table. The host handed them menus and vanished.

Beneath the table, Kelly worked to pry her heels off. They looked great, but they were digging into the sides of her feet. While removing her left shoe, she accidentally kicked Lance's shin.

"Hey—I am *not* a soccer ball."

Kelly laughed.

Then she noticed K2 had a clear sightline from the bar. The pressure was on.

A waiter appeared with a bottle of chardonnay that he insisted went great with anything on the menu. Kelly and Lance each requested a glass. The waiter poured their drinks and Kelly took a sip. The wine was smooth and dry. Delicious. Lance caught her smiling and told the waiter to leave the bottle.

"Excellent," the waiter said. "Are you ready to order?"

"Shrimp salad," Kelly said.

"Same here," Lance said.

"Excellent. Any appetizers? Perhaps the lobster bisque?"

"I'll try it," Kelly said. More eating meant less talking.

"I'll try it too," Lance said.

"Excellent." The waiter collected their menus and left.

A stiff breeze pushed against Kelly's bare shoulders. She hugged herself. "So, we ordered the same things, huh?" *Great conversation starter. Real romantic.*

Lance shrugged. "Didn't know what to get. Seafood is miles beyond my comfort zone."

"Really?"

"Yeah, the smell usually knocks me on the floor."

She grabbed her chardonnay glass, reminding herself that she needed to appear as though she were having a good time. She smiled pleasantly but wasn't sure where to steer the conversation. What did you talk about when you wanted to sabotage a date while still pretending you were having fun? She couldn't talk about Norwell—that was too freaky. Emma's hospital visit was too morbid. Work was too dull. She could talk about Aiden and Zach, but if the conversation drifted toward yesterday's game—

Her phone buzzed inside her purse.

She glanced inside at the bar.

K2 sat glaring with her burner phone pressed to her ear. First strike.

Damn.

"So, the other day at work," Kelly said, collecting herself, "I left a customer on hold for twenty-seven minutes."

"Twenty-seven minutes? What were you doing that whole time? Thinking about me?"

"You wish, creeper. I was talking to myself about how much I hate my job."

"Sounds like it's time for a new job then."

"I don't really feel like searching for one."

"My neighbor runs a gym. I think they're hiring. You like fitness routines, right?"

She swilled her wine. "I like fitness, but not routines."

"You'd be enforcing them, not following them."

"Still..."

The waiter dropped off a steaming basket of biscuits. They smelled delicious, but the thought of eating one made her nauseous.

"So, no routines," Lance said, tearing apart a biscuit. "Okay then. What's your dream job?"

"Professional soccer player."

"Great gig," he said. "Sucks there aren't more open positions."

"Right? They should build more stadiums."

"Hell yeah." He chewed his bread and nudged the basket toward her. "Got any other dream jobs?"

"I don't know." She nudged the basket back. "Something with variety. And nothing big on math. And it's gotta be high paying."

"I said dream job, not dream salary."

She shifted in her seat. Her mind went blank. She feared K2 would buzz her again, so she blurted, "What about you? What's yours?"

"Professional soccer player." He grinned. "But if we're being realistic, I'd say airline pilot."

"Ooo, I could be your copilot." Her words came out more seductive than intended. To dial down the temperature, she added, "Actually, wait. There's math involved, right?"

"Yeah. That's why I never went after it." He set his bread down. "But I'd love the freedom to go anywhere. I mean, obviously I'd have to fly along scheduled routes, but what's not to like about sitting up in the sky with no traffic, no stop signs, and you got the whole world down below." He sipped his chardonnay.

Kelly gulped the rest of hers.

Those soups were taking forever.

Her phone buzzed a second time.

Shit.

Over at the bar, K2 had her burner phone pressed to her ear. Her piercing stare reminded Kelly of the way Superman's eyes burned in some of Zach's comic books. Strike two.

Kelly asked about flight school requirements when her

phone buzzed yet again. This time, however, K2 didn't appear to be calling. Kelly wondered if it was Rick, but when she checked the caller ID, it was DJ.

The phone continued to buzz.

"Gonna answer that?" Lance asked.

Kelly accepted the call. "H-hello?"

"Where you at?" DJ said. He sounded pissed.

"I told you, I went to see Emma."

"At her house?"

"Yeah."

"Really? Because I'm there right now."

Heat burst across her face. Her stomach dropped. "Really?"

"Yeah, Rick invited me and the kids over for dinner, but I don't see you or him anywhere. Olivia said you never even stopped by."

"Oh."

"Where are you, Kelly?"

"Next chance I get, I'll call you." She hung up and silenced all incoming calls from her husband.

"Who was that?" Lance asked.

She rolled her eyes. "My boss. I'm out of vacation time and—"

"That was your husband, wasn't it?"

"What? No."

"You can be honest." Lance scratched his eyebrow. "I know our situation is...unusual."

She sighed. "Okay, you're right. It was him. He's having a tizz because I lied about where I was going tonight."

"Gotta say, I was stunned when you invited me here." Lance poured more chardonnay into their glasses. "What happened behind the bleachers yesterday seemed like a heat-of-the-moment thing."

"No, not exactly."

"Oh yeah? Then why exactly are we here?"

"Well, I..." She cleared her throat. That soup couldn't arrive fast enough. "I...want us to get to know each other."

"So do I. But let's make one thing clear. If the reason we're here is because you're trying to piss off your husband, I'm not that guy."

"Nonono, I don't want you to be that guy." She could sense K2 reaching for her phone. "Lance, what happened between us—I'm trying to decide if it should keep happening. And if so, how long would you stay interested in someone like me?"

He squinted. "Someone like you?"

"You know what I mean."

"Actually, I don't."

She twisted her wrist while trying to find the words. "I mean...me."

"What about you?"

"Everything."

"Can you be more specific?"

"Look," she said, huffing with frustration, "I'm eight years older than you, I've got three kids from two guys, a shitty job, no degree, and enough baggage to sink the nearest cruise liner. That's me. That's who you're sitting with."

A soothing coolness spread across her face. It was like the relief that came after vomiting into a toilet.

Lance sat blinking, his hands folded beside his glass. He looked toward the road, where a sedan zipped by. It seemed she had dumped out too much and scared him. She didn't blame him for feeling uncomfortable, but she needed to maintain this conversation till the soup arrived.

"And honestly," she said, "you don't even know the worst of it. I could go on."

"So could I."

"About me?"

"No—about *my* worst." He grabbed his wine glass. "What, you think I'm some brand-new sports car that never had its paint scratched?"

"No, but—"

"I have a kid too, you know?"

"Your nephew doesn't count as a kid."

"I don't mean my nephew." He gulped wine. "I mean my five-year-old son. He lives in Seattle with his mom. She's got full custody."

Kelly's jaw dropped. "I'm sorry. I didn't know."

He shrugged. "Wasn't ready to tell you. If you don't mind, let's save that discussion for another time."

"Sure." She sipped more wine.

"Question," he said. "Do you want tonight to be a good night?"

She'd been so focused on survival that she never even considered that question. But the answer was obvious. "Yeah, I want it to be a great night."

Lance smiled. "Then let's make it one."

Her soup arrived moments later. It tasted like relief.

47

Dinner didn't kill either of them. It turned out Lance could stomach seafood and Kelly could stomach a candid conversation. After finishing her shrimp salad, she eased back into her seat and gazed down the forest road. Nightfall had blackened the path between the trees, the darkness broken only by the occasional glow of oncoming headlights.

When the waiter came by before closing time, Kelly ordered the raspberry cheesecake.

"Excellent," the waiter said.

After the waiter left, Lance said, "Guy needs to pick a new adjective. Everything is 'excellent' to him. You order wine, excellent. You finish your salad, excellent. You throw him over the patio railing, excellent."

Kelly laughed and tipped sideways. She grabbed the table edge to keep from falling off her chair. When she looked up, she locked eyes with K2, who was smiling wistfully over a beer glass. Kelly winked at her. K2 winked back.

Dessert arrived on a ridiculously long dish. A trail of

raspberry syrup wove toward a tall wedge of cheesecake. It looked like something from a gourmet magazine.

"This looks *excellent*," she said, giggling as the waiter walked away.

"I think he heard you," Lance said in a conspiratorial tone. "He's probably hiring an excellent hitman to take you out."

Suppressing laughter, she grabbed a fork and slid it through the cheesecake. It parted like foam. When she popped it into her mouth, sweetness burst across her tongue. Delicious. She finished slow-chewing and said, "Mmm. You have to try this."

"I'm not a cheesecake guy."

"You are tonight." She sliced off a piece and lifted it to his mouth. It took some coaxing before he bit down. After she pulled the fork from his lips, he started chewing. His eyebrows hopped with approval. She lowered the fork. "What do you think?"

"Not bad," he said. "That raspberry syrup is great."

She dabbed her little finger in the syrup and touched it to her tongue. He gazed wide-eyed while she sucked it. "Mmm. Delicious."

"Yeah," he said stupidly.

"The sooner we finish this," she said, "the sooner we can leave."

"I better ask for another fork."

As Lance turned to signal the waiter, the patio door opened. Kelly thought she was hallucinating when her husband appeared on the threshold in his sand-colored polo and wrinkled black slacks. The moment he spotted her, DJ adjusted his glasses and marched toward the table.

Kelly turned to stone. She couldn't believe it. How could he have found her? Then again, he'd seen the menu on her computer yesterday. It wasn't that hard to connect the dots.

Lance faced her with a sober look in his eyes.

She wondered what to say. She was good at lying, but it was hard to craft anything convincing when you were seated at a fancy restaurant with a hot guy.

DJ stopped beside their table. His arms hung at his sides. Slowly his fingers curled into fists, the knuckles whitening as he studied Lance. The patio went silent. People at the other tables glanced sideways, pretending not to watch. The moment stretched on.

DJ inhaled, his chest visibly expanding, and studied Kelly. "New dress."

"I've had it for a while, actually."

"Did you hide it in the van?"

"No, the closet."

DJ glared at her, his eyes ablaze.

The waiter returned. Without skipping a beat, he set a check holder on the table. "Will you need a box for the cheesecake?"

"Yes," DJ said, eyeing Lance. "He'll be taking it home with him."

The waiter strolled back inside.

DJ's fists remained clenched.

Kelly took a breath but forgot how to exhale. She wanted to scream, to run, to cease existing.

Lance pulled out his wallet. He slid his credit card inside the check holder.

DJ removed the card and tucked it into Lance's shirt pocket. "Dinner's on me."

Lance scratched an eyebrow, rose from his chair, and walked toward the patio door.

Once he was gone, DJ said, "Let's go, Kelly. Olivia's watching the kids. We gotta pick them up."

She collected her purse and began to rise when she realized something. She sat back down. After a sip of wine, she gestured toward the empty chair. "Please sit."

"We're leaving."

"But I want to talk."

"If that's the case, call me sometime on your burner phone."

She sighed. "DJ, please. Give me two minutes."

Begrudgingly, he took the seat across from her and folded his arms in disgust. "So how was dinner?"

"The food was good."

"And the company?"

She chewed her lip. She eyed the road as Lance's Ford Explorer vanished into the darkness. "Can I be honest with you?"

"I don't know." He scowled. "Can you?"

She shifted in her seat. Her gaze followed the trail of raspberry syrup to the half-finished slab of cheesecake. "I'm not happy."

"Yeah, it must suck to get caught cheating."

"That's not what I mean. You know what I'm saying."

"No, I don't. I don't know anything because you never clue me in. You disappear every night, you use Emma's health as an excuse, and apparently you meet other guys for dinner."

"Tonight was the first time."

"And I'm supposed to believe that?" He shook his head, his expression ripe with dismay. "I knew our marriage wasn't paradise, but I never thought things were *this* bad. When did you stop being happy?"

"I don't know. Years ago."

"Why didn't you say anything?"

"I did. I said, 'Take off that stupid mask, it's our wedding night.'"

DJ grimaced. Turned red. "It's just a mask. You're acting like I did something wrong."

"Well, we've been together for nine years, yet I've never gotten an explanation for why I can only fuck Batman. It's like I don't even know you."

"I could say the same about you, Kelly. You've shut me down before when I asked personal questions."

"Then why didn't you push a little harder?"

"Because I was giving you space."

"No." She shook her head. "You were doing the same thing I was doing—lying. Keeping secrets. Trying to ignore the shameful stuff." She tapped the tabletop. "That all needs to stop."

"So, what, are we gonna be honest with each other from now on?"

"I don't know," she said. "Are we?"

DJ leaned forward, arms on the table. "If we are, let's start now. Tell me… If I didn't come here tonight, would you have gone home with that guy?"

Her eyes landed on a smear of raspberry syrup. "We didn't have any plans."

"I didn't ask if you had plans," he said through gritted teeth. "I asked whether you would've gone home with him."

She wasn't sure. If Lance had walked her out the door with an arm around her shoulders, there was no telling where the night would've taken them. Maybe he would've kissed her. Maybe she would've kissed him. Maybe he would've invited her back to his place. And if he did...

"I really don't know," she said. "Tonight I was living in the moment."

"A moment I wasn't part of."

She winced. That one stung. She didn't know what to say. An apology wouldn't fix this. Part of her wanted to admit defeat and commend him for finally calling her out on her bullshit. Crashing her date tonight was a bold, necessary move, a step in the right direction, but they'd been veering the wrong way for too long.

Her phone buzzed. She checked the caller ID and didn't recognize the number. She answered anyway, if only to escape the hardest conversation of her life. "Hello?"

A hissing noise came through. It sounded like spraying water. A loud voice asked, "Hi, is this Kelly O'Neill?"

"Who's this?"

"Officer Pete Jankowski. I'm with the Scranton Police Department." His voice was interrupted by a siren. "You live at 22 Byron Street, correct?"

"Yeah, why?" Her voice came out thin. "Is something wrong?"

"I'm afraid so," he said. "It's your house."

"What about it?"

"It's on fire."

Orange traffic cones and a flashing police cruiser guarded the entrance to Byron Street. Kelly steered the minivan toward a gap between the cones. There, a uniformed officer gestured for her to lower her window. The moment she did, a noxious burning odor filled her nostrils. In between coughs, she explained that she lived on this street. The cop waved her through.

Down below, her next-door neighbor's pine trees blocked the view of her home. All she could see was smoke rising. A firetruck sprayed a watery beam toward her property; onlookers crowded the opposite sidewalk. Some watched grimly. Others filmed on their phones.

"How bad's the damage?" K2 called from the cargo area. She had snuck back to the minivan after DJ arrived at the restaurant. "Huh? How bad?"

"Quiet," Kelly said in a choked voice. "Lotta people around."

As the van rolled closer, she glimpsed her front porch. The sight knocked the air from her lungs. Her home—her family's home—was scorched from foundation to roof.

Chaotic black marks covered the white siding. Smoke leaped from shattered windows. Sections of the roof exposed holes large enough for her kids to crawl through. Not even the garage was spared; the rolling metal door hung wrinkled within the frame.

In the side yard, men wearing mustard-yellow suits and red hats ran through the grass where she had taught her twins to play soccer. Embers flickered along the lawn and floated toward a parked ambulance.

She swallowed hard and felt her throat crack like a glass tube. This home had been the backdrop of her life for eight years, the place where she lived out the good and bad, the laughs and frustrations. Judging by the damage, she would never again snooze on the office couch or cook a mac-and-cheese casserole in the kitchen or hear the staircase creak like an old galleon when she carried her kids to bed. Never again.

A uniformed officer approached the van. When she lowered the window, he said, "Ma'am, you need to turn around."

"But I live here."

"You're Kelly O'Neill?" he said. "Rick's ex-wife?"

"Yeah." She eyed her scorched home. "What happened?"

"Arson," he said. "Someone dumped gasoline and set the fire."

"Do you know who did it?"

Behind her, DJ parked his car and sprinted toward the porch.

"Sir!" The officer chased after him. "Do not approach the building!" The officer grabbed DJ by the elbows and dragged him backward.

Kelly ran out to intercept her husband. "Hon, calm down."

"Our stuff is in there," he said, struggling within the cop's grasp. "All the kids' stuff—their clothes, their school supplies, their games. My computer rig, my hard drives—"

"It's okay."

"What about your jewelry?" he said, lunging. "And our emergency cash?"

"It's okay." She stepped in front of him. "You said the kids are at Rick's, right? Long as they're safe, that's all that matters."

"I know, but... Ugh."

The cop steered DJ into his car and shut the driver's door. Her husband gazed at the house with a desperate, helpless expression.

She approached the cop. "Do you know who started the fire?"

"We suspect it was a woman named Nancy Norwell."

"Norwell?" Kelly flinched. "But she's in your custody."

He squinted, confused. "What're you talking about?"

"Rick said she was being held at the station."

The officer glanced at a nearby police cruiser. "I just started my shift, so maybe I'm outta the loop. Let me check with my superior." He hurried over to another officer, yapped for a bit, then came running back. "No, ma'am, Norwell was never booked."

"Never?" Kelly brought a hand to her mouth. "But Rick said she was in your custody. He arrested her outside a cemetery. He called for backup."

"Not what I heard."

Kelly shuddered. She grabbed the cop's arm to steady herself. If what he said was true, Rick had lied to her. But why would he lie? Was he involved with Norwell? Had the woman reached out to him? Blackmailed him? Forced him to get Kelly's family out of the house so she could torch the place?

After I lost my daughter, I lost my home. Do you know what that feels like? Join me out on the streets.

Kelly was out on the street right now.

Was Norwell watching?

"Officer," she said, eyeing the surrounding woods. "Do you know where Nancy Norwell went after she set the fire?"

The cop scratched behind his neck. "I'm not supposed to say anything—we're waiting for confirmation—but we believe she's no longer a threat."

"Why not?"

He nodded toward the ambulance. "We found her body."

49

After midnight the police confirmed that the charred body inside the ambulance was Nancy Norwell—or at least one of her. Kelly operated under the assumption that there were likely two Norwells. She insisted the woman might've had an accomplice—perhaps a sister who resembled her—but the police barely acknowledged that possibility. They operated based on evidence, and nothing suggested to them that a second Norwell was prowling around.

As the emergency vehicles cleared out, Kelly realized she needed to leave. Her kids were at Rick's, and his lies about arresting Norwell worried her. Why her ex-husband would deceive her like that was beyond understanding. She recalled how he reacted to the Murder House. Was it possible that the place had warped his mind or manipulated him? She needed to find out.

Rick's truck was absent from his driveway when Kelly pulled in. She cut the engine and noticed she reeked of smoke and chemical odors. She needed a shower and a change of clothes—especially a change of clothes, because she didn't want her kids seeing her in this dress.

She yelled back to K2 about swapping outfits, but Aiden and Zach ran outside chirping her name. Aiden tugged her door open. Both boys climbed onto her lap.

"Mommy," Zach whispered, his nose tickling her ear. "Did a secret agent set our house on fire?"

"Yeah," Aiden said, "was somebody trying to hurt Aunt Kay?"

Kelly shushed them. "Both of you, keep quiet about her."

"We didn't tell anyone," Aiden said.

"Good," she said. "Are you two okay?"

"Yeah, can we go home now?" Aiden asked.

Zach whimpered. "They put the fire out, right?"

She swallowed hard. The truth might wreck them. Better to keep hope in their tiny hearts. "I'll check tomorrow. You two should be asleep."

"We can't sleep," Aiden said.

"I wanna go home," Zach said.

Kelly blinked back tears. She needed to stay strong. Carry herself like everything would be okay.

She ushered the kids inside. The house was well lit at this late hour, and the air smelled of reheated pizza. Olivia appeared at the kitchen entrance in a purple bathrobe, her honey-gold hair wrapped in a tight bun. She narrowed her eyes with suspicion, or perhaps jealousy, at the sight of Kelly's dress.

"Where's Rick?" Kelly asked.

"Thought you would know," Olivia said.

"He's not here?"

"Haven't heard from him in hours. He won't answer my calls or texts."

Kelly swallowed. Had nobody seen him since that deceitful phone call? "Where's Emma?"

"Basement," Olivia said. "She's been acting strange all night."

Kelly ventured downstairs to Rick's man cave. The place emitted a nasty odor, like rotten chicken left in the sun. She couldn't remember the last time she'd been down here, but there hadn't been any furniture then. Now, three couches surrounded a wall-mounted TV. A pair of framed Dallas Cowboys jerseys flanked the TV, along with police award plaques and photos of Rick and Emma hiking together. Beside one of the couches was a game-ready pool table. Beyond that was a bar counter with four stools. One seat was occupied by Emma, who sat hunched over a paper plate.

Emma wiped her mouth. Swallowed something. A brown smear of barbeque sauce decorated her plate, along with what looked like pulled pork. Kelly took another step and realized it wasn't pork—or any animal meat for that matter.

She grimaced. Turned away. Fought the urge to gag. She hated to think what was inside the fridge behind the counter.

"Sorry, Mom. I know it's super gross, but I have to eat it every few hours. Otherwise my legs start hurting." Emma pinched her nose and pushed another forkful into her mouth. After she finished chewing, she washed it down with Sprite. "Usually I post pics of my food on Instagram, but I don't think this would get many likes."

"No, probably not." Kelly claimed the adjacent stool. She tucked a strand of Emma's long red hair behind her ear. "You poor thing."

"I'm okay." Emma frowned at her plate. "I miss her though."

Kelly wrapped her arm around Emma and pulled her close.

Emma rested her head against Kelly's neck. "Sorry about your house."

"Thanks." Kelly sighed. "I don't know what I'm gonna tell Aiden and Zach."

"In psych class, we learned that little kids are more resilient than adults."

"Well, that's encouraging."

"Yeah." Emma untangled herself from Kelly's grasp. "I like your dress."

"Listen," Kelly said, "has your dad contacted you tonight?"

"No. Why?"

"Earlier he called and said he found Norwell. Claimed he took her to the station. But when I spoke to the police tonight, they said Norwell was never booked. I even called the station on the drive over here, but nobody had seen her —not until her body was found."

Emma gasped. "Norwell's dead?"

"One of her is."

"There are two of her?"

"I think so. I'm worried she might be controlling your dad."

Emma blinked. Her eyes filled. "You mean... He's a hostage?"

Kelly rubbed her daughter's shoulder. "If he is, we'll find him."

"Oh no," Emma said, breathing rapidly. "No, not Dad. No."

"Honey, when did you last see him?"

"This afternoon."

"How did he seem? Normal?"

"I think so. When we got home from the Murder House, he moved E2 down here and put her in the fridge. Then he cooked me some of this...food. After that, he had coffee, got the mail, changed clothes, and left. He said he was gonna look into that diary we found. Actually, now that you mention it, he was acting pretty sus."

"Sus?"

"Suspicious. Like, he gave me a kiss and told me he loved me—he only does that on holidays. I figured it was because of everything going on, but what if he was acting weird because of Norwell?" Emma reached into her pocket for a piece of multicolored rope—her good luck charm. She squeezed it like a stress ball. "Has anyone else heard from him?"

"Not since he called me about capturing Norwell. That was when—wait. You said he got the mail? When was that?"

"Um, right before he left. He rushed upstairs after he opened a green envelope."

50

Kelly and Emma spent all night searching the house for the green envelope. They checked every cupboard, every drawer, every nook of every room. DJ tore apart furniture and checked behind heavy appliances. Olivia sifted through Rick's private safe and filing cabinets. By sunrise, the entire house had been searched, but no green envelopes turned up.

Neither did Rick. The wait for his return stretched on. Whenever vehicles motored past the house, Kelly dashed to the front window hoping to see his truck. He never showed.

Around noon, the mail carrier arrived. Kelly tensed as the gray-haired mailman tucked a short stack of envelopes into the box and drove off. She rushed out. A green envelope lay sandwiched between the others. With trembling fingers, she plucked it free.

Her name—not Rick's—was scribbled above the address. Norwell must've anticipated that Kelly would stay here after the fire. The lady was three steps ahead of her, and suddenly the cozy, crime-free neighborhood of Peachwood Acres became hostile territory. The houses and parked cars across the street seemed to be watching her.

Kelly ducked back inside like a soldier taking cover and ripped open the envelope. It contained a twice-folded letter. Her heart and stomach switched places as she unfolded it. The message read: "My husband died of grief after Anissa's death. One loss after another. Can you imagine losing the man you love?"

Kelly warned DJ, then called the police. Within an hour they arrived. Along with the security team came detectives who asked countless questions about the green envelopes and Rick's disappearance. Officers marched around the property. She worried they might check her van and spot K2, who had spent all night in the cargo area hidden under blankets and soccer equipment.

At the kitchen table, DJ typed furiously into a laptop he'd borrowed from Olivia. His expression was tense as he Googled Nancy Norwell.

Kelly sat beside him. "You'll be okay, hon."

"Not if Norwell has an accomplice." He tapped the Enter key. His breathing accelerated. He scrolled through news articles until he slapped the laptop shut in frustration.

She rubbed his back. "Relax. The cops won't let anyone hurt you."

"Why me?" His breathing grew faster. "Why do I have to die?"

"You won't die."

"Just like our house won't burn?"

"That was different. We weren't prepared."

"Oh, but now we're prepared? Prepared how? Some psycho could be waiting across the street with a sniper rifle." He removed his glasses. Wiped sweat from his face. Stared at the closed laptop. "I love you, Kelly. I don't say it enough, but I want you to know in case something happens."

His words pained her.

Kelly slid her hand toward her husband's. She curled her pinky finger around his and squeezed tight. She had done the same on their first date many years ago when they sat poolside at a Fourth of July party. It had been an odd choice for a first date—the pressure of meeting all his friends was overwhelming—but she loved the way he welcomed her into his life with his heart on his sleeve. By the time fireworks splashed the night sky, she knew she'd found someone special.

Now, however, he pulled his hand away. After a moment, he scratched his beard and said, "This morning I was thinking."

"About what?"

"Your assistant coach. Even though we've got bigger problems, I thought about going after him. Yelling at him. Punching his teeth out. Then I realized he's just a guy who's interested in you. Can't blame him for that. But you... You dressed up for him."

She rubbed her neck. "DJ, I..."

"Hang on. I'm not finished. You see, I got really pissed at you. I couldn't believe you'd do that to me. I thought you were the worst woman on Earth. And then it hit me that I would never marry the worst woman on Earth." He met her eyes. "What you did last night was wrong, but you were right about one thing—I should've been more honest with you."

"About your mask?"

"About everything." He pulled his chair closer to hers. "Ever notice how we only talk about surface stuff? Our jobs, the kids, what's for dinner... We never touch on anything personal. It's always been that way, like we're coworkers instead of husband and wife."

She squirmed in her chair. "You had your secrets, I had mine."

"That's the problem. Remember the first time we went to bed together? You asked me about my mask, and I didn't tell you anything because I was afraid you'd dump me. I always thought you'd ask again, but you never did." He wiped his palms on his shirt. "Know what's pathetic? Last night when I saw our house burning, my first thought was that mask. I didn't know what I'd do if it melted into a puddle of sludge. But now, having a target on my back... Everything's in perspective."

"DJ..."

"Let me finish. I don't know what's gonna happen to me, but I want you to know about that mask." His chair creaked as he slid it closer. "See, in high school I had this girlfriend. Nicole. I was nuts about her. She was my first, so naturally I wanted to grow old and wrinkly with her. We went everywhere together, and she never missed any of my soccer games."

"You played soccer?"

"Yeah. Striker. Everybody called me the Scoring Machine. Before our games, Coach would ask me if I was powered up and ready to go. I'd reply with 'Can't fucking stop me!' and my teammates would go nuts. It was our battle cry."

Kelly smiled. "How come you never told me about this?"

"I'm getting to that. Anyway, when senior year rolled around, I got a bunch of soccer scholarship offers. Nicole applied to each school so we could stay together. My top choice was Michigan, but she didn't get accepted there.

That led to a nasty fight. She demanded I pick another college, but I told her that I didn't want my talent going to waste, that I would go pro someday, that nobody could fucking stop me. Nicole told me I'd struggle against D1 opponents but my confidence held strong.

"About a week after our fight, she and I made up. Then I committed to Michigan. When I broke the news in math class, she stormed out and went home for the day. That was a Friday, and she avoided me all weekend.

"On Monday people were giving me funny looks, snickering behind my back. I figured it was because of Nicole's outburst. Then at lunch, half the soccer team was missing from our table. The remaining guys wouldn't look at me, like they were afraid of hurting my feelings or something.

"I asked what was going on. One guy pulled me into the hall. He took out his phone and showed me a text from Nicole. It said, 'Scoring Machine. Can't fucking stop me.' Beneath it were photos." DJ swallowed hard and stared at the kitchen table. "Nicole was naked in them. And she was with all these different guys. Guys I knew, guys I didn't, guys from the soccer team. She had someone take those pictures, then she sent them to all my friends."

Kelly grimaced.

DJ removed his glasses and set them on the table. "Nicole got expelled. I ended up transferring to another school to finish my senior year. I still went to Michigan but got kicked off the soccer team within weeks. My brain shut down every time I stepped onto the field." He pinched the bridge of his nose. "Anyway, I stayed single for two years. When I started dating again, I couldn't get anything going in the bedroom. Whenever a girl took off her clothes, I thought of Nicole's photos and went limp. It was humiliating. I didn't want to go near a woman ever again.

"Then Halloween happened. I dressed as Batman, met a girl at a party, and went back to her place. She called me her Dark Knight and told me to keep the mask on. That time I got it up. I felt like a different person. Felt human again. But next time—without the mask—my problems returned. From then on, I always wore it. Most girls thought it was creepy, but then I met you, Kelly. You didn't seem to mind, so I kept wearing it. And now here we are. And I'm not sure why it took me so long to tell you."

His cheeks were crimson.

She felt awful. She wished this conversation had happened years ago. Then she could've discussed her suicide attempt, failing out of college, losing custody of Emma, and all the other things that led her to believe she was a worthless piece of garbage who should cling to the first "safe" guy she met. DJ was that guy, and though they had chemistry, more importantly they had boundaries. She ignored his secrets, he ignored hers. It was a perfect match.

Except hiding from each other was no way to sustain a relationship.

She took his hand while he collected himself.

Emma wandered into the kitchen in a gray zip hoodie and black shorts. Her skin looked healthy, but her eyes looked sleepy. "Mom? Why are the police outside? Did they find Dad?"

"No, honey. We got another envelope."

"Oh no." Emma darted over. "Is Norwell coming after us?"

"We'll be fine. Don't worry."

"What'd the note say? Anything about Dad?"

"No."

"Well, why not?" Emma snapped. "Norwell should at least tell us if he's alive. I mean, he's been gone a whole day.

Shouldn't she be demanding ransom or something? You don't think she hurt him, do you?"

"Em, settle down." Kelly got up and hugged her daughter. "The police are looking for him. There's nothing else we can do."

"What if there is?"

"Like what?"

Emma glanced at DJ. In a small voice, she said, "Mom, can we talk outside?"

"Of course."

"You sure it's safe to leave the house?" DJ asked.

"We'll be fine." Kelly led Emma into the backyard. Overhead, the sun was bright and hot. A cop patrolled along the garden. Good thing Rick had moved E2's body into the basement fridge.

Kelly lowered her voice. "What's up, Em?"

Emma squirmed. Guilt tinted her expression. "Um, so... I remember who dared me to enter the Murder House."

Kelly grabbed her daughter's shoulders. "Who?"

"A guy from my class." Emma averted her eyes. "Mike Manganaro."

"Mango? Why didn't you tell me sooner?"

"Sorry, I didn't think it was a big deal."

"Not a big deal?" Kelly said, raising her voice. "If I had known, I might've been able to stop Norwell from torching my house. Now Aiden and Zach don't have a home or toys or clothes or anything because you were, what, embarrassed to admit you liked this guy?"

"Ew, no. I don't like him."

"Then why didn't you tell me about him?"

Emma twisted free. "Look, Mom, it doesn't matter. You know now. Isn't that enough?"

"*Enough?*" Kelly snapped. "Unbelievable, Em. I should

drive you down to Byron Street and show you what's left of my house. It's a charred husk—all because you kept this from me. Oh, but when your father's in danger, that's when you chime in."

Emma shrank away. "Sorry."

"Why don't you go tell Aiden and Zach how sorry you are? Explain to them why they're staying in your guest room. Explain to them why I can't pick up any of their toys."

"Mom, I..." Emma lowered her head. "I don't know what else to say."

"Then stop talking and get your shoes on."

"Huh? Why?"

"Because we're going after Mango."

51

Mango didn't answer the doorbell. His dog barked like a shotgun, but the door remained shut. According to Emma, the Mazda in the driveway belonged to Mango, and school had let out hours ago, so he should've been home. Emma offered to message him, but Kelly wanted to catch him at least somewhat off guard.

Frustrated, she started pounding the door with her fist. When her hand throbbed from the blows, she stepped back and surveyed the property. Emma and K2 tried coaxing her back to the minivan, but Kelly stormed into the backyard. There she saw an attached enclosed patio. She put her foot through the screen door and let herself in. The house's rear door was unlocked, and she stepped into a cramped kitchen with sticky floors. Emma and K2 followed.

"Mom, are you crazy?" Emma said, tugging on her arm. "This is burglary."

"Actually, it's breaking and entering," K2 said.

"I don't care what it is," Kelly said, storming toward the hallway.

The dog growled and bounded after her. Teeth flashed within its snout as it snarled toward the kitchen. She retreated toward the patio until Emma placated the animal in a sing-songy voice. Her daughter rubbed its dark brown fur before guiding the dog toward the living room.

With the dog subdued, Kelly and K2 searched every room before reentering the kitchen. Kelly opened a door beside the fridge and discovered wooden steps leading to the basement. The lights were off. The air was redolent with the skunky odor of freshly smoked weed.

"Smell that?" Kelly said.

K2 nodded. "Maybe he fell asleep."

Kelly flicked on a light and headed downstairs. The basement's near corner was cluttered with stacked canned goods, bottled water, and a dusty treadmill. At the far end was a massive flatscreen TV and enough video game consoles to make her kids squeal.

Facing the TV was a cracked and peeling pleather couch. Mango lay on it, his head denting the armrest. Dark shaggy hair covered his eyes; a pair of noise-canceling headphones hugged his ears. The idiot didn't have a clue she was here.

Kelly turned to K2. "Guard the staircase."

K2 hesitated. "Why?"

"So he can't escape."

Kelly stepped around the couch, careful not to bump the coffee table, which was covered with glass bongs, beer cans, and Dorito bags. When she turned to face Mango she noticed something concealed under a burger wrapper.

It resembled the diary from the attic.

She grabbed it. The first entry was dated January 13, 1934—months before anything in the other diary. The opening line read, "I must write this down before I stop believing it." She flipped pages, skimming through messy handwriting for anything that looked important.

Beside her, Mango stirred. He pushed his hair away from his face. His bloodshot eyes located her. Blinked with confusion.

Before he could react, Kelly reached for the top of his head. She bumped the headband of his headphones, then seized a fistful of his hair. With one swift motion, she yanked upward. His scalp offered sharp resistance, but still she lifted him halfway to the ceiling.

His startled cries echoed through the basement. Like a fish on a line, he flopped and floundered. His lighter clattered to the floor. His feet frantically kicked at the seat cushions.

"What the fuck?" He swatted her arm. "Let go!"

She lifted the diary. "Where'd you find this?"

"I-I didn't."

"So it magically appeared on your coffee table?"

"Someone gave it to me."

"Who?"

"Some lady."

"Norwell?" Kelly lifted him higher—they were face-to-face. Her forearm ached, but she was too furious to care. "Was it Nancy Norwell?"

"I didn't get her name."

"Did she tell you to send Emma into the Murder House?"

He hesitated. "No."

"Don't lie to me. Emma said you dared her to enter that house."

"It was a joke, okay? Everyone was afraid of that house

except Em. I thought it'd be funny if she went in, so I dared her."

"When did you last see Norwell—the old lady?"

"I don't know. The other day."

"What day?"

"Uh, Thursday."

That was the night E2 was murdered. "Where'd you see Norwell on Thursday?"

He hesitated. "She came here."

"What did she want?"

"She told me to take Emma to a party."

"And you listened?"

"I had to." Fear was written across his face. "The lady said she'd hurt my dad."

"When you took Emma to the frat house, did you race her?"

His eyes widened like targets.

"So you were the one." This part surprised Kelly. She had marched down here for answers on how E2 came into existence, not how E2 died. But it seemed Mango was more involved than expected. "What happened after your race?"

"Nothing."

Kelly's arm trembled with effort. She strained to keep her grip. "Whoever wins the race can make the loser do anything. What'd you make her do?"

He looked away. "Nothing."

"Tell me before I rip your scalp off."

"Nothing happened!"

Kelly dropped the diary. With her free hand, she tugged a clump of his hair.

"Shit! Okay—stop!" Mango caught his breath. "Please stop."

"What'd you make Emma do?"

"Nothing... Just a blowjob."

"*Just* a blowjob?" Kelly felt herself boiling. "Did I hear you correctly? Are you saying that ordering my daughter to... Are you downplaying what you forced her to do?"

"It was part of the game. I never forced her."

"Oh, you're a real fucking prince." Kelly dropped him to the floor. He landed hard between the couch and coffee table. Before he could sit upright, she pressed her foot against his crotch. "Later that night Emma was in the woods. Somebody hurt her. Was it you?"

"No—get your foot off me."

"Who took Emma into the woods? Norwell?"

He hesitated. "I don't know."

She stomped him. The impact created a clapping sound, followed by a boyish grunt. He coughed a series of nasty wet hacks before rolling onto his chest and vomiting. The puddle spread around his head like a grimy halo. He moaned.

"Where is Norwell now?"

He panted.

"Where is she?"

He kept panting.

Kelly squatted beside him. The moment she reached for his hair, he whirled around and shoved her onto her back.

Before she knew it, he'd pounced on her, dropping his knee onto her stomach. The impact knocked the wind out of her. She tried pushing him away, but something struck her face.

She saw a flash of light. Warm, stinging pain followed. Her ears rang. Her vision doubled. She realized he'd punched her.

Then another punch rocked her skull.

Light burst beneath her eyelids. Her cheek exploded with heat.

She twisted away. Tried to catch her breath but gagged on the skunky air. She considered grabbing the revolver from her purse, but another blow struck the side of her head. A hot, stabbing sensation arrived as her earring punctured the skin behind her jawbone. Heat zinged through her head.

He drew back his fist for another blow.

Then Kelly's shout echoed through the basement. But it hadn't come from her mouth.

Red hair whipped past as K2 tackled Mango against the coffee table. The wooden legs screeched against the concrete floor. One of the bongs tumbled and shattered. K2 flattened him against the ground and pinned a forearm against his throat. Mango grunted.

Head pounding, Kelly picked herself up and crawled there.

"Where's Norwell?" she asked in a dazed tone.

"Ugh..." He struggled beneath K2. "I don't know."

Kelly's patience was gone. Plus her head was throbbing and her ear was on fire. When she reached up to check it, her fingers came away bloody. The blood gave her an idea.

She dug through Mango's hair and found his ear buried within. A silver hoop earring hung from the lobe. She hooked her index finger through the earring. "Tell me what happened to Emma outside the frat house. Did you strangle her?"

"Huh? No!"

She tugged on his earring. He groaned as his fleshy lobe stretched like a piece of gum. She pressed her free hand against his cheek to keep him pinned. "Answer me."

"Let me go—I didn't do shit!"

She ripped the earring upward. There came a snapping sensation, like a popped rubber band.

He roared. Blood spurted from his torn earlobe. He spazzed against the concrete.

Somewhere above, the dog barked. The basement door opened and slammed.

Emma yelled, "Mom!"

"Stay upstairs!" Kelly shouted, her voice drowned out by Mango's screams. She slapped his mouth to quiet him then twisted his head to find his other earring.

Footsteps rapped against the concrete. "Jesus, Mom!"

"Enough!" K2 said, grabbing Kelly's elbow. "Emma doesn't need to see this."

Kelly shrugged free. Then, with her forearm barring Mango's neck, she curled her finger through his earring. "Why are you protecting Norwell?"

"I'm not." He panted. "Really, I'm not."

She gave a slight tug. "Then tell me what you're hiding."

"Not hiding anything—I'm serious."

"So am I." She tightened her grip. "You just blew your last chance."

The moment she drew her arm back, he screeched, "Closet! Closet!"

"Which closet?" she asked.

"Under the stairs."

She turned her head and noticed a wooden door beneath the basement staircase, not far from where Emma was standing.

"Em, open that door."

Inside, two people wrapped in duct tape were crammed between the closet walls, stacked on top of each other. Kelly craned her neck for a better look and flinched when she recognized the one on the bottom. Her friend Brittney.

"Britt? How did you—"

Before Kelly could finish, the top prisoner twisted into view.

A frightened kid who looked exactly like Mango.

52

The sight reminded Kelly of when she'd imprisoned K2 in the backyard shed. At the time she had considered herself cautious, but looking back, it had been a cynical, inhumane move. And what she saw in the basement closet was even worse. Brittney and the other Mango sat soaked in sweat. Duct tape wrapped them from ankle to throat like silver mummies. Their mouths were taped shut, and they smelled like diapers in desperate need of changing.

Emma gawked in disbelief. Her hand slid from the doorknob.

Kelly peeled herself off the hostile Mango and approached the one trapped in the cubby. He mumbled behind his gag. Brittney was squashed beneath him, her eyes blinking desperately. Within this cramped space, they slumped, their backs curled against one wall and their feet mashed against the other. Though both looked eager to crawl out, they couldn't move.

Kelly knelt beside the doorway and reached for the kid's ankles. He moaned in pain. "Em, help me move him."

"That's...Mango."

"I know, honey. Let's get him out so he can stretch his legs."

Emma reached behind his shoulders. Kelly slid an arm under his knees. On three, they lifted him. The closet was so narrow that Kelly had to tilt him upright to fit him through the doorway. She almost freed him when K2 abruptly howled in pain.

"Kay, what's wrong?" Kelly said.

Footfalls hammered against concrete. The other Mango dashed toward the stairs.

"Stop him!" Kelly shouted. "Hurry!"

K2 stumbled after him, clutching her forehead.

Kelly dragged the prisoner onto the couch and joined the chase. The moment she reached the bottom step, barking thundered above.

"Shit!" K2 shouted. She yanked the basement door shut. The dog thrashed against it. She turned heel and hurried downstairs. Blood trickled from her forehead in a thick red line.

"Hold up—you're bleeding," Kelly said, brushing hair away from the wound. She grabbed a tissue from her pocket and applied pressure. "What happened?"

"Mango cut me with a piece of his bong. Asshole."

Kelly checked the damage. Despite the bleeding, it didn't look deep. "You okay?"

"Yeah," K2 said woozily, "but he got away."

"He won't get far. Not without his double." Kelly grabbed another tissue. "Here. Keep pressure on it."

"Does it look bad?"

"You'll survive. By the way, thanks for the save earlier."

"He had no business hitting you."

The dog slammed into the door, barking nonstop.

"C'mon," Kelly said. "Let's help Britt."

They lifted Brittney out of the closet and lowered her onto her back. As her knees unbent, she moaned. Kelly peeled tape from her friend's lips. A slimy rag was stuffed between her teeth. Kelly gently removed it. "Britt, what happened?"

All Brittney could manage was a faint cough. Her lips were dry, her tongue shriveled. Kelly grabbed a water bottle from the coffee table, then cradled Brittney's head and helped her drink. Meanwhile, K2 ripped tape from Brittney's torso, revealing her work apron as well as nasty bruises along her arms. The stench of sweat and stale urine filled the air.

Over by the couch, Emma peeled tape from Mango's mouth. He spat out a rag, then coughed like an old lawnmower. He looked desperate to say something, but his voice was a raspy, inaudible whisper. Emma offered him water. His lips shifted hungrily toward the bottle.

"Thanks," he said after three gulps.

Kelly lowered Brittney's trembling head to the floor and crawled to Mango. "How're you feeling?"

"Unngh." He writhed against the seat cushions. "You Emma's mom?"

"Yeah. How long were you trapped?"

"Since Labor Day."

"*That long?*" K2 said. She held Brittney's hand. "Britt, what about you?"

Brittney struggled to speak.

"It was hell," Mango said as Emma unraveled more tape. "My legs kept turning to ice, and they only fed me once a day."

"They?" Kelly asked.

"My double and my dad's double."

"Your dad too? So you both went into that attic?"

"Yeah." He gulped more water. "Last month, after that house burned, I walked my dog past it every morning. Then one day a brand-new house appeared. I couldn't believe it, and I didn't think anyone else would either, so I went inside and took pictures. Then I climbed up to the attic and..." He made a slicing gesture with his hand. "When I woke up, I freaked out and called my dad. He thought I was crazy till he found me in the attic."

"Is that when he got split?" Kelly asked.

"Yeah. Then we both had doubles. My dad didn't trust them, so he tried locking them in the closet. But they got the upper hand and stuffed us in there."

Emma shuddered. "Where's your dad now?"

"No idea. When Brittney came along, they took him away. Haven't seen him since."

Emma finished unwrapping his legs. They were covered in faint bruises—likely the result of tight tape and cramped positioning. The kid had indeed been through hell.

"Think you'll be able to walk?" Kelly asked. "Once your dog settles down, we can—"

Her phone buzzed. Rick. His timing worried her. The other Mango—M2—had escaped only minutes ago.

She stepped away from the couch. "Rick, where've you been?"

"Wait, that's Dad?" Emma rushed over. "Put him on speaker!"

Reluctantly, Kelly switched to speaker.

Rick's staticky voice came through. "Kell? You there?"

"I'm here too, Dad!" Emma's voice cracked. "Are you okay?"

"Fine, chief. What about you?"

"Things have been crazy," Emma said, her voice thick with emotion. "Where are you?"

"Long story," he said. "Your mother there?"

"Right here," Kelly said. "Rick, you lied to me about Norwell."

"I had to. Got a green envelope in the mail yesterday. The note said I could save Emma if I followed instructions."

"What instructions?"

"I can't tell you."

Kelly swallowed hard. "Then why'd you call?"

"Because I figured out who wrote that diary."

"Really? I just found another diary." She glanced at the book she'd dropped near the coffee table. "An older one."

"Well, the one you gave me was written by a guy named Walter Webber. He owned a clothing store in Las Vegas and moonlighted as a stage magician. Before then, he lived in Separtown, Arizona—that place I told you about on the phone yesterday. He's the only one who survived the blaze. And, get this—when the authorities found him the next morning, he kept repeating the words 'We burn.'"

She gasped. "That's what was carved into the attic safe."

"I know. And it had a number lock, right? The code might be the date of the fire. March 4, 1934. Try entering 3-4-34."

"Hold on," Kelly said, nervously clutching the phone. "You expect me to march up to that attic? After you just said Norwell's blackmailing you?"

"Kell, I'm limited in how I can help. This is the best I can do."

"How do I know this isn't a trap?"

He sighed. "Do you want to discuss this in person? Where are you right now?"

Kelly rubbed her throat. Though she wanted to believe

him, the timing of the call and the urgency of his request were red flags. She couldn't risk it.

"Bye, Rick."

She hung up.

"Mom, what the hell?" Emma moaned. "What if he's telling the truth?"

"Forget it. We'll find another way." Then she realized the basement was silent. No more barking came from upstairs. Seemed the dog had settled.

Kelly approached Mango. "Let's get you and Brittney to a hospital."

He coughed. "Are you sure? What if they ask what happened to me?"

"Play dumb. And pretend you didn't see your captor's face." Kelly offered him more water. "Before we go, do you know where your dad's double might be?"

He shook his head.

"What would your dad normally be doing on a Tuesday?"

"Working. He's a mailman."

Her scalp tingled. "Where's his postal route?"

"Down near Scranton."

The news jolted her. Her mind flashed with the image of a mail truck pulling up to her house. The arrival time of those green envelopes had been spot-on this past week. His father's double must've had a hand in delivering them.

"What's your dad's name?" she asked.

"James."

Kelly faced K2. "Call the post office and ask about James Manganaro. Say that he misdelivered a package and see if they can tell us where he is."

K2 took out her phone. "On it."

Kelly tensed at the thought of confronting the man.

Finding his mail truck should be easy, but there was no telling how dangerous he was—especially if M2 warned him. She needed to hurry.

"Em, let's walk Mango upstairs. We'll drop him off at the ER, then go after James."

Together, Kelly and Emma hefted Mango to his feet. He was reluctant to walk, but with some help, he climbed the stairs. Upon reaching the kitchen, Emma lowered him into a chair and dabbed a damp paper towel along his grimy face. Anyone with functioning eyes could see she was crazy about him.

Kelly returned to the basement, where K2 was thumbing away at her phone.

"Any luck reaching the post office?" Kelly asked.

"Yeah." K2 still sounded woozy. "They helped me narrow it down. I'm checking a map now."

"Worry about that once we're on the road." Kelly spotted the diary on the floor. "Grab that book and help me with Britt."

Together, Kelly and K2 hoisted Brittney to her feet. Their friend was in obvious pain. Every step was a struggle. Upon reaching the stairs, she finally spoke.

"Keh...Kelly?"

"Hey, Britt." Kelly kept a firm hold on her friend's upper arm. "You're gonna be okay."

Brittney winced as she climbed another step. "Didn't know you had a twin sister."

"Long story. How'd you end up here?"

Brittney shut her eyes and sobbed. "All I remember is the bathroom."

"What bathroom?"

"At the liquor store. I was on the toilet, then the lights went out. I tried to leave the stall, but...that's all I remember."

Kelly's chest tightened. She hated the thought of her friend being attacked in total darkness. She dreaded one thing even more. "Britt, how are your legs?"

"They hurt."

"But are they cold? Colder than the rest of your body?"

"A little, yeah."

Kelly and K2 exchanged a knowing glance. Rather than burdening Brittney with the details, Kelly reassured her friend and guided her upstairs.

Once everyone was in the kitchen, Emma led Mango toward the front door. Kelly and K2 followed, Brittney in tow. The dog started barking, but thankfully Emma had lured the animal into a bedroom and shut the door. That made for a hassle-free exit.

They reached the van. Emma opened the passenger door for Mango. He stretched one foot inside before someone yelled, "Stop!"

Kelly turned her head. Standing beside the garage was the other Mango. M2. He held a polished black pistol. His blood-smeared face held a hostile glare.

"Real simple," M2 said. "If he gets in the van, I start shooting."

Rick's revolver was in Kelly's purse. Problem was, her purse was zipped shut. She couldn't imagine drawing her weapon before M2 fired.

"What do you want?" she said.

"The prisoners." He gestured with his gun. "Rest of you, lay flat on the ground and put your hands on your heads. You move, you bleed."

Kelly knelt then lowered her chest to the blacktop, her eyes facing him. Emma and K2 did the same.

M2 popped the trunk of his Mazda. He shoved Mango

inside and did the same with Brittney. Then he slammed the lid shut.

"Anybody follows me, these two die."

M2 slid behind the wheel and started the motor.

The car left the driveway and sped toward the Murder House.

"We have to help them," Emma said, tugging Kelly to her feet. "Hurry, Mom!"

Kelly didn't argue. She climbed behind the wheel of the minivan while Emma and K2 rushed to their seats. The afternoon sky had turned cloudy, and a faint drizzle tapped the windshield. Kelly raced down Red Trail Road and swerved into the Murder House driveway. Her tires battled uphill until she reached the front lawn.

Mango's car idled beside the front porch. The trunk was open and empty.

Kelly reached into her purse and gripped the revolver. She turned to Emma in the passenger seat. "If anyone shows up, run."

"I'm going with you, Mom."

"Absolutely not."

Emma unlocked her door.

Kelly snatched her elbow. "*Emma.*"

"But you need backup." Emma's voice cracked. "I told you, I wanna be a cop like Dad. I wanna protect people. You can't go alone, Mom."

"Then I'll take K2."

"But she looks ready to pass out."

In the backseat K2 leaned against the window, her forehead smeared with blood.

"See?" Emma said. "She can't go."

"Don't tell me what I can't do." K2 opened her door. Stumbled outside. Took three steps before she wobbled sideways. "Shit."

Kelly dashed into the drizzle to help her.

At first K2 protested, but her words trailed off. She blinked. Her eyes held no focus.

Panic struck Kelly. She guided K2 to the backseat again. The woman twitched with awareness. They met each other's eyes. Then Kelly pressed another tissue to K2's wound. "Hold this in place. I'll be right back. Emma, if you want to protect me, protect K2. Stay with her and make sure she doesn't lose any more blood."

Emma sighed. "Okay. Careful, Mom."

Kelly approached the house holding her gun in one hand and an LED flashlight in the other. The front door hung open. Ominous shadows waited inside. She crossed the threshold and snapped the light toward the living room, down the hall, and then up the staircase. No sign that anyone was lurking.

Glass crunched underfoot as she climbed the stairs. The second-floor hallway was empty. Inside the master bedroom, the soiled mattress lay at the foot of the attic ladder.

From above came arguing voices. One she recognized as Mango's, the other as Brittney's. Both sounded strong—nothing like the two raspy prisoners from the basement. Which confirmed that Brittney had a double, just as Kelly had feared.

A third voice—a commanding, masculine one—interrupted the argument. "Will you two shut up and quit wasting time? Do what the note says. Brittney, you go first."

"Me?"

"Hurry up—stand over the dividing line."

Kelly killed her flashlight and climbed into the sweltering attic. Yellow lantern light glowed near the center. She carefully navigated the maze-like setup, sneaking toward the light. Mannequin parts rattled underfoot, but the argument went on—a sure sign that the doubles hadn't heard her.

Then came two honks of a car horn.

Was that a warning from Emma? Had something gone wrong outside?

"Shit, somebody's here," M2 said. "I don't get it—I warned them not to follow me."

"Apparently you weren't convincing enough," the commanding voice said. "Brittney, enough hesitating. Kill her already."

"No!" the original Brittney croaked. "Please don't—"

Her words abruptly stopped, replaced by a gagging sound and thrashing plastic.

Kelly rushed past a wall of cardboard boxes. Pointing her revolver ahead, she turned the corner and spotted the yellow lantern blazing on a cluttered table. Dust particles floated within the light.

Below, along the polished dividing line, Brittney lay in her work uniform. Her double—wearing a trim athletic outfit—straddled her, both hands gripping the original's throat. M2 seized Brittney's arms so she couldn't resist. Another guy in a sweaty gray tank top, presumably James Manganaro, stood nearby, his back turned to Kelly. He clutched a sheet of wrinkled paper—a diary page, she guessed.

"Everyone, stop!" Kelly raised her weapon. "Leave her alone!"

James turned around. His gray crew cut matched his tank top. His upper arms sported tattoos. Familiar ones. Kelly recognized him—this was the guy who'd slept with K2 the other night. He must've targeted her while she was out barhopping, probably to scout out Kelly's house before Norwell torched the place. Whatever his motive, Kelly could worry about that later. Right now she needed to help her friend.

"Let her go!" She pointed her gun at Brittney's double. "Now, or I'll—"

James reached under his shirt and pulled out a pistol. He pointed it at Kelly, who ducked behind a wooden cabinet. She cursed herself for hesitating before she gripped her revolver with both hands, trying to decide her next move.

Over by the attic entrance came the sound of clicking plastic—someone was rushing through the maze. Another double perhaps. Kelly tensed and aimed toward the noise.

From behind a dusty grandfather clock, Emma emerged. "Mom!"

Kelly lowered her weapon and exhaled a big gust of breath. "Stay back!"

Before Emma could respond, a bizarre scream tore through the attic, subhuman, a glass-on-glass screech so harsh it threw Kelly off balance.

Brittney?

Kelly popped out from behind the cabinet.

What she saw left her and everyone else stunned.

The original Brittney twitched along the floor, still in a chokehold. As if zapped by electricity, her limbs jutted outward until her body resembled a five-pointed star. A skillet-like hiss sounded as the sweat along her forehead sizzled. Steam rose from her face, arms, and legs. It poured from under her uniform. A cloud formed in the attic, dimming the light and boiling the dusty air.

Heat thrust toward Kelly, scalding exposed flesh. She reached to cover her face, hearing the others howl in agony. Plastic crunched as everyone staggered and stumbled.

Then the temperature abruptly dropped. Fire to ice. The haze thinned, revealing a bizarrely different Brittney on the floor. The skin along her arms and legs was a smooth, milky gray—identical to the mannequins. Kelly noticed the hair on Brittney's head had vanished. Her eyes, nose, and cheeks were glossy. Gray. Plastic.

Kelly gawked in disbelief.

Emma frantically gripped her shoulder. "Wh-what happened?"

The others remained silent, staring at the newest mannequin.

Brittney's double stood and patted her waistline. She traced her fingers from stomach to face, then pinched her cheeks. She snorted with glee. "It worked. I feel whole again. No disconnect—none at all. It actually worked!"

"What worked?" Kelly snapped. "Turn her back!"

Brittney's double faced M2. "Try it. It's just like that note said."

M2 tugged the pistol free from James' hand and moved toward the rear wall. There, along the dividing line, lay two unconscious people. One was the original Mango, the other presumably the original James. Without hesitation, M2 touched the barrel to Mango's skull.

"No!" Emma shouted.

A gunshot roared. Steam erupted from Mango's body, clouding the air, spreading another wave of hellish heat.

Kelly threw her arms around Emma in a protective net. She clutched her daughter, growling through the burning vapor. After it passed, another gunshot boomed. More steam erupted. This time, she presumed, James was the victim.

As the air cleared, plastic rattled in the direction of the attic entrance. Kelly pointed her flashlight toward the sound. The beam bounced back from a tall mirror, momentarily blinding her. She blinked to clear her vision and noticed the blurred silhouette of a woman marching toward her. Shadowy hair fluttered along her shoulders. In her right hand was a pistol.

It was pointed at Kelly.

Norwell, Kelly thought. *She's here.*

The silhouette approached, less blurry now. The pistol stretched toward Kelly and Emma as light flickered across the woman's face.

At that moment, Kelly realized she was wrong.

It wasn't Norwell. It was K2.

54

Maternal instinct kicked in. Kelly yanked her daughter sideways, out of the line of fire. Plastic clattered noisily around her feet before K2's pistol thundered. Maybe Kelly should've returned fire, but she was already scrambling in the opposite direction.

Gripping Emma's elbow, she charged past the lantern toward the other doubles. They seemed to be preparing to stop her. James—rather, J2—stretched down for his pistol on the floor. Before he reached it, Kelly fired a round into his shoulder.

He collapsed. His son rushed to help him. Brittney's double ducked beneath a table.

That cleared a lane. Kelly barged through and rounded the corner, dragging her screaming daughter toward the dark end of the attic. They stumbled past filing cabinets and then reached the area where they'd found the diary.

Kelly squatted behind a cluttered table and rapidly breathed in and out. Plastic rattled in the distance. Her ears rang after the gunfire, and she couldn't determine whether people were chasing her or fleeing the attic.

She readied her weapon.

"Mom, look." Emma pointed at the safe. The door hung open. Apparently someone had entered the code.

"Anything inside?" Kelly asked.

Emma hurried over. "No. Who opened it?"

"Probably that older guy—James."

"But how'd he get the code? Did my dad tell him?"

Kelly felt her stomach sink. "If anyone told him, it was K2. She must've texted him while we were at Mango's house."

"Wait, she knows James?"

"Yeah." Kelly thought back to K2 and James asleep on the air mattress. At the time, Kelly had considered it a reckless hookup. Now, however, it appeared the pair had been working together, apparently scheming to replace their originals.

Her thoughts were disturbed by the nearby sound of thrashing plastic. Someone was approaching.

She nudged her daughter toward the front of the building. "Em, get outta here."

"What about you?"

"I'll create a distraction."

"But K2 tried to kill you," Emma said. "If I distract her, you can shoot her when she's not looking."

"Honey, I can't risk you getting hurt."

"But, Mom—"

"Shhh!" Kelly grabbed Emma's shoulder and steered her toward the front of the building. "Head back to the entrance. I'll make noise so nobody follows you. Now go!"

With reluctance, Emma crept toward the front wall.

Kelly rushed in the opposite direction. She ducked behind a filing cabinet and kept her focus on the lantern light. A shadow shifted. She aimed toward the light and fired.

Come on, Em. Get out, get out, get ou—

Return fire boomed.

Kelly flattened herself against the wall. Three more shots sounded, each louder than the last. The shooter was closing in. Kelly fired blindly. Following the loud report was silence.

Then a voice called out.

"Poor thing," K2 said. "You're in quite a tizz, aren't you?"

Kelly peered around the filing cabinet. She couldn't see anyone, and her ringing ears couldn't pinpoint where K2's voice was coming from.

"Stop shooting," Kelly snapped. "If you kill me, you'll end up in the hospital like Emma."

"Emma's not in the hospital," K2 said. "She's been home for two days. And she seems to be adjusting to her new diet."

Kelly tensed. Her double wasn't supposed to know about that. "What diet?"

"You know exactly which one," K2 said. "And for some reason, you never told me about it. Why is that?"

Kelly struggled to determine K2's location. Though it had been years since Rick took her to a shooting range, she knew she could hit K2 if the woman revealed herself. Kelly needed to keep this conversation rolling until then.

"I didn't tell you," Kelly said, "because I didn't want to scare you."

"Scare me?" K2 scoffed. "I'm not the one who gets scared. You are. That's why you locked me up. I terrify you because I'm the person you're afraid to be. I'm the one who can make the hard choices and do what's best for us."

"Oh, yeah? If you're so wonderful, why are you trying to kill me?"

"You saw what happened with my friends just now, didn't you? That locked safe had the answers we needed. Inside was the diary's missing page. It said that when someone is split in two, both halves will suffer until one ends the other's life along the dividing line."

"For all we know," Kelly said, trying to buy time, "that missing page could've been planted by Norwell."

"It wasn't."

"But she orchestrated this whole thing."

K2 laughed. "No she didn't. Want to know the truth? Last week James and I found her in the cemetery. We captured her, then framed her as the arsonist who torched your house. James lit her on fire to make it look like a suicide."

"What? Why?"

"Because she deserved it. All those nagging letters, year after year—they poisoned us, ruined us. I did what you should've done a long time ago. I put a stop to her."

"Wait. If Norwell was captured last week, who sent the most recent letters?"

"I did."

"No. That's impossible. That was her handwriting on the envelopes."

"I forced her at gunpoint to write them."

"But... No... I got a letter while you were still trapped in this attic."

"Are you sure I was trapped?" K2 said. "The night we were chopped in half, I woke up long before you did. James found me and explained the situation. He warned me that you would turn against me, just as his other half had turned against him. At first, I wanted to believe otherwise—I wanted to believe in you, Kelly. But in case I was wrong, I needed insurance. Those letters were my insurance. If you remember, the first one said to bring your*selves* to Anissa's grave. My hope was that the letter would bring us together. I wanted us to be friends, teammates. I thought we could accomplish amazing things together—I thought we could rebuild our lives. Instead you repeatedly let me down. Then I learned you were hiding the truth about Emma's new diet. That was the final straw. That was when I realized you and I can't coexist."

Kelly trembled. The revelations were hitting so fast that she was struggling to keep up. But one thing stood out. One thing needed to be answered for. "If Norwell wasn't involved, then does that mean...you killed E2?"

K2 remained silent.

"It was *you*?" Kelly snapped. "You killed her? You strangled our daughter?"

"I had to." K2 grew quieter. "E2 was reckless. She tried to—"

Kelly aimed in the direction of K2's voice and pulled the trigger. The revolver roared and punched her palm. Beneath one of the tables, a shadow shifted. She fired at it until her ammo ran out. A cry of agony followed the last shot.

Kelly approached the dividing line in a crouch and listened for sounds. When she stepped into the light, she spotted K2's legs twitching behind a toppled stack of boxes.

Before Kelly could take another step, K2 sat up and fired.

Kelly fell backward, landing awkwardly on her hip. Pain zinged up her side.

Ahead, K2 entered the light, her eyes as cold and

emotionless as a mannequin's. She squared her shoulders, lifted her pistol, and aimed for Kelly's chest.

Kelly shut her eyes, bracing for the worst.

Instead, a hard *thunk* sounded, followed by a growl from K2.

Opening her eyes, Kelly watched a thick plastic leg strike the woman's shoulder. The impact sent her crashing against a cabinet.

Into the light stepped Emma, wearing a fierce expression. She swung the plastic leg like a baseball bat, connecting with K2's elbow. When the leg snapped apart after a blow, Emma seized the woman's gun hand. They faced each other, wrestling over the weapon, spinning in violent, uncoordinated circles. Emma growled and steered the barrel toward K2's neck.

Kelly grabbed a plastic leg from the floor and stormed toward them.

K2 drove her foot into Emma's shin. That knocked Emma off balance, allowing K2 to twist the gun away. The barrel wavered between the floor and ceiling and everywhere in between. It targeted Kelly, targeted Emma, targeted K2, then disappeared from sight.

Rushing forward, Kelly lifted the plastic leg overhead. She swung at K2 with all her might.

That instant, the muzzle flashed.

A deafening report sounded.

Blood sprayed the air.

Kelly completed the swing, smashing K2's forearm. K2 lost her grip on the pistol. The weapon hit the floor. So did Emma. Everything happened so fast that Kelly wasn't sure what *had* happened.

She located the pistol and pointed it at K2, squeezing the trigger twice.

K2 fled behind a wall of cardboard boxes, and both shots missed.

Kelly didn't give chase. She turned to check on Emma. Her daughter lay on her back clutching her stomach. Clutching a bleeding wound.

55

Blood darkened Emma's pale gray hoodie. The pouch turned black beneath her trembling red fingers. Her eyes wide and confused, she stared at the ceiling. Took a series of hitching breaths. Then a weak sob escaped her mouth.

Kelly moaned and pressed her hand against the wound. Emma twisted and growled. The blood flowed hot as Kelly applied pressure. Never had she felt so powerless. She was no doctor. She didn't know first aid. She needed to call 911.

"Honey, look at me."

Emma sobbed. Sweat and tears rolled down her face.

"I know it hurts," Kelly said, guiding Emma's hands toward the wound, "but you have to keep pressure on it."

Emma whimpered.

Kelly wiped her bloody hands on her pants and grabbed her phone from her pocket. She dialed 911. The call didn't go through.

Shit.

"You'll be all right," she said, trying to convince herself as well as Emma. "Let's get you outta here. I'm gonna pull you to your feet, okay?" She stood behind her daughter and positioned her hands beneath Emma's armpits. "On three. One, two, three."

The moment Kelly tried lifting her, Emma groaned in protest.

Kelly let go.

Might need to carry her, she thought. *Lifting her is asking a lot, though. Nowadays, I can barely lift Aiden or Zach.*

Kelly curled one arm around Emma's back and the other under her knees. Straining, Kelly pulled her daughter toward her chest. With Emma now cradled against her, Kelly set her feet and stood upright. Adrenaline surged through her arms, shoulders, and back. It was like those miraculous stories about mothers lifting flipped cars to save endangered children. Never had she been so strong.

And never had her senses been so sharp. She expertly navigated the dark attic, her mind's eye guiding her along the correct path. She felt unstoppable—until she reached the attic entrance. She realized she'd have to dangle Emma through the opening into the bedroom below.

"Em, you with me?"

Emma moaned, supporting her stomach.

Kelly settled her in a sitting position on the floor beside the opening. She rotated Emma so the girl's legs hung over the edge. "I'll lower you down. Then you need to grab the ladder."

With Emma's butt resting along the edge, Kelly reached under her daughter's armpits and lifted her forward. The angle was awkward and uncomfortable, but Kelly managed to lower her through the opening.

Emma gasped when her shoes knocked against the

ladder. At Kelly's urging, Emma grabbed the railing and set her feet on a rung.

Kelly exhaled with relief. Heat burst through her shoulders, followed by tingling coolness.

"Em, can you climb down?"

Emma whimpered.

"Okay, okay," Kelly said breathlessly. "Don't move. I'm coming down."

With the grace of a novice gymnast, Kelly stretched a leg past Emma's shoulder and stepped onto the ladder, which creaked under their combined weight. Kelly descended, maneuvering around her daughter until she reached the bedroom floor. Then she peeled Emma off the ladder and hoisted her into her arms.

Ice prickled between Kelly's toes. Though uncomfortable, the sensation meant K2 had fled the vicinity, which would allow for a clean escape. Finally, something was going right.

Kelly carried Emma outside into the afternoon drizzle. Mango's car was gone. The van remained parked. She opened the passenger door and buckled Emma into the front seat. Then Kelly motored down the driveway, making a fierce turn onto Red Trail Road.

Emma slumped against the window, clutching her belly. The bloodstain looked worse in daylight. Kelly feared the bullet might've shattered bones and ricocheted through various organs—those worst-case scenarios she often heard about on TV.

"Hang on. Hospital's ten minutes away. Maybe even less if I run some lights."

Kelly swerved through the next turn. The van threatened to flip, but its tires stayed true to the road. When she reached a straightaway, she dialed Rick.

He picked up on the first ring. "What, Kell?"

"I'm heading to the hospital. Listen, don't panic, but Emma got shot."

"*Shot?* Where was she hit?"

"Stomach area."

"Shit. Put pressure on it."

"I can't, I'm driving." Kelly blared her horn as she approached a red light. She held her breath as she streaked through the intersection. "I'll have her at the hospital in five minutes."

"I'll call and notify them," he said. "Emma, you there?"

"Dad…" she croaked.

"Love you, chief." His voice cracked. "Keep pressure on the wound and keep fighting. I'll see you soon."

"Wait, Rick," Kelly said. "One more thing. Norwell didn't send those green envelopes."

"Really? Then who did?"

"It was K2. I'll explain later. But be careful if she reaches out to you."

Kelly ended the call before she ran a stop sign. Gaining speed, she wove into the oncoming lane to pass a few cars. Ahead lay the sprawling hospital campus. Pine trees and white buildings waited atop green hills in the distance.

She glanced at Emma, whose bloodstained hands had fallen into her lap.

Kelly squeezed one of them. "Hey—keep pressure on that wound."

Emma's hand remained limp.

"Em, wake up!" Kelly squeezed harder. She dug her nails into Emma's palm.

Emma didn't respond. She gazed ahead.

Kelly waved a hand before her eyes.

The girl didn't blink.

No... No.

A horn blared ahead. Kelly looked up and realized she was still in the oncoming lane. A flashing ambulance was barreling toward her.

Without thinking, she swerved back into the right lane. She overcorrected, sending the van over the shoulder and into the nearby woods.

She stabbed the brake. Her weight was thrown forward against the steering wheel. The vehicle screeched but maintained its speed, rumbling over uneven terrain.

A thick pine tree appeared.

She cut the wheel left.

Dodged one tree.

And hurtled toward another.

In the moment before impact, Kelly glanced at Emma. Her daughter's head rested against the dashboard. Her eyes were open. There was no fear in those eyes. No concern. Nothing at all.

The impact shook the van with a loud *crunch*.

Kelly was slammed forward.

And all went black.

56

Though Kelly couldn't open her crusty eyes, she recognized she was in the hospital. The chemical smell, the chilly air, and the chatter of nurses were unmistakable. Strangely, she didn't remember arriving. *I must've fallen asleep while visiting Emma.*

Kelly reached up and rubbed the crust from her eyelids. She pried them apart and stared ahead at a white blur. Two blinks brought the room into focus. On her right was a computer monitor. To her left, an IV pole. When she glanced down, she saw bedsheets. Her legs were underneath them.

Gently, she twisted her neck and spotted DJ sitting in a chair, his eyes closed. His hands were folded beneath his chin, and his bearded lips whispered what she assumed were prayers.

"Hey," she croaked. Her throat was dry as dust. "DJ!"

He leaped upright. His bright blue eyes widened. "Kelly? How you feeling?"

"Thirsty."

He offered her a plastic cup filled with water. She drank slowly and said, "Why am I here?"

He gestured to her head. "Concussion."

She touched her forehead. It ached. "How'd I get a concussion?"

"Accident," he said in a choked voice. "On the drive here."

"When?"

"Two days ago."

"Two days ago?" She glanced at her legs, trying to remember. Images blipped within her mind. She recalled driving Emma somewhere. Her daughter had been leaning against the passenger window. She'd been clutching her stomach. Clutching at blood.

Kelly sat bolt upright. More memories poured in. Brittney and the Manganaros turning to plastic. K2 and Emma fighting over a pistol. The gunshot. The wound. The escape.

She grabbed her husband's arm. "Where's Emma?"

He looked away. Scratched at his beard.

"DJ, where is she?"

He headed for the door. "Let me get Rick. I'll let him explain."

She yelled after her husband, but it was no use. She sat there, a bundle of worries. Then Rick trudged in. His face appeared to have aged a decade. His eyes were bloodshot, and there were puffy bags beneath them. He dropped into the chair that DJ had vacated. "You okay, Kell?"

"Forget about me—how's Emma?"

Rick swallowed hard and made an odd clicking sound. "Not sure how to answer that."

"Where is she?"

"Couple rooms down from here." He sighed. "They put her in a coma."

Kelly hesitated. "So she's alive?"

"Yeah, but she's getting worse. Having problems with her legs. The doctors think it's a post-surgery complication, but you and I know what the real problem is."

"Have you tried feeding her one of E2's fingers?"

"Emma's in a coma. She can't eat or drink anything."

"Oh, God... There's gotta be a way. Think, Rick."

"What do you want me to do? Pour E2's remains into an IV bag?"

"I don't know. We gotta do something." Kelly felt as though she were floating through another dimension. This couldn't be real. There had to be a way to help Emma. "How long till she's out of the coma?"

"They don't know. Could be weeks."

"Are you sure?"

"*Am I sure?*" he snapped. "*Am I sure?*" He launched to his feet and grabbed her bed rail, white knuckled, enraged. He looked ready to flip her hospital bed. Then a sob escaped. He turned away. Stared into an empty corner.

Kelly bit her lip.

"I'm going back to her room," he said, rubbing his eyes. "Listen, you'll be contacted by the police soon. At the time of your car accident, you had a pistol in your pocket that was registered to James Manganaro. James and his son Mike went missing after Emma got shot, so they're the suspects, but the police will question you. When they do, don't tell them anything. Mention your concussion and say your memory's foggy. Got it?"

She could barely think straight, but she nodded.

He stepped out of the room.

She wanted to follow him, but her legs were numb. She

groaned at the thought of Emma and how unfair the situation was. Why couldn't Kelly be the one in the coma? After all, she deserved it. All her lies, secrets, and bad decisions had led to Brittney being suffocated and Emma getting shot. Had Kelly done things differently, Emma would be visiting her now instead of lying comatose down the hall.

A uniformed officer stepped in and interrupted her chaotic thoughts. He asked if she could handle questions, but she insisted her head was foggy. He said he'd stop by later.

DJ returned to her bedside and took her hand. He updated her on the twins, who were staying with Olivia. When he offered to bring them to visit, Kelly declined.

"I don't want them seeing me like this," she said.

"But they miss you," he said, tucking a strand of hair behind her ear. "Zach especially. He asks about you every five minutes. Babe, I know you're hurting over Emma, but—"

"You don't understand. Emma shouldn't be here. She stepped in to protect me—that bullet was meant for me, not her." She pointed to her abdomen. "Me. I deserved that bullet."

"Don't say that."

"It's true, though."

He scratched behind his neck. "Can I ask you something? Who was it that tried to shoot you? Rick mentioned the Manganaros. Was it them?"

"No."

"Then who?"

Kelly swallowed hard. Met his eyes. "K2."

"K2? Who's that?"

She went quiet. After a deep breath, she said, "Let me start from the beginning."

57

After Kelly finished her story, DJ went silent. He sat like a block of stone. His bright blue eyes stared at the opposite wall, as if the past week's events were being projected onto it. Aside from an occasional cough, he made no noise. He kept shaking his head, as if refusing to believe everything he'd heard.

"Hon," she said, "are you okay?"

He wobbled to his feet and left without a word.

Kelly lay in her ICU bed, her legs cold and twitchy. She began to worry. She couldn't just lie here. Not while K2 was out there planning another move. There was no telling what the woman would do next. Attack Kelly in the hospital? Kidnap her? Drag her into the attic and kill her?

And if K2 did erase Kelly from this world, what would happen to Aiden and Zach? Surely K2 wouldn't stick around to raise them. K2 wanted out. She would abandon them. And the boys would have to endure that abandonment.

Kelly clenched the bedsheet with both fists. She couldn't let that happen. But what could she do? She was stuck in a hospital bed with frosty legs. Then again, cold legs were like a map to K2. All Kelly needed was someone to drive her around until her legs warmed up.

She slapped the Nurse Call button and requested that someone find DJ. Hopefully he was done processing everything. Now, more than ever, she needed his help.

Shortly after sundown, a nurse knocked on the doorframe. "Someone here to see you."

Kelly sat up hoping to see her husband. Instead, a skinny girl with ghostly blonde hair entered wearing a pink zip hoodie. The girl wiggled her fingers in a timid wave.

"Cassie?" Kelly felt her chest tighten. On Saturday, she had confronted Cassie outside Mango's house. The girl had spent all afternoon with Mango's double, and there was no telling how involved she was now. She herself could be a double.

Kelly swatted the Nurse Call button.

Cassie didn't seem fazed. Hands in her pockets, the girl tiptoed over to the chair beside the bed and sat. She lowered her head and sighed. Platinum hair curtained her face. When she pushed it back, her eyes were moist with tears. "Hiya, Mrs. O'Neill."

Kelly shifted toward the opposite side of the bed. "Get the hell out of here."

Cassie flinched. "Is now a bad time?"

"Who sent you?"

"Sent me?"

"Was it Mango?"

"Huh? No. I came here to talk about...about Emma." Cassie burst into big anguished sobs. They didn't sound fake.

A nurse raced in. "What's wrong?"

Kelly hesitated. "Nothing. False alarm."

The nurse left.

Kelly leaned toward Cassie. "What'd you want to talk about?"

Cassie dabbed her eyes with her sleeve. "I... You saw Emma's rope, right?"

Rope? At first Kelly didn't understand. Then she remembered Emma's good luck charm. "Yeah, I've seen it. Is it a friendship bracelet?"

"Not exactly." Cassie unzipped her purse and grabbed a matching piece of rope. She pulled her chair closer, squeaking against the floor tiles. "I promised Emma I wouldn't tell people about this. I hope she won't be mad."

Kelly nodded. "It's okay."

Tugging her hair into a sloppy ponytail, Cassie said, "Last year, me and Em were like the biggest losers ever. I met her in the bathroom one day while I was crying on the toilet. She was sobbing over in the next stall because her friends hated her. I guess during the quarantine, everybody kinda shunned her. Nobody liked me either because my family just moved here from Indiana. I didn't know anybody, and everything sucked, but that day in the bathroom was like, a moment, y'know?"

Kelly smiled sadly.

"First time we hung out, I invited her to my house," Cassie said. "We watched movies and drank my mom's wine coolers. It was fun. We started hanging out more until her dad decided I was a 'bad influence' because Emma came home one night smelling of weed. I don't even smoke weed, but whatever." She snorted. "Anyway, we still hung out. Our lives were, like, crazy similar. We both got bad acne around the same time, got dumped by our boyfriends the same week, got humiliated on social media—it was like a misery competition. 'Whose life can suck the most?'" She picked at the frayed multicolored rope. "Then one day I gave her the idea."

Kelly leaned closer. "What idea?"

Cassie struggled for a deep breath. "In Emma's garage, we found these jump ropes lying around. Kiddie ropes. We cut off the handles and threw the ropes over the rafters and tied them in place. Then we stood on chairs, and..." She gestured toward her throat. "We put the ropes around our necks."

Kelly's eyes widened. Her insides turned hot.

"We were supposed to hop off our chairs at the same time," Cassie said, trembling. "I was too scared. Em, though... She didn't hesitate. But the moment she went, I saw it in her eyes. She didn't want to die. Neither did I, so I undid my rope and cut hers down. And that was it. Afterward, we swore we'd never do it again. We each kept a piece of rope to remember the promise we made."

Kelly lowered her eyelids and flinched at the thought of a noose digging into Emma's neck. It was like discovering E2's body all over again.

Warm tears trickled down Kelly's cheeks.

Now it made sense why Emma had spent the past year distancing herself from Kelly. After the jump rope incident, Emma would've wrestled with countless emotions. Brutal, ugly emotions. The kind that forced you to take a hard, unforgiving look at yourself. There was no telling what went through her mind then, but at some point she must've sought to blame someone other than herself.

She blamed me, Kelly thought. *Her silence, her avoidance, her grudge—it all started last year. She probably blamed me because I swallowed all those sleeping pills when she was little. I tried to take my life, and she saw me on the floor. That was her first encounter with death. She had to carry that horrible image with her until she hooked that rope around her neck. All because of me.*

Sobs erupted from Kelly's mouth.

"I'm sorry," Cassie said, sniffling. "If Emma hadn't been my friend, she never would've gone inside that stupid Murder House."

"Don't blame yourself," Kelly said, wiping her eyes. "It's not your fault."

"Yes it is. I'm the reason she was able to enter in the first place."

Kelly blinked. "What do you mean?"

"Em figured out why certain people can go inside the house while others can't."

"Really? Why?"

"Everyone was afraid of the place," Cassie said. "Everyone except Emma and Mango. And everybody knows that Mango tried to kill himself after his mom died."

"Wait," Kelly said, leaning closer. "So you're saying that the Murder House..."

Cassie nodded gravely. "It only lets you in if you've attempted suicide."

58

Cassie sat still, staring at the torn piece of rope.

The truth about the Murder House left Kelly trembling in her hospital bed. She had spent the majority of her adult life trying to forget her suicide attempt. She never discussed it with her husband or her closest friends; whenever Rick or Emma brought it up, she changed the subject and hid behind small talk.

But the Murder House knew. It had accepted her near-fatal overdose as an entry ticket. Then the attic split her into two identical people with clashing mentalities. Throughout this past week, Kelly had wondered what exactly K2 was. Now it was clear: K2 represented who Kelly had been prior to her suicide attempt—a reckless thrill-seeking college girl who craved competition and thrived on manipulating others. That version of Kelly took no interest in adult values like stability, responsibility, and family.

Now came the question of what K2's next move would be. Obviously the woman intended to lure Kelly back to that attic and kill her, but how would K2 pressure her into going?

What would I do in her position? Probably kidnap Aiden and Zach.

The thought startled her. When she looked up, she spotted DJ waiting outside her room. He seemed to be giving her and Cassie space. Kelly nudged the girl's arm. "Thanks for telling me about Emma. Can I have a minute with my husband?"

"Oh, sure." Cassie stood up and left the room without a backward glance.

DJ wandered inside, still shaken, silent.

"Hon," she said, "I need a ride to Rick's house."

"But...you're in the hospital."

"Not anymore." Kelly smacked the Nurse Call button.

A trauma specialist insisted she stay, but Kelly signed an AMA and climbed out of bed on cold, shaky legs. DJ helped her change into a long-sleeve t-shirt and jeans. She zipped her jacket and took careful steps as he escorted her to the parking lot.

Under a moonlit sky, she dropped into the passenger seat of his car. It smelled like chicken nuggets despite the three air fresheners hanging from the rearview mirror. DJ started the engine and drove to Rick's. A police cruiser was parked across the street. The officer waved as DJ pulled into the driveway. Surprisingly, Kelly's minivan sat in front of the garage. The front fender was crumpled, but the rest seemed to have survived the crash. DJ parked beside it and asked if Kelly needed help getting out.

She massaged her thighs. Both legs were frosty but warmer than they'd been at the hospital. Shaking off the chills, she marched up the sidewalk toward the front porch. Her legs continued thawing. That meant K2 was getting closer. The woman might be heading here now.

DJ unlocked the front door with a borrowed key. Light

spilled onto the porch. The sound of Olivia's voice echoed faintly from the second floor. She was yelling at Aiden.

Kelly hurried upstairs and down the hall toward the guest room. There were two beds inside. On the closer one lay Aiden, kicking his feet like a fussy baby who needed his diaper changed. Olivia sat on the mattress trying to wrangle his legs. Zach, meanwhile, cowered behind a rocking chair in the corner of the room.

Olivia glanced over her shoulder. "Kelly? They discharged you already?"

Kelly rushed to Aiden's bedside. "Are the twins okay?"

"They were asleep until fifteen minutes ago." Olivia pinned one leg to the mattress. The other kicked wildly. "Quick, grab his other leg."

Kelly snatched his ankle and wrestled it down to the mattress. "Settle down, bugger. You should be asleep."

"I'm not tired!" Aiden snapped.

"Hey!" DJ said, appearing in the doorway. "Don't talk to your mother like that. She just left the hospital."

"But I'm not tired!"

Kelly felt a tug on the back of her shirt. Now Zach wanted her attention.

"Mommy." He sounded raspy. "I'm sick."

"With what? Sore throat?"

"No, I'm cold."

Kelly released Aiden's leg and touched the back of her hand to Zach's forehead. "Olivia, do you have a thermometer?"

"Already took their temps," Olivia said. "They're both normal."

"I'm freezing," Zach said, rubbing his arms. "Aiden said he's cold too."

"Crawl under the covers," Kelly said, steering him

toward the other bed. "That way you won't..." Her voice trailed off when she noticed Aiden's arms lying at his sides. Lying motionless.

Kelly faced Olivia. "When did they start complaining about being cold?"

"About fifteen minutes ago."

Around the time Kelly had left the hospital.

"Boys," she said with mounting dread. "Where do you feel cold?"

Aiden's mouth opened in a jagged, mechanical way. His tongue floated, unable to form words.

She turned to Zach. "Where do you feel cold?"

"Up here." He patted his head. "Freezing."

Then Zach's arms fell at his sides. He stumbled sideways and collapsed onto the carpet, his legs jerking wildly.

Kelly dropped to her knees beside him. Her heartbeat thrashed in her ears while she stroked his hair, trying to comfort him. As she stared into his terrified eyes, she wondered about the boys' upper bodies. Was it possible they had entered the Murder House? Could K2 have abducted them and taken them into the attic?

"Kelly, what's wrong with him?" DJ asked.

"We should take them to a doctor," Olivia said.

"No. Keep them here." Kelly lifted Zach onto the bed and draped the covers over him. She grabbed DJ's arm and tugged him toward the hall. "C'mon, I need you to drive."

"Where are you going?" Olivia asked.

"I'll explain when we get back."

59

Kelly sat in the passenger seat, her eyes closed, her mind focused on the temperature of her legs. DJ drove. He asked questions she didn't answer; she said they'd find their kids faster if he allowed her to concentrate. That quieted him. Now the only noise came from the steady hum of the motor as they shot down I-81 South.

With each passing mile, warmth spread from her thighs toward her feet. Soon her toes wiggled without hindrance. Farther down the highway, a faint chill returned.

"Turn back," she said, opening her eyes. A motorcycle's red taillight glowed ahead. "Where are we?"

"Just drove past the Scranton Expressway," he said. "I'll get off at the next exit." The steering wheel squeaked as DJ clutched it tighter. "I can't believe this. How'd she kidnap the twins? The police have been watching Rick's house for days."

"She must've snuck in at some point."

"When?"

"I don't know. But if you and Rick were at the ICU, then Olivia was all alone watching the kids. She had to sleep at some point. That's probably when K2 grabbed them."

"Then why didn't their bodies freeze up sooner?"

An explanation came to mind. One that made Kelly's stomach float. "They were probably kept near Rick's house until recently."

"Kept where? In someone's home? In the woods?"

"I don't even want to think about it."

"Swear to God," he said, increasing speed, "when we find her, I'm running her over with this fucking van."

"You can't. Remember, I need to kill her myself—and it has to be done in that attic."

DJ stared ahead at the road. Bloodlust filled his bespectacled eyes. After getting off at the next exit, he blazed past a Wendy's and veered onto Pittston Ave, which led them into Scranton.

Evening traffic was thin around Courthouse Square. As they maneuvered through the city, Kelly's toes warmed to their normal temperature. K2 was near. Very near. Kelly was wondering about potential hiding places when her phone buzzed. It was her father.

She answered in a panic. "Dad? Are you okay?"

"Me? I'm always okay." He chuckled. "How about you? Heard you left the hospital."

"Yeah. Who told you?"

"Monica."

"Monica? You mean your bartender?"

"Yeah, she just called. Said you threw her out so you could work the counter."

Kelly hesitated. "But I didn't—"

"No need to explain yourself," he said. "Some people get through rough times by staying busy. If it helps, you can bartend to your heart's content."

Kelly now realized the implication of Monica's dismissal. "Actually, Dad, I might leave the bar soon."

"Oh yeah? How soon?"

"Let me call you back once I figure this out."

"Don't overdo it, my dear. I'm sure Emma will be fine."

"Thanks." She hung up and turned to DJ. "K2's working at the bar."

"Your father's bar? Out in public? Why?"

"She wants to be found. Probably wants to talk. Negotiate."

"*Negotiate?*" He spat the word as he turned onto Adams Ave. "Here's a better idea. We'll go inside and drag her out the door."

"Forget it. She has our kids, remember? I need to figure out where she's keeping them."

"Then let's force the information out of her."

"Won't work. If we grab her, she'll make a scene. Trust me, I know how she thinks."

He grumbled under his breath.

"Drop me off at the bar," she said, clenching her fists. "I'll handle this."

60

The O'Brother Bar glowed along the dark street corner like a neon illusion. Behind the front windows, the evening crowd drank and dined. Every seat in the building was taken. Tables, booths, barstools, everything. Patrons gobbled sandwiches and ESPN analysis while Springsteen's "Dancing in the Dark" pumped from the sound system. The up-tempo riffs filled the street as Kelly's minivan approached the entrance.

Finding nowhere to park, DJ dropped off Kelly at the corner. Before exiting the vehicle, she checked the glove compartment for something to conceal her identity. A shaggy white beanie hid under the vehicle registration. That and an old pair of aviators were the best disguise she could muster.

"You sure about this?" DJ asked as she stepped onto the sidewalk. "Want me to go with you?"

"Stay in the van. Circle the block and be ready in case I need to leave."

He scratched his beard. "I don't like this."

"Me neither. But K2 chose a public place for a reason. She wants to talk."

"What're you gonna say to her?"

"That she's not leaving till she tells me where the kids are."

Kelly slammed the door. Her body brimmed with adrenaline as she marched into the noisy glass chamber that was her father's bar. Behind the counter, striking red hair whipped by as K2 spun away from the cash register. In a low-cut tank top she leaned forward, flaunting cleavage as she handed two crisp bills to a customer.

The moment Kelly met K2's eyes, everything around her faded—colors dulled to gray, noise thinned to silence, the smell of frying potatoes vanished, and even her muscle aches dissipated.

A customer vacated a corner stool. Kelly climbed onto it like it was her destiny.

K2 strolled over, face glistening with sweat. She planted her fists on her hips. "Can I get you anything?"

"Two things," Kelly said. "You know exactly which two."

"How about a drink instead?" K2 grabbed a bottle of Jameson and filled two shot glasses. She knocked back her whiskey and slapped the glass down.

Kelly badly needed a drink, but she pushed the glass aside. She resisted the urge to smash the bottle against her double's arrogant face. "Where are my kids?"

"Somewhere," K2 said. "By the way, nice hat."

"How about I take it off? Let everyone know our secret?"

"You won't."

Kelly set her hat on the counter.

K2 frowned. Crossed her arms.

Kelly did the same.

"So..." K2 said. "How's Emma?"

Kelly slammed her fist on the counter. "Don't you dare ask."

Her outburst startled nearby patrons. Eyeballs swung toward her. She reached for her hat.

K2 laughed it off and said, "Anybody need refills? No? Okay then." She returned her attention to Kelly. Leaned in. "I don't blame you for being furious, but you have to understand that I never meant to hurt Emma."

"Bullshit," Kelly said, trying to keep her voice down. "You pulled the trigger."

"I panicked. It was an accident."

"Just like when you strangled E2? Was that also an accident?"

K2 sighed. "No, that was intentional."

"Everything was." Kelly removed her sunglasses and glared into K2's eyes. "Sending those letters, torching my house, snatching my kids—all of it was intentional." She grabbed the whiskey bottle and lifted it like a weapon.

K2 forced a laugh to draw attention. The social pressure subdued Kelly, and K2 wrestled the bottle away. When the guys returned their focus to their beers, K2 wiped her brow. "Believe it or not, I *am* sorry about Emma. Now, E2...that's another story. As I was trying to explain back in the attic, E2 was reckless. She tried to kill you."

"Me?"

"Yeah. You. She wanted to kill you in order to test a theory."

"What theory?"

K2 leaned in and lowered her voice. "You know how you've been wanting to get rid of me? James Manganaro felt the same way about his double. He had a theory that if he killed his double, everything would go back to normal—no more icy legs, no more freaky situation, nothing. But when he tried to kill J2, he hesitated. Then J2 also hesitated. Do you know why?"

"Because it was too risky."

"Exactly. You'd be a fool to kill your other half without knowing what the outcome would be. That's why you need a guinea pig. And that's how Emma got involved."

Kelly narrowed her eyes. "The Manganaros targeted her?"

"Not exactly. Last week M2 led a bunch of his class-mates to the Murder House. Emma was the only one willing to enter. Then, of course, she became split. But he didn't want to kill her—he liked her too much. Instead, he welcomed E2 aboard, and the next day *she* decided who the real guinea pig should be."

"Me?"

K2 nodded. "Remember when Emma asked us to find her purse? That was E2's idea. She convinced Emma to lure us into the attic. Once you and I became split, the Manga-naros were supposed to strangle you, but they lost their nerve. Instead, they woke me and explained the situation. After I settled down, I told them about Norwell—about how she would make a perfect target. They liked the idea, and they welcomed me into the tribe, which pissed E2 off even more. From that point on, she became fixated on killing you."

Kelly squinted in disbelief. "But why?"

"Because Emma has hated us since she was little. You like to pretend her grudge was a recent development, but it started long before she gave us the silent treatment. Remem-ber, we were absent throughout her childhood. Rick and her grandparents raised her while we went to school, soccer, and parties. Then we swallowed those sleeping pills; that hurt Emma as much as it hurt us. She never got over it, and later on, she blamed us for things like divorcing Rick and replacing her with Aiden and Zach."

"I never replaced her."

"That's not how Emma saw it. And unlike Emma Number 1, E2 couldn't control her anger. She would've killed you if you'd gone inside her house on Thursday morning."

"Thursday? You mean the morning I met E2 in the garden? But she was thrilled to see me. She even asked me to...watch TV with her." Kelly felt her throat constrict. She faced a grim realization. That morning, E2 had practically begged her to go inside. At the time it seemed like girlish enthusiasm, but now it reeked of an ulterior motive. "No... She wouldn't..."

K2 wiped the counter. "That night, you and Emma searched the attic. When E2 learned where you were headed, she begged the Manganaros to drive her there so she could kill you. Soon as I heard about her plan, I told them to drive her to the frat party. I'd been planning to head there anyway so I could take pictures for a future green envelope."

"Wait, how'd you even get to the frat house?" Kelly asked. "You were locked in the shed."

"Did you forget the spare key behind the garage? The Manganaros released me. Anyway, when I found E2 at the frat house, I confronted her. She ran into the woods, and I chased her. Then she tried to slash my throat."

Kelly laughed humorlessly. "No. You're lying."

K2 grabbed her purse from beneath the counter. She unzipped the side pouch and pulled out a blue keyring. Attached to it were a bottle of pepper spray and a pocketknife. "She sprayed me blind before she tried to kill me. Remember that cut on my arm?" K2 lifted her sleeve, revealing the scab. "I didn't get this from the shed. I got it from her knife. Had she been more accurate, she would've cut my throat. Instead...I grabbed hers."

Kelly clenched both fists atop the counter. "You monster."

"Monster? If I had let her go, she would've killed me. And you."

"You expect me to believe that? After everything you put me through?"

"What about everything *you* put *me* through?" K2 said. "Locking me up, punching me in the mouth, plotting to kill me and eat me... And let's not forget all those years you buried me in the back of your mind."

"That's where you belong."

"I belong out here." She spread her arms in display. "Unfortunately, you and I can't peacefully coexist out here. Only one of us can win."

"Win? Is that what you want?" Kelly leaned closer. "Tell you what, if you want a competition, give me my kids back. Then we'll fight to the death in that attic."

"Love the idea, but there's one little problem. How do I know you won't double-cross me? I'd hate to hand over the kids and then have Rick send in a SWAT team."

"I don't want Rick involved," Kelly said. "I want to fight one-on-one."

"Ooo, I like that attitude," K2 said with an intrigued smile. "Y'know, it's a shame... Ever since Anissa Norwell took our goalie spot, it's like your spirit died. But now that competitive fire seems to be roaring again."

"This isn't a joke. If you don't give me my kids, I'll kill you. Inside that attic or out."

"Just like twelve years ago, huh?"

"This time, it'll be different. This time, I'll strangle you like you strangled Emma."

K2 shrugged, evidently unimpressed.

Kelly glared at her. "Tell me where my kids are."

"Only if you visit our favorite attic alone without backup."

"Not happening."

"Then you're stuck with Aiden and Zach's doubles."

There had to be another way. Something K2 wasn't expecting. Something that appealed to K2's competitive nature. Something that could give Kelly a chance to win.

"We're at a stalemate," Kelly said, "which makes sense, considering we're equals."

"Equals?" K2 scowled. "I'd argue otherwise."

Kelly was hoping to hear that. "You really think you're better than me?"

"I don't think it," K2 said. "I am."

"Then prove it."

"How?"

"Here's an idea. Winner-take-all scenario. You and I will head to the frat house tonight. We'll do a race."

K2's eyebrows rose at this idea. It was no surprise—she was ultracompetitive. She represented the period of Kelly's life when she lived and died between the extremes of winning and losing. A challenge like this was irresistible.

"Interesting," K2 said. "And we would follow the standard racing rules?"

"Right," Kelly said. "Winner gets to demand anything of the loser."

K2 gave her an appraising glance. "How do we guarantee that the winner gets what she demands? If I win, you could easily run away."

"And if I win, you could easily lie about where my kids are."

"Here's what I can do." K2 grabbed a notepad from beneath the counter. "I'll write down their locations. Then I'll let you choose either one. We'll drive there now, grab one boy, then head for the frat house. If you win, you can take both kids home."

"How do I know your friends won't interfere?"

"I could say the same about Rick and DJ." K2 took out her phone. "I suggest we power off our phones. No outside communication till the race ends. And I saw DJ drive you here, so have him park the van and take an Uber back to Rick's. Once he's gone, you and I will drive the van to Aiden or Zach's location."

"How do I know those locations aren't traps?"

"Because I'm certain I'll win that race," K2 said with steely eyes. "Hell, I'm stunned you even suggested it. For fuck's sake, you were in the hospital two hours ago."

That comment struck Kelly like a claw hammer. The desperate energy that had been fueling her suddenly dissipated. She became aware of the aches and bruises that peppered her legs, lower back, and chest. Running sore wouldn't be easy. Even if her adrenaline showed up full flow, she would be competing against a healthier, well-rested version of herself. No wonder K2 was so quick to accept the offer.

K2 tapped her pen against the notepad. "Do we have a deal?"

Under the circumstances, it was the best deal Kelly could hope for. Aside from her recent injuries, her only major concern was K2's friends. The other doubles might be watching the bar, waiting to follow at a moment's notice. They might also be waiting at either location K2 was about to jot down. Everything could be a sham, and a million things could go wrong, but Kelly was banking on K2's competitive nature—the one thing about her former self she could trust. This was a chance worth taking.

Kelly eyed the notepad. "Write down those addresses."

61

Both addresses were soccer fields. The closer one was the site of Emma's final game. The other was the boys' practice field. According to K2, Aiden and Zach were waiting inside concession stands at each location. "Waiting" sounded like a euphemism, and Kelly feared her sons were taped and gagged in total darkness. It took all her resolve to keep her hands steady on the wheel while driving toward the practice field.

"I swear," Kelly said, glancing at K2 in the passenger seat, "if Aiden or Zach suffered so much as a paper cut, I'll rip your face off."

"Settle down. I didn't harm them."

"You chopped them in half."

"They were asleep when I carried them into the attic. They didn't feel anything."

Kelly squeezed the wheel tighter, pretending it was K2's throat. A growl escaped through gritted teeth.

"Ever wonder where it comes from?" K2 asked. "All your self-hate?"

"Doesn't matter."

"It started when we got knocked up in high school. We weren't ready for Emma, and whether you'll admit it or not, back then we resented her for being born. She wasn't a daughter, she was an obligation. A chore. Baggage. The first time we held her in our arms, we felt nothing. No maternal high, no pride, no joy—only despair because we knew our own story had been cut short."

Kelly clenched her jaw. She was too furious to reply.

K2 leaned back against the headrest. "Before we even collected our high school diploma, the whole world expected us to marry Rick and be Mother of the Year. But you know what hurt the most? It was that we had to settle for Caraway's soccer team while we had the legs for UCLA. I mean, we could've been something. We could've been anything other than what we are now."

"And what are we now?"

K2 sighed. "A shattered woman who's been at war with herself for nearly half her life. And that war has hurt everyone around us. You can blame me for E2's death, but remember... You chose to hate me—hate us—long before you stepped into that Murder House. Every choice you made in life brought us to this point."

Kelly shook her head. "You're insane. Completely insane."

"So are you."

Reaching the practice field, Kelly flicked on her high beams. Shadows surrounded the area. The place looked empty, but to be safe she drove a loop around the field before pulling up behind the concession stand. Her headlights gleamed off the back door.

"It's unlocked," K2 said. "Want to grab Aiden yourself, or should I bring him out?"

"You." Kelly refused to exit the van. If this turned out to be a trap, she would step on the gas and leave.

K2 disappeared inside the concession stand. Moments later she stepped out into the glare of the headlights. Cradled in her arms was a sobbing Aiden. Kelly's jaw dropped at the sight. He was shaken and scared, his face redder than his hair. Duct tape covered his mouth, upper body, and ankles.

Against her best judgment, Kelly stormed out of the van after her son. "Get that tape off him!"

"It has to stay on."

"The hell it does."

"Our deal was we'd pick him up," K2 said. "The tape stays until the race is over."

Kelly clenched both fists. "Take it off."

"If I do, he could run and alert someone."

Kelly melted when Aiden's frightened eyes bored into her. "At least let me talk to him. I won't race unless he says he's okay."

K2 lowered his feet to the grass. "You have one minute."

Kelly gently peeled the tape from his lips. Aiden flinched and released a muffled cough. She noticed something in his mouth—a saliva-soaked rag. She pried it free, and he coughed again. She hugged him, fixed his hair, and dabbed his eyes with her sleeve. Poor kid smelled of sweat and urine. "Bugger, you okay?"

"My legs are cold." Tears slid down his cheeks. "I'm really scared. Aunt Kay took us. She said it was top secret. That you'd die if we didn't go with her."

"Oh, sweetheart." She massaged his stiff little shoulders. What disturbed her most was that Aiden had believed K2 could be trusted. He believed it because Kelly had lied to him—lied to her own kids to spare herself some embarrassment. She hated to imagine what they'd gone through in that attic.

"I wanna go home," he said.

"Listen, can you be brave until we find your brother?"

"Mom, I really wanna go home."

She brushed his hair. "I know, but—"

"Time's up," K2 said, slapping the hood. "Replace his gag and put him in the trunk. Then we'll change into our gym clothes. You better give me your best tonight."

Kelly intended to. No way was she losing that race. Not after this.

62

S hadows smothered the frat house's backyard. If not for the orange firelight flickering along the forest edge, the racetrack would've been a dark mystery.

Minutes earlier, Kelly and K2 had scouted the dirt trail in preparation for their race. The path was a straight shot until the midway point, where two referees with lanterns stood drinking beers. From there, the trail snaked between scattered oaks and bushes, weaving senselessly until it reached the steep hill upon which the all-important banana box waited.

Each curve in the trail offered a potential shortcut, provided Kelly was willing to dash through tangled shrubs. Tree roots, fallen branches, and other woodsy debris might trip her, but it was a gamble she would have to take. Of course, K2 was likely thinking the same thing, so this race would ultimately come down to who wanted it more.

The smell of burning firewood invigorated Kelly. She stretched her legs behind the starting line. K2 did the same. They were waiting for their gorilla masks. Once those arrived, they would strip down to their underwear and literally run for their lives. The last time Kelly had run one of these races, she ended up destroying Anissa Norwell's life. Tonight she intended to win for the right reasons.

A bottle shattered near the campfire. Laughter followed. More than a dozen people had gathered around the flames, everyone sporting long-haired wigs and bandanas for tonight's 80s theme. A remix of Rick James' "Super Freak" boomed from inside the house. K2 clapped excitedly and started dancing.

Go right ahead, Kelly thought. *Burn all the energy you want.*

"Kay, who you racing?" a drunk guy asked.

"Why, none other than my twin sister Kelly," K2 said.

Kelly felt the cold stares studying her. It had been forever since she competed in front of spectators. She could sense the fire pit crowd wishing she would lose. In the past, she fed off such animosity, but now it dropped snowballs into her gut.

"Kay, when you win," the drunk guy said, "will you let us watch what you make her do?"

K2 threw her head back, laughing. "Nope, sorry. But at least you guys get the honor of wrapping the loser in duct tape." That was one adjustment Kelly and K2 agreed to. To ensure the winner got what they were promised, the loser would be taped up and hauled out to the van.

Cheers sounded as two guys in baggy blue tracksuits exited the house. Each carried a gorilla mask in both hands as though it were a sacred idol.

Kelly's mask reeked of cheap rubber and stale sweat. She knew from experience that once she started running, the mask would bounce around, making it hard to see. She fastened her hair into a bun before putting on the mask.

The hair-bun somewhat stabilized it. Hopefully that would give her an advantage over K2, who opted for a ponytail.

Someone tapped Kelly's shoulder.

"Yo," a guy said. "Want me to hang onto your stuff?"

"What stuff?"

"Your clothes."

"Oh. Right." Kelly's cheeks burned beneath the mask.

"C'mon," K2 said, dropping her shorts around her ankles. "Tear those clothes off."

Kelly retreated into the shadows for privacy. She set her mask aside and stripped down to her underwear. Before arriving here, she had changed into her gym clothes, which included her sports bra. It was more supportive and less revealing, but she still drew sleazy stares as she approached the starting line. With trembling hands, she adjusted her mask and focused on the trail ahead.

Beside her, K2 bounced in place.

Kelly took a deep breath of rubbery air. Anissa's memory haunted her, but she shoved her guilt aside and set her feet.

I'm winning this. Doesn't matter what happened back then. I'm winning this. I have to.

For Aiden.

For Zach.

For Emma.

A referee holding a whistle approached. He sipped from a can of Coors Light. "You both know the rules, right? First to grab a banana and come back is the winner. Loser has to do whatever the winner says." He glanced at Kelly's feet. Then at K2's. "Who requested the race?"

"I did," Kelly said.

"Cool. Race'll start once you finish getting undressed."

"*Excuse me?* I'm down to my underwear."

"I can see that. But your shoes are on."

"So? Girls always keep their shoes on."

"Actually, whoever requests the race has to take them off."

Kelly gawked at K2. "No way. If I can't wear shoes, neither can you."

"Sure I can," K2 said, cracking her neck. "Back at the bar, we agreed to race according to the rules. That was the deal."

"But you'll have a huge advantage."

"Not my fault. You're the one who asked me to race."

Kelly stomped the dirt. "This is bullshit."

"Listen," the referee said. "Either take off your shoes or forfeit."

The crowd roared its disapproval.

Two guys holding duct tape approached.

With a pounding heart, Kelly undid the laces on each shoe. She slipped them off, then peeled away her socks. She pressed her bare feet against the hard dirt. Debris itched the arch of her foot. A rock nipped between her toes. She hadn't taken a single step, yet her feet were already uncomfortable.

Staring into the woods, she realized she didn't like her chances. But she recalled an old saying from her high school soccer coach: *You don't have to like your chances. But you do have to take them.*

"Ready?" the referee asked, grabbing his whistle. "On your marks..."

Kelly and K2 took their positions.

"Get set..."

They adjusted their masks.

The whistle blew.

63

Kelly sprinted off. Her feet slapped hard dirt. The first few footfalls landed with prickly discomfort, but once she found traction, she burst ahead. Her knees pistoned, her arms pumped at her sides. The pregame nerves in her chest vanished as she entered the woods. The race was on.

The campfire crew roared. For a moment she believed they were lauding her toughness. Then K2 stormed ahead in a pair of Asics trail runners. The footwear advantage was monumental; Kelly continually lost ground as they approached the midway point.

There, two frat boys with lanterns sipped from beer bottles and watched K2 increase her lead to about three car lengths. To Kelly's dismay, K2 used her shortcut strategy and dashed between the bushes along each curve in the trail. All Kelly could do was follow and shake off the pain after stepping on pointed rocks.

I've stepped on worse, she told herself. *Stepped on Aiden's Legos before. Those hurt a thousand times worse.*

Kelly pumped her knees faster. The exertion made her

mask bounce like crazy. It was hard enough to see by moon-light, and the added handicap of bouncing plastic eyeholes made it nearly impossible.

While that thought crossed her mind, K2 cried out, "Fuck!"

The profanity was followed by the *thump-thump* of her tumbling body.

Kelly steadied her mask and spotted K2 on the ground. The woman pushed herself up and kicked to her feet.

As they approached the next turn, Kelly pulled even. She kept adjusting her mask, which threw off her stride but kept her upright. After hopping a tree root, her heel came down hard on a broken branch. The impact jolted her leg. She growled between her teeth, gaining speed until she broke into a full sprint, pacing with K2.

They reached the bottom of the banana hill. K2 climbed straight ahead while Kelly shifted away from rocky terrain. Her smoker's lungs struggled for air, but adrenaline poured and pushed her uphill. At the top she came within an arm's length of her twin.

K2 reached inside the cardboard box and grabbed an entire bunch of bananas. She ripped one loose and turned to run when Kelly bashed into her. The contact broke K2's stride.

Kelly snatched her own banana and bolted downhill. She stretched her legs forward, one foot after another, fighting through the pain of each step. Her feet soon became one with the terrain, sensing the right places to push off with the ball of her foot. She imagined that her cave-dwelling ancestors must've run like this while hunting to feed their young.

Ahead, K2 attempted a shortcut and crashed into a tree trunk. She staggered, reached up to adjust her mask, and tripped over something. The moment she struck the ground, she fumbled the banana among nearby ferns.

Kelly dashed past, her confidence growing with each step. Near the midway point, the lantern guys roared. They were really into it, leaping and clapping, urging her to hurry.

Then Kelly noticed something scattered along the trail, glinting in the light. *Maybe rocks?* Then she realized that the guys hadn't applauded earlier because each was holding a beer bottle. If they weren't holding the bottles anymore, that meant—

Before she could finish the thought, her heel slammed down on something sharp.

Fire exploded up the back of her left leg.

She went down screaming. More glass splinters tore into her legs and forearms. She seethed through the pain. When she attempted to crawl forward, her palm landed on another jagged fragment.

K2 huffed behind her.

Pulled even.

Shot ahead.

Kelly pictured Zach locked in a dark room miles away. She couldn't lose this race. Couldn't lose her kids.

And so, she did the only thing she could do. She stood up. Her wounded heel screamed as it struck solid dirt. She took off, her gait uneven but fierce. She clenched her fists, pumping her arms at her sides.

Her heel burned hotter until a surreal coolness spilled in, dulling the pain. She felt nothing now—nothing but the terrain underfoot and the wind rushing against her bare skin. Her legs carried her, one foot after the other, as she raced with inhuman desperation.

K2 glanced over her shoulder and stumbled.

Kelly sprinted to full speed. Her mask bounced around her face until she saw nothing but a mental image of the trail ahead.

Cheering sounded. She and K2 were closing in on the finish line.

Ahead, K2 huffed with exhaustion. With fear.

The woman's panting grew louder. Closer.

Then Kelly heard it alongside her.

Finally, the panting faded behind.

And that was it.

Kelly crossed the finish line. The whistle blew. The crowd exploded.

She ripped off her mask in celebration and flung it into the dirt. Adrenaline flooded her body as the campfire crew erupted with raucous cheers.

She roared. Roared till her throat felt raw.

She had won.

K2 limped across the finish line. She dropped her banana. Her shoulders dipped. Her head hung. With a trembling hand she removed her mask. There was a shattered look in her eyes.

"Tape her up," Kelly said to the crowd.

Two guys holding tape rolls approached K2. They each peeled off a foot-long strip, making a rip-squeak noise. K2 grunted as her wrists were bound together. She didn't resist. She accepted defeat until—out of nowhere—a laugh burst from her lips.

Grinning, she nodded her chin at Kelly, indicating something around her hip area.

"What?" Kelly said, spotting a cut along her thigh. "You think it's funny I fell in broken glass?"

K2 smiled. "No, not that."

"Then what is it?"

"You lost."

Kelly scoffed. "Oh please. Everyone saw me beat you—barefoot, no less."

"Sure, you outran me," K2 said, "but you lost."

"Shut up already. I won against all odds."

"Really?" K2 flashed a smug grin. "Then where's your banana?"

Kelly looked down at her hands. They were empty.

64

No matter how many times Kelly opened and closed her fingers, she couldn't conjure a banana. Nor could she remember dropping the thing. She must've lost it when her heel came down on that broken glass. The pain had been so intense that she'd forgotten about the banana. All she had thought about was getting up. Running. Saving her kids. Beating K2.

And she *did* beat K2. Against all odds. Without any socks or shoes.

But someone seized Kelly from behind. Strong hands gripped her elbows. She pried one arm free and raked her fingernails into someone's neck. While the guy grunted, two others snatched her wrists and wrangled them behind her back.

Struggling, she shifted her weight onto her bad foot. A bomb went off below her ankle. She collapsed. Her mind turned hot and fuzzy. Adrenaline faded as duct tape wrapped her wrists, knees, and ankles. Thunderbolts tore through her wounded heel. She growled in agony.

A damp sock was stuffed into her mouth, silencing her cries. Her tongue pulled back from foul-tasting cotton. Someone taped her lips shut, sealing the sock inside.

Two people hoisted her. Someone grabbed her left foot, detonating hard sparks of agony. By the time her head cleared, she was being loaded into the trunk of an ancient sedan that smelled like spilled wine. A hand reached up to shut the lid while a familiar voice said, "Tough break, K-Lady."

Kelly looked up and saw Brittney—or rather B2—leaning over the trunk. Tousled hair hung across her face. There was no sympathy in her eyes. She shut the lid, plunging Kelly into darkness.

Somewhere ahead, K2 squawked out orders. The motor rumbled as the car shook to life. Within seconds they were vrooming along, undoubtedly heading toward the Murder House.

Fear greased Kelly's stomach. Her nose was clogged. Her mouth tasted of bile and sweaty cotton. She lay on her side, her hands and ankles bound tight, her left heel burning as if it'd been dipped in hellfire.

Thankfully, her fingers hadn't been bound. All ten wiggled, unobstructed. They couldn't quite grasp the tape binding her wrists, but when she bent her knees, she could pinch the tape around her ankles. She tried ripping it free without success.

The car struck a pothole. Her hand slipped, bumping her left heel. Pain nuked her foot. She chewed on the sock until the worst passed.

Then she noticed her little finger was hot along the knuckle, sticky with sweat. No, not sweat—blood. She must've cut herself on the glass sliver embedded in her foot. That gave her an idea.

With shaky fingers, she reached for her left foot. Her thumb grazed something stiff and pointed—a glass shard. As she traced the triangular tip, she realized it was embedded sideways in her heel. How she had managed to run on the foot was beyond belief.

Stretching her wrists backward, she touched the tape to the shard. She blinked back tears as she wiggled her hands, trying to cut through the makeshift bindings. Her first attempt ended in agony when the glass rooted deeper into her foot. But on her second try, she felt a satisfying snag before the tape tore.

It energized her. She maneuvered her arms, expanding the rip until cool air pushed between her sweaty wrists. Soon both hands rested free at her sides. She peeled the tape from her lips and spat out the gag-sock. Then she inhaled cool, merciful air.

She unwrapped her ankles and traced her palms around the trunk lid, seeking an emergency release handle. She couldn't find one.

Suddenly she felt her weight sliding toward the rear of the trunk.

The car was heading uphill. A steep hill. The Murder House driveway.

This was it. Any moment now, the doubles would park the car and pop the trunk. Kelly could try to run, but she couldn't picture herself escaping on foot. Nor could she picture herself fighting back. She wasn't Schwarzenegger— she couldn't grab their heads and slam them together. Hell, in her current condition she probably couldn't take one of them.

Then she considered the glass stuck in her foot. She could remove it. Use it as a weapon—*if* she could get it out.

With her thumb and forefinger, she pinched the edge of the

shard. She pulled gently, hoping it would slide free, but it didn't budge. She bit down on her lip and twisted her fingers into the throbbing meat that was her heel. She buried her fingernail into the wound and nudged the shard outward. The heat intensified. She saw stars. Her entire leg felt like it was shredding.

Then the shard popped free and fell into her palm. It was barely larger than a postage stamp. She pinched it against her foreknuckle and shifted onto her stomach, prepared to attack.

The car jerked to a halt.

The trunk popped. A line of faint moonlight glowed along the edge.

Then a pair of hands lifted the lid.

Pushing off with her good foot, Kelly lunged at B2. The woman wasn't expecting it. Kelly wrapped both arms around her neck, the way a little girl might hug her best friend after prolonged separation. B2 yelped in shock as she caught Kelly with her arms and stumbled backward.

The moment Kelly's good foot touched the grass, she shifted behind B2 and curled an elbow around the woman's throat. B2 released an odd hiccupping sound. Then Kelly jammed the glass shard into her cheek and pulled it out again.

"Ow, fuck!" B2 cried.

"K2!" Kelly shouted. "Get out here."

The passenger door swung open. K2 stumbled out, her mouth agape. She held up both palms. "Let her go, Kelly. She's our friend."

"Not my friend." Kelly poked the shard under B2's chin.

"Calm down," K2 said, genuine worry in her eyes. "There's no reason to hurt her."

"There was no reason to hurt the real Brittney either," Kelly said. "Now give me my phone. Leave it on the passenger seat. And leave yours too."

K2 hesitated.

Kelly pushed the sliver into B2's neck. The woman thrashed and whimpered within her grasp. "Put both phones inside the car and shut the door. Now!"

K2 didn't move. "You won't kill her."

"Oh yes I will."

"Kelly, think. This is the only Brittney left. If she dies, her family and friends will mourn her. And what about her parents? Who's gonna take care of them?"

Kelly hesitated.

"See?" K2 said. "Now let's talk about—"

Kelly stabbed the glass into B2's cheek. The woman shrieked.

"Phones in the car—now!" Kelly yelled.

"Okay, okay!" K2 held up both phones before tossing them in the car. "Just so you know, you won't reach Zach in time. James is heading there now."

"Walk up the porch steps," Kelly said. "Put your hands against the front door."

K2 stepped backward until she reached the front porch. "Let Brittney go."

"Not until your hands are on the front door." Kelly needed to buy herself enough time to reach the driver's seat. "And get on your knees."

Flustered, K2 slapped both hands against the front door and lowered herself to her knees. "Happy now?"

Kelly sliced upward, dragging the glass from cheek to temple. B2 screamed, and Kelly shoved her on the grass. She hobbled toward the driver's side door. She opened it, dropped behind the wheel, locked the doors, and started the engine.

B2 was still screaming when Kelly swerved onto Red Trail Road.

65

Kelly motored through the dark, twisting forest, her good foot firmly on the gas. The headlights struggled against the shadows; tree trunks repeatedly popped out of nowhere, forcing her to cut the wheel. She considered lowering her speed but couldn't afford to—not while Aiden waited for her back at Caraway campus.

When she reached I-81, she dialed Rick on her phone. He answered with gloomy news about Emma's condition. Kelly cut him off and explained that K2 had kidnapped the twins.

"I'm heading after Aiden," she said, passing a tractor trailer. "Listen, Zach is inside the concession stand at Emma's soccer field."

"Fuck," Rick said. "I'll send someone to get him."

"No, we can't have the police involved. Everything's a mess. There are two Aidens and two Zachs."

"You're shitting me."

"Get in your truck and go after Zach. Don't waste a second. And be careful. James Manganaro is heading there."

"All right. Leaving now. Watch yourself, Kell."

She hung up and called DJ. He answered on the first ring. "Kelly, where are you?"

"On my way to get Aiden. Rick's going after Zach."

"Are they okay?" DJ's tone was thick with emotion. "Are you okay?"

"I will be once the kids are safe. Did you head back to Rick's?"

"Yeah, I took an Uber. Everything's fine here. Olivia coaxed the boys—er, their doubles—back to sleep. Gotta say, I don't like thinking of them as duplicates."

"I don't either. Listen, we'll talk later. I need to focus on the road."

"Okay. Love you, Kelly."

She ignored the speed limit until she reached Caraway. Her minivan remained parked outside the frat house. She pulled up behind it in the borrowed car and hobbled out the door, still wearing blood-smeared underwear. She must've looked like a neanderthal, but nobody seemed to notice other than drunk girls frolicking down the sidewalk. They pointed, giggled, and carried on.

Kelly reached the van and popped the tailgate. Writhing among soccer nets and orange cones was Aiden. His eyes widened when he saw her. She shoved gear aside and pulled him close into a bear hug, petting his soft red hair. He was taped, gagged, and shaking, but now he was safe. Her scalp tingled with relief.

She peeled the tape from his mouth, and he spat out the rag and dropped his head against her shoulder. His breath tickled her neck. He trembled.

"You're okay, bugger. I'm here."

She ripped the tape binding his wrists. When his hands were free, she urged him to remove more tape while she dressed. She found an old workout bag, filled with clothes she hadn't worn in forever. She tugged on a t-shirt and shorts, and then she checked her foot. Her heel looked like ketchup-slathered meatloaf. Tears soaked her eyes when she tugged on a sock and stepped into a pair of worn-out sneakers.

With reassuring words, she buckled Aiden into the backseat, then drove off.

She'd barely left the campus when Rick called.

"Bad news, Kell. Concession stand's empty. The door was hanging open when I got here. Manganaro must've left in a hurry."

Kelly swallowed a lump. "Any clue where he might've taken Zach?"

"We'll find him. Let's head back to my place and regroup."

Kelly drove to Rick's and parked in the driveway beside his truck. DJ ran outside to get Aiden. The two shared a tearful embrace while she hobbled toward the porch.

DJ hurried after her, carrying Aiden. "Hon, you're limping."

"I'm fine," she said, grimacing. "Just need to sit."

Rick let her inside. She collapsed into his living room recliner. He extended the footrest and removed her shoe. After one look at the bloody sock, he said, "DJ, grab the first-aid kit. Bottom cabinet in the bathroom. Hurry."

DJ set Aiden down and retrieved the kit.

Rick snapped it open and poured the contents onto the coffee table.

"What happened to your foot?" DJ asked.

"Broken glass," Kelly said.

"That or a landmine," Rick muttered. "DJ, how about grabbing a bucket and peroxide?"

DJ raced back to the bathroom. When he returned, he slid a wastebasket under the footrest and handed Rick a brown bottle of peroxide.

Rick unscrewed the cap. He tilted the bottle toward Kelly's foot. "Brace yourself."

She bit her lip. Shut her eyes. Clutched the armrests.

Liquid splashed her heel. She growled between her teeth as heat shrieked inside the wound. Her shoulders whipped back against the recliner, rocking it in place. When the pain passed, she realized Aiden was patting her arm sympathetically.

She put on a brave smile. "You okay, bugger?"

Aiden leaned over the armrest and hugged her. His cheek touched hers, and he yawned in her ear.

"You sound tired," she said. "You should lie down."

Aiden nodded and climbed onto the couch, lowering his head against a pillow. His eyelids drooped. Within moments he was snoring. That should've brought her peace, but all she could think about was Zach.

Rick pressed a strip of gauze against her heel. He wrapped her foot with discolored white bandages, replaced her sock, and slid on her shoe. The whole process hurt beyond description. She was gasping by the time he tied her shoelaces.

"I'll grab you some painkillers," he said, packing up the first-aid supplies. "They should get you moving again." He speedwalked to the bathroom.

Kelly lowered the footrest, pressed her feet against the carpet, and winced.

DJ knelt beside the recliner and took her hand. "Anything I can do for you?"

"Forget about me. We need to find Zach."

"Oh—that reminds me." DJ snapped his fingers like he'd

just solved some computer problem. "I had an idea. You know how you said your body gets warmer as you move closer to K2? If that's the case, let's drive Zach's double around. He can guide us."

"K2 will be expecting that," Kelly said tiredly. "She's using Zach as bait. If we get close, her friends will attack."

"Are you sure?"

"I know how she thinks. We'd be playing right into her hand."

"Is there a way to make her play into ours?"

Kelly mulled that thought until Rick returned with a bottle of pills. He shook one into her palm. She dry-swallowed it and hoped it would kick in fast.

DJ snapped his fingers again. "Got another idea. K2 needs to kill you in that attic, right? Why not use the attic against her? Set a trap or—"

"Burn it," Rick said.

Kelly flinched. The thought of torching the Murder House sent a warm tingle across her scalp. She remembered reading diary entries that mentioned sacred flames in the Arizona desert. There was no evidence to suggest that burning the Murder House would erase her problems, but still, the idea tempted her.

DJ stood up defiantly. "Rick, we can't burn it. Kelly and my kids need to visit that attic again. If it burns, we're stuck with two Kellys, two Aidens, and two Zachs."

"I guess you're right," Rick said.

"Wait." Kelly steepled her fingers beneath her chin. "What if I *threaten* to torch the Murder House?"

"Threaten?" DJ said. "What would that do?"

"Think—K2 has leverage now because she has Zach. But if I pour gasoline inside the house and wait there with my lighter, I'll have my own leverage. She knows I care more about my kids than anything else. If I threaten to destroy the house, she'll have to give us Zach."

DJ stroked his beard. "Will K2 actually believe you'll do it, though?"

"I'll convince her." She faced Rick. "Do you have any gas?"

"Got some five-gallon containers in the garage."

"Perfect. Load them into the van. I'll drive them over."

"We'll go with you," DJ said, looking to Rick for support.

"Actually," she said, "you both have to stay behind."

"No way," DJ said. "I'm not sitting this one out."

"You don't understand." She shifted uncomfortably in her seat. "You guys can't go near the Murder House."

DJ scoffed. "Why not?"

"Because," Rick said gravely, "that house'll fuck with your head. Take it from me—I set one foot inside and lost my damn mind. Couldn't think straight or control my actions. I ran right outside and threw myself at a speeding truck."

DJ's eyes widened. "But...Kelly and Emma went in."

"Right." Rick glanced forlornly at Emma's portrait above the fireplace. "They were on the guest list."

"Guest list?" DJ looked from Kelly to Rick to Kelly again. "What's that supposed to mean? Can someone please clue me in?"

Kelly rubbed her hairline. "Hon, don't worry about it."

"Too late for that—I'm beyond worried. How do I get on this guest list?"

"You can't."

"Then how'd you and Emma qualify?"

"We..." She lowered her head and sighed. "I'll tell you another time."

"There might not be another time." He knelt beside the recliner and took her hand. "C'mon, just be honest with me. Give me a chance. Maybe I can help."

Kelly recalled his confession at the kitchen table the other day. She supposed she owed him the truth.

After making sure Aiden was still asleep, she met her husband's eyes. "I'll tell you, but once I explain, you don't get to ask follow-up questions. Got it?"

He nodded.

Her throat constricted. She leaned toward his ear. "The house only lets you in if you've attempted suicide."

He pulled back slowly, his face pale as chalk. "Wait, Kelly, you—"

"No follow-up questions. If you've attempted before, you can enter. If you haven't, you'll lose your mind like Rick did."

"I...haven't. I'm sorry."

"There's nothing to be sorry about. Now let's drop the subject."

"Hold on." He squeezed her hand. "What if there's another way into that house? I mean, how could Aiden and Zach have entered? They're just kids. They couldn't have...attempted."

"That's been bothering me too," she said, eyeing Aiden. "I guess when they drank laundry detergent, that qualified as an attempt."

DJ balked at the idea. "No way. They just wanted to skip school. That couldn't have counted. There's gotta be another way to enter."

"If there is, we don't have time to figure it out. Just let me do this alone."

"Wait—what about Rick?"

"What about me?" Rick grumbled.

DJ rose to his feet and faced him. "You said you threw yourself at a speeding truck. Wouldn't that count as a suicide attempt?"

Kelly and Rick traded a look.

"Tell you what," Rick said, rubbing the back of his neck. "I'll let Kell drive me up to the Murder House. If the place spooks me, I'll stay in the van. If not, I'll join her inside."

"Thanks," DJ said. "That's better than nothing."

"All right then." Kelly struggled to her feet. "Let's get going."

"Before we do," Rick said, cocking a thumb over his shoulder, "let's head into the garage. Got a bulletproof vest I want you to try on."

66

The moment Kelly pulled out of Rick's driveway, the rain started. First a silent drizzle, then a frantic pattering against the windshield. Her wipers could barely keep up. It was as if the moonless sky was dumping a warning: *Don't go. Turn back. Stay away from the Murder House.*

She ignored it and drove on.

In the passenger seat, Rick wore a tactical vest covered with ammo pouches. He tinkered with a 9mm pistol, checking the magazine repeatedly before he holstered the weapon.

When they reached the highway, chills crept from Kelly's ankles toward her knees, as though crushed ice were being poured inside her legs. By the time she reached Red Trail Road, her thighs were frozen. Though uncomfortable, it was a good sign. It meant K2 was miles away. Hopefully the other doubles were with her. They could, of course, be lurking inside the Murder House, but given recent events— Brittney's face being slashed and the Manganaros rushing to recapture Zach—the building was likely empty.

The rain settled into a fine mist as Kelly parked across

from the porch and killed her headlights. Beside her, Rick glared at the Murder House with fierce, unwavering eyes. The half-burned structure no longer intimidated him. Without looking away, he said, "Let's do this."

They left the van. Kelly winced as her left foot touched the lawn. *Those painkillers must be the slow-release kind.* It didn't help that she was wearing a heavy bulletproof vest beneath a hiking jacket. The extra layers and weight meant that every step impacted harder.

Rick popped the trunk and strapped a semiautomatic rifle over his shoulder. He grabbed two five-gallon containers of gasoline and reminded Kelly to have her weapon ready. She reached into her pocket and closed her fingers around the pistol he'd given her.

Side by side, they climbed the porch steps. Silence blanketed the property, interrupted only by the creaking wood beneath their feet and the nighttime drizzle on the roof. Rick set the containers down and gripped his sidearm before he opened the front door.

A damp odor escaped the building. Rick shined his flashlight down the main hall and peered into the living room. "Place isn't furnished, huh? Good. Nowhere for those assholes to hide. Stay here while I do a quick search."

Holding his pistol and flashlight, he stepped inside. Broken glass crunched as he checked each room. Soon he called out, declaring the area clear.

They headed up the stairs, Rick leading. She lugged both containers, which added extra weight on her bad foot. She toughed it out while he checked each second-floor room, moving rapidly until he reached the master bedroom. He paused at the sight of the bloodstained ladder. He ran a finger along the steps, flinching at the touch of Emma's dried blood.

"Can't believe this place." He glanced around. "It's so empty."

"What were you expecting?"

"I don't know. When I came here with you and Emma, it was like staring into a nightmare. I can't even remember what I saw—only that it was terrible." He kicked the filthy mattress aside. "Thought there'd be more here. Was hoping I could fight through the nightmares and find a way to save Emma." He stared up into the attic. "This place... It wants to burn. Can you feel it?"

What Kelly felt was chest-tightening dread at the thought of K2's arrival. Kelly's legs were warming up. Her double must be on the move.

She set down the fuel containers. "We should hurry."

He nodded.

They each grabbed a container. She splashed the upstairs rooms then spilled a trail down the staircase. Rick doused the first floor. Before long, the whole building reeked of the foul, heady odor.

They regrouped in the living room, where he emptied his container to the last drop.

"Fuck this place." He flung the container aside. "Where's your lighter?"

"We're not starting a fire, remember? We just want it to look that way."

"Right, right." He paced around. "But the energy here... This place wants to burn."

"I think you've inhaled too many fumes."

"Not enough, actually. I'd like to forget that Emma ever came here."

"Maybe after this is over, we can start forgetting."

"Yeah." He crushed a glass shard under his heel. "Still can't believe Emma tried to...y'know." He gestured to his neck. "It never should've come to that. I should've paid more attention to her. Should've been there for her."

"Don't beat yourself up. You could've been Father of the Year and it might not have changed anything. Besides, if anyone deserves the blame, it's me."

"You? You didn't do anything wrong."

"Sure I did. I swallowed all those sleeping pills."

"That was forever ago."

"Still, it was one of Emma's first memories. It left a mark." Kelly spotted her reflection in a puddle of gasoline. She shook her head in dismay.

A thumping sounded nearby. Toward the back of the house.

"Stay here," Rick said. "Have your gun ready."

Kelly held her pistol firmly and pressed her shoulder against the living room wall. She braced herself as the thumping grew louder and more erratic. It sounded like someone was trapped inside the walls. She worried it was Zach.

Glass crunched as Rick moved in the hallway. "I think it's coming from next door."

They rushed outside and pulled open the burned house's back door. A heavy chemical odor poured out. Rick charged toward the ruined kitchen, where the thumping had become nonstop. Kelly shined her light on the cabinet below the sink, the one K2 had stared into the other day before abruptly shutting it.

Rick yanked it open.

A pair of dirty Nikes twitched inside. They were too big to be Zach's shoes, and they were attached to a pair of thick, taped-up legs. Rick opened the adjacent cabinet to reveal an old gray-haired woman with tape wrapped across the lower half of her head. She mumbled into the tape.

The woman's eyes found Kelly, glaring with deep black hatred.

"You know her?" Rick asked.

"Yeah." Kelly swallowed hard. "That's Nancy Norwell."

67

Rick tugged Nancy Norwell free, onto the scorched, debris-covered floor. He unraveled the tape from her head, taking some hair with it. When he pulled the rag from her mouth, she growled like a rabid dog. Her eyes never left Kelly's. Never blinked.

"Who trapped you in here?" Rick said. "Who taped you up?"

Norwell ignored him. She maintained her glare.

"She thinks I'm K2." Kelly squatted beside the woman. "Nancy, I'm not the one who captured you. That was the other me."

Norwell growled behind clenched brown teeth. She lay on the floor wearing a filthy blue jacket and urine-stained sweatpants. She smelled like garbage—so bad that her stench overpowered the house's burnt chemical odor.

"What do you want me to do with her?" Rick asked.

"Pull that tape off her."

"You serious?"

Kelly nodded. Since the other Nancy Norwell had died a few days ago, this one likely wouldn't have much energy.

She'd be suffering like Emma had in the days after E2's death. The only question was whether this Norwell was the original or the double.

Rick used a tactical knife to cut through the tape wrapping her arms, knees, and ankles. After her legs were free, they began kicking wildly.

"This is Norwell's double," Kelly said. "I can tell by her legs."

He frowned. "Then the original burned alive at your house."

Strange waves of emotion crashed within Kelly's chest. Norwell had tormented her for so long that Kelly had spent years wishing for the woman's death. Any method would do —cancer, a car accident, a fatal shooting, whatever. K2 had granted that morbid wish, and now Kelly couldn't help but feel responsible; that desire had festered in her soul for years.

"Rick, can I have a minute alone with her?"

"You sure that's a good idea?"

Kelly patted the gun in her pocket. "I'll be fine."

Once he exited out the back door, she helped Norwell sit up so they were at eye level. Kelly inhaled, expelled the breath, and said, "I got your letters. All of them."

Norwell didn't blink. Her mouth twisted like a vortex, as if trying to form words. Her teeth clicked. In a garbled voice she hissed, "You never visited her grave."

Kelly frowned. "No. I didn't. But I think about Anissa every day. Even when I'm completely distracted, she never leaves my mind. She's always a part of me. Always there. That's why I never visit her grave. Because—" Kelly patted her heart. "Because I'm always at her grave. I'm always wishing I hadn't taken her from this world...taken her from you."

Norwell blinked. Her head twitched, as if shaken by an unseen hand. Trembling, she reached up and peeled tangled gray strands from her cheek. Her arm dropped to the floor. After a long pause, she said, "You're not the one who captured me?"

"No. That was the other me."

Norwell stared.

Kelly leaned closer. "That other me and her friends are the ones who brought you here. If you know where they went or you overheard them say anything, please tell me."

Norwell said nothing. Something in her eyes suggested she knew more.

"Please." A lump formed in Kelly's throat. "They took my son. If you know anything—"

An odd expression shifted across Norwell's face. It was hard to tell if she was commiserating with Kelly or mocking her. The woman grimaced and then fell onto her side.

"Nancy?" Kelly pushed the woman up against the cabinets. "What do you know?"

Norwell stared back. A faint smile curled across her wrinkled mouth.

"Please." Kelly squeezed the woman's shoulders. "Tell me what—"

The back door burst open. Rick stormed in.

"They're here," he shouted.

Kelly rubbed her chilly legs. "Are you sure?"

"Saw headlights coming up the driveway." He tugged her elbow. "C'mon, Kell. It's time."

Kelly cast one last glance at Norwell, who hadn't stopped smiling.

68

Beyond the gas-soaked living room curtains, a Honda CR-V was now parked next to Kelly's minivan. The Honda doors opened, and the Manganaros stepped outside. They faced the house. Both wore camo hunting vests and carried pistols. They paused and glanced toward the backseat.

Kelly tapped Rick's shoulder. "Could Zach be in there?"

"Let me check." He pulled a handheld scope from his pocket and peered outside.

"See anything?" she asked.

"Yeah." He adjusted the scope's magnification. "Two assholes."

"What about Zach?"

"It's too dark to tell. If he's here, we'll get him after we ice these shitbirds. They both lured Emma into this place, right?"

"Mango, the younger one, did."

"What about the old man?"

"He orchestrated everything."

Rick pocketed the scope. "Go lock the front door." After she did, he added, "Now hide in the kitchen. When they come in through the back, try to distract them." He readied his rifle. "That'll make my job easy."

She hesitated. Not out of some moral quandary—these weren't the real Manganaros, after all—but out of concern for Zach. If he wasn't in the car, he was likely with K2, wherever she was. "Shoot to wound, okay? We'll need to ask them where Zach is."

"Got it. Now get ready."

The Manganaros tried the locked front door. They stomped along the veranda, heading for the rear entrance. Rick took position by the staircase, giving himself a clear shot at the back door. Kelly, meanwhile, crouched behind a kitchen cabinet.

Footsteps quieted at the back door.

The knob squeaked. A breeze whistled in from outside.

Mango muttered, "Fuck. Gas."

"Where's my son?" Kelly yelled. "Tell me, or I'll burn this place to the ground."

Mango snorted. "Go right ahead."

The door slammed shut. Retreating footsteps pounded the veranda.

Kelly hobbled into the living room. "Rick, they're leaving."

"The hell they are." Clutching his rifle, he opened the front door. "Fuck!"

James stood on the porch aiming his pistol.

Two shots thundered simultaneously. The noise echoed through the building. Rick dropped. James dropped. Kelly shrank against the wall before she pointed her weapon at the doorway where both men had collapsed. Rick lay on his back, clutching his stomach. He grabbed his sidearm and fired into the shadows.

James moaned in agony.

More gunshots boomed outside.

Amid the chaos, Kelly froze. Though she'd survived a shootout in the attic two days ago, live bullets weren't something she was accustomed to. Instinct urged her to run, but the pain in her left foot kept her anchored. She squatted against the wall and watched Rick writhe in the entranceway. He tried picking himself up, but he collapsed.

More gunshots.

The staircase banister exploded with splinters.

Then came a noise like a harsh whisper. In the hallway a gas puddle hopped to life with blue flame. It hovered along the ground and began spreading outward. The blaze snaked toward the staircase, leaping with orange light as it engulfed the fuel-splattered walls.

Rick yelled as the fire raged toward him.

Kelly didn't think. She sped ahead, reaching him as the flames did. Heat swallowed her as she rolled Rick outside. He was heavy, but he slid out the door onto the porch next to James, who lay bloody and motionless.

She slammed the door behind her, cutting off the flames. Rick grunted. She checked his wound and sensed movement from the building's near corner.

Mango emerged from behind it. He aimed for her and fired.

A bullet whizzed past her knee.

She stumbled away from Rick toward the charred side of the porch. Another bullet struck the ground near her feet. She took cover behind the burned corner. Pressed a hand over her pounding heart. Filling her lungs, she snapped clear of the corner and squeezed off three rounds. She didn't bother to aim.

On the front lawn, the Honda's motor growled. Headlights flickered. Kelly realized Brittney's double sat behind the wheel. She swerved parallel to the porch and extended a handgun out the window.

Kelly ducked.

For a moment there was silence.

Then gunshots.

Rick roared in agony.

"C'mon out," Brittney yelled, "or I'll shoot him again."

Kelly considered firing at the Honda, but Zach might be inside.

More shots boomed.

A front window must've shattered—smoke escaped and cast a haze over the porch. Kelly's nostrils became dry. Her throat itched. She worried about the blaze intensifying. If the flames ate through the structure and collapsed the attic, she and her kids would be in serious trouble. Somehow, she had to get this situation under control.

Squatting against the siding, she poked her head around the corner, barely glimpsing Mango before he fired. The bullet kicked up splinters ahead of her. Another low shot. Seemed he was shooting to wound.

She returned fire. Mango vanished behind cover.

Smoke poured thicker, obscuring her view of Rick. He was hacking and wheezing on the floor. She couldn't let him die. She needed to act now.

Gripping the pistol in both hands, Kelly snapped around the corner and dashed ahead. Adrenaline surged, like in the closing minutes of a soccer game. She fired two shots at the Honda's front tires. Brittney ducked low. Kelly barreled into the smoke cloud. She hopped over Rick's outstretched legs and continued toward the far end of the porch.

The moment she swung around the corner, she blasted Mango three times. One hit him square in the throat. It happened so fast she thought she'd imagined it.

He dropped his gun and collapsed to the floor like the sack of shit he was.

Blood leaked from his neck. He didn't move. Didn't blink.

Mango was dead.

Before she could turn around, gunshots thundered behind her.

Something whizzed past her hip.

She flung herself to the ground beside Mango's corpse. Her elbows banged against the floorboards. She braced for more shots. When they didn't come, she rolled onto her back.

Then something slammed down on her bad foot.

Pain bolted through her leg. She howled in agony. Sparks burst beneath her eyelids. When her vision cleared, she found herself staring up at Brittney, who was stepping firmly on Kelly's damaged foot.

The double pointed a gun at her.

Kelly tried lifting her own weapon before she realized her hands were empty. She spotted her gun an arm's length away.

"Don't even think about picking it up," Brittney snarled through gritted teeth. Her sliced-up cheek was covered in blood-darkened bandages. "You try anything, I'll stomp you."

"Britt—"

"Shut up and put your hands on your head."

Kelly obeyed.

Brittney grabbed her phone from her pocket and called someone. "Hey. I got her. She's at the Murder House—which is on fire, by the way. What do you want me to do?" She paused. "Sure you don't want to come here before it burns down?" Another pause. "But what if we're wrong?"

Kelly noticed a shadow stretching behind Brittney. Someone was staggering across the porch.

Please, Rick. Get over here and shoot her.

Brittney ended the call and pocketed her phone. She pointed her gun at Kelly's leg. "We're leaving. Keep your hands on your head and stand up slowly."

To buy time, Kelly said, "Wait, where are we going?"

"Don't worry. You'll find out."

C'mon, Rick. Faster.

"Are you taking me to Zach?" Kelly asked, watching the shadow.

Brittney extended her weapon toward Kelly's thigh. "Get up. Now."

Kelly sat up slowly. She fought the urge to reach for her fallen gun. Instead, she eyed the staggering shadow. It grew darker. A hand clutched the corner wall. The fingers were too slim to be Rick's.

Nancy Norwell stepped into view.

Kelly cleared her throat. "Britt, you should apologize."

Brittney squinted. "For what?"

"For what we did to Anissa."

"Fuck Anissa. Now get up."

Immediately, Norwell slammed into Brittney from behind. The pair coiled like hostile dancers before they crashed against the veranda railing. Norwell grabbed Brittney by the hair and dragged her to the floor. They struggled, twisting and rolling. Then two muffled shots sounded.

Norwell gagged wetly and fell silent, sprawled on top of her opponent.

While Brittney heaved herself free, Kelly grabbed her fallen pistol and jammed it into the woman's side. It landed like a punch. Kelly squeezed the trigger.

The gunshot knocked Brittney onto her back. She clutched at her wound, screaming.

Kelly launched to her feet and aimed for Brittney's leg. "Where's Zach?"

"Go find him yourself."

Kelly shot her thigh.

"Ow, fuck!" Brittney writhed in agony. "Fuck."

Kelly aimed for the woman's face. "Tell me where K2 is hiding Zach."

"Your house."

"On Byron Street? Why there?" Kelly stretched the gun closer to Brittney's nose. "Answer me."

"Or what? You'll kill me?" Brittney smirked. "You won't. You can't."

Kelly touched the gun to the woman's forehead. "Why Byron Street?"

"Think about what you're doing. Would you really kill your best friend?"

"You're not my best friend." Kelly clenched her teeth. A teardrop salted her upper lip. "You murdered my best friend."

"I saved her." The double's eyes widened with intensity. "I saved the idea of Brittney Mathis. My other half, all she ever did was settle. She wasted her life working at that stupid liquor store and playing nurse to Mom and Dad. It was pathetic. She could've been special, and K2 recognized that. That's why K2 brought out the real me. Because I deserved better. And you deserved a better friend. Not some pathetic—"

Kelly squeezed the trigger.

Blood splattered the floorboards. Smoke rose from the barrel. Maybe she should've kept Brittney's double alive longer, but she couldn't listen to another second of that. Now she needed to help Rick and do something about this fire.

Back on the front porch, Rick was blanketed in smoke. She checked him for injuries. He'd taken two bullets to his leg and another two to his tactical vest. One had struck an ammo pouch. The other had gone through the zipper near his stomach.

Not another stomach wound. Please no.

"C'mon, Rick!" She tugged on his elbow. "Let's get away from the house."

"Ugh, shit." He grimaced. "Those assholes dead?"

Kelly shot James in the head to be safe. "Yeah, all three of them. Now help me move you."

He dug his heel into the floorboard and pushed himself away from the door. She grabbed him by the vest and guided him down the porch steps. Her bad foot was killing her, but she dragged him out beside the minivan; it seemed a safe enough distance away. She called 911 and requested an ambulance and firetruck.

Rick told her to remove her belt and wrap it around his leg like a tourniquet. She followed his instructions. Once the belt was tightened, she pressed both hands over his stomach wound.

Ahead, the blaze intensified. Fire consumed the Murder House. Everything burned, from foundation to roof. Glass cracked. Shingles tumbled. Black smoke leaped into the moonlit sky.

"It's burning, Rick." Her eyes focused on the attic. "How do I stop it?"

The left side was flickering now—like a staticky old TV. The right side stood firm while the left twitched and fizzled. At first she thought it was an illusion caused by the smoke, but the smoke wasn't affecting the right side in the same way.

Then, all at once, the entire left side vanished. Completely vanished. Cracking sounds became silent. Flames extinguished in midair. Only smoke remained.

No. Impossible.

As the air cleared, the right-side unit rose into view. It stood alone, without a trace of the left unit. Embers glowed in the dirt where it had stood, but there was no porch, no veranda, no building, nothing. Even the doubles were gone.

Rick called out, "Where'd it go?"

Kelly didn't have an answer. She stared at the remaining housing unit, at the char-markings on the siding, a brutally familiar sight. They reminded her of the damage done to her own home.

"Where'd it go?" Rick repeated, his voice full of wonder.

"I don't know," Kelly said, maintaining pressure on his wound, "but K2 has Zach. They're on Byron Street. Soon as the paramedics get here, I'll go and—"

"Leave now," he said tiredly. "I can take care of myself. Just promise me one thing."

"What?"

"That you'll save Emma." His voice faded to a whisper. "There's gotta be a way."

"Okay." Kelly pressed both his hands against his wound. "I promise."

He steadied his gaze at her. "Good. Now get going."

She climbed into her van and drove off.

Storm clouds smothered the night sky as Kelly took the exit toward her neighborhood. Wind howled. Rain splattered her windshield. Her wipers swung wildly to keep up. She was battling an all-out downpour, but determination fireballed within her. She stomped the gas pedal. Charged past red lights. Surged through intersections.

With each passing moment, her legs became warmer. She tightened her grip on the wheel and pictured herself squeezing K2's throat—squeezing tight until the windpipe crushed beneath her thumbs.

The morbid fantasy was interrupted by her buzzing phone.

It was DJ calling. She put him on speaker.

"You find Zach?" he asked.

"Not yet." She slammed her horn to scare away traffic. "I'm on my way."

"On your way?" His voice was high and anxious. "Thought you were already there."

"K2 and Zach weren't at the Murder House. I'm going after them now."

"Where at?"

"Our house."

"On Byron Street?" She heard the sound of a chair sliding on tile. "I'll head right over."

Kelly didn't argue. She was grateful for the offer, especially now that she couldn't depend on Rick. "Be careful. There's no telling what K2 has planned."

"She'll probably try to capture you and take you to the Murder House."

"That's not an option anymore."

"What do you mean?"

She swallowed hard. "The Murder House is gone."

"Gone?" Alarm in his voice. "You mean you burned it?"

"Yeah. Things got complicated."

"Shit. How bad's the damage? Is the attic still intact?"

"No."

"So it's a pile of rubble?"

"No, it's gone. Completely gone. It vanished like a ghost."

He paused, taking this in. "So now what?"

"I don't know." She blew through a stop sign. "Mango dared me to light the house on fire, so maybe he and the other doubles knew something. Maybe the Murder House isn't permanently gone. If it reappears, I'll take the kids and get them back to normal."

"Not sure I'm willing to pay that price."

"What price?"

"Kelly, do you realize what Aiden and Zach will have to do to get back to normal? They'll have to take their doubles into the attic and...I can't even say it."

Things had been moving so fast that she never stopped to consider that her children would have to commit murder. She was prepared—and rather eager—to kill K2, but the thought of her sons doing the same left a foul taste on her tongue.

"Let's worry about that later." After ignoring another stop sign, she turned onto Byron Street. Breathed deep. "I'm almost at our house."

"Any sign of K2?"

She wiggled her toes. They were warm. "She's somewhere nearby."

"Do you see her?"

Kelly couldn't see anything. Thick sheets of rain pounded her windshield as she descended the hill. Her wipers swung at max speed but failed to carve out a view. It wasn't till she reached her driveway that the storm finally eased up.

After another sweep of the wipers, her house came into view.

And there, right beside it, stood the unthinkable.

Attached to the scorched ruins of Kelly's home was its mirror image—an unburned replica. The pristine roof extended from the charred roof of her original home. The new building intruded into her side lawn, where a duplicate garage had smashed through the tree line of the nearby woods. Like a misty reflection, this bizarre structure flickered in the rain.

"DJ, it's here," she said.

"What is?"

"The Murder House. It's right here. It attached itself to our home."

As her wipers cleared the windshield, white light flashed behind a second-floor window. Someone was upstairs. A moment later, panicked cries sounded. Zach's cries.

"Zach!" Kelly rushed out into the rain. The soggy front

lawn splashed under her feet as she raced up the Murder House steps and threw herself at the front door. Her key unlocked it, but the door didn't budge, as though a couch were propped behind it.

Holding her pistol, she ran to check the back door. That too was stuck, but it shifted after she rammed it with her shoulder. She heard a rattling near her feet. It sounded like marbles spilling onto the concrete porch.

She angled her flashlight toward the noise and saw dozens of white disc-shaped pills. They looked eerily familiar. She squatted for a closer look and recognized the code etched into each tablet—the exact code that had been on the pills she'd tried to kill herself with twelve years ago.

The Murder House appeared to be overloaded with these tablets. On Red Trail Road the floors were covered with broken glass, but here an excess of pills replaced the shards. If there were enough to block the doors, there must be millions inside.

But millions wouldn't stop her. With renewed urgency, she slammed her shoulder against the door. Heat and soreness spread down her arm as more tablets spilled through the slim opening. She kept shoving until there was a wide enough opening to push through. She stepped onto a mound of pills, packed tightly enough that she could walk on them like snow.

With her flashlight she scanned the kitchen. The Murder House had copied her home down to the furniture and photos hanging on the walls. Pills swamped the place. Massive white lumps covered the fridge, stove, and dinner table. A narrow gorge cut toward the living room, where more furniture was buried under white mounds the size of snowdrifts. The only thing visible was the TV, which poked above the surface like a shark fin.

Her bad foot nagged her as she climbed the staircase. The pill-covered steps proved steep and shifty. She grabbed the banister, fighting to maintain her balance. Tablets slid underfoot. She powered ahead until her left ankle abruptly buckled.

Sharp pain jolted her. She cried out, lost her footing, and tumbled backward.

For a moment she was in freefall. Then the back of her head struck the staircase. Next thing she knew, pills were avalanching on top of her, burying her. Everything went dark. She opened her mouth to scream, and pills poured onto her tongue, coating it with a bitter, chalky taste.

She spat without success. Her face grew hot. Tablets clogged her throat. The grainy edges dissolved, and nasty chemicals oozed into her stomach like they had twelve years ago.

But the pills hadn't killed her then, and she refused to let them kill her now. With desperate strength, she twisted onto her side—bad foot be damned—and pushed herself up. She drove her head above the surface and coughed up everything she could. Pills, covered in webs of saliva, dropped from her mouth. Even so, she could feel some of them bobbing in her stomach.

She gripped the gun tightly and scrambled upstairs. She pointed her flashlight down the second-floor hallway. Gooseflesh bristled along her neck as she pushed past her office, the kids' room, and the bathroom.

Finally, she entered the master bedroom. Her walk-in closet stood opposite the bed. The door was open.

The attic entrance waited inside the closet.

A ladder invited her to climb into the attic.

Dusty, hellish heat pulsed down from overhead. Kelly shined her light toward the rectangular opening in the ceiling, where mannequin limbs dangled into view. They wobbled, threatening to spill down onto her. High above them hung a familiar sight—the exact wooden roof beams from the Red Trail Road attic. Though the exterior of the relocated Murder House had mimicked Kelly's home, the attic remained unchanged. Remained its own dark entity.

She stepped onto the ladder and climbed toward the heat. Her tongue, still chalky from the sleeping pills, dried out even more. A fuzzy calm settled over her brain. She shouldn't feel calm. Not now. That meant the pills were kicking in.

She stopped midclimb. She needed to hurry but couldn't just rush up there. Not while K2 had all the leverage. They both knew Kelly would do anything to save Zach, and once she entered the attic, she would be vulnerable. K2 might be perched beside the entrance holding a knife or waiting behind a filing cabinet with a gun. The entire attic was a potential death sentence.

Somehow, Kelly needed to take the upper hand. She held only one advantage: her life—or rather, her death. If she died outside the attic, K2 would lose the opportunity to become whole again.

Kelly pointed her pistol at her head. "I have a gun. I'll shoot myself if you don't give me Zach."

"That's a lie," K2 said, her voice distant.

"No. For once, I'm telling the truth," Kelly shouted. "Believe me, *I will do it*. Far as I'm concerned, climbing into that attic is suicide. At least if I blow my brains out down here, you'll rot along with me." Her pulse drummed in her ears. With conviction in her tone, she added, "I'm counting to three." Her finger grazed the trigger. "One...two...thr—"

"Mommy!" Zach shouted. "We're behind the—"

His words were cut short by the sound of slamming metal.

K2 yelled, "I locked him in the safe. You remember the code, don't you? Better get him out before he suffocates."

Spurred by her son's predicament, Kelly completed the climb into the sweltering attic. Darkness surrounded her, along with countless mannequin parts. At the far end of the attic glowed a yellow lantern, on top of the locked safe. K2 was baiting her. It couldn't be more obvious, yet Kelly had no choice but to press on.

Powering off her flashlight, she rushed toward the nearest row of tables. Adrenaline zipped through her veins. Her entire body trembled. She used boxes and cabinets for cover as she navigated the maze.

Plastic clacked and rattled. The attic's dividing line waited ahead, along with rows of cluttered tables. She crossed over and rounded the corner of a table.

A gunshot thundered.

She ducked.

More shots boomed. Ahead something flashed between two cardboard boxes.

Kelly aimed for them. Squeezed off two quick shots.

Silence.

She ducked behind a filing cabinet. Through ringing ears, she listened intently.

And waited.

Waited.

Wai—

A shadow swept through the darkness. She chased after it, squeezing the trigger again and again, panic-firing until her gun was empty.

Silence swallowed the attic. All she heard was the sound of her own nervous breath. There was no telling how much air Zach had left.

With no ammo remaining, she pulled her pocketknife from her jeans pocket and unfolded the blade. Ducking low, she stepped out from behind cover. Plastic clattered as she crept along the near wall. Her eyes dashed in all directions before she turned the corner and rushed toward the light.

The lantern was impossibly bright. She couldn't have felt more exposed if a thousand cameras were pointed her way. She squeezed the knife grip and reached for the safe.

Rattling sounded behind her.

Kelly turned, and something struck her like a hammer to the chest. Next thing she knew, she was on the floor, gagging for air. Rough heat spread along her left breast, right beneath the collarbone. Similar pain throbbed along her abdomen, though she didn't remember being hit there. Only now did her ears register the gunshots. Was this what it felt like to be shot? Was she dying?

Plastic rattled nearby. To her right. Maybe to her left. Nothing made sense anymore.

She pressed a hand to her chest and winced. She lifted her hand to check the bleeding, but her fingers came back pale. No blood.

The vest, she remembered. *Thanks, Rick.*

More clattering. She turned her head. Beneath the table she saw K2's legs moving.

Kelly rolled onto her stomach and readied her knife. The moment K2's leg came within reach, she thrust the blade forward and felt it pierce flesh.

K2 howled and stumbled. The knife handle slid from Kelly's grasp as her twin collapsed to the floor.

Chest throbbing, Kelly threw herself onto K2. They were both within the lantern's orb of light now, and Kelly spotted the pistol in K2's grasp. They wrestled over it, tugging back and forth. K2 fired repeatedly until the gun clicked. Then she dropped it and pulled the knife from her wounded leg.

The blade darted for Kelly's face. She winced at the hot scrape along her cheek. Blood trickled into her mouth. She spat, then retreated from the stabbing blade.

Panicking, she claimed a plastic leg from the floor and swung wildly at K2. It struck the woman's head, the impact snapping the leg apart at the knee.

K2 dropped the knife.

Kelly reached for it, but a fist rocked her cheek. Her ears rang. Hot discomfort shot through her neck.

She shuffled backward. Raised both fists.

K2 raised her own. "Good. Hand-to-hand. Kelly-versus-Kelly. I love it." K2 staggered to her feet. Her left leg was bleeding through her jeans. "It all comes down to who wants it more."

"If that's the case," Kelly said, rising to her feet, "you have no chance."

She threw an angry punch that sailed wide, leaving her vulnerable, and K2's fist cracked her in the teeth. Heat exploded between her cheeks. K2's follow-up shot struck Kelly along her eye socket and knocked her sideways against the locked safe.

When she turned her head, she registered an incoming punch. Her nose exploded. Cartilage snapped with a crack audible both inside and outside her skull. Blood flooded from her nostrils.

Another punch rocketed toward her face.

This time, Kelly dodged.

K2's knuckles struck the metal safe. The woman growled.

Shaking off the pain, K2 lifted both fists. Kelly did the same. They mirrored each other, inching closer until they were an arm's length away.

Kelly circled to her right, forcing K2 to shift weight onto her wounded leg. The woman hesitated, and that gave Kelly the opening she needed.

Swinging her right leg, she slammed her toe into K2's knife wound, kicking with enough force to launch a soccer ball downfield. The impact dropped K2 to the floor.

Kelly pounced and drove a fist into K2's nose. The sound of cracking cartilage was immediately followed by a wet smack as Kelly poured on more punches. She pounded K2's face, throat, collarbones, chest, and anything else she could hit.

Blood leaped from K2's mouth.

Kelly kept going. She drilled K2 in the forehead.

Then the cheek.

Then the other cheek.

One shot for Brittney.

One for Aiden.

One for Zach.

One for Emma.

And another for Emma.

Kelly kept punching until K2 twisted her bloody, broken face away. Muffled sobs escaped her ruined mouth. There was no fight left in her.

Kelly rushed to the safe. Her hands were sore, damaged from punching, but she managed to unfold her fingers and twist the dial. She entered the code. The lock clicked and the door swung open.

But the safe was empty.

She whirled on K2, who lay among the mannequins. "Where's Zach? Where is he?"

With a trembling arm, K2 pointed behind Kelly at an antique storage trunk against the wall. It was shut, a keyhole embedded in the lid.

"Where's the key?" Kelly demanded.

"It's...not locked."

Kelly hurried there and lifted the lid. Zach lay curled inside, tape across his mouth. His eyes were wide with fear, his wrists and ankles bound.

She peeled the tape from his lips. "Cutie, you okay?"

He spat out a rag. "Mommy!"

Kelly lifted him from the trunk. Hugged him. Kissed him. "Oh, Zach..."

"Mommy, can we leave?"

"Sure. But first I have to finish something."

She lowered him back inside the storage trunk so he wouldn't have to see what happened next.

She grabbed K2 by the ankles and dragged her to the dividing line. Kelly straddled K2's midsection and seized her neck. With both thumbs, Kelly pressed down on her throat.

"Please," K2 croaked. "I spared him. I—"

Kelly applied more pressure. She glared into K2's eyes, the only part of her face that wasn't swelling or bleeding.

K2 tapped Kelly's wrist. "Please... I'm only what you made me—made us."

Kelly pushed her thumbs harder against the windpipe.

K2's eyes bulged. "I...saved...you."

Her cheeks reddened.

Her eyelids drooped.

At that moment, the air in the attic hissed. Steam swirled around them. An odd discomfort flushed through Kelly's gut, reminding her of standing on the sideline in college and watching her soccer team tear itself apart. Back then, part of her had wanted to intervene, but her feet remained anchored in the grass. She could've taken action, but instead she let the team destroy itself. That led to Anissa's death. To Kelly's self-destruction.

Now, the only person left to destroy was K2.

With the attic air swirling toward the boiling point, Kelly squeezed tighter.

Behind her, Zach whimpered in terror. Her son was so timid. She couldn't imagine him suffocating his double. The mere thought left her dizzy. How could she possibly order him and Aiden to commit murder? And what if they refused—would she have to force them? Worse yet, what about afterward? How would they cope? Would they resent her? Would they someday shut her out like Emma had?

Emma...

Kelly recalled what Emma said last week in the school parking lot. About how she felt warm and at peace whenever she embraced her double. Kelly had experienced a similar sensation when she and K2 held each other after E2's death. The warmth along her waist had been undeniable. But could it have meant something more? Could it save her now?

Kelly released her grip on K2's neck.

The steam began to fade.

K2 coughed. Blinked.

For a moment Kelly and K2 stared at one another.

Then, with great reluctance, Kelly slid her arms under K2's back and pulled her close. She didn't forgive the woman. Didn't accept her. Didn't love her. But deep down, Kelly knew she needed her. Needed to hold onto this twisted, broken part of herself.

As she embraced K2, a surreal heat burst along her waist. Warmth spread in both directions, toward her head and toes. Tears soaked her eyes as she leaned her chin on K2's shoulder. Their cheeks touched, swollen and slick with blood. Kelly held tight.

K2's arms curled around Kelly's lower back—faint yet firm pressure.

The heat along Kelly's waist intensified. Hotter and hotter until the air around her boiled.

Steam surrounded her. Burned her. Melted her.

Before long, she knew no other sensation.

Together, Kelly and K2 clung to each other until all went black.

71

Next thing Kelly knew, she was embracing cool, empty air.

Shivering, she lay alone, covered in bruises and soaked with blood. Her cheek rested against a hard plastic torso.

Now that the battle was over, the adrenaline faded. Pain consumed her. Her knuckles hurt like hell. She tried uncurling her fingers, but both fists were rigid and sore. Everything ached. Her busted nose burned, her forehead throbbed, and her swollen jaw made her want to scream—not that she could scream.

Behind her in the storage trunk, Zach whimpered nervously. She needed to remove his tape. Needed to carry him out of this godforsaken attic.

Hoping to boost herself up, she propped both forearms underneath her shoulders and pushed. She lifted her head upright. Blood seeped into her mouth, soaking her tongue with a nauseating flavor. She tried climbing to her feet, but sharp heat hissed below her knee.

She collapsed. Pain chewed through her leg.

That didn't make sense. She'd suffered many blows

during the battle, but none below the waist. Yet when she touched her leg, her fingers came back wet with blood. Her jeans were soaked—right around the spot where she'd stabbed K2.

Something squealed nearby. Then came a metallic bang. A flashlight beam wavered along the ceiling. Her ringing ears heard the sound of someone climbing. Climbing closer.

Frantically, she crawled toward Zach. A familiar voice called out.

"Kelly?" DJ said, panting. "You up here?"

"DJ?" She shuddered with relief. "How'd you get inside the house?"

"I went in through the burned side."

"The burned side..."

"Daddy!" Zach rumbled within the storage trunk. "Daddy, I'm inside a treasure chest!"

"Zach's stuck," Kelly said. "Help him."

Mannequin parts rattled as DJ stepped into the attic. He hurried closer, then stopped as his flashlight beam illuminated Kelly. "Oh God. Hon, are you okay?"

"Help Zach."

DJ shined his light around. "Is K2 here?"

Kelly wasn't sure how to answer that. Her leg throbbed as if to say yes, but there was no trace of her double anywhere. "It's just me."

72

ONE MONTH LATER

Kelly paced along the sideline, clapping and shouting for Aiden to dribble downfield. He got the message and zipped past a clueless defender. Kelly hobbled after him, her calf aching. She'd only been off crutches for two days, and the indoor turf was wearing her down. She was tempted to sit on the bleachers, but she wanted to rally her team. It was the first game of the autumn season, and they were losing. That needed to change.

Aiden burst toward the net and went one-on-one with the goalie. He dribbled left, then launched the ball to the right—just like DJ taught him.

It went in.

"GOOOOAAALLLL!!" DJ roared beside her. He pumped his fist in celebration, then turned to hug her. He lifted her off feet, spun her around, and set her down gently on her good foot. "What'd I tell you? Like father, like son. Can't fuckin' stop him."

Kelly laughed. "Tie game, hon. We got this."

"Let's win it."

"Come on, green team!" she hollered out to the players. "Keep attacking!"

The other team kicked off. Zach intercepted the ball and whacked it toward the opponent's end. Aiden chased after it. He and five other kids battled for control, Kelly and DJ shouting encouragement from the sideline.

Her phone buzzed. It was Rick. She backed toward the facility wall and answered.

"Kell, I'm at the hospital," Rick said, sounding excited. "They're sending Emma home today."

Kelly gasped. "Really? That's great! How's she feeling?"

"She's walking without help. Needs a breather after every dozen steps or so, but that beats lying in a hospital bed. Let's hope she can climb stairs—and that ladder."

Kelly swallowed hard. "Are we going there today?"

"Yeah, meet at my place in an hour." He blew out a nervous sigh. "Hope this works."

"It will," she said. "It has to."

They hung up. She returned to DJ and excitedly slapped his shoulder. "Guess what, guess what, guess what!"

Keeping his eyes on the game, he said, "You got a job interview at that gym?"

"Better—Emma's heading home."

"Really?" His head swung toward her. "Rick must've pulled some serious strings."

"Yeah. Just gotta hope our plan actually works."

"It worked for you and the twins."

"Yeah, but our doubles were *alive*."

He smiled. "You'll find a way. Just like I found a way into that attic."

The whistle blew. Cheers sounded from the field. Zach

danced in celebration near the opposing goal. The ball was in the net. He had put them in the lead.

Kelly grinned at her husband. "Can't fuckin' stop any of us."

The clock ran out. They won. The kids celebrated on the field. Kelly kissed DJ hard on the mouth and congratulated him on their first win as a husband-wife coaching duo.

It was refreshing to enjoy a victory, especially after all her recent ordeals. Despite defeating K2 and rescuing her kids, Kelly had endured plenty of heartbreak lately. Helping the twins cope with their kidnapping was an ongoing process, and although Emma had awakened from her coma weeks ago, her daughter hadn't fully recovered from the gunshot wound.

And then there was Brittney. Kelly's best friend was gone, and her body would never be found. Last week, Kelly shared the morbid truth with Britt's family, but they didn't believe her. They continued to hold out hope while Kelly carried the burden of her friend's death.

Pain and regret persisted. All Kelly could do now was fight to establish a somewhat normal life. It felt like the nightmares would never end, but seeing her twins laughing together on the soccer field brought her momentary peace.

After the teams exchanged handshakes, Kelly and DJ wrangled the twins into the van and drove to Rick's house. The driveway was empty. Then Rick's truck bolted down the street. He parked along the curb. The passenger door opened, and out stepped Olivia. She turned to help Emma climb down.

The moment Emma's feet touched the grass, she yelled out, "Mom!"

Kelly was already hobbling across the lawn. Emma limped toward her. They met with a warm, clumsy hug.

Kelly shook with relief at seeing her daughter standing upright.

Rick was still recovering from his own abdominal surgery, so DJ retrieved E2's triple-bagged body from the basement fridge. He loaded it into the cargo area and asked if everyone was ready to leave. The twins, of course, would stay here with Olivia, but everyone else planned to head to the Murder House.

"I'll ride shotgun," Rick said. "You know the new address, right?"

The Murder House had relocated again since attaching itself to Kelly's home. After she and the twins had restored themselves to normal, she asked DJ to set fire to the place. It had been an act of caution; she dreaded how the world would react if the Murder House remained on Byron Street. After it burned, it vanished to a new location. Rick spent days searching before he discovered it on a secluded road near Taylor, a few miles south of Scranton.

Now DJ drove them through the streets of Taylor, passing homes, churches, and gas stations. Rick gave directions in the passenger seat. Kelly sat in the back, her arm around Emma, who yapped about hospital food, abdominal stitches, and her physical therapy regimen. It felt as though she might never stop talking.

Then she abruptly went silent. Her gaze drifted back toward the cargo space.

Kelly enclosed Emma's hands with her own. "Hey. This'll work out."

Emma inhaled deeply. She looked ready to say something. Instead, she reached into her pocket and grabbed her good luck charm.

They arrived at the Murder House. This one stood on flat grass. The right-side housing unit was scorched; the left side shined in the late-October sun. The two-story building offered a spacious front porch, concrete stairs, and more windows than Kelly could count in a single glance. Trees surrounded the property, appearing to keep their distance.

"Let's finish this," she said.

The group exited the van. Rick wasn't supposed to lift anything heavier than ten pounds, so Kelly and DJ carried E2's body into the burned side of the house. The place stank of smoke and melted plastic. In an upstairs bedroom, they found the attic entrance and hoisted the body into the sweltering attic. After setting E2 near the dividing line, DJ left and sent Emma up.

Emma climbed the ladder slowly, careful not to disturb her stitches. When she reached the top, Kelly guided her toward the dividing line.

Kelly sliced open the bag. The putrid smell made her eyes water. She buried her nose in her sleeve. Emma knelt beside her double, tears in her eyes as she leaned forward. She slid both arms beneath the body and hugged E2 against her.

Nothing happened.

Nervous pressure mounted within Kelly's chest. *No. It can't end like this.*

In an act of motherly desperation, she grabbed E2's dangling arms and wrapped them around Emma's back, bending the stiff arms into place. The air around her steamed hotter and hotter until she could take no more.

She held on anyway.

When the steam cleared, Emma sat up. A mannequin lay where E2 had been.

"Em? How you feeling?"

Emma rubbed her knees. She stood slowly, wincing in pain. "My legs hurt."

"Hurt?" Kelly tensed. "They shouldn't hurt. You should be whole again."

Emma scratched her thigh. "I feel whole, but my legs hurt. It's not that bad though."

Kelly stood up. "Are you sure?"

Emma tapped each foot against the floor. She took a step forward. Then another. After a moment's hesitation, she threw her arms around Kelly. They held each other.

Emma started crying. "I'm sorry, Mom. For everything."

Kelly squeezed tight. "You have nothing to be sorry for."

"But I put you through all this."

"I put you through worse."

They stood along the dividing line, hugging it out until Emma said she was ready to leave. They descended the attic stairs, hopefully for the final time.

Outside, Rick and Emma shared a tearful hug. DJ grabbed the five-gallon fuel container and soaked the porch while Kelly eyed her daughter's twitching legs. Pain was part of life, but she hoped Emma's pain would relent—if not soon, then someday.

When DJ had emptied the container, he nervously backed away from the building. "Who wants to light it?"

Kelly had quit smoking, but she kept her lighter handy. She offered it to Emma, who accepted it and climbed the porch steps. The girl squatted near the gasoline trail and struck a flame. She hesitated and then gestured for Kelly to join her.

Kelly knelt and closed a hand around her daughter's. Together they lowered the flame to the floor.

Thin blue fire spread across the porch. Kelly and Emma backed away and rushed to the driveway. They held each other, side by side, watching while flames wrapped the building. The blaze charred the porch, melted the siding, and cracked the windows. Heat and smoke escaped the house like silent screams. The blaze leaped higher and higher toward the roof.

The attic burned. Smoke darkened the sky.

Before long, the Murder House vanished.

Kelly and Emma remained.

AUTHOR'S NOTE

Thank you for reading this book!

Please consider leaving a review on Amazon, Goodreads, Barnes & Noble, and Bookbub. Reviews are vital to authors like me, and your support goes a long way toward encouraging others to read my books. If you could spare a few moments to write a review, I would greatly appreciate it!

For updates on future novels and stories, join my mailing list at www.brandonmcnulty.com. It's a private list and your email address will never be shared with anyone else. You'll also receive a free gift for signing up!

Finally, be sure to connect with me on social media:

youtube.com/WriterBrandonMcNulty

x.com/McNultyFiction

facebook.com/McNultyFiction

amazon.com/author/brandonmcnulty

goodreads.com/brandonmcnulty

bookbub.com/authors/brandon-mcnulty

ACKNOWLEDGMENTS

Normally I say nasty, rotten, horrible things about Samantha Zaboski, but after all the editorial support she provided, the only thing I can say is "Thank you." Sam keeps leveling-up as an editor, and her insights—everything from structural criticisms to sentence-level tweaks—made this book stronger and snappier. Her critiques, line edits, and friendship are invaluable.

Vic Rushing unleashed an editorial beatdown and helped me tighten the story when it was loose and out of control. His developmental edits are always soul-crushing and—more importantly—always worthwhile.

Shell Steiner helped me inject heart and realism into this book. She critiqued two separate drafts, suggested countless improvements, and challenged me to revise the book's original ending. The story is significantly better because of her.

Chris Bauer beat me over the head with honest feedback that I needed to hear. He never hesitates to tell me when things suck, and I can't thank him enough for it.

Brandon Ketchum tackled an early draft and provided tons of detailed feedback. His writerly insights helped me restructure the plot, and his soccer knowledge especially came in handy. Thanks, Bubby!

Kate Lytle Rushing not only answered numerous medical-related questions, but she also critiqued the book and spotted several inconsistencies. Her patience never ceases to amaze.

Sue Ducharme provided yet another phenomenal copy-edit. She worked her magic on almost every page and made this book infinitely more readable.

Major thanks to everyone who provided feedback on the manuscript. Adora Michaels and Jenn Waterman helped me believe in this story. Devin Olshefski pointed out tons of hideous dialogue. Victor Bryan helped me rethink several critical scenes. Jack Hambrose spotted embarrassing errors that no one else did. Carol and Denny McNulty caught tons of typos. Zack Hammond, Heide "Stormcloud" Wenzel, and Elicia Messier provided clutch last-minute feedback. Fred Himebaugh, M.G. Martin, Karl Gallagher, Paul Miscavage, and Mark Bearden offered valuable insight and encouragement.

Special thanks to everyone who helped with medical, legal, and other research. Mike Dorbad, Steph Harkins, Dave Scherer, Genel Gronkowski, Christine Martin, and Tom Meluskey all helped shape this book for the better.

Finally, I'd like to thank you, reader, for taking a chance on this story. I hope you enjoyed it!

www.ingramcontent.com/pod-product-compliance
Lightning Source LLC
Chambersburg PA
CBHW031000190726
48285CB00004BB/1395